THE HUNT FOR THE BUNYIP

BUNYIP BOOK 3

TRISTAN A. SMITH

To my parents, Ross and Pauline, with all my love and gratitude.

A DREADFUL MEETING

THIRTY-YEAR-OLD PYRAN ZUMSTEIN sat on a large, stringy-bark log and stared into the campfire. Rich orange flames reflected in his green, red-rimmed eyes. His long red hair framed his pale, gaunt face. It was lank and greasy – he hadn't had a shower for two days.

He smiled absently at the drunken laughter, filthy language and stoned humour that droned around him.

The stars twinkled above on yet another warm, late spring night near the Goldcoast of South-east Queensland. The sun had set only a few moments ago, and so there was still a bright glimmer of light in the west. Not a breeze stirred the surrounding gum trees of the bush.

The site of the camp was a favourite haunt of Pyran's group. It was a sheltered little clearing beside railway tracks a mere ten-minute drive out of town. Many a Friday and Saturday night had been passed there. Many a fight had taken place in the clearing, and much fornication accomplished under the nearby trees.

There were about fifteen or sixteen there, and they were a

1

mix of white and Murri blood. The sex ratio was even. The girls were aged between fifteen and nineteen, but the boys' ages varied much more – the youngest was fourteen, the oldest thirty-five.

Pyran had slept with at least half of the scrawny, laughing girls that were there that night. So, had his mates. Whilst the female company varied from party to party, the males were mostly the same.

Pyran sat in dazed reflection. He had marijuana smoke in his lungs and the taste of cheap, bitter beer in his mouth. His head was heavy, and he was uncomfortably close to the fire. His shins were too hot, and his can of beer was nearly empty.

With a final swig, he finished the can. The beer was warm and unpleasant.

"Fuck." He grumbled and threw the empty can into the fire.

Pyran was normally talkative on nights like these. His ambitions on most occasions were simple: he would play a little acoustic guitar, laugh at jokes, listen to stories and make moves on an easy girl for the night. These were distractions. Pyran didn't like to think too deeply for too long. However, tonight he couldn't help himself.

What the fuck am I doing with my life?

He sighed deeply and gazed sadly at his friends. They were doing and saying the usual things. The same sort of fights were brewing, the same sort of debauchery was being planned. Bitter hatred, drunken escape, unrealistic dreams...

Fuck it. This is a party. Snap out of it.

"Man..." He drawled. "I wanna get more drunk without havin' to drink more of this fuckin' warm beer, eh?"

Brian sniggered at his side. The smile was a temporary relief from his perpetual snarl. He was thirty-five but looked forty. His once pitch-black hair was now starting to grey. He was well muscled, with a broken nose and a lazy eye.

"You didn't have to pay for it, so just shut up and drink it, ya ungrateful cunt." Brian muttered.

Pyran let out a guffaw. "What are ya talkin' about, bruz? I gave a twenty to Rick before."

"Well, go an' fuckin' get it off him. We five fingered these fuckin' slabs, la."

"What? Ya fuckin' jokin'?"

"Nah, bruz. It's true. Rick! Rick, ya theivin' cunt! Give Pyro back his twenny!"

A skinny Murri called Rick smiled broadly from across the fire at Pyran. He was about eighteen with smooth dark skin and wavy, coal black hair.

"I'll pay ya back next week, bruz." He promised.

Pyran waved him away. "No worries, bruz. But gimme some of ya smokes, eh?"

"I only got four left, la. I'll scab some off Brian for ya though, eh?"

"Fuck off." Brian scoffed.

Pyran laughed drunkenly. "Why do I hang around you fuckin' povo cunts?"

His companions laughed with him.

"Have anothery, bruz." Rick smiled and tossed Pyran another can of beer.

"Thanks."

Rick then realised that the card-board slab box was empty.

"Aw shit, bruuuuuuz!" He wailed comically. "I think we've finished the grog, eh?"

"What? Bullshit." Brian glowered. "You said yous got enough for the night."

"Someone's gotta go to a bottle-o, la. We're cleaned out, bruz!" Rick shrugged.

Brian's face set cruelly. Violence simmered in him.

Rick's shoulders sank under the bully's glare. However, he was spared by a sudden distraction.

"Hey, who's that?" Pyran frowned.

The group turned their attention to the railway tracks.

A stooping figure in a trench-coat and floppy hat was balancing his way along one of the rails on the railway line. His arms were stretched out to his sides to help him balance, yet he seemed very unsteady. With the last of the dying light in the west behind him, he was a perfect silhouette.

"Haw! I reckon that cunt's more pissed than we are." Rick muttered with a drunken grin.

Chuckles followed as the figure got and more unsteady. His arms were making rapid circles and he swayed erratically.

"Fuck, even I can walk along the rail when I'm pissed. This cunt's got somethin' wrong with him. Look at his legs." Brian drawled.

A feeling of dread accosted Pyran.

As the figure got closer, they could see that one leg bent at an unnatural angle.

"Hey look – he's only got one boot, man! His other one bare foot, la!" Rick laughed.

"Man, I gotta bad feelin' about this." Pyran murmured.

There was something familiar and disconcerting about the figure that was now just a few metres from their camp.

"What are ya talkin' about, bruz?" Brian asked.

"Dunno. I just got a bad feelin', eh? Do ya know him, Bri?"

"Nup. He's just an old man, eh? Shit, here he comes. Stop grippin', bruz. He can't fuck with all us brothers, eh?"

As the figure left the track and shuffled towards them, Pyran noticed that one of the girls was whispering urgently to the others. Within a minute all the girls and four of the boys had began to move away towards their cars.

4

"Oi!" Brian shouted. "Where the fuck are yous goin'?!"

He did not receive an answer.

Now, only Pyran, Rick, Brian and a twenty-four-year-old called Brett remained by the fire.

"Man, this is not good." Pyran muttered.

Suddenly the figure was only a few feet away. They could see that he was an old aboriginal man. His left leg was encased in a knee-high leather boot, his right foot was bare and heavily calloused.

"What's up, my niggers?!" The old man suddenly shouted, then burst into a rattling cackle.

"Who are you?" Brian asked flatly.

"I'm just a lost old coot, eh?" The old man drawled. He lifted his head up so that the light from the fire flickered upon his face. Orange eyes gleamed at them with amusement.

"Fuck..." Rick murmured. "He's got trippy eyes, la."

The old man let out a bark of laughter.

"It runs in my family, unna?" He burbled. "What's the matter? Ya grippin', bruz? Ya freakin' out? Can't help da eyes ya born with, unna?"

"Sorry." Rick blushed. "Didn't mean no offense."

"Oi...where ya mates goin'?" The old man asked with playful disappointment. "One da girls gimme filthy look, unna? Look, she's got em all grippin'."

They heard car doors slam, and then the engines started and two car-loads of people drove away.

"Hmm." The old man mused. "Maybe they'll be back directly."

"Fuckin' cunts." Brian muttered.

The old man suddenly reached into his pockets. He pulled out three fifty-dollar notes.

Rick and Brett's eyes lit up.

"I know what'll bring em back, boys. Don't worry. I heard

one of ya say that ya all out o' grog." The old man smiled. His teeth were small, yellow and sharp. "Got a remedy, la. Whose gonna go get it then?"

"You serious?" Brian asked, his attitude to their visitor now much more amiable.

"Yeah, bruz. Gotta look after ya own, unna? Here ya are. One fiddy each. Come back with plenty, eh?" The old man beamed.

"Shit! That's deli, man!" Rick clapped.

Brian stood up and shook the old man's hand. "You're alright, eh?"

"I do what I can, unna?" The old man grinned. "Now, why don't you three fellas bugger off and get the grog, then come back directly. Let the others know I'm alright, eh?"

"Fuck, yeah!" Brett clapped.

The three Murris were on their feet.

"Oi, ya cunts, what about me?" Pyran objected petulantly.

"Stay here with me. You'll be right." The old man smiled wolfishly. "Unless ya think I'm gonna rape ya or somethin'."

The lads laughed heartily.

"We'll be back in less than half an hour, bruz." Brian smiled. "Just stay here, eh?"

Pyran wanted to flee. Yet he could think of no excuse to leave, so he sighed and said. "Hurry back. I'm gettin' sober, eh?"

With a whoop of joy, Brett ran to the last remaining car. Laughing, Brian and Rick ran after him.

When the sound of the car engine had faded, the old man came and sat on the log beside Pyran. He was just a little too close for comfort.

Pyran raised his eyebrows, then let out a long sigh.

"So... how's it goin'?" He asked wearily, staring at the campfire.

6

The old man turned to face him. He waited for Pyran to make eye contact before he spoke.

"They say that it takes all sorts to make a world." The old man suddenly announced. The brim of his floppy hat shadowed his eyes, yet they gleamed.

Pyran grunted. "So they say."

"I've met so many people, ya know, over the years. All sorts. Yet – many of them the *same* sort. Know what I mean?"

"Yep. Sure."

The old man grinned impishly.

"So, be honest. What sort do you reckon you are?" He asked.

"Eh? What sort am I? I dunno." Pyran grinned sheepishly.

"Ya dunno, eh?"

Pyran shrugged. "Yeah. Look...I'm just an easy-going sort of guy, eh?"

"An easy-going sort of guy? And what does a guy like that want to do with his life?"

Pyran frowned thoughtfully. "Funny you should ask that."

"Nah, mate. When ya as old as I am, ya know what's brewin' in a young fella's head when he stares a long time into da fire, with the chatter of his brothers swirlin' round him..." The old man answered, his voice becoming musical as he spoke. "It's usually one of the da big questions, unna? Whether he should stand up an' do somethin', or he misses someone, or he doesn't know what to do with himself. But for all da big questions, one thing come first, unna? And dat's what sort ya are. See?"

Pyran nodded his appreciation for the philosophical pearl.

"I'm an artistic sort, eh? I want to be an actor."

"Yeah?" The old man beamed. "What sorta actor?"

"Oh...well, you know – the tragic hero type." Pyran grinned amiably.

The old man returned the smile. "Oh yeah? Is that all? I see a guitar there, is it yours?"

"Yeah." Pyran nodded softly. "I also wanted to be a musician."

"A musician?"

"Yeah..." Pyran chuckled gently at his admission.

The old man smiled at him fondly. He reached into his trench-coat and pulled out a hand-rolled cigarette. He held it out to him. "I'll swap ya, kordah."

Pyran tilted his head politely. "Swap me for what?"

"The beer. I'm thirsty as, unna?"

Pyran shrugged, then gave him the can. He accepted the cigarette.

"Cheers, eh?" Pyran smiled, as he lit it.

The old man watched him take a drag.

Pyran nodded thoughtfully at the smoke. "This is different. Fruity."

Crow's feet tightened about the old man's eyes. "Yeah. I've heard a few people describe it that way. Ya should roll yer own, brother. Better for ya, unna?"

"Yeah...yeah, I reckon you're right there." Pyran agreed.

Suddenly the old man's eyes sparkled cheekily.

"Oi, I gotta question for ya." He said.

"Yeah?"

"Do you know why we don't generally fuck our mothers and our sisters?"

Pyran sputtered in surprise and then laughed. "Aside from the obvious, you mean?"

The old man grinned. "Yeah, aside from the obvious."

"I dunno. I s'pose most of us aren't attracted to our mums and sisters that way." Pyran answered.

"It's the smell." The old man rejoined.

"Eh? Their smell?"

"Yeah."

"Oh yeah. Like pheromones or somethin'?"

"Yeah. Somethin' like that. Point is, they give off a certain smell that turns ya off em. Most people don't even realise that they are reactin' to a smell. But they are. The closer the bloodline, the more attractive they are unless it is *too* close – like a sister or a mother." The old man explained. He took a sip of beer.

Pyran gave a bemused frown. "So why are you telling me this?"

"Hmpf." The old man grunted with amusement. His eyelids drooped languidly. "Because, I can smell the bloodlines, you know."

"Eh?" Pyran asked. A shudder went through him.

The old man turned to stare into Pyran. Suddenly he spoke in a clear, bell-like voice with a sophisticated English accent.

"You smell very much like someone I once met. A *cousin*, perhaps."

"Is that right?" Pyran breathed.

"Oh yes. He would be about your age by now. Though he has more English blood, and you have more German...and Italian."

Pyran sat and stared into the old man. "I know who you are."

The old man smiled like the Cheshire cat. "Indeed?"

Pyran swallowed nervously. "I wasn't sure at first, but you're him, aren't you? You're...Dinewan?"

The old man's eyes sparkled dangerously. "Yes, I am. And you are?"

Pyran did not answer.

"Well?" Prodded Dinewan mockingly.

Pyran steeled his nerves and spoke very carefully. "Please. I don't want any trouble with you. And I don't want to disrespect you, but I am not going to tell you my name."

Dinewan shrugged. "Have it your way, Pyran."

"Oh *shit*." Pyran groaned.

Dinewan chuckled merrily. "Hmm. I like you already."

"OK. What do you want with me?" Pyran asked warily.

Dinewan looked to the stars and sighed. "I want you to tell me a story."

Pyran frowned. "A story? What do you mean?"

"Tell me a story...about the opal, the boy...and the monster." Dinewan continued, his eyes gleaming in the fire-light.

"I dunno what you're talkin' about." Pyran answered flatly.

"Hmm." Dinewan drawled. "According to the story I heard, a little boy named Tristram and his cousin *Pyran*, went down to a water-hole in a gully deep in the High Country of Victoria. There, they met a monster – a *bunyip*. According to the story, their lives were spared by the bunyip because Tristram gave it a magic opal."

"You're nuts." Pyran rejoined.

"Come, come, Pyran. Let's cut to the chase, shall we? I know that Tristram once had a very special opal. I know that you have seen it. I know that he believes that he has lost it. I also know, that he and you saw a bunyip."

"Man, that's just a story that Tristram tells based on what we imagined when we were kids." Pyran waved dismissively. "Look, what do you want with me? You already tried to take the opal from Tristram all those years ago, and he told you then that he doesn't have it any more. So why are you talking to me?"

"I no longer care about the opal. It is lost. I want to know where to find the bunyip." Dinewan announced.

"There is no such thing as a bunyip!" Pyran shouted. "We were just wound up by the stories that a koori elder told us!"

Orange eyes rolled in thought. "The watchdog. The man you called Fred Morris."

"Yeah...how the fuck do you know about him?"

"I heard that he died two days ago. Pity." Dinewan's eyes betrayed a dreadful glee.

Understanding dawned on Pyran. "Fred Morris knew about you." He breathed. "He told us that you could never come into East Gippsland."

"Nonsense, Pyran." Dinewan laughed. "I would have visited Tristram a long time ago if only I knew where he lived. But I don't really need to now. I just need you to tell me where you saw the bunyip."

"I don't know! No one knows where to look!"

"Tristram does."

"He won't help you."

"Yes, he will. You are going to talk to him for me."

"Like hell!"

"You are, Pyran. You are going to deliver this to him personally." Dinewan rejoined sternly. He pulled out a small, yellow padded envelope.

"What's that?"

"It is a message. The time is coming for Tristram and I to meet again. The tide for magic is rising."

"Magic? Tristram told me about your plastic skulls and your..." Pyran suddenly realised something. He looked at his cigarette and then violently threw it into the fire. "You fuckin' cunt!"

"Settle down, Pyran. There is no need to be uncivil." Dinewan chuckled.

"Listen, you are not going to fool me. I know that you aren't really magic. There is no such fucking thing!" Pyran growled hotly.

His pulse was now racing, and he had to fight a growing panic within him.

Dinewan held Pyran's eyes coldly. He shook his head mockingly at the frightened young man. Then he slowly reached down and pulled the long leather boot from his left leg.

Pyran nearly fainted at what he saw.

Instead of a human leg, it was an emu's leg...complete with a three-toed foot.

Dinewan lifted the leg up for Pyran's inspection. The flames reflected in the grey scales, and the toes wiggled grotesquely.

"Magic is a fact of life, like murder, sex and monsters." Dinewan crooned. "Now, just sit there and relax, Pyran. We have lots to talk about."

THE COURAGE TO BE ORDINARY

"Welcome to Emu Post, this is Tristram."

Twenty-nine-year-old Tristram Jones worked in a call centre for a rival postal company to that of Australia Post. He was excellent at his job – and he hated it with all his heart.

Today he was taking calls, which was unusual these days, as he was a team leader. However, the centre was under-staffed and so he found himself on the phone again.

"Oh thank God, a real person." The customer responded. She was a well-spoken woman in her fifties.

"We are programmed to sound real." Tristram answered with a gentle hint of humour. "How may I help you?"

The customer laughed politely.

"I have a complaint about your Speedpost product." She began.

Tristram sighed inwardly. It's always the same – a lost or late parcel, or a failed redirection...

"Oh Yes?" Tristram responded courteously. "What's the complaint?"

"Well, how can I put this? A three-legged tortoise could have delivered my satchel faster than Emu Post."

Tristram responded drily. "We did look into using three-legged tortoises as couriers, however the vet-bills for removing the fourth leg made the whole thing unprofitable."

This will either backfire and make her angrier, or...

"Heh."

We're OK.

"Alright, so the Speedpost satchel was late?" Tristram resumed.

"Worse. It is lost."

"I see. Did you keep the tracking number?"

"Yes. It's SJK764531."

"Thank you. And may I have your name, please?"

"It's Judy Wilson."

"Thank you, Ms. Wilson. I will just put that number into our system for you and see what comes up. What date did you post it?"

"A week ago. The thirteenth of November."

"Thank you."

"You know, the first time I used your service, I posted my package in one of your ordinary Emu Post satchels." Judy informed him coolly.

"Oh yes?"

"You lost that one too."

"Oh. I'm sorry to hear it."

"That is what the last operator said. Apparently, you can't track the ordinary satchels, so she recommended the Speedpost Satchel. However, you have lost that one too, so tell me: what's the advantage of Speedpost?"

"Well, I can prove that we lost the Speedpost satchel faster." Tristram quipped.

"Ha!"

"I have a scan here showing that it went through our delivery centre on the fourteenth of November."

"Well, it didn't get to my mother." Judy sighed.

"OK...I know I seem to be taking a light-hearted view of the situation, Ms. Wilson, but I assure you, we will sort the issue out." Tristram continued amiably.

He then explained in detail what searches they would do and took the details of both the ordinary and speed-post satchels. He advised that he would organise compensation on both if they could not be found and sent her two speed-post satchels for free as a gesture of good will.

"I must say, your service is an improvement over the first operator I spoke to." Judy said warmly as the call came to an end.

Judy Wilson was one of the good customers. In fact, most people were good. Yes, they had a question or a complaint – but they were generally reasonable and civil. However, the minority of rude people still represented over a dozen calls per operator per day. They ranged in attitude from petulant and sarcastic, to downright aggressive and abusive. The worst offenders were generally escalated to Tristram Jones. This was punishment, Tristram supposed, for being good at diffusing irate customers.

Tristram finalised Judy's inquiry file and sent a fax off to the delivery centre. He then checked another computer screen beside him for the current statistics. He gave a deep sigh. There were twenty-one calls in the queue and some of them had been waiting over twelve minutes. He lifted his head above the wall of his cubicle to see how his team were doing.

All of them were talking to customers – none of them were doing after-call work. He smiled to himself. They were a handful at times, but they were on the whole a good team.

"Tristrammmmmm..." Whined a tall, blonde girl.

"Yes, Tiana?" Tristram smiled coolly.

What will it be this time? Headache? Stomach cramps? Over-it syndrome?

Tiana was twenty-two and well aware of her sexual attractiveness. Today she wore a black top that clung to her lean figure like a glove. Her chocolate business pants accentuated her long, shapely legs. Long honey-blonde hair with dyed cherry highlights played over her delicate neck. She had warm hazel-nut eyes and a white, elfish smile.

Tiana sauntered over to Tristram and sat on his desk. She eyed him coquettishly.

"I haven't been late to work for two weeks now." She began.

"So?"

"So, you should give me a Tarot reading."

Tristram scoffed. "*What?*"

"Come on! You're so good at them."

"I don't think so." Tristram grinned.

"But it's only fair!"

"It's only fair that you get back on the phones. We have twenty-four in the queue now." Tristram answered with an authoritative smile.

"*Excuse you*, I'm on my break." Tiana responded with a censuring raise of her eyebrows.

"And you're spending it talking to me?"

"You're fun to talk to. You're different."

"Don't you want to go outside for a smoke?"

Tiana sighed petulantly. "Whatever. I quit."

"Really?"

"Yes, really. Didn't you think I could?"

"Well, congratulations."

"I also quit pot."

"Glad to hear it. Good for you."

"And I quit alcohol."

"Alcohol?!" Tristram expostulated. "*Why?*"

Tiana giggled. "Actually, that one is just for Sunday to Thursday."

"Ah. Fair enough. No more whiskey with breakfast."

"I quit my boyfriend." Tiana watched Tristram's face carefully as she spoke.

Tristram waited for her to say more.

"Yeah?" He rejoined finally.

"Yup."

"How are you holding up?"

"You know we have been together two years. And we have been on and off all year. I think it's for the best."

Tristram nodded kindly. "I hope so."

"I know so. Like you said, I am an attractive specimen with many choices." Tiana parodied a sultry supermodel pose. "Right?"

"Right." Tristram beamed.

"So how are things going with your chick?"

Tristram sighed. "You know how I said a week ago that we were finally back on track?"

"Yeah. She liked the story and the present – you won her over again for like, the eighth time this year. Man, I hope she knows how lucky she is to have you. I wish some guy would write stories just for me."

"Yeah, well...I don't think she does feel lucky to have me. We are on the rocks again."

"*What?* Why?"

Tristram shrugged. "She's had another change of mind."

"Dump her. Just dump her – and go out with me." Tiana smiled charismatically.

"Ha! A gorgeous thing like you has far better choices than me."

"Yeah right. I know that you don't think I'm intelligent enough..."

"Tiana..."

"Relax, I'm joking, man!" Tiana smiled warmly. "I don't think either of us are ready for a new relationship. But if you and I are both still single in five years...we should so give it go."

Tristram nodded. "Thanks. Although, you know what they say. You should be careful what you wish for."

"I am being careful...this time."

Tiana gave Tristram a look that made him blush. Her smile broadened.

Tristram sighed sheepishly. "Um. OK. Right. You're on. Five years. If we are both still single, we'll go out."

Tiana sighed longingly. "Do we really have to wait five years?"

Tristram grinned shyly. "Where do you think you'll be in five years?"

"I dunno. Not here, that's for sure."

"Amen to that."

Tiana thought about the question. "Five years, eh? By then I will be a successful dancer and you will be in the middle of a jungle somewhere being Mr. Zoologist."

"You want to be a dancer? What happened to being a famous painter?"

"I'll do that, too. I will be very successful, you know. And once I leave this call centre, I will never answer the phone again."

"Heh. Me neither. There will be no reception in the jungle anyway."

Tiana fixed him a stern, flirtatious look. "I heard that you were going back to zoology and that you haven't told anyone."

Tristram's eyes sparkled. "I wish. No, it is just a rumour. I'm taking a few days off from tomorrow – going back to Bairnsdale for some much-needed fishing. But, before I go down, I am helping my old supervisor out with a practical class at the university."

"You should do that for a living instead of working here." Tiana answered.

"Not enough hours."

"You would like to, though, wouldn't you? It's your passion."

"It was. Now, though, my zoology career is looking like it will never happen."

Tristram's face hardened.

"I wouldn't say that." Tiana rejoined kindly. "You have nearly finished your Masters, yeah?"

"That's the story. But I don't know if it is really true. Over six years ago, my supervisor told me that I had only two weeks to go."

"What's the hold up?"

"It's a long and boring story. And I believe that your break is almost over." Tristram returned with a sympathetic grin.

Tiana sighed and a give a little *moue* of disappointment.

"Now, now." Tristram soothed. "We must have courage. As my father once said to me – and still says, from time to time: we must have the courage to be ordinary."

"What?!"

"Heh. That was my first reaction, too."

"The courage to be *ordinary*?"

"Uh-huh. Once, when Dad and I went to the supermarket

19

in Bairnsdale, he asked me to consider all the people working around us. He pointed out a few different people: some who were serving at the registers, some who were the cleaners, and the guy who was collecting the trolleys. Then he pointed at a guy driving a delivery van – and then the butchers working behind the meat counter, the bakers in their bakery and so on..."

Tristram paused and looked into Tiana.

She took the bait. "Yeah, and?"

Tristram grinned. "That's just what I said. Well, Dad just reminded me that all of these people would have had childhoods full of dreams of what they wanted to be when they grew up. And it was a fair bet that most of them did not imagine a boring nine to five job. But they all have obligations and responsibilities – families and what-not – and so they put aside their own dreams and have the courage to be ordinary. And because they have that courage, the rest of us have the things we need every day."

Tiana considered the idea. "I see the point your Dad was making. But why would he tell you something like that?"

Tristram smiled. "Because I was bitching and moaning about being in a call centre instead of being a writer and zoologist. I was telling him how humiliated I felt working in a place like this. And Dad was just trying to tell me that most people are doing jobs like mine – and that the job I was doing was not demeaning, but an important service to others."

Tiana winced. "So, he wants you to suck it up and be happy with the ordinary lot?"

Tristram laughed gently. "Again – that's what I said. And then Dad said this: sometimes we don't succeed straight away with our dreams – if at all – but the ordinary things we do to meet our responsibilities in the meantime are not without dignity and virtue. They are important services to others – even if they don't realise it at the time – and we should show courage as we do our best in them every day."

"Hmm. Well, I still don't want to be here forever." Tiana shrugged with a sigh as she sauntered away to her desk.

"You won't be." Tristram called after her.

And neither will I.

PROFESSOR BURT. D. WHITESIDE

"Science is a lot like sex. It is much better to do it than to read about it – but if you read about it, you'll be better at doing it."

That was Professor Burt. D. Whiteside's opening sentence to the two thousand first year Biology students that sat expectantly in the Copland Theatre. It was delivered with roguish abandon, and his bright blue eyes sparkled cheekily at his young audience.

Tristram smiled at the memory, as he sat on the morning tram that made its way up Elizabeth Street in the central business district of Melbourne. It was the day after his conversation with Tiana. He was on his way back to a place that he loved: the Parkville Campus of The University of Melbourne, where he met the best teacher he had ever had and finally got a real taste of his childhood dream, zoology.

Tristram would never forget that first encounter with Burt, in the first semester of First Year Biology, 1997. It was a late lecture that began at five pm, well after the time that students had an attention span. A lot of the students were settling down for an hour's snooze – Tristram among them. Tristram took biology very seriously, but he found that he learned more about it by reading the textbooks and paying attention in the practical classes, than by listening to bored old academics drone through a dry lecture. Furthermore, the conditions of the Copland Theatre were designed to send students to sleep. The seats were very deep and comfortable, the lighting was low, and the monotone of senior academics was very soothing – perfect conditions for catching up on sleep – and Tristram had a *lot* of sleep to catch up on.

Tristram's first year at university hurtled by. The curriculum was year twelve all over again – but with double the material in half the time with three hundred times the students – most of whom seemed to be much richer and much smarter than he was. Furthermore, Tristram was staying at University College, which was like being in a hotel with a hundred and fifty of his friends. His social life exploded. He was surrounded at all times by young, intelligent and stimulating personalities. Tristram embraced it all – drinking, movies, restaurants, plays, parties – and just hanging around in the common room of the college, talking into the small hours of the morning. Tristram got little sleep even when he finally went to bed, as his room at the college was right next to the very busy Royal Parade. Hence, he was wide awake from the noise of heavy traffic early in the morning. It was a blessing in disguise, for he had to be up early anyway for classes or to go to the gym.

When could he sleep? Evening naps were out of the question. He worked evenings at the supermarket on Lygon Street near the university – college fees were expensive. He also had late chemistry practicals that ran from six in the evening until nine. If Tristram thought that he was exhausted in year twelve, it was nothing to what he crammed into his first year at university. There was only one good opportunity for sleep, and that was during lectures...

However, for Professor Burt Whiteside's lectures, Tristram was enchanted and wide awake from the very beginning.

Before that first lecture began, the theatre was abuzz with chatter as the students awaited their lecturer. He was five minutes late. Then suddenly, he appeared.

Burt had an enormous presence – he loomed into view like an elephant in a parade. He was six feet, five inches tall and had very broad shoulders. Though he was very tall, he did not stoop. Burt had a thick mane of greying black hair that hung well past his shoulders, and a long, grey bushy beard that stopped at his navel. Burt had large, round blue eyes that blazed out at the world from under wild bushy black eyebrows. He had a large forehead, and a strong jaw. His demeanour could easily have been intimidating, were it not for the deep crow's feet about his eyes that were formed from a lifetime of cheeky smiles.

"My name is Burt Whiteside." He had continued in a dry, booming voice. "I am one of the two current professors in the Zoology department. The other one is the head of the department. Me? Well, I'm just wanking off in the Faculty somewhere. I teach the third-year Animal Physiology course, the second year Cell Biology and Bio-med. You'll also probably see me for a couple of your practical classes. And yes, I also give three or four lectures in this course – First Year Biology. So... today, we are going to talk about echinoderms. These animals are among my real favourites..."

Burt had then launched into a fascinating lecture on the physiology and behaviour of starfish and sea-cucumbers.

Burt was a perpetually animated spectacle. He gesticulated widely as he injected wit and warmth into every piece of information. He took the great, complicated puzzle of science and delivered it as a humorous after dinner anecdote – with copious warnings that he was oversimplifying things.

Eighteen-year-old Tristram Jones had found his academic mentor. He wanted to teach the way Burt taught. He wanted to speak and think like Burt. He knew from that very moment that he must follow the colourful and ingenious giant – that the presence before him would change his life and illuminate the way to his destiny.

Tristram attended all of Burt's lectures with relish – he even went to the lectures for the other two streams just to watch him in action some more. Tristram discovered which subjects in second year would be taught by Professor White-side and ensured his enrolment. It was during his second year that he became known to Burt, and by third year Tristram had secured him as his supervisor for a research project on the sea cucumber *Lipotrapeza vestiens*. They were trying to elucidate the physiology behind the mutable connective tissue of these fascinating animals. Seacucumbers resemble a muscular sausage, and via chemical changes unknown at that time, can make themselves as pliable as playdough or as rigid as concrete within a second.

Tristram was not the most scientific or brilliant student that Burt had had, but Burt did concede that Tristram could write better than all but one of the students that he had taken on in the last forty years.

"*And* you also have another quality which is absolutely essential in this game." Burt continued in his deep, rumbling voice. He was frowning seriously at his young student, as they sat outside Burt's lab with a cup of coffee.

"What's that?" Tristram asked earnestly.

"You're decidedly odd."

"Thanks." Tristram smiled ruefully.

"I'm being deadly serious. And complimentary. You should

lap it up, Jones – I don't stroke egos if I can possibly avoid it. The only thing I stroke on purpose is my wang."

Burt then exploded into a helpless, smutty guffaw. Tristram could not help but join him. The man's often self-induced laughter was incredibly infectious. It echoed down the corridors of the Zoology building and brought a smile to people working quietly in their offices.

"Seriously, though." Burt continued. "You *are* odd."

"Um...right."

"And you *need* to be odd. Of course, you have to be odd! You know what interests most people? I'll tell you. It's what's on television. Or who's sent them email, or what's for lunch or when they're gonna get their next root. That is what occupies the mind of most people. But us? We wonder how a bloody sea cucumber can make its body go from limp to concrete and back again. We wonder how a toad can regulate its heart rate if we take the cardiac nerves away. These are fucking odd interests, and you need to be fucking odd to pursue them."

"I see. And you think I have this oddness?"

"Oh yes. These plays that you write – what the hell was the last one called?"

"*A play for Kate.*" Tristram answered. He had given Burt a free ticket to the first play that he had ever written and directed.

"That's the one. I've told you what I thought of it."

"You said that you enjoyed it."

"I did. You managed to write a musical play with a coherent and interesting plot that included an alien, a robot, a zoologist, drag queens, a giant penguin, God, The Devil and host of others. And you managed to include *pirates*. The song they sang about mermaid fillets had me and Nathan totally enthralled. The lyrics were a stroke of genius. Remind me, what was the chorus again?"

"Mermaid fillets: you can kiss one half and eat the other." Tristram grinned.

"That's it. Heh. It was clear to both of us that you are madman – but a talented madman, and that's what I'm getting at."

"Thank you."

"Don't get too excited. Talent is nothing if you can't back it up with good work. And that is what I think you are: undirected talent. Your results so far at uni are middle of the road, aren't they?"

"They are getting better with each semester. Most of them are second class honours." Tristram answered defensively.

Burt's eyes twinkled. "Relax. You are not bottom of the class, but you are not at the top. And I think that is more a reflection of how you have scattered your energies rather than your actual ability. But that's the point, isn't it? Sooner or later, ability has to be proven before it is rewarded."

"I agree."

"Tristram...you are clearly intelligent enough, and you are clearly odd enough – but are you actually a scientist? I don't know. But next year, if you get the necessary results from your third year, we'll work together on something and find out."

"You'll be my honours supervisor?" Tristram smiled eagerly.

Burt chuckled. "Yes. But do me and yourself a favour and get some good second semester marks, alright?"

Twenty-nine-year-old Tristram's reverie was broken by announcement of the tram driver.

"Next stop: Melbourne University."

Tristram smiled to himself. *My old stomping grounds.*

Within a minute, he was at the next stop and disembarking.

He strode across Royal Parade and made his way to the Zoology Building of the University of Melbourne.

Everyone is so young. Tristram mused ruefully. *Young, and for the most part, attractive.*

Tristram reached the door of the Zoology building.

He stopped and sat down by the brick wall. When they had arranged the meeting, Burt didn't know whether they were running the practical class in Zoology or one of the biology labs in the Redmond Barry Building, so they decided to meet at Zoology and go from there. Normally Tristram would go upstairs to the third floor and wait outside Burt's office – but Burt had retired a year ago. The professor now had neither a laboratory or an office.

As he waited, Tristram reflected on his tumultuous honours year.

IMPLANTED HEARTS

TWENTY-ONE-YEAR-OLD TRISTRAM HAD BEEN WAITING outside Professor Whiteside's office for an hour. It was early February in 2000, and Burt was late. Tristram knew he would be, and it did not bother him. He had plenty of scientific papers to read.

Burt's office was a large one at the very end of the third-floor corridor. The space outside his office had been made into a private waiting area, with a grey metal bookcase acting as a wall to the rest of the corridor. There was a bar fridge and a kettle, and two comfortable chairs.

Suddenly, Tristram heard a breathless, heavy stride up the corridor.

"Jesus fucking Christ." Burt groaned as he reached his office.

Tristram smiled.

Burt peered around the bookcase and gazed amiably down at Tristram.

"Well fuck my old boot, you're on time." Burt beamed.

"And you're late, Professor." Tristram beamed back.

Burt frowned and looked at his watch. "What? I said eleven, didn't I?"

"You said ten. You always do this."

"Well, it takes all my strength of character to come into work. Especially now that I have an obstreperous little bastard like you as an honours student." Burt retorted with a twinkle in his eyes.

"Glad you made it, Sir." Tristram grinned.

"Right. Let's get this kettle on..." Burt sighed, as he slumped heavily into the chair beside the bar-fridge opposite Tristram. "Christ, I feel like I'm a million years old."

"I put some chocolate biscuits in the fridge." Tristram chimed.

"Excellent!" Burt answered, breathless. "That's a good start."

"You OK? You seem a little worse for wear."

"Oh Jesus..." Burt moaned as the kettle gurgled to life. "I'm so fucking out of breath these days with the mildest exercise. It's because I am a fat bastard who has smoked most of his life – and I probably have emphysema."

Tristram didn't know what to say, so he nodded kindly. It seemed to amuse Burt.

"So... let's get on with it, Jones." Burt grinned drily. "What the fuck is your Honours project going to be about?"

"Not sea-cucumbers." Tristram answered. "You promised. Besides, those Japanese scientists have already figured all that out. The sea-cucumbers change the viscosity of their connective tissue with four bio-active peptides, remember?"

"Mm-hm." Burt nodded seriously. Then he frowned thoughtfully. "Yes, Tristram. But you know, I haven't been able to verify their results in my lab. It has left me *fantastically* suspicious of their literature."

"Well then, I guess their findings must be complete nonsense." Tristram returned cheekily.

"Ha! Of course. Anything that I can't verify in my lab must be bullshit. But fine, you've had enough of sea cucumbers." He eyed Tristram playfully. "My, what a petulant little fellow you are."

"You said last year that I would be doing a broad project, measuring heart rate during feeding in a variety of simple vertebrates – cane toads, other frogs, maybe flathead fish – and maybe also turtles." Tristram continued.

Burt considered him. "I do remember talking about that. So, that appeals to you, does it? A kind of general *stamp collecting* exercise?"

Tristram detected a hint of contempt. "Stamp collecting?"

Burt grunted good-humouredly. "Don't get me wrong, stamp collecting has a very important place in science. It is the collection of facts from which more interesting experiments are devised. But stamp collecting itself is, well, boring."

"It was your idea." Tristram shrugged.

"Every honours project should have two basic components." Burt continued. "One is a good, solid, piece of bread and butter. Stamp collecting – a nice, safe set of experiments or data collection, that furthers our knowledge on a particular subject, is a good example of what I mean by bread and butter. It is important to have a good piece of bread and butter to show examiners that you can do science and get results. But the more interesting second component – the jam – is what will distinguish an honours student from all the others."

"Right. So... what's our jam?"

"That is what I need to discuss with you. The project I have in mind is risky, because if it goes wrong, you are not left with any bread and butter."

"What's the project?"

"Postprandial tachycardia in *Bufo marinus*." Burt announced, looking into Tristram.

Tristram blinked. "The rise in heart-rate after feeding in cane toads?"

Burt grinned. "That's right."

Tristram frowned. "Didn't Lucien's student do that last year?"

"Yes and no." Burt answered. "She demonstrated once and for all that postprandial tachycardia happens in toads and that they increase their blood volume after feeding – and that the volume remains increased for at least six hours after feeding. She also showed that if you take water away from the toad, it is unable to expand its blood volume and most of the postprandial tachycardia goes away."

Tristram nodded. "That's right. It confirms Lucien's idea that the heart rate increase is caused by the change in blood volume."

Burt leaned forward with playful suspicion. "And just how would an increase in blood volume increase heart rate?"

"The greater blood volume stretches part of the heart and that makes it beat faster."

"Which *part* of the heart?" Burt prodded.

"The pace-maker." Tristram answered. "The sinoatrial node."

"The *WHAT*?!" Burt bellowed incredulously.

Tristram's smile turned sheepish. "Is it not the pace-maker?"

"The *sinoatrial node*?! Do toads even *have* a sinoatrial node?"

"I'm guessing...no?"

"Sinoatrial node in a *toad*! How outrageous!" Burt boomed with theatrical disgust.

"Sorry."

"You're thinking of the mammalian heart, Tristram. The pacemaker in mammals is the cluster of cells called the sinoatrial node. However, toads and frogs do not have a sinoatrial node. They have a separate structure that sits above the atria called the sinus venosus." Burt explained.

"I see."

"Lucien's theory – which he based on one of my ideas from a paper I did in the late eighties – is that the sinus venosus is stretched by the increased blood volume after feeding, and *that* causes the sinus venosus – and therefore the rest of the heart – to beat faster. Right?"

"What about nerves?" Tristram asked.

"We got rid of them. Or so we thought. What do you know about cardiac nerves, Tristram?"

"Not much."

"Give me a better answer. What did you learn in third year physiology? Or even first year biology?"

"OK. Well, there are two nerve groups. The sympathetic nerves which speed the heart up, and the parasympathetic or vagal nerves which slow the heart down."

"And? What else? How do nerves work?"

"They release chemicals which act on tissue receptors."

"These chemicals are called?"

"Neurotransmitters."

"Good. What are the main neurotransmitters for each type of nerve?"

"It is acetyl-choline for the vagus and... for the sympathetic nerve it is...ah... noradrenalin?"

"That's basically right. Mammals use more noradrenalin, but in toads, the sympathetic uses mostly adrenaline."

Tristram frowned. "But I thought that adrenaline came in the blood-stream from the adrenal glands?"

"Remember that there are two main types of adrenaline receptors, alpha and beta."

Tristram sighed. "Should I write this down?"

"Heh. You'll get used to these facts, trust me. You will be thinking about them a hell of a lot over the coming year. But yes – you are basically right. Now, there are two ways to take out the cardiac nerves – one way is to use drugs, the other way is surgery. In the past, we have used a combination of both. Sympathetic denervation is relatively easy – vagal denervation is bloody hard."

"Wouldn't surgery also cause more stress on the body?"

"Well yes, that is a basic problem with doing animal physiology. But remember, we don't have to do surgery to take out the sympathetic nerves. We can use bretylium or phentolamine to take out the neurotransmitter from the sympathetic. We can block the circulating adrenaline from the adrenal glands with propranolol. And finally, Mr. Jones, just to cheer you up: we use atropine to block the acetyl-choline from the vagus."

"I see." Tristram lied. He was deeply lost.

"So, we have all the influences blocked. Right?" Burt barked, his blue eyes ablaze.

Tristram's mind was overwhelmed with terminology.

"Right." He bluffed.

"Wrong!" Burt beamed, with a sparkle of glee. "There is a problem. A problem that, as far as we can tell, is unique to the cane toad."

"Yes?"

"The fucking cane toad has *two* neurotransmitters in the vagus nerve!"

"Bummer..." Tristram shrugged with a hint of humour in his eyes.

Burt chuckled. "Yes, it is a bummer. In fact, it is an act of *spectacular bastardry*."

"Why?"

"Atropine treatment blocks the acetyl-choline, right? But within an hour the vagus nerve recovers function and it is *not* because the atropine has worn off. We discovered a few years ago, that cane toad vagal nerves have not just acetyl-choline but also *somatostatin*."

"You can't block somatostatin with drugs?"

Burt smiled broadly. "Nope. And there you see the problem. In all past experiments, we can be confident of removing the sympathetic effects – AND – the adrenaline hurtling through the blood stream – BUT – *not* the actions of the vagus – because we have blocked only *one* of the *two* neurotransmitters. You see?"

"I think so. So, are there only two neurotransmitters in the cane toad vagus? Are we sure about that?"

"A few years ago we did some good old histology to see what the fuck else is hidden in their cardic nerves. That is when we found somatostatin and galanin – but we don't think that galanin has any cardiac effect."

"Fair enough."

"So, we know that the vagus *can* operate with somatostatin when its acetylcholine is blocked by atropine. And THAT has completely *fucked* all of our conclusions about previous experiments." Burt concluded with comic dismay.

"I see. But why are you so worried about it? I mean, Lucien's student has made it clear that it is the expansion of blood volume that increases heart rate anyway. So, who gives a shit about the nerves?"

Burt chuckled derisively. "Sorry, Tristram. We can't blithely dismiss the nerves just yet. There is a flaw in Lucien's theory. Have a look at this..."

Burt handed Tristram a graph. It was a plot of heart rate against blood volume.

"Um...what am I looking at?"

"This is from Lucien's student's data. We know that blood volume goes up after feeding, we also know that heart rate goes up after feeding. So, if there is a causal relationship between the two, then a high blood volume should be concurrent with a high heart rate. Yes?"

"Yes." Tristram nodded. He frowned as he stared at the graph.

"Well? Anything strike you about that graph?"

A whirl of terminology clouded his thinking. He took a deep breath.

Just look at the graph...

"Huh." Tristram suddenly grunted as the penny dropped.

"Yes?" Burt asked eagerly.

"The blood volume and the heart rate are both higher after feeding – but they don't get higher at the same time."

"Exactly!" Burt thundered triumphantly. "Blood volume takes at least an hour to get high – but heart rate is up *instantly*. So, for the *start* of postprandial tachycardia, you cannot use expanded blood volume as the explanation. AND you can't use adrenaline, because we blocked that with propranolol. *And* the sympathetic is out, because in these experiments, it was surgically removed."

"So... that just leaves the vagus...but hang on, that can't be. The vagus...lowers heart rate...right?"

"Yes." Burt nodded happily.

"But heart rate is *higher* – and it is not adrenaline or the sympathetic nerves doing it in these experiments." Tristram added, perplexed.

Burt beamed. "You are forgetting one very important fact. Do you know the *resting* heart rate of cane toads?"

Tristram shook his head.

"Look at the graph."

"Oh...right. Um...looks like it is around twelve to fifteen beats a minute. Shit. That seems low."

"Lower vertebrates typically have a low resting heart rate. Now, do you remember the experiments we did last year with isolated toad hearts in organ baths?"

"Yes."

Tristram remembered them vividly. The toad heart, if placed in Ringer's solution, will continue to beat spontaneously for hours – sometimes a couple of days. It was a macabre spectacle, the little toad heart beating in a test tube.

"What was the resting heart rate of those isolated hearts?" Burt continued.

"I can't remember. It wasn't as low as fifteen beats a minute."

"Right. It was around twice that or more – thirty to thirty-five beats a minute."

"Obviously, the answer lies with the lack of cardiac nerves." Tristram concluded. "The heart rate is high, because there is no vagus to slow it down?"

"Exactly."

Tristram nodded understanding. "The pace-maker. It naturally beats at a *higher* rate than what we see when the animal is at *rest*."

"Spot on. The default rate of the pacemaker is about thirty beats a minute in the toad. The vagus nerve is therefore *holding it down* to fifteen when the animal is at rest. So, the theory for the postprandial tachycardia – at least for the first hour – is that the vagus nerve stops holding the heart rate down."

"So, you have it all worked out then." Tristram shrugged.

Burt's eyes twinkled. "How high was the heart rate after feeding?"

"It got as high as..." Tristram looked at the graph. "Fifty to sixty beats a minute... Wait. That's higher than the default rate of the pacemaker by about thirty beats! Shit. So, it is not as simple as the vagus doing its thing…"

"It is not as simple as reduced vagal inhibition." Burt clarified.

"OK. But the sympathetic is not raising heart rate. So, it must be hormones – but not adrenaline, because that is blocked…um…my head hurts."

"To be absolutely sure to rule out reduced vagal inhibition, we need to see if the postprandial tachycardia goes away if we remove the influence of the vagus – and that is the whole problem. The surgery to remove the vagal nerves to the heart is fucking difficult and we can't block the nerve with drugs, because there is no drug to block somatostatin."

Tristram nodded as he understood the problem. "I see."

Burt's eyes twinkled. "So, what do you suggest we do, Tristram?"

"Huh?"

"This is the challenge for your honours project." Burt announced.

"Oh shit." Tristram winced. "Um…do I have to do the feeding experiments on toads whose vagal nerves have been removed?"

"Are you a good surgeon?"

Tristram blinked. "I don't know. Probably not."

Burt chuckled. "Well, what are you going to do then, Jones?"

Tristram considered the question. "Use isolated hearts?"

"Why?"

"Because they can't be impacted by nerves." Tristram shrugged.

Burt looked into Tristram. "True. But how are you going to use them to demonstrate that reduced vagal inhibition is not the cause of at least some of the increased heart rate after feeding?"

"I'm not. That seems too hard."

Burt laughed heartily. "You lazy bastard!"

Tristram smiled. "I want to tackle the other side of the problem. Heart rate goes beyond the *default* rate of the pacemaker. The default rate is thirty beats a minute, but after feeding, it goes up to sixty beats."

"Yes. So?"

"So, what causes those extra thirty beats a minute? It isn't the sympathetic nerves or circulating adrenaline. Both of those were removed in the earlier experiments."

Burt nodded thoughtfully. "Go on."

"I think...we should set up organ baths...then, ah...alright... we feed the toads, right? Then we take blood samples every half hour and put that blood into the organ bath, to see if the isolated heart beats any faster."

"So, you are testing for blood-borne chemicals that act directly on the heart, other than adrenaline?"

"Yes." Tristram answered, grateful for the clarification.

Burt smiled drily. "I foresee some practical difficulties there. You can't just keep sucking blood out of a toad, they don't have much. And if you throw it into an organ bath you will be diluting it considerably..."

Suddenly, Burt seemed to drift away. His eyelids drooped and he let out long, heavy exhalations through his nose. Tristram knew that he was in intense thought.

"I've got an idea." Burt finally announced. "Rather than use organ baths, we will implant the heart with its own electrodes into a host toad. Then we will feed the host toad. If anything is released into the bloodstream after feeding that raises the heart rate, we'll see it in the implanted heart."

"OK..." Tristram reacted with quiet awe. "But how are we going to implant a heart?!"

Burt smiled faintly. "Let's be simple-minded about this. We may be able to get results from a partial implant. Say, just the sinus venosus."

Tristram frowned as he considered the idea. "Even so, the sinus venosus would be too big to put in a blood vessel. And what about the problem of clogging up a blood vessel?"

Burt thought some more. "Again, let's be simple-minded. If there really is a cardio-accelerating hormone released into the blood stream, then it is probably also going to appear in the lymph fluid. Toads have large sacs for holding lymph. In fact, they have two particularly large dorsal lymph spaces just under the skin. We could try an implanted sinus venosus into the dorsal lymph space with very little trouble to the host toad."

Tristram nodded absently as he tried to imagine how he could ever really do what Burt was suggesting.

Suddenly Burt clapped his hands sharply. "Well? Are you game or not?"

"I'm game." Tristram answered automatically.

"Right. Well, I do need to clear this idea with the ethics committee. That should be easy, as we are not doing anything too invasive to the host toad. I also need to clear this with Lucien – postprandial tachycardia is his baby, so I want to make sure that we are not trodding on his toes. In the meantime, why don't you bugger off to the library and refamiliarise yourself with the cardiac and circulatory systems?"

Tristram beamed. "Righto, chief."

He made it all sound so easy...Twenty-nine-year-old Tristram smiled ruefully as he remembered the year that followed the above conversation.

WARNING SIGNS

An uncomfortable sentiment plagued Tristram throughout his honours.

"I feel as though I am on the right train, but that we have just passed my stop." He confessed to his parents one day. "I think I like learning about science – but that I don't like doing it."

The work was tedious and demoralising. He hated to be trapped in a laboratory away from daylight. He got sick of setting up experiments that failed. He got sick of experiments that worked for the first few hours, but then became ruined by a restless toad or implant failure. He was heartily sick of analysing the long paper traces that made up the tachograph...

Tristram could tell at a glance that the heart rate had gone up after feeding in both the host toad and the implant – but he could hardly paste metres and metres of trace paper into his thesis. He had to measure the heart rate from the raw data – and that took ages. It was torture to a meandering intellect such as his.

Burt was supposed to be with him, and when he was, Tristram was very happy. His mentor was always interesting – he educated Tristram on a broad canvas of topics: science, history, politics, literature and otherwise. He made Tristram laugh. He gave encouragement and discipline in the right balance. He even shared his fears, follies and regrets with Tristram, so much so, that Tristram counted the man a close friend. However, Burt was rarely in the lab or his office for long. He came in late to work and left early to pursue his interest in history. He was absent due to teaching commitments – or a plethora of personal issues. He was not there when things went wrong. Tristram nearly failed his honours because of it.

Three weeks before Tristram was to hand in, he discovered a flaw in the experiments. He had finally gotten a series of implant experiments to work – but there was an important element missing from his control data. When Burt pointed this out to him, he felt that his zoology career was over.

"That's it, then. I'm going to fail." Tristram murmured with surreal detachment as they sat in the little area outside Burt's office.

"You're not allowed to fail. That would make me look bad, and I can't have that." Burt joked.

It was late in the evening and Tristram was in no mood for humour.

"I'm sorry." He sighed bitterly. "I've done my best. I know you thought I'd be a good honours student, but now that it hasn't worked out, too bad."

"Listen to me carefully, Tristram." Burt began kindly. He waited for Tristram to make eye contact before he continued. "There are a lot of people better at science than you or me, but you are the only person I have met that has written a play. You are talented, you are clever, and you are hardworking – but there is no virtue in hard work, only results."

"I get that. Thank you. It's been a blast." Tristram retorted.

"Do you really want to do science?" Burt suddenly asked.

Tristram blinked. "What?"

"Do you really...want to do science?" Burt repeated, holding Tristram's gaze.

Tristram blushed. "Of course, I do. Why? Don't you think I have what it takes?"

"Actually, Tristram, I think you *do* have what it takes. Don't get me wrong here, I have a lot of time for you. But just because you *can* do something doesn't mean that you really enjoy doing it. You seem to have gotten more joy out of play-writing and classic literature than science."

"That's because the science hasn't worked. It has been repetitive, frustrating, and boring – and ultimately, unrewarding."

Crows feet tightened around Burts eyes. "I hate to break it to you, but that's science. For much of the time, you will be reading through dry academic papers and attempting things that don't work. Occasionally, you will have successes and make a worthwhile contribution to science. However, you will probably have to wade through a lot of tedious shit to have those successes. If you don't like the slow, careful, repetitive nature of scientific experiment and *data analysis*, then you won't like the vast majority your time as a scientist."

"What are you trying to say? That I should give up?"

Burt smiled patiently. "I am saying that I don't honestly know what you are going to end up doing with your life. If it's science, I can help you. If it is writing plays and novels – well, I'll do what I can for you. The point is, I want to know what you really give a fuck about, so I can help you along the right path."

"I want to do both." Tristram answered stubbornly.

Burt nodded with a proud smile. "Fine. Then stop panicking and focus."

"I can't win this one, boss!" Tristram exclaimed angrily. "There are three weeks to go before I have to hand my thesis in, and I have not finished my experiments. Most of the other students have collected all their data *weeks* ago. Most of them have already started their thesis."

"So fucking what?" Burt frowned. "Your fellow Honours students had no choice about collecting their data by now – they are field ecologists and behaviourists. Your work is lab-based. You can make great progress in a very short time if you design your experiments carefully and *focus*."

"In three weeks?"

"No. You will need to do them in two."

"*Two*?! Fine. Excellent. That will give me one week to write up. *One week* for an *entire Honours thesis*. Ten thousand words in *one week*. Yeah right." Tristram glowered. "The head of Honours says we need at least three weeks for the *first draft*."

"*Other* students need three weeks. You'll need one. You are the second-best writer I have ever had. Writing up is the very least of your worries."

"If you say so." Tristram muttered incredulously.

"I do say so." Burt answered firmly. "As to the experiments, I'll be working with you side by side. The two of us should be able to knock them over if we work every day, including the weekends. I will even help you with the clerical work of analysing traces."

Tristram was stunned. "Why would you go so far out of your way to help me?"

Burt grunted, and then appeared to be embarrassed. "Frankly, I am not overly happy with my supervision of you this year. You have made mistakes that I am paid good money to make sure don't happen."

"No." Tristram returned kindly. "I think the world of you as a supervisor. These were my mistakes."

"It's not that simple. You are not a scientist; you are not even a PhD student – you are an Honours student. That is the whole reason you have a supervisor. Your failing in this case is my failing. I have been indulging in my own shit and I just haven't been here anywhere near as much as I should have. I honestly believe that, Tristram – and you know me, I'm not one to blow smoke up anyone's arse. I fucked up, and you should not have to pay the penalty."

Tristram could hardly believe what he was hearing. His respect for the professor deepened immediately.

"Um...thanks."

"Heh. Don't thank me yet. We have a busy three weeks ahead."

The three weeks hurtled by. Tristram and Burt set up multiple experiments and ran them back to back, every day. Tristram stayed up late every night analysing the data. They finished the experiments with very exciting results – they discovered that the implant showed postprandial tachycardia – and it was not due to nerves, circulating adrenaline or mechanical stretching of the pacemaker. It was a blood-borne cardioactive substance that was new to science.

Then, in less than one week, Tristram completed his ten-thousand-word honours thesis. The result was far better than he dared hope. He missed out on getting first class Honours by one mark.

Tristram was once proud of his Honours year – yet, seven years later, as he reflected on the Masters that followed, he couldn't help but wonder if life would have been better if he had failed.

"I am thirty in less than a month, and I still haven't finished this fucking Masters." Tristram murmured to himself bitterly.

Where the hell is Burt? He is now twenty minutes late.

Suddenly Burt appeared from around the corner.

"Well, fuck my old boot, you're on time." The professor beamed.

PROMISES, PROMISES

"I DIDN'T THINK I would ever be doing this again." Twenty-nine-year-old Tristram smiled gently, as he made a ventral incision with a fine scalpel on a freshly dead cane toad.

"Heh. That goes double for me. I fucking retired last year!" Burt boomed from the other side of the work bench.

"Well, it beats the hell out of the call centre – I can tell you that much." Tristram sighed.

They each sat with a large microscope in front of them, gathering different tissue samples for the second-year animal physiology practical class. Burt had tucked his great shaggy beard down the collar of his bright pink shirt to keep it out of the way of the dissection.

"So why are you doing this?" Tristram asked.

"Oh, the department needed a favour and Harold kind of guilt-tripped me into it." Burt answered airily, as he pulled the skin off his toad's legs.

Harold Hildebrandt was the current Head of Zoology. He was an austere, grey man with a pointed face. Everything about him seemed elderly and brittle – except for his brilliant lilac eyes that perceived everything at a glance.

"Why would Professor Hildebrandt do that? You are retired. He has no hold over you." Tristram observed drily.

He had no hold over you even when you weren't retired. Tristram added with silent resentment.

Last year, and the year before, Harold had pursued Burt relentlessly for the assignments of the Honours students to be marked. However, Burt continued to procrastinate. He took days off to be in the library researching his personal history project or stayed at home 'sick'. In the end, Harold tried to shame Burt by publicly declaring that Burt was holding back the Honour's students from receiving their results. Burt had responded with genuine shame and apology – and yet *still* failed to mark the assignments, despite having ample time to do so. Finally, with great disgust, Harold retrieved the assignments from Burt's office whilst he was out to lunch and marked them himself. Burt offered no excuses, in fact he declared himself entirely guilty and irresponsible and left it at that.

Burt looked up from his microscope to eye Tristram cheekily. "I suppose Harold doesn't really have any power over me anymore. But he was niggling me about my responsibilities towards my fucking Masters student, so I agreed to do this to make him shut up for a bit."

Tristram did not smile in response. The day had started with pleasant memories of his time as an undergraduate, but now that Burt was there in front him, making jokes and excuses with a cavalier air, he was reminded of just how much Burt had failed him.

"So, have you gone through my introduction yet?" Tristram asked, as he cut through the toad's epicoracoids to expose the beating heart.

"Nope. I really haven't done a fucking thing. I'm sorry.

Every time I sit down to read it a huge resistance builds up in me and I just can't seem to get into it." Burt answered. His face was apologetic and sympathetic, but Tristram was tired of it.

"Well then, why don't you let Reginald and Mike help?" He returned. "Reginald shot me an email only a month ago saying that he and Mike were willing to help us finally nail this thing."

Reginald and Mike were both senior, retired colleagues of Burt. They had taught with Burt in the undergraduate courses and often sought his opinion on their papers and exams. Tristram was known to them and liked by them, and he was deeply gratified when Reginald had emailed him with an offer of help after he had heard on the grape-vine that Burt was once again not meeting his responsibilities.

Burt nodded reluctantly. "Yes, Reginald has contacted me. He would be good for reading a draft after we have decided what is going to be in it. As for Mike, well, he would be good for reviewing a draft as well, but he and I have never really seen eye to eye on how to present an argument."

Tristram sighed helplessly. "Well, you can't ask Lucien."

Lucien Hooker was the other senior Lecturer in the Animal Physiology Lab – and a long-time colleague. In fact, Lucien was Burt's first PhD student. He was as tall as Burt but seemed to take up a third as much space. He was in his mid-fifties but seemed much younger. His eyes were an intense amber under a crazy mop of jet-black hair. His humour was quick and quirky, and he fascinated Tristram almost as much as Burt. Lucien would be the only academic that Burt would trust with his work. Burt was in awe of Lucien's ability to think around corners, just as Lucien was in awe of Burt's ability to absorb every paper ever written on a particular subject, and then produce a coherent and persuasive story. However, their relationship had soured, and in Tristram's opinion, it was entirely Burt's fault.

Tristram's Honours year had sparked what Burt called his 'second coming' – and Lucien Hooker was to be a very important part of that. They were going to form a new, productive laboratory again – the 'physiology dream team' – and Tristram's Honours project represented Burt's first sortie into that venture. For years, Burt had not produced any scientific papers or taken on any students, as he had suffered a divorce and two heart-attacks – and then a triple by-pass operation. The divorce was particularly painful to Burt. He loved his ex-wife and their three children dearly – but after his first heart-attack, Burt had looked death in the eye and decided rather abruptly that he might be gay. He began a homosexual relationship with an antique dealer called Nathan who was twenty years his junior and ended his marriage. For those that knew Burt well, these events were unexpected but not out of character. What Tristram found remarkable, was Burt's mysterious power to maintain the affection of people that he had deeply hurt.

During Tristram's third year, Burt decided that he would rebuild the animal physiology lab. He and Lucien would each take on more third year and Honours students, with some of them such as Tristram, continuing as post-graduates. Tristram would be a head demonstrator for the second and third year practicals, and Burt and Lucien would continue to teach the third-year Animal Physiology course.

At the end of Tristram's Honours, with a very promising scientific discovery, Burt was full to the brim with enthusiasm. He took on three more Honours students, with Tristram doing a Masters. Tristram did not want a PhD in animal physiology; he wanted to do animal behaviour. However, his Honours mark was not quite enough to get him into the animal behaviour group, so he agreed to do a Masters with Burt and whilst he completed that, help as a demonstrator and colleague to the new Honours students.

For the first year, the plan seemed to go exceedingly well. The 'dream-team' was a happy-go-lucky, raucous bunch of students. Burt and Lucien were truly inspiring as teachers and mentors. Tristram was a good ear to the new students and helped them with their projects. The lab meetings were full of humorous, stimulating debate.

Yet, towards the end of the year history repeated itself. All three of Burt's new Honours students had projects with serious deficiencies that needed frantic last-minute correction. Once again, Burt was off in the library researching his personal history project. Once again, he was 'too stressed' from lectures or exam papers to give any of his students proper supervision. Whatever time Burt did give his students, there was very little left over for Tristram.

The Honours students were riddled with anxiety, but Tristram assured them that they must have faith in Burt. Yes – the man was haphazard and irresponsible at times – but he was also a genius that would not let his students fail. Tristram and Lucien helped them with drafts of their theses, and Burt vindicated Tristram's faith by pulling last minute miracles and guiding his students successfully to the finish line.

However, once the dust had settled after the Honours students had submitted, Burt's energy levels had been severely depleted. He was no help to Tristram, who had spent a year struggling with a very difficult series of experiments. Furthermore, the project was not interesting to Tristram. It felt more like a duty to Burt than the pursuit of his own aspirations. The Honours project that he had done at least had the benefit of novelty and innovation. The Masters project on the other hand, was essentially a repeat of all of Burt's earlier experiments – with no expectations of interesting results. In Burt's previous experiments on feeding, exercise and stress, the vagus nerve was thought to have been blocked – but of course, the presence of somatostatin destroyed that belief. Hence, Tristram was repeating the experiments exactly as Burt had done them, only this time he was surgically removing the vagus nerve – surgery which Burt had rightfully called 'fucking difficult'.

Tristram was miserable. He found the lab-work frustrating and excruciatingly tedious. Not only that, his conscience plagued him in two ways. First, was the thought that he was failing Burt after all the good-will that had been nurtured between them. Second, Tristram felt that the experiments that he was doing were cruel. Unlike the Honours project, the surgery was very invasive to the host toad. It was open heart surgery, which required that Tristram open the chest and sever the muscle and bone that the toads used to move and support themselves. Even though the Ethics Committee had approved the experiments, and Tristram was using anaesthesia and analgesics, he knew that he was causing the animals pain. He was making them run on a treadmill with a cannula tube coming out of the right lateral aorta – one of the two major blood vessels coming from the heart. For some of those experiments, the animals had undergone open heart surgery only four weeks before, when Tristram had surgically removed the vagosympathetic nerve branches just as they entered the heart. Tristram wanted to give the animals longer to recover from the surgery, but the toads could re-grow the severed nerves after five weeks.

The Masters was supposed to be only a year, but it dragged on for two. Tristram was living on very little money and was becoming seriously fed-up with the whole situation. However, Tristram persisted with the Masters – he had a debt of honour to Burt. Tristram reminded himself constantly that Burt had helped him greatly with his Honours, had been an inspiring teacher and mentor, and also...a friend. Tristram felt that Burt would be a man that he would know and care about deeply for the rest of his life.

Finally, Tristram could not confront Burt when he could see that Burt's world was falling apart. First, two of Burt's colleagues retired – Mike Hartford and Reginald McKenzie. Three months later, Burt's own mentor died. He was a notorious physiologist who had written a textbook on pharmacology still in use by many labs and a personal hero to Burt. It brought Burt's own mortality sharply into focus yet again. Nathan Panagiatidis – his lover – had an affair behind Burt's back with a man who turned out to be HIV positive. Aside from the emotional gauntlet of betrayal and humiliation, there was the risk that Burt himself may be infected. Burt eventually forgave Nathan, but it was an uneasy forgiveness.

The final straw was the fight with his dear friend and long-time colleague, Lucien Hooker. Lucien and Burt taught the third-year Comparative Animal Physiology class together, but it was really Lucien's baby. It was his absolute passion, and the culmination of his professional life. Success in the world of professional science is usually measured in terms of publications, of which Lucien had precious few. It was not that Lucien was not brilliant – in the opinion of many, including Burt and Harold Hildebrandt, the man was a genius. It was just that Lucien did not measure his success by a pile of publications in his name. Lucien loved teaching more than anything else, and he was exceptionally good at it. He got the highest student reviews ever recorded for a subject. However, despite that impressive achievement, Lucien was told that due to budget constraints, he would have to stop his class. He received no support from his colleagues. Burt plaintively shrugged his shoulders and basically told Lucien that he just didn't have the energy to fight for him.

Lucien was bitterly disappointed in his once mentor and friend. He retired in disgust.

Burt took Lucien's departure deeply to heart, and when Lucien's office was cleaned out and then occupied within a day by a graduate student from a competing physiology lab, Burt saw the end of his own career and what was left of his spirit died.

Meanwhile, Tristram struggled to finish a Masters that he hated more and more as the months went by. The pitiful scholarship finally ran out, and Tristram was forced to take a job.

Now, Tristram had begun to hate that job and bitterly resent the fact that his twenties had slipped away without anything to show for them. What if Burt never came through? Tristram had given the man six years – they were into the seventh year – would they really result in a failed Masters?

No. Don't be negative. Burt swore in front of Harold that my project has legs. It will result in a passable Masters – he said so. I just have to persist. I just have to be firm with him one more time…

Suddenly Burt sighed heavily from the other side of the workbench. "I know that I am in a thorn in your side. I know things in my personal life keep fucking me over and distracting me from your project. But you have completed the experiments and although the results are far from ideal, the material *is* there – I just need to get the momentum up to get into it."

Tristram nodded. "Burt, I have waited more than five years now. I am twenty-nine and working in a Call Centre for fuck's sake – I should have handed this in a minimum of three years ago. I should be half-way into a PhD in Animal Behaviour by now. But you won't let me hand it in without your approval, you won't let anyone else help me finish…"

"I never said that. When have I ever said that?"

"Burt, you have never explicitly forbidden me to seek help. But..."

"I believe that I have always encouraged it." Burt returned with a defensive frown.

"To a degree. When it comes to a second opinion or something like that – but when it comes to something more solid like an approach to the thesis, you have subtly steered me away from others with a promise that you will soon help me."

"Look...I won't deny the truth of what you say. You have been very patient with me – more patient than you really should have had to have been."

"Burt...with all due respect...you have been...outrageous." Tristram swallowed hard, after he said the words. He felt a strong pressure building behind his eyes.

Burt considered him with a guilty silence. Then he spoke gently.

"I deserve that criticism. I have fucked up...and I am sorry."

"You are always sorry. Don't be sorry. Just...say when you will look at my introduction." Tristram pleaded.

"Alright. Alright, that's fair. It's a good idea – we'll set a date, eh?"

"Please."

"Shall we say...end of this month? The thirtieth of November?"

"Yes." Tristram nodded eagerly.

"Right!" Burt clapped decisively. "I really will have made some solid progress on reading your introduction by then. Now...have you got anything that you can do in the meantime – or are you still busy with Australia Post?"

"I don't work for Australia Post. I work for Emu Post."

"Oh, yeah, that's right. I forgot."

"That's OK. I have done a fair bit of productive reading on

pain reception via the phrenic innervation of the epicardium – it is mostly histological, but it lends substance to our argument about shams in this study being more of a hindrance than a help as a control. I could try to write a section of my discussion on that stuff."

Burt nodded. "Good. I think that is a good idea."

A silence passed between them as they each dissected their own toad for tissue samples. It was eventually broken by Burt.

"Tristram..." The old man began. He waited for his student to make eye contact. "You deserve some reward for your persistence through a whole bunch of shit that you should not have had to deal with. I fully acknowledge that. I know you have heard all this before, but we really will knock this one on the head. I am retired now, and I have nothing else to deal with in my life. It's time."

Tristram sighed. "Thanks, boss."

Suddenly Tristram's mobile phone beeped loudly in his pocket.

"What was that?" Burt asked with alarm.

"That was my lie-detector." Tristram quipped as reached for his phone.

"Heh. Girlfriend?"

"I wish." Tristram answered. "No, this is from my cousin, Pyran."

"I see."

Tristram frowned as he read the message.

It said: "We need to talk. Dinewan is back and he has a message for you. See you tomorrow at Fred's funeral."

THE RETURN OF IVAN MACALLISTER

ELSPETH LAWSON WAS A GOOD LISTENER. Her smiles were tailored to the dialogue – sympathetic here, encouraging there and kind no matter what was being said. She laughed in the right way at the right time. Her deep-sea blue eyes gleamed with a caring intelligence. Her style was Bohemian – she wore a heavy purple dress that had a sapphire, floral pattern. Her long hair had the swirling shades of grey of an approaching summer thunderstorm.

Tristram knew that he was going to miss her, even though only an hour ago she was just another stranger on the train.

"You know something?" Tristram suddenly mused. "I just realised that I am doing to you what other people normally do to me."

"And what's that?" The old lady asked amiably.

"Chewing your ear off with my personal stuff, even though we have only just met." Tristram answered with an apologetic smile.

"Well, in your case it is a pleasure." Elspeth answered charmingly.

Tristram blushed and looked away. "Thanks."

"Seriously. I haven't a conversation this stimulating in quite some time." Elspeth continued. "You are an intelligent, funny, and charming young man. I think you will accomplish great things."

Tristram sighed and shook his head. "Thankyou."

"You don't believe it?"

Tristram met her perceptive eyes. "I want to believe it."

"But you don't."

"No." Tristram answered firmly.

"Why? Tell me, right now, why you don't believe it." Elspeth demanded.

Suddenly Tristram understood why he liked the older lady so much.

"You know, Elspeth, you remind me very much of my grandma, Joan." He smiled.

"Wonderful. Now I feel old." Elspeth sighed with playful rebuke.

"Heh. Actually, I never thought of my Grandma Joan as an old lady. She always had a youthful energy to her. She liked nothing better than a laugh with a glass of wine and good company. She was also very interested in young people and what they were up to. She even watched Big Brother." Tristram chuckled. "I loved her very much. She was a cool lady that I had a very special relationship with and I miss her deeply. Comparing you to her is a big compliment."

"In that case, I thank you. But you have dodged my question and I want an answer." Elspeth rejoined.

"Fine. I am nearly thirty. I work in a call centre. I have wasted seven years pursuing a Masters that is a mere stepping stone into a field that I don't think I want anymore – and in my heart, I don't think I will ever finish it. I have no money – just credit card debt and student loans. I have no assets. And the love of my life is not speaking to me. Needless to say, my morale is *low*." Tristram answered.

"Heh. Well, I'm sure you will find a way to turn it all around." Elspeth grinned warmly. "Your life is far from over – there is much more to come."

Tristram shrugged. "Yeah, there's more to come. But I am not excited about any of it."

"What?!"

"Oh...I still have dreams and ambitions...but at the moment they are abstract concepts rather than driving forces. Look: my life in a nutshell? I'm a failure until further notice."

"Oh, what a load of *rubbish!*" Elspeth exclaimed.

Tristram laughed heartily.

"*Seriously.*" Elspeth continued with theatrical disdain. "You can not think of yourself as a failure. You may certainly have failed to achieve some of your ambitions thus far, and you may have failed to make certain relationships work and what have you – but so has *everybody else!* As a person – as a specimen of human being, you are far from a failure. You have skills and talents and strength of character – and you have *time* to make very good use of all that you are. *Failure until further notice?* Pish! You need to change that attitude, young man – right now."

"OK. Thankyou, I'll think about it."

"Don't *think* about it. For heaven's sake, just get on with it! Change it! Change it now!" Elspeth expostulated.

"Alright, I will!" Tristram expostulated back.

"Well? Instead of 'failure until further notice' what are you changing it to?"

"I don't know."

"Wrong! And by wrong, I mean that you are getting there." Elspeth grinned.

"Heh. Alright then, do you have a suggestion?" Tristram chuckled.

Elspeth thought about it.

"Yes." She decided brightly. "Instead of 'failure until further notice' we will say: 'on the path to success'."

"On the path to success?"

"Yes. Why not? It doesn't say that you have succeeded yet – but that you are on your way. And there is nothing negative in there – nothing about failure."

Tristram nodded with a fond smile. "Alright."

"I am on the path to success." Elspeth reiterated with a proud sparkle in her eyes. "Say it."

"I am on the path to success." Tristram obeyed.

"Very good." Suddenly her expression changed. "Oh dear, here we go..."

Tristram gave a curious frown. "What's wrong?"

In answer, Elspeth leaned to one side and let out a rattling fart.

"Lentil curry." She explained with a charismatic grin. "Followed by crimson seedless grapes. The wretched things do it to me every time."

"Oh..." Tristram returned, suppressing a giggle. "As long as it wasn't the conversation."

Elspeth laughed merrily. "That would be one way to signal boredom, wouldn't it? I shall try and do it deliberately next time any of those wretched Witnesses come hassling me at my door."

"Heh."

"In all seriousness, Tristram, I am sorry about that."

"No worries. It will help me remember the conversation." Tristram answered congenially.

"Oh fantastic." Elspeth blushed chagrinously. "Now you

will forever remember me as the disgusting old lady who farted at you on the train."

Tristram chuckled. "Not at all – I will remember you as a nice lady who made me feel much better about my life."

"Before she immersed you in her own personal gas crisis. Phew! This rancid fog is the last thing you need! Oh well, when things next stink in your life you will remember that you are on the path to success."

They enjoyed a cackle at the quip.

As they settled down again there was an announcement over the speakers.

"Ladies and Gentlemen, we are approaching Traralgon Station."

Suddenly Tristram shuddered.

"Hmm." He mused as he wondered why.

"Yes?" Elspeth asked languidly.

"Dunno...just a shiver." Tristram shrugged.

The train slowed and then stopped.

"Oh wonderful." Elspeth sighed sarcastically. "Here he comes again. I don't think we can avoid him this time."

Tristram turned to see an aboriginal man shuffling down the aisle towards them. He was probably in his early forties, as his oily black hair had started to grey. The man was shabbily dressed and reeked of cheap beer and cigarette smoke. His eyes were red and glazed.

Elspeth and Tristram had noticed him when they first boarded the train. He had no sooner got on board when he started asking the other passengers for spare change. After he had obtained enough to buy a can of beer, he sauntered away to the refreshment bar in the middle carriage. Elspeth and Tristram had observed him repeat this procedure three times, and each time his begging would start at seats closer to theirs.

"Maybe if we both just look out the window, he will walk past us?" Tristram suggested.

"Heh. Good luck." Elspeth muttered as she turned to stare out the window.

The train started moving again.

Within a moment Tristram sensed the shuffling man approach. He continued to stare out the window as the scent of sweat, beer and smoke swirled into his nostrils.

"Oi...'scuse me, brudda." The aborigine drawled, patting Tristram on the shoulder. "You gotta spare cigarette, mate?"

Tristram turned to face him.

"Nah...sorry, mate, I don't smoke, eh?" He answered amiably.

"Oh..." The man mumbled.

The aborigine considered Elspeth briefly. She was unapproachable, as she looked resolutely out into the night.

As Tristram looked into the man's face he recognised him...

A year or two before, Tristram had driven past a shabby house in East Bairnsdale on the way to the river for some fishing. There were some kooris on the veranda, having a few beers. On the thick grass of their nature strip, the man now standing in front of him was lying prostrate, motionless and bleeding from a large cut on his forehead.

Tristram had asked the kooris if the man was alright, and they had simply laughed.

Tristram asked the man if he needed help, and when all he got was a nonsensical mumble, he decided to take the man to the hospital.

When Tristram had walked the man into the emergency room, he saw that it was empty, aside from a friendly looking elderly nurse and a tall young doctor. They had seemed to be having a pleasant conversation. However, as soon as they had noticed Tristram and the koori man, their smiles had dropped.

"Hey guys, just thought I'd better bring this chap in." Tristram began congenially.

The elderly nurse had sighed drily. "Oh, did you? Why?"

"I found him lying beside the road, barely conscious."

"Is that right?" The nurse had returned deadpan.

All of her former friendliness had evapourated. Hard, pale blue eyes considered Tristram.

Confused at the sudden hostility, Tristram had looked from the tall young doctor to the sour old nurse. "I'm sorry, have I made some sort of mistake?"

"I don't know, have you?" The nurse returned flatly.

Tristram had then held the nurse in a cool stare. "Is this the emergency room?"

"Yes."

"And would you consider someone barely conscious with a head wound as somebody who should probably be taken to the emergency room?"

The nurse grunted. "Sure. In *most* cases."

Tristram frowned incredulously and was about to take the nurse to task when the young doctor interjected.

"He's a regular here." He had explained with a patronising grin.

"*Very* regular." The nurse had added with contempt.

The doctor shone a pen-light into the koori's eyes.

"You'll be alright." The doctor concluded. "You know where to go, don't you?"

"Yep. Thanks, mate." The koori muttered, then wandered down a hallway and into one of the rooms.

The nurse rolled her eyes, then shook her head at Tristram before she had wandered after him.

Tristram gave a bewildered shrug. "Well...I suppose that's that, then. Sorry to be an inconvienience."

The doctor smiled kindly. "You did what you thought was right. In fact, to be fair, you did do the right thing. I don't want to sound racist but...the fact is, we get guys like him in every weekend. They always drink too much and then injure themselves. Where did you find him? Just up the road?"

"Over in East Bairnsdale."

The doctor had given a confused frown. "How did you get him here?"

"I drove him."

"What? In *your* car?" The doctor asked incredulously.

"Yeah. In *my* car." Tristram returned sardonically. "I let him sit in the front seat and everything."

"Heh. Oh well. Good on you. Have a nice day." The doctor had smiled, before he patted Tristram on the shoulder and strode away.

Tristram came back to the present.

The koori man before him on the train was still looking at him.

Do you recognise me at all? Tristram wondered.

"Goddolla?" Asked the aborigine.

"Hmm?"

"You got any spare change?"

"Um...yeah, let me just check – I might be able to help ya." Tristram pulled out his wallet and gave the man all his spare change – about eight dollars. "There ya are – that's all the change I got."

"Good on ya, brudda. Thanks, mate. Take it easy, eh?"

"No worries, mate. You too." As the man shuffled away, Tristram smiled and shrugged at Elspeth.

"You could have pretended not to hear him." She suggetsed.

"No...that'd be rude, and there's no need for that."

"*He* was rude. His behaviour was disgraceful. Putting people on the spot like that – it just isn't appropriate."

"Well, he won't bother us anymore." Tristram rejoined.

"Not on this trip. But he or someone like him is going to go on asking us for spare change. As your hero Oscar Wilde once said, charity creates a multitude of sins. You've done more harm than good."

"Hey look – nobody is perfect, alright." Tristram retorted. "He who is totally uncharitable cast the first stone!"

Suddenly an empty drink bottle came spinning towards him. He caught it quickly just before it hit his face.

He frowned, then looked up at the man who had thrown it.

Even in his forties, Ivan MacAllister was strikingly handsome. His eyes were still a dark, penetrating sapphire. Though his once raven locks had now lightened with faint ribbons of grey, it only served to make him more interesting. Ivan's choice in clothing accentuated his lean figure – tight blue denim jeans, white t-shirt, long leather boots and a deep coffee coloured, leather bomber-jacket. Though Ivan's skin was still fairly smooth and youthful, he now had fine laugh-lines and very dark circles under his eyes.

"This is *not* a stone." Tristram beamed at Ivan.

"Greetings, Tristram Jones." Ivan began suavely.

"Salutations, Ivan MacAllister."

"May I join you?"

Tristram stood up and shook Ivan by the hand heartily.

"I don't believe it! I have been thinking of you all day!" Tristram exclaimed.

"No kidding? I was coming to Bairnsdale to seek you out."

"But I live in Melbourne now."

"I figured you would be back in Bairnsdale this Saturday morning." Ivan answered with an enigmatic smile.

Tristram returned the smile. "So, you *did* get my email. But what are the odds of us meeting on a train?! I normally drive, but my car died in Bairnsdale last time I was down – and surely you have your own wheels?"

Ivan shrugged ruefully. "I tore the under-carriage out of my Landcruiser last week, driving carelessly in the bush."

"Really? Well, sorry to hear it. Anyway, man, sit down and let's catch up. It's only been *twelve years!*"

Ivan hoisted his back-pack up onto the bag rail and sat down next to Tristram.

After a polite introduction, Tristram and Ivan began a light-hearted argument about the merits of the modern high-school teacher, which Elspeth found very amusing. Ivan was charming and articulate, just as Tristram had remembered him.

Suddenly their conversation was interrupted by a loud, ocker young mother.

"Bradley! Stop fuckin' around and give me back me smokes! Jesus Christ, don't ya know how to behave in public?"

Ivan, Elsepth and Tristram turned their attention to the young woman. She was half drunk and heavily made-up.

"Now siddown an' drink ya Coke before ya dad goes crook at ya again." She continued. "What? Ya finished? Alright, hang on, hang on. Look – here, ya can have the rest of this UDL."

"UDL?" Tristram scoffed. "Christ. That would be soft-drink with *vodka* in it."

Elspeth sighed. "It's disgraceful, isn't it?"

"Disgraceful?" Ivan answered with a sudden hostility. "Try thoughtless, moronic and irresponsible!"

Tristram searched Ivan's face. *That was a rather passionate response.*

"Children are precious things." Ivan continued with

palpable bitterness. "Do you know what I mean? I mean children are precious. I mean more valuable, more important, more special than anything else in this farce we call life and yet...they are given by chance to any pair of deadshits who fuck, aren't they?"

Ivan noticed that Elspeth was taken aback. He calmed himslef, then gave us both an engaging smile.

"Excuse me. It's been a long day – a long year, actually."

Elspeth nodded politely. "Things like that do make you wonder how we made it this far as a species."

Tristram continued to look into Ivan. "Not really. Evolution is not survival of the fittest – it's survival of those who breed."

"So anyway, Tristram..." Ivan began.

"Yes?"

"I was going to ask you something before that bogan woman distracted me. I noticed that you gave some spare change to that drunk aborigine."

"Yeah. So?"

"Would you have given that man your spare change if he was white – or indeed, any nationality other than aboriginal?"

"I don't know. Maybe...maybe not." Tristram shrugged gently.

Ivan's dark sapphire eyes sparkled. "Perhaps a recent event has influenced you?"

As Tristram met Ivan's eyes, he couldn't help but smile.

You still want to be my teacher. You still want to play little games to make me think.

Tristram sighed. "OK, Ivan. Just like old times, you got me. The real reason that I gave that guy my spare change? I felt a bit guilty."

"Why?" Ivan prodded.

Tristram turned to Elspeth. "When I was growing up, I

knew an aboriginal elder called Fred Morris. He liked me, and I liked him, and we shared a special friendship – or at least, we should have. But I never really visited Fred as often as I meant to – in fact, I haven't seen him in years. And tomorrow, tomorrow Ivan and I are going to his funeral."

Elspeth nodded understanding. "You were unconsciously giving change to your old friend, Fred?"

Tristram sighed. "Yeah, maybe. I don't know...maybe."

As the conversation continued, Tristram realised that Ivan had deliberately deflected the attention onto him and away from speculation as to why Ivan was so wound up by the young mother giving alcohol to her child. Tristram promised himself that he would get to the bottom of Ivan's reaction.

Ivan, however, was a step ahead of Tristram.

"So, Tristram, I recently reread your novella." He began cheerily. "I must say I enjoyed it. You have certainly improved it since I read your first attempt at it nearly fifteen years ago."

Tristram smiled.

"You wrote a novella?" Elspeth asked.

"Yes. It is now part one of a three-part novel." Tristram answered.

"And? What's it about?"

"Have you ever heard of the bunyip?"

"Yes, of course I have."

"Well, I wrote the novella about a bunyip – and my novella was inspired by an account that our good friend Ivan had inherited from his great, great grandfather. Ivan believes, rather optimistically, that there might be some truth in that account, and that one of his ancestors was eaten by a bunyip."

"Really? Well, that *is* interesting." Elspeth returned. "I'd love to read these stories."

Tristram suddenly stood up and searched through his bag

up on the bag rail. He pulled out several folders, each with pages of text. He handed the thickest one to Elspeth.

"This is my novella." He announced with mock pride. "I've called your bluff, Elspeth. If you really want to read it, now is your opportunity!"

To Tristram's surprise and delight, Elspeth was keen to read some of his novella.

"I even have some new reading glasses which I got in Adelaide." She smiled brightly, as she accepted a folder of text from Tristram.

"I have some reading glasses too." Ivan grinned, as he retrieved some stylish glasses from inside his jacket. "Why don't you give me the chapters that come after the novella?"

Tristram was happy to oblidge.

With their glasses on, looking down onto the pages, Elspeth and Ivan suddenly seemed rather supercilious. As he watched them read, Tristram was filled with a contrary mix of pleasure and anxiety. He felt a childish need for the approval of his old English teacher and the nice stranger who reminded him so much of his grandma.

When it was time for Elspeth to disembark at Rosedale, she said the nicest thing to Tristram that he had heard in years.

"Well, Sir." She began, as she looked into Tristram seriously over her reading glasses. "You must publish this novella. I haven't read all of it, but what I have read is lovely. Yes, it needs some polish, but the bones of it are there – and they are *very solid bones*. You, Tristram Jones, are a writer. And you *are* on the path to success."

"Thankyou." Tristram murmured sincerely.

Ivan's reaction to his writing was less complimentary. When they were alone, he locked angry eyes on Tristram.

"Tristram, listen to me very, very carefully: you are not allowed to publish this."

"Excuse me?" Tristram returned coolly.

Ivan held firm. "You can't just write about other people's lives. What you have written is very autobiographical. And it is clear which characters are people from your life – and any one who reads this will be reading about them."

"What I have written is true – but not factual." Tristram shrugged.

"Ah – but it is a mix of what is true and what is not." Ivan rejoined.

"Are you embarrassed by what I have written about you?" Tristram prodded.

"Not at all – you paint me in a very positive light – so far..."

"Heh. You have all the charm of a fictional character, Ivan." Tristram joked.

Ivan's brilliant sapphire eyes gleamed with an animal malice. He leaned forward.

"Tristram, if you continue on this autobiographical course you are going to reveal things about my past that I do not want in the public eye. And you must understand that I will not allow that."

Tristram blushed.

"Ivan, I would never publish this without your permission." He murmured with a nervous, conciliatory smile.

"Well, if you want my permission, try a little more respect." Ivan snapped.

At that a defiance brewed in Tristram. "Actually, you know what? Bugger the consequences, I am going to write as I see fit."

"I beg your pardon?"

"Look: my inspiration comes from life, but it is not dictated from it. I will weave my story with fact and fiction – with no distinction between the two. Only those who know me very well will have some idea of what is real and what is not – and even then, they won't be able to tell about everything."

"Tristram..." Ivan began, but Tristram had not finished.

"Ivan... just... cut it out. Don't try and intimidate me – don't try and stare me down like a sensei in his dojo. I have a right to tell my story, I have a right to choose what is real in it and what is made up – and if you are uncomfortable with your impact on my story – bad fucking luck."

Suddenly Ivan seemed very tired, as though he had just aged a year in an instant.

He sighed heavily. "Will you at least have a disclaimer?"

Tristram parodied Ivan's sigh. "Yes, alright – if it will make you feel better."

Ivan allowed himself to smile. Then he suddenly leaned back and chuckled heartily.

"Oh Jesus...I have no idea why I am being so... intense." He frowned with bewildered good humour. Then he laughed again.

Tristram began to wonder what had happened to Ivan in the last twelve years. The man seemed pale and haunted. He lacked his old *savoir faire*.

"Ivan, something tells me that you have accumulated more painful memories since we last knew eachother." Tristram said kindly.

Ivan winced. "Heh. Yeah...but that's life, isn't it? Although...you know what? I'll have you know that I have also accumulated my best memories. Memories that are deep and powerful...and joyful."

"Yeah?"

Pain and pleasure fought in Ivan's smile. "Yeah...yeah. The very best memories of my life are those that have happened in the last twelve years."

Tristram nodded softly. "That's true for me too."

At that, the conversation eased into silence.

At Sale station, they disembarked and boarded the bus to Bairnsdale. Soon after they had taken a seat, Ivan began to read more of Tristram's novel. Tristram knew that Ivan was doing so to avoid conversation, but he did not take offense at that. In fact, he identified with it. He and Ivan were comfortable in each other's silences, and each allowed the other his own private reflection.

It's true. Tristram mused, as he watched the paddocks go by under a clear, starry night. The most deep and powerful memories I have are those from the last twelve years...particularly the last two.

PRAWNING

As THE BUS hummed through the night, Tristram mused on the beginnings of the most important relationship of his life so far.

It all started two years ago in the week before New Year's Eve. That was what she told him. Tristram had thought that it had begun four months later, during a cocktail party at Easter...

"No. You obtuse goose. Easter was when we finally crossed the line – not when it started. Our fiasco began with a message you sent to me New Year's Eve."

"Really? Well, I wasn't trying anything." Tristram smiled.

She laughed gently. "I believe you. But what you said on that night got the ball rolling."

"What did I say?"

"Remember I sent you a message asking you if you were coming to our New Year's Party? I said that there were a lot of single girls and that you should come along, remember?"

Tristram shrugged. "Yeah? So? I never came to your party."

73

"You said...hang on, I still have the message on my phone, I'll show you." She pulled out her phone.

"You keep all my messages?"

"Hell no. I delete most of your bumf as soon as you send it." She returned with a cheeky smile.

"Thanks."

"But some messages I keep. The ones that really...I dunno – the ones that change how I feel after reading them." Her dark eyes betrayed a sudden vulnerability.

Tristram swallowed. "This one changed your feelings?"

"Yeah." She blushed.

"Well, what did I say?"

She grunted. "I don't think you'll really get this."

"Just tell me already!"

"You said: "nah, the only girl there worth having is already married"." She looked deeply into him.

Tristram sighed. Then he smiled. "I wasn't trying to seduce you there. I was just paying you a compliment."

"I know. But it got me thinking. That's why later that week, when you and Lachlan went out prawning, and Chris was away, I wanted to come out with you."

It was a warm and humid summer night four days into the new year, 2007. The Eastern King Prawns were running in large schools through the Gippsland lakes, and they had grown bigger after the recent full moon. They could be caught by wading with dip-nets in the shallow bays that shouldered the mouths of the major rivers. In the same territory, flathead, flounder and sole could be had with hand-held spears. Tristram, his family and friends were regular visitors to the bays either side of the Tambo River. Tonight, Tristram, his father and Tristram's long-time fishing mate, Lachlan

Pendergast, were getting ready on the shore of Swan Reach Bay.

The air was steeped with the fresh, savoury smell of the estuary: seaweed and rich, sandy mud. The still surface of the bay was a perfect mirror for the universe above. There was no moon on this night, yet there was light. In the distance, across the bay to the north west, white town lights glowed like a puddle of fallen stars.

The day had baked the landscape as it had done for the last few weeks. Thunderstorms had rumbled briefly in the afternoon, but the quick soak of warm rain had all but evapourated by sunset.

Tristram smiled with deep contentment as he stepped into the luke-warm water of the bay. His bare feet registered the soft, sandy mud. It was only an inch or so deep, before the bottom became hard, so it was very easy to walk on.

Perfect conditions.

Suddenly he detected the sound of heavy wings, then the deep, muted notes of eight black swans flying overhead.

"Boom-boom!" Lachlan called, as he always did when they saw any animal.

Lachlan was of Tristram's age and had been friends with him since year ten at secondary college. He was a giant – six foot four inches tall with very wide shoulders. He helped his father repair bridges through-out East Gippsland. Great strength was in his limbs, and his legs, face and arms were permanently tanned. His sandy brown hair was cut very short, under a dusty base-ball cap that was forever upon his head. Lachlan had a round face with a small nose and cheeky brown eyes. These features would have given him a boyish expression, were it not for his goatee.

Tristram smiled. "I dunno if swans would be any good eating, mate."

Lachlan and Russell wandered over with their nets, spears and waders.

Lachlan shrugged, as he lit a cigarette.

"I wouldn't know." He drawled. "Although me granddad ate a pelican once."

"What?" Russell and Tristram scoffed in unison.

"He did." Lachlan rejoined.

"That's illeagal." Russell said.

Lachlan remained deadpan. "I know. He got fined for it."

"How much was the fine?" Tristram grinned.

"I can't remember. But just before the judge fined him, he said 'just outta curiosity, what did it taste like?' And me granddad goes 'Oh...mid-way between platypus and koala'."

Tristram and his father groaned.

"Is that true?" Tristram asked.

"No, you idiot!" Russell laughed. "It's an old joke."

"Well, you never know with this bastard." Tristram answered. "Anyway, come on, fellas! Let's get out there!"

"Yeah, yeah – in a second! Russ and I just have to get our waders on." Lachlan rumbled.

"Waders. What a pair of *pansies*. I know that Dad has always been a pussy but why do *you* wear waders?" Tristram smirked.

"Hey!" Russell objected. "Unlike you, Lachie and I don't have to worry about cut feet."

"There is nothing out there that can cut your feet." Tristram scoffed.

Suddenly headlights shone across the paddocks, and the sound of a small car engine grew louder as it approached.

Tristram sighed. "Ah well, it's too good a night for there not to be others here."

"It's Eve." Lachlan announced.

"Eve Hong?" Tristram asked surprised.

"You mean Eve Saintly." Russell reminded him.

"I know, I know. I keep forgetting."

"I reckon she might like to forget it, too." Lachlan quipped drily.

"Lachlan." Russell censured.

"What? I'm just sayin'."

"Things are good with Chris and Eve." Tristram rejoined.

"Yeah, things aren't always what they seem." Lachlan crooned cheekily.

"Oh, you bloody great shit-stirrer!" Russell responded, punching Lachlan lightly on the arm.

Lachlan laughed. "Ease up, Russ – I'm windin' Tris up, not you!"

"Why is she here?" Tristram asked.

Lachlan shrugged. "I caught up with Chris and Eve before Chris went off to Melbourne this arvo. I told him he was gonna miss out on a good night for prawning and then Eve piped up and wanted to come out with us. That's alright, isn't it?"

"Yeah, that's fine." Tristram shrugged good-naturedly as Eve's little hatch-back pulled up beside Lachlan's old 1978 Holden Premier.

As the engine shut off, Lachlan gave Tristram a surreptitious grin.

"I reckon she has a bit of a thing for you, all jokes aside."

Tristram laughed gently. "Chris has nothing to worry about."

"It took you a while to catch up, didn't it?" She asked, thoughtfully.

"We were prawning. I was happy to see you. As a friend." Tristram answered.

"Well, on New Year's Eve the seed was planted. But it was

on that night we went prawning that I decided that I wanted to be with you."

As the bus continued through the starry night, Tristram continued with his memories.

It was that night. At what moment in that night did it begin?

"Hello!" Eve called cheerily, as she got out of her car.

"G'day, Eve." Lachlan and Russell answered.

"Hey." Tristram grinned.

"How do I look? Will it do for a prawning wench?" She chuckled.

Lachlan shone his headlamp upon her.

Eve Saintly was a beautiful half Vietnamese, half Caucasian woman. She was slender and graceful, with olive skin and fine, shoulder-length hair that was usually raven coloured. Tonight, she had died it a vibrant sky blue. She had large almond hazel eyes, and when she made eye contact, she smiled fondly. It was a smile that always found a smile in return.

Even in old sneakers, old beige board shorts that seemed over-sized, and black t-shirt, Eve seemed elegant and at ease.

You're as gorgeous as ever. Tristram thought warmly.

Yet, there was no longing in him.

"What's with the blue hair? Did you shower with toilet cleaner?" Russell teased.

"You're mean, Russ." Eve smiled cheekily. "I dyed it for you, don't you like it? Blue is your favourite colour, yeah? Come on! Don't you like it?"

"I like it." Tristram smiled.

"There! Like father like son, yeah?" Eve beamed.

Russell chuckled. "It's lovely."

"I'll just get me waders on and we'll be off." Lachlan announced.

Eve suddenly looked concerned. "Do I need waders?'

"No. I'm not wearing waders." Tristram answered. "They're for wimps. Are you a wimp?"

She frowned at him playfully. "Hell no. Should I at least leave these sneakers on?"

"It would be a good idea, Eve." Russell answered as he pulled his waders up. "You never what's out there, but you be your own judge."

Eve took her shoes off. Then she poked Tristram in the chest. "If I cut my feet, I am holding you personally responsible."

With that, they entered the water.

They had two prawning boxes – plastic tubs about the size of a laundry basket, lined with polystyrene foam an inch thick, with a rectangle cut out of the middle for an old car battery to sit. The boxes were tied to a fine orange rope, which was looped around the waste of the person who held the prawning light and towed the box. The prawning lights had a stem about a metre long, and at their end a large light bulb protruded at a right-angle to the stem.

"Make sure you keep the light under-water – the glass gets really hot in the air, and if you let the bulb get hot and then put it under-water, it will crack." Lachlan reminded every-one.

Russell towed one box, Tristram encouraged Eve to tow the other.

"Is there a special way to do this?" Eve asked, as Tristram tied the rope around her waist.

"Not really, just do a gentle sweep with the light from side to side as we walk, so that we light as much of the ground as we can." Tristram answered. "By the way, you hold this dip net in your other hand. I'll carry the spear."

"Aren't girls allowed to have spears?" Eve teased.

"Not at all, it's just that when we come across prawns, it is usually easier for the person with the light to net them."

Soon the troup was in water up to their knees. Hundreds of tiny grey-green fish darted away from them in the clear water.

"We might be a bit early." Lachlan drawled. "The tide is still out a bit, I reckon. We might get a good run later in the night."

"I'm not sure that we can stay out very long." Tristram answered deadpan.

"What? *Why?*" Lachlan demanded.

"Oh...just looking up at the stars...I reckon a storm's comin'." Tristram grinned.

Russell chuckled heartily.

"Good on ya." Lachlan grunted.

"Am I missing something?" Eve asked.

"No." Lachlan answered firmly.

"Just an in-joke." Tristram rejoined.

"Here we go." Lachlan sighed.

"Me, Sam, Dad and Lachlan were out fishing one night." Tristram began. "It had been quiet for a while, and then Lachie breaks the silence with "Arp. Storm's comin'." We asked him why, and he pointed up to the sky and said "handle of the Big Dipper's pointin' the other way.""

Eve and Russell chuckled.

"It was a joke." Lachlan retorted

"No, it wasn't!" Russell interjected. "You were deadly serious. And I said "that's cosmologically impossible, Lachlan.""

"That's not the only pearl we have from Lachlan." Tristram smiled gleefully.

"Oh, here we go." Lachlan groaned. "I tell you guys things

to try and cheer you up, and then you turn around and take the piss."

"Only last week, Lachie and I were fishing down on the Grassy Banks of the Mitchell." Tristram continued. "And then Lachie suddenly turned to me and said "caught a carp on a plover egg the other day.""

Eve frowned incredulously. "What? How?"

"It's not true, obviously." Tristram teased.

"It is true!" Lachlan bellowed. "Last time I tell you anything, ya prick."

"I'm jokin', man!" Tristram laughed.

"Come on, Lachlan. Tell me how you did it." Eve prodded.

"I'd just run out of garden worm, when I noticed this plover nest nearby. There were two eggs in it, so I threaded one on me hook and then landed an eight-pound carp." Lachlan shrugged.

"It was only six-pound last week." Tristram smirked.

"He told me five-pound on the day it happened." Russell added.

"Fine. Whatever, I still caught a carp on a plover egg." Lachlan concluded.

"You have to watch him, Eve." Tristram continued. "His stories always start with a seed of truth, but then they spin wildly out of control."

"You love it." Lachlan grinned.

Russell chuckled. "Tell her about the onion incident."

Tristram let out a short bark of laughter. "You're right! That one's a pearler!"

Russell turned to Eve, jerking his thumb at Lachlan.

"This big thug killed a rabbit from his front porch by throwing an onion at it."

"What? Why with an onion?" Eve frowned.

Lachlan shrugged. "Gun wasn't handy. There was an onion on the kitchen window sill."

"You're a natural killer." Russell grinned. "If it wasn't for you, we probably never would have started the wildlife shelter."

Lachlan grunted. "Heh. Yeah – it all started with that little swamp wallaby, didn't it? Didn't know the wallaby I shot had a joey – and I thought Holly might want to look after it, so I brought it to your joint on the front seat of Dad's ute."

Suddenly they saw a small eel, about a foot long. It swam languidly into the pool of light made by the troup.

"Look out!" Lachlan whooped. "We're at the point in the night where we watch Tris shit himself!"

Russell bellowed with laughter.

"Well?" Eve shouldered Tristram.

"Dad will tell this one."

"One night out here, Sam, Saffi, Tris and I – and I think Lachie, you were here?"

"Yep." Lachlan grinned broadly.

"Well, we came across this bloody great big conga eel, and Tris had the bright idea of spearing it for shark bait. Sam and Saffi were right behind him, and just as Sam said 'nah, you'll never get it' Tris struck and pinned it just behind the head. Well, it wriggled and fought furiously, and then escaped. Then came charging back!"

"A truly, terrifying spectactle." Tristram added firmly. "This eel was a monster – big golden eyes and a mouth gaping with teeth like a wild dog – and it was seriously pissed off."

Lachlan chuckled. "Russ and I were fine, we were in waders."

"Anyway, the three of them panicked." Russell continued. "Saffi belted off so fast that the light became disconnected from the box, plunging us into darkness. Sam was shrieking at the top of his voice, Saffi was charging through the water towards the shore and Tris was climbing up onto my bloody shoulders like some crazed gibbon!"

"Brave boy, aren't you?" Eve teased.

"You weren't there – it was a bloody monster." Tristram returned. "In hindsight, I should not have speared it. It would have been a very old creature, probably a large sterile male."

"But to you, just shark bait?" Eve rejoined.

"Not anymore. Too tough. Too mysterious. Even though I have heard that they really are the best shark bait." Tristram grinned.

"Second best." Lachlan contradicted.

"What's the best?" Eve asked.

Lachlan sighed. "Alright, I'll tell ya something. But Russ and Tris: don't tell Holly, alright? I'd never hear the bloody end of it."

"Oh, this ought to be good." Russell groaned.

"Couple of weeks ago, me and Johnno were out at his farm near Sale, when we saw his neighbour's cat. It had been givin' Johnno the shits for ages 'cause it kept comin' after his budgies – and then there it was in the drive-way, so we shot it and cut it into four bits for shark bait." Lachlan recounted.

"That's horrible! You used a cat for shark bait!? Why?" Eve gasped.

Lachlan shrugged. "Neither of us had the heart to shoot a dog."

"Was it the stories?" Tristram asked.

"That was part of it, actually." She answered. "They made me feel connected to something...I don't know exactly what, but it was good. It was something I had been missing."

"Family? Friends?"

"Not exactly. I mean, I have a good family. And I have good friends. I can't explain it. But I felt something stir awake in me. And I knew that something big was going to change."

83

. . .

Tristram shook his head and exhaled deeply as he stared out the bus window.

What was it about that night?

"We might have more luck if we split up." Lachlan suggested. "With four people trudging in the water, we're scaring everything away."

"OK. You and Dad go towards shore, me and Eve will head towards that old dead tree." Tristram answered.

As the night wore on, Tristram and Eve saw baby sole and flounder, gelatinous orange eggs that puzzled Tristram, a yellow seahorse the size of Eve's little finger and a tiny purple squid that flashed irridescent colours as it hovered in the torchlight. They saw five inch-long, electric blue garfish with bright red knobs on the end of their needle-like snouts. They saw spherical clear sea-jellies and olive spider-crabs. They also saw two very large conga eels.

Eventually, they started to come across King Prawns of a good size. Tristram showed Eve how to catch them, and they collected enough for a good feed the next day.

Finally, they came across a large flounder. It was a mottled olive green and about the size of a dinner plate.

"Jackpot!" Tristram exclaimed, then pointed the spear. Then he noticed the look of nervous distaste on Eve's face.

"We don't have to spear it." Tristram sighed with a grin.

"No, don't mind me. If you want it, kill it." She replied.

"They *are* delicious. A sweet, white flesh. We could bake it in the oven with some butter, lemon and chilli." Tristram explained. The thought made him salivate.

"I don't like eating fish."

"What fish?"

"All fish. They all taste the same." Eve grimaced.

"What? What do you mean they all taste the same? And what do you mean you don't like fish? What sort of Asian are you?" Tristram grinned.

"I'm half Asian, remember? Just shut-up and spear it already, before it takes off on you." Eve shot back.

Tristram chuckled. "Flounder are not as skittish as flathead. He'll sit there quite smug, thinking that we can't see him until he feels the spear in his back."

"That's so horrible!" Eve groaned.

"Alright. I won't spear him. Watch this."

Tristram then placed his foot on the fish and pressed it to the sandy mud.

"Have you actually got it?" Eve asked.

"Yep." Tristram smiled broadly. "This is another reason that I go bare-foot. You can't do a foot-catch of flounder in waders – well you can, but you will likely injure the fish."

He reached down and grasped the flounder firmly by the head.

"What a wierd animal." Eve frowned. "It's mouth is in a really strange position..."

"Flounder are not like sting-rays." Tristram explained. "They start off swimming around like a normal fish. Then, the eye migrates around the head to join the other one."

"What?"

"It's true. Then they turn on the now eye-less side and start to swim along the bottom. The side facing the bottom loses all pigment to become milky white, and the side facing the sky changes colour to resemble the sand."

"Its eye moves around the head?"

"Yep."

"Which one?"

"Depends on the species. Some the left eye moves, others the right."

"Huh..."

"Don't tell me. It was the zoology lessons." Tristram grinned.

"Heh. No."

"I bored you with all that stuff, didn't I? I noticed you were quiet whenever I was showing you things and talking about them."

"I loved it." She murmured.

"Right."

"I'm serious. I was quiet because I loved it." She smiled into him. "A certain kind of joy emanates from you when you are talking about nature, and it is very catching."

"Yet it wasn't the zoology lessons?"

She shook her head. "No."

Tristram sighed at the memory. He noticed that the other passengers on the bus were getting restless. They would be at Bairnsdale very soon.

So what was it then? All that remains is the walk back towards the car...

They waded through knee-deep water towards the small light of the kerosene lamp in the distance. The sloshing of the water the only sound between them.

"Do I seem unhappy to you?" Eve asked.

Tristram smiled. "I thought this was one of those comfortable silences? I have been waffling on all night, I thought you were appreciating the break."

"No – I don't mean now. I mean in general. Do you think I am unhappy?"

Her tone was casual, but Tristram sensed something behind it.

"*Are* you unhappy?"

"No."

"Good."

"I love Chris."

"And poultry farming?"

"I don't really like poultry farming. I used to – when it was just Chris and I and a few rare breeds of chickens. And pheasants – until we learned that they were unprofitable around here. I miss the pheasants, actually – they were very dirty but at least they were pretty to look at."

"Dad says that pheasants are just chooks in drag." Tristram grinned.

"Heh. Anyway, originally Chris and I used to be a good team, you know, we were on equal ground."

"Is that no longer that case?"

"No. I mean, Chris respects me and loves me, I know he does. But in the last two years he has kinda expanded the whole operation without me. I mean – I understand why he has taken over the financial side of things – because he used to stress me out by borrowing too much money – I hate owing money – but the business has grown and been very successful, so I can't fault him there. And I agreed to it – I mean I agreed to stay out of the finances of the business and just do my thing – which was to deal with customers and distributors and feed orders and keep the pens tidy...it was for the best."

"Out with it, Eve." Tristram demanded, yet his tone was kindly.

"Fine. OK, I'll tell you something... I feel like... he has left me behind."

"Go on." Tristram nodded thoughtfully.

"I don't feel a part of the direction of the business anymore. I do all the hard work – all the grunt stuff – while he is off shmoozing potential partners and looking for different markets and special stock. He is designing all the pens and all the product lines – and borrowing more and more. You know how he bought a house in town, recently?"

"Yes."

"He didn't ask me about that."

Tristram turned to her, surprised.

"What do you mean? He told me that you guys had agreed to do that so that you would have some collateral to borrow against. I thought it sounded like a good business decision. Chris is a very talented businessman."

"Is he? How do you know?" Eve demanded.

Tristram shrugged. "He has always been a clever, business-oriented kind of guy."

"And you think it's OK to just go on ahead and buy a *house* without talking to your wife?"

"I admit that I don't." Tristram answered gently.

"I didn't even see the house before he bought it." Eve added angrily.

"I am surprised that Chris did that." Tristram returned carefully. "But this I do know: he loves you dearly and he has only your best interests at heart. I'm sure he did not mean to upset you."

Eve sighed heavily. "I know that. But still...it just feels like I am doing all the shit work – and I am tired and stressed and there just isn't anything left for me anymore."

Tristram stopped and looked into Eve.

"So, what do you want?"

"I don't know. What do you mean, what do I want?"

"You said that there isn't anything left for you anymore. What is that anything?"

Eve put her hands in her hips. Then she seemed lost for words.

"I... have not really thought about it." She answered finally.

Tristram raised his eyebrows. "Really?"

"Well, there was stuff that I wanted to do, but it just didn't pan out." Eve sighed irritably.

"Like what?"

"Art. I wanted to do arty things."

"Art. OK. Like what? Painting? Music?"

"Jewellery." She announced decisively.

"No kidding? I didn't know you were ever into that."

"I've only done a little bit. But I really, really liked it and I wanted to do more. I liked working with beads and stuff...but what I really want to work with is silver. What are you grinning at?"

"Do you have dry hands?" Tristram asked.

"*What*? Why?"

"Pull the light leads off the battery a minute, I want to show you something."

Eve hesitated with playful suspicion. "Am I going to get shocked?"

"Not if you have dry hands."

Eve unhooked one of the leads and the light went out.

"Now what? What are you up to, Mr. Jones?" She asked.

"Notice anything?" Tristram asked.

They were two shadows in a dark lake, with the stars shining brightly above them.

"The view has improved – I can't see you anymore." Eve teased.

In answer, Tristram splashed gently in the water.

"Is there a point to this?" Eve retorted. Then she noticed. "Hey...wow..."

Each splash of the dark water caused electric blue bubbles that gleamed in the night.

They began to splash more vigourously, filling the water about them with faint blue light and bubbles.

"Magic, isn't it?" Tristram smiled.

"What is going on with this water!?" Eve exclaimed.

"Bioluminescence. It is caused by tiny creatures called dinoflagellates. When they feel a disturbance in the water around them, they think that there must be predators around. So, they give off a flash of light, which has the effect of attracting the things that will eat the things trying to eat them."

"Heh. Now it's even cooler."

"Now, about your situation..." Tristram began. He continued to splash gently about him, so that they were bathed in the faint blue light.

"Yes?" Eve asked seriously.

"It is about to get a whole lot better. *Because*, you have identified something that makes you happy. You are going to explore making jewellery."

"Yeah right. Haven't you been listening? I don't have the time."

"That is something that you have to remedy. Talk to Chris and together work out a way to get a bit more of what you want. You deserve it, and I know that Chris will be very happy to make it happen."

"You make it sound easy." Eve murmured.

"I would have settled for possible. But yes, when you come to nutting out the details, it will seem absurdly easy." Tristram assured her. "And you just watch the effect it has on you. Suddenly you will start to enjoy life again, and you will be a whole new person. Doing what you truly love has that effect."

"Are you doing what you truly love?" Eve asked him seriously.

Tristram reached into the box and reconnected the battery lead. He got a shock.

"Ouch." He chuckled. "Let's go."

As they walked, Eve persisted. "You didn't answer me."

Tristram nodded sadly. "I'm happy right at this moment."

"Just not in the rest of your life?"

"No, my life is not yet where I want it to be. But the wind will find my sails and I can see my guiding stars."

"You always were wierd." Eve grunted.

"Gee thanks." Tristram drawled.

"But you know something? I know you will get there." She added sincerely.

"On that night, I realised that I really was unhappy in my marriage. And I also knew that I was interested in you and I was thrilled by that. I don't think I intended to do anything about it. I mean, I wasn't seriously thinking that I wanted to end my marriage or have an affair with you. But..."

"*But?*"

"*When I went home that night, I crawled into bed and had a very nice time... thinking of you.*"

"*Jesus.*"

"*No. You.*"

COCKTAILS

THREE MONTHS after that night of prawning it was Easter, and Tristram, Saffi and Sam had arrived late to Chris and Eve 's cocktail party.

"What the hell, mate?" Chris chuckled as music boomed and happy drunken people careened through their lounge room. "You were supposed to come early to learn how to make cocktails – and you bloody well turn up late!"

Chris was a stocky, well built man with an even more boyish face than Lachlan. He had tanned, flawless skin and large, open eyes the colour of a tropical blue lagoon. His smile was wide, white and engaging. He was handsome and stylish. His auburn hair was in a short, fashionable cut with blonde highlights. Though a few inches shorter than Tristram, Chris's presence was often larger as he had a cheerful, managerial disposition.

Tonight, Chris was dressed in black slacks with a white business shirt, open at the collar. Tristram wondered if he was under-dressed in his kaki cargo pants and black denim shirt – but he soon saw that everyone else at the party was casually dressed. He noticed with a grin that Lachlan was in his beige work shorts, thongs, and a navy singlet under a red flannellett shirt.

"Yeah, sorry we're late, mate." Tristram answered with a roguesh smile and a big hug. "I was waiting on a ride with Saffi and Sam, but they were late back from Sam's parents. We bought the lemons though."

Suddenly Eve appeared in front of him. She had red and blue feathers through her hair, which she had dyed a dark purple. She was wearing a low-cut black top and a long scarlet skirt. Her feet were bare, and she was very drunk.

"Oi. You didn't answer my text!" She began with playful scorn.

"What text?" Chris asked.

Tristram pulled out his phone. "This one: when are you coming over to ravish me in the rhubarb patch?"

Eve laughed raucously, and Chris shook his head.

"What were you going to answer? That's what I want to know." He said with mock suspicion.

"I dunno, some suave bull-shit." Tristram shrugged. "But I didn't get around to it because someone has turned the predictive text on in my phone and it's giving me the absolute shits."

Saffi glared at him with incredulous disgust. "*I* turned it on. Don't you find it much quicker?"

"No. Turn it back off." Tristram answered handing her the phone.

"*Caveman!*" Saffi exclaimed.

"What do you mean 'caveman'?! I have a bloody mobile phone, don't I?" Tristram retorted.

Sam laughed, his blue eyes twinkling under his blonde fringe. "Ease up, Saff'. This is Tris, remember? He is ten years behind everyone else – it was only last year that he swore he would never even get a mobile phone!"

"Jones, I will teach you later how to use predictive text." Chris declared. "But right now, you were all late getting here so now you all have to catch up!"

Chris then lead them to his make-shift cocktail bar in the kitchen.

Eve eyed Tristram coquettishly before she sauntered away to mingle with the other guests.

"So!" Chris began with a decisive clap of his hands. "What are you having first?"

"Just start from the beginning. Give me one of everything that has gone out since the start of the party." Tristram answered with a swagger.

"We've been drinking for two hours, mate." Chris warned playfully.

Tristram gave a cavalier shrug and then grinned at Sam. "I reckon Sam and I can do it all in twenty minutes."

Sam grinned back. "Shit. Alright, you're on!"

Saffi rolled her eyes.

Tristram and Sam were true to their word. In just twenty minutes, they had drunk a Cowboy, a Grasshopper, a Quick-fuck, a Rusty Nail, a Screw-driver, an Illusion, a Screaming Orgasm, a Slippery Nipple, a Zombie and then finally, a straight shot of Absynthe.

Tristram had thought that his university days had prepared him for such an intake of alcohol. So had Sam.

They were both wrong.

For about forty-five minutes, Tristram and Sam were the life of the party. They danced and joked and laughed. Then Sam disappeared into the garden to throw up for a while. Chris and Lachlan lead three cheers for Sam as he lay on the back lawn, hurling vomit at the foot of a rhododendron. Sam grinned sheepishly when he finished and gave the crowd the finger when they gave him a round of applause.

Meanwhile, in the lounge room, the world continued to spin wildly for Tristram. He noticed after a while, that Eve was spinning with him.

They tangoed, and slow danced and giggled stupidly.

Suddenly, Tristram's system could take no more and he felt himself on the verge of collapse.

"Are you going to join Sam in the garden?" Eve whispered flirtaciously in his ear.

"Heh. No. But I am going to pass out and there's nothing anyone can do about it." Tristram burbled.

"Just when I was having fun, too." Eve drawled. "Well, so much for a ravishing in the rhubarb patch. Come on, I'll take you to our spare room."

The next thing that Tristram remembered was lying on a thin matress across a springy wire frame, with a flimsy blanket over him. The room was dark and warm, and the party was deafening as it boomed through the open door. The bright yellow light from the hallway was in Tristram's eyes, but he was good-natured about it. People came in to chatter around him, and Eve was lying on top of the blanket beside him.

Tristram talked to everybody, but mostly to Eve, and he could not remember anything that he said, though apparently, it was funny. It was as if he had a conversation auto-pilot and he could tune his own conversation out as if it were someting on the radio.

"OK, we better let this boy pass out." Eve suddenly announced.

Tristram realised that he must have dozed off for a second.

"Thanks." He mumbled with a goofy grin.

Once everyone had left the room, Eve climbed onto the bed and straddled him playfully. He was under the blanket; she was above it.

"Good night." She grinned.

Tristram sighed. "Yes. It was."

"You didn't want any of the girls here tonight?"

"Only you." Tristram grinned cheekily.

"Well, you could have had me in the rhubarb patch." She crooned. As she spoke, she massaged his chest through the blanket. "But the fact is, you are going to be with someone else soon enough. And I will be jealous, but it's all good."

Tristram frowned drunkenly. "Is that a serious note I detect in your voice, Ms. Hong?"

"That's *Mrs. Saintly.*" She reminded him.

Tristram grinned and closed his eyes. "Of course. Well, perhaps in the next lifetime, you will marry me instead of Chris..."

"Next lifetime?" Eve asked whistfully. She continued to massage his chest, and Tristram was about to fall into a deep, drunken sleep.

"Yes. Next lifetime." Tristram mumbled. "I think we could have an amazing romance..."

He heard her scoff flirtaciously. "Must be amazing, if you fall asleep at the thought of it."

Tristram grunted. "The sooner I fall asleep, the sooner I can have you in my dreams."

"That is the lamest thing I have ever heard." Eve answered, slapping him on the chest.

Tristram opened his eyes and smiled cheekily at her. She was looking down into him, with a sleepy, sad smile.

"What is it?" Tristram asked.

"Next lifetime is a long time to wait." She murmured.

Eve leaned closer to him, so that he felt her long hair and the feathers touch his face. She was wearing a pink crystal necklace, and it swung in the promising shadow that held her cleavage.

"That is the way of it." Tristram sighed.

"I suppose." She sighed back.

"Good night, Eve Saintly." Tristram whispered with a smile, yet he felt a sudden longing that made him very sad.

Eve laughed gently. "Good night, Sir Tristram."

She kissed him on the forehead, and they both giggled.

"Night." Tristram mumbled.

Then Eve kissed him full on the mouth.

Tristram kissed her back, and then they stopped to look into each other.

Suddenly Eve got up and walked to the door. She closed it, and then ran back to the bed. She pulled the blanket up and crawled in on top of Tristram.

They kissed passionately and wildly.

Barely a minute passed before the door flew upon and somebody switched on the light, banishing the surreal scene like a bolt of lightening.

"Hey, what's going on in here?" Lachlan boomed cheerfully.

"We're having an affair, what does it look like?!" Tristram shouted jovially.

Other people piled in behind Lachlan, pointing and laughing drunkenly.

"Eve!" A plump woman gasped with mock rebuke. Her hair was dishevelled, and her mascara was running. "I am so proud – whoops, I mean so disappointed in you!"

Suddenly Chris entered.

"What's going on here?" He demanded jovially. "Jones, are you fucking my wife?"

"Well, I was trying to. Can you come back in like forty-five minutes?" Tristram returned.

Chris laughed, but his eyes betrayed a glint of anxiety.

"Actually, he is very boring and keeps passing out." Eve announced. "Let's get out of here and let him sleep."

"Fine! Get out of here you tease!" Tristram expostulated.

With that, they left. The door closed, and the light went out. As Tristram lay in the dark, a slow, terrible understanding engulfed him.

Something extremely bad just happened.

Sleep was now impossible, so he lurched out of the room, made a comical good-bye to the people still in attendance and then hugged Chris tightly.

"You alright?" Chris asked with genuine concern.

"That hug was a bit overboard, I know." Tristram drawled roguishly. "I think those bloody cocktails have made me bi-curious or something."

Chris, Lachlan and a few others laughed.

"I thought you were going to pass out?" Chris smiled incredulously.

"So did I. Second wind, I suppose. Anyway, I'm outta here. See you all later!"

With drunken laughter fading behind him, Tristram staggered out into the night for the forty-minute walk back to his parent's place.

"Folks, we shall shortly arrive at Bairnsdale Station." The Bus Driver announced.

Ivan turned to Tristram.

"I'm glad you gave me your novel to read." He smiled gently. "Otherwise I would have sat here the whole time brooding about everything that went wrong in my life."

Tristram blinked. "You're welcome. Thanks for reading it."

SHIT HAPPENS

A WARM, starry night greeted Ivan and Tristram as they exited the bus at Bairnsdale station. A full moon glowed tranquilly above them.

"I reckon summer's here a week early." Ivan grinned as he gave an exaggerated stretch. "I could almost go for a swim!"

Tristram shook his head. "Nah, the weather may have been very warm this week, but the water in the rivers will still be a bit chilly."

After they had collected their bags from the belly of the bus, they made their way north through the quiet streets of Bairnsdale, passing under the shadow of the heritage listed Catholic church. They shared a cynical smile at the fact that the austere monument was right next door to a brightly lit MacDonald's restaurant.

Only a few minutes had passed when they had reached Ivan's Aunty's house.

It was strange to be standing face to face with Ivan again after all these years, especially in the night. Tristram was suddenly reminded of their adventure in the small town of

Donald, when they had rushed to keep the old witch doctor in sight, as he had lead them out of town and into the vast, dry paddocks.

Should I tell him about the message from Dinewan? Tristram wondered.

He decided against it.

If I tell him about Dinewan's message, we will end up talking for awhile and I really want to check the messages on my phone...

"I'll be seeing you shortly, won't I?" Tristram said.

"Yes." Ivan nodded.

"Tomorrow, in fact."

"That's right. Eleven in the morning."

Tristram sighed sadly. "Life goes on..."

"So..." Ivan smiled. "Are you going to give me the rest of what you have written?"

Tristram shrugged. "Do you really want to read it?"

"If you don't mind."

"Alright." Tristram beamed.

He opened his backpack and handed Ivan the loose folders of text.

"Many thanks, Sir." Ivan grinned.

"These are more bits of the novel." Tristram explained. "They are fragments, really. I don't know where they fit yet, but I know that they are important."

"Have you have written more about me that I won't like?" Ivan asked drily.

Tristram chuckled. "So, your true motive is revealed."

"Part of it, yes." Ivan returned. "But in fairness to you, what I have read so far is readable."

"Readable?" Tristram grunted. "Well, that's something, I suppose."

A silence passed between them, in which Ivan seemed to be on the very edge of saying something. Yet, he said nothing.

In the semi-darkness, Tristram sensed a keen, sad longing in Ivan. The silence became too uncomfortable, so Tristram broke it.

"Well, I'd better get going if I want to get home before midnight."

Ivan nodded gently. "You're walking?"

"Yeah – I can't surprise my folks if I ask them to pick me up. Besides, I enjoy the walk. I get to cross the river."

"The good old Mitchell. It's been...well, years since I have laid eyes on it." Ivan mused whistfully.

Another pregnant silence began.

There is more here. Tristram thought. Ivan has an agenda that has something to do with me. And why is he even down here? Well, I don't want to get into this now...

Tristram cleared his throat. "I'm gonna keep going. I will see you at the funeral tomorrow, yeah?"

Ivan nodded, his reverie broken.

"Yes. Yes, you will. See you tomorrow, mate." Ivan said, and shook Tristram's hand firmly.

Good. Tomorrow I will find out what's going on with you. Tristram thought to himself as he turned and walked away.

Once Tristram was out of sight of Ivan he pulled out his mobile phone and checked it for messages. There were none, and he sighed with disappointment.

No response. She just won't respond to me.

Tristram quickened his pace in frustration.

There was a time when she wouldn't stop texting me...

· · ·

"Hi. Sorry I got so touchy-feely last night."

That was the text that Eve had sent the morning after the cocktail party. It was not the first text that he had received after he had staggered out the door, but it was the first one that Tristram could be certain had been sent from Eve. Chris had taken her phone and sent him messages supposedly from her to catch him out.

Tristram shook his head at the memory as he marched out of the town and down into the Mitchell River Valley.

Sorry I got so "touchy-feely" last night? Touchy-feely – the understatement of the century.

"So, what do we do now?" Tristram had messaged back.

His phone chimed softly as the reply was received. He would hear that chime a lot more often in the weeks and months to come.

"Don't tell Chris. I don't want him to know and I hope you want that too." Eve had responded.

I disagree. Tristram had thought grimly. *We have to face up to this.*

"Can we talk now?" He messaged back.

"Yes. Where are you?"

"I took a ride with Saffi and Sam back to Melbourne this afternoon." Tristram answered, and then he rang her.

"Hi." She answered miserably. Tristram felt his heart sink with guilt.

"Eve...I am so terribly sorry..."

At that he heard her sob and it hurt. He waited for her to say something back.

"I don't feel guilty. I know I should, but I don't." Eve finally murmured.

Heartbeats passed.

"You are probably still in shock." Tristram offered finally. "I know you, Eve. You are a good person and I think...well... the two of us were very drunk, weren't we? I was certainly totally out of my brain. And we were... playing a nice game of pretend... and then we took it too far. I promise you, that it will never happen again."

He heard more sobbing before she answered. "I feel like shit – but it's not guilt."

"Well, I can tell you that I feel guilty." Tristram returned seriously. "I feel guilt on a giant scale and I think we have to tell Chris and just get it out in the open, over and done with."

"No. Please don't tell him." Eve whispered anxiously.

"Eve..." Tristram began kindly.

"No. He won't take it well."

"Of course he won't."

"Look. If you tell him, I am dead."

"You won't be dead. Chris would never..."

"He would leave me. Our marriage would be over."

"Over a kiss?"

"You don't know this, but I told him I had a thing for you a while back as a joke, and he totally snapped. He said that if I ever did anything with you, that would be it."

Tristram sighed deeply.

"OK. I will tell him that it was my fault." He said.

"But it wasn't just your fault."

"I will take responsibility."

"No. It won't make a difference to Chris, he will end things either way."

"Eve, we have to tell him."

"No! Don't tell him!" Eve pleaded. "You don't know him like I do! Please don't tell him."

Tristram gave another heavy sigh. "Eve..."

"Please, Tris. Just trust me." Eve implored.

"Alright, Eve. I won't tell." Tristram promised. "So... what do we do now?"

"I don't know. Maybe I should hang myself." She retorted bitterly.

"Don't say things like that." Tristram replied earnesty. "I know we both feel like shit right now, but time will pass, and we will deal with this."

"How?"

"Well, if we are not going to tell Chris, then we just have to carry on as normal, don't we? Let's...bury this atrocious deed under a lifetime of good behaviour and leave it at that."

"Just like that?" Eve snorted bitterly.

"No... not just like that." Tristram rejoined gently. "This will take a bit of doing. It is going to be awkward, and we are going to feel bad and that is a natural consequence of doing the wrong thing. But we will get through it. We will get through it."

"Maybe" Eve sobbed.

"No maybe about it." Tristram assured her. "What we need is time...and distance."

"That sucks."

"Heh. Yes, it does. But everything will work out."

"OK."

"Eve...?"

"Yeah?"

"I think we should leave it there for now. I think we both need time...time to process this. OK?"

"OK." Eve sniffed. "Sorry."

"You don't have to say sorry to me. I should be saying sorry to you."

"Well, this certainly makes life interesting." Eve murmured.

Tristram grunted. "That's an understatement...Well...um... Eve... I am going to say good-bye now, OK?"

Eve hesitated before she responded. "OK."

"I mean...that's not good-bye forever, it's just...you know... bye for now." Tristram qualified.

"OK." Eve sighed. "Bye for now."

"Right. Bye for now."

"Tristram?"

"Yes?"

"I don't feel guilty." Eve stated with a quiet resolution. "I don't feel good, but I don't feel guilty."

Tristram didn't know what to say, so he simply whispered "good-bye".

Tristram was now at the Lind Bridge over the Mitchell River. At this point, the river runs roughly west to east, before it curves south around the main part of town on its way towards the Gippsland Lakes. He walked along the footpath on the east side to the middle of the bridge and looked down-stream. The water was running slowly, smooth and deep. The light of the full moon caught gentle ripples made by surface-feeding fish.

Just watch the fish...

Another memory stirred.

Eve had texted him at 3.17am, distraught.

"I don't know what the fuck to do with myself. I'm going insane. I can't take my life anymore. I'm in hell."

"Just sit. Just be. Just watch the fish in your fish tank. You won't solve anything tonight. That's OK – just let some time pass. For now, just watch your fish and let it all go."

Tristram feared that his words were useless, but he sent the message anyway.

He waited anxious moments in the darkness of his room in Melbourne, before his phone chimed softly, and cast pale blue light towards the ceiling.

"I just don't know what to do." Eve had responded. "I know in my heart that I don't love Chris anymore, but I feel trapped. I can't leave him. I can't stay with him. I don't know what to do."

"Patience, dear-heart." Tristram had returned.

She looked into him.

"The things you say reach into me and calm me down. Just the simple things."

"Like what?"

"When you said "patience, dear-heart". I can't describe the feeling – but it made me feel...just...it made me feel really good."

Tristram sighed with deep longing as he watched the soft, silver-green flashes of the school of fish below the bridge.

Let's bury this atrocious deed with a lifetime of good behaviour... Tristram mused with a sigh.

"I can't talk to anyone else about what we did because nobody else knows." Eve often said.

So Tristram listened. Tristram comforted, joked, reassured and cared. Tristram also tried to steer Eve back to her husband – and his good friend.

Tristram tried to return to being a man of honour.

Chris Saintly was a good, kind man. He listened to his friends, Tristram among them, and two months after the cocktail party, Chris and Eve finally had a meaningful conversation about the state of their marriage.

Eve texted Tristram about it afterwards.

"Chris and I have had a massive talk." She wrote. "He is going to get someone to help me with my work-load and I will get some time to get into jewellery. Then we made up and tried again for a baby. Looks like you saved our marriage against the odds." She wrote.

At those words, Tristram had nodded to himself and mouthed the word "good".

Yet he felt far from good. He felt somehow swindled.

"You see?" He wrote back. "All's well that ends well. He always was your knight in shining armour, Eve. All you need do is let him know what your heart wants, and he will always win it for you. As for us, well, we have moved on from our mistake, and things are going to get better. In years to come, when you look back, you can think of me as the good friend that you almost had an affair with – and be glad that you didn't, and that we all stayed the best of friends. And now, if you don't mind, I think it's best that we don't communicate for a while."

As Tristram waited for her reply, he felt a wave of resentment.

Then we made up and tried again for a baby. That's just a bit too fucking insensitive.

His phone chimed, and he read the message.

"I understand. I know you must fly away for now Superman, but I hope you occaisionally come back down to earth to visit us poor mortals some day."

Tristram sighed.

Well, Tristram, what did you expect? He had thought to himself. *This situation was totally wrong from the beginning, and now you have finally fixed it. It's over – this drama is over, and it really is a good thing. Just be gracious and get the hell out.*

Two days later, as he was riding a tram to work, he received a text from Eve.

"I just heard a song from our childhood. Sheep are cute, sheep are beaut, sheep are soft and curly."

Tristram smiled to himself, and then replied with more of the chorus. "But when I take them into town, I have to start off early."

He waited for her response, and his phone chimed with it straight away. "Because they never go the way I want, So I need someone to help me..."

Tristram replied. "I just give a whistle – And I call for Bob the kelpie."

"Who wrote that?" Eve messaged.

"Don Spencer."

"It came into my head this morning and it made me happy. It seems like years since I have been happy."

Tristram sighed sadly as he typed his next message. "Glad to hear that you are happy again."

He waited for another message, but nothing came. Just as he put his phone back into his pocket it chimed again.

"It was a happy thought and I wanted to share it with you."

Tristram replied. "Thank you. It did cheer me up."

His phone chimed again with another text.

"We are going to be seeing each-other again soon. Chris has bought us all tickets to that new *Cirque Du Solei* show."

"I know. You guys are staying at my place." Tristram replied.

Suddenly the thought of them doing what couples do

accosted Tristram, and an angry bitterness washed over him.
He sent another message:

"Gotta go. I am about to go into work and we are not
allowed to have our phones on, so there won't be any more
messages from me for a while."

The response came, just as the tram reached his stop.

"OK."

Tristram grunted at the anticlimax as he put his phone back
in his pocket.

He marched up La Trobe Street in the central business
district of Melbourne, feeling very resentful. Just as he reached
the building of his work, his phone chimed again.

"The happy thought wasn't really Bob the Kelpie. The
happy thought was that my life is sad, and lonely, and busy and
boring, and going nowhere – but in two weeks I will be coming
to Melbourne to see a show. And I will be seeing you again."

Tristram held his breath. He blushed, then exhaled slowly.
Anxiety and elation duelled within him.

You are going to break my heart, aren't you? Tristram
thought to himself.

This situation is not going away...

Tristram sent one last message.

"Have a nice day, Eve. I will be happy to see you too."

The circus show was amazing, but the real performance of the
night was that of Tristram and Eve. They flirted and made
jokes and enjoyed themselves – and it all seemed totally
innocent.

As they walked away from the Big Top, Eve slapped Tristram firmly on the behind.

"We need to find a bedroom." She whispered.

"Easy, tiger." Tristram warned playfully.

"Life is very interesting, isn't it?" Eve returned.

"That it is. A little too interesting."

"I'm going to divorce Chris." Eve announced.

Tristram turned to her sharply and she held his eyes. She was so sad and serious – and there was a longing within her. A longing for his support.

The moment was interrupted by Sam, Saffi and Chris.

"Hey, do you guys wanna go get coffee somewhere?" Chris asked.

Tristram shrugged. "Yeah, definitely. I never say no to coffee and tiramisu, you know that."

"Tiramisu?" Chris laughed. "Bloody good idea. What do you reckon, Eve?"

"Whatever. Sounds good." She grinned flatly.

The night rolled merrily along and in the fleeting nanoseconds of opportunity within the wit and chatter, Eve and Tristram's eyes found each other.

A few weeks later, Eve was crying in Tristram's arms at his parent's place. Her tears were gentle and silent. It was late, and his parents had gone to bed.

Eve had come around for some home-made pumpkin soup and crispy garlic bread. They had then watched *Tenacious D: The Pick of Destiny*. They had sat on the couch a chaste distance apart, yet Eve 's hand had found his half-way through the film.

And then, after an evening of chatter, Tristram's parents went to bed, and Eve crawled over to Tristram and hugged him.

Then, he felt her sobbing.

"He doesn't deserve this." She murmured. "Chris doesn't deserve this."

Tristram sighed. "I know. Maybe you guys need to try marriage counselling?"

"No. If we can't work it out ourselves, then it's over."

Suddenly the lounge room door opened, and Russell appeared in his navy dressing gown.

"Still here, Eve?" He asked politely.

"This isn't what it looks like, Dad." Tristram began, still holding Eve in his arms.

"I know that, Tris. You are a man of honour."

Tristram of the present grimaced. *I was.*

Russell had then listened as Tristram explained Eve's predicament. Tristram left out the kiss at Easter.

Russell had then been as comforting and understanding as he could be, and in the end advised that Tristram should let Eve go home, and then allow her and Chris to try marriage counselling.

"And hard as it may be, Tris, I think you should stay away from both of them to give them a fair chance to try and work things out." Russell finished.

"Agreed." Tristram answered resolutely.

Eve had given a non-comitall nod.

Then Tristram had followed Eve up the steps to the top of his parent's property, and just before she got into her car, she turned to him grimly.

"So this is good-bye again, I suppose." She grunted.

Tristram sighed deeply. "Yeah. But it's the right thing to do."

"Are you OK?" Eve asked.

Tristram nodded. "Yup."

"You don't seem OK."

"It's hard." Tristram admitted. "That's all. You know?"

Eve nodded glumly. "Yes. I know...I'm sorry."

"I'm sorry too. Good luck."

Eve then got into the car.

"You too." She said, before she closed the door.

The very next night, as Tristram was driving back to Melbourne through pouring rain, his phone chimed with another text from Eve.

"I've done it. I've left him. I've told him that it's over and I am moving out tomorrow. He is crying in our room."

Tristram pulled over as he was suddenly short of breath.

Shit. He remembered thinking. *So much for marriage counselling. Shit, shit, shit, things are never going to be the same for any of us.*

Dismay and exhilaration, guilt and resolve – all battled fiercely within him the whole night. None had a lasting victory.

"I have been talking with Eve." Saffi had said a couple of weeks before the night Eve left Chris. "It looks like very bad news for Chris."

"Yeah. I know." Tristram had answered.

"She didn't seem at all concerned for him, you know?"

"She is going through the toughest time in her life."

"Maybe. But she was going on and on about what she felt, but she didn't say a single thing about Chris's feelings. It was very selfish – and selfish people make me extremely uncomfortable – *especially* when they are getting involved with *my family*." Saffi looked into Tristram seriously and he met her gaze.

"It is a messy situation. But I think I love her, Saffi." Tristram returned.

Saffi sighed heavily. "Well...try to be classy about all this. Class and style, and you can't go wrong. Just..." She put on a cockney accent. "Don't mug yourself, mate, don't mug yourself."

Class and style and you can't go wrong...

"Mate, we need to talk."

Tristram had no idea how this was going to pan out.

It had been five months since the kiss at Easter, but so much had happened it had felt like a year.

Tristram had juggled so many things – and at this moment he was going to drop some of them...

"Is this about you and Eve?" Chris asked quietly.

He stood in Tristram's kitchen in Melbourne, as he had so often done over the last few months. The kettle was reaching its boiling point behind him.

"Yes, it is." Tristram answered carefully, holding his friend's gaze.

Tristram was sitting down at the kitchen table, but he had turned his chair in such a way that he could quickly stand and defend himself should the need arise.

I could take him – but on the other hand, maybe I should just let him hit me?

"I can't say I am surprised, mate." Chris answered kindly. "You and her have been talking so much. She talks to you more than me."

Tristram felt pressure building behind his eyes. "Yeah. I

think you should know that she has developed feelings for me. And they are returned."

Chris turned his bright blue eyes to the floor. "I know."

"At this stage, we have not had sex or anything." Tristram added quickly. "But we have talked – as you say – we have talked a lot."

Chris nodded. Then he made Tristram and himself a coffee, brought them to the kitchen table and sat down opposite Tristram.

"Thankyou." Tristram said as Chris handed him the coffee. He could hardly believe how civilised Chris was being.

Chris looked into Tristram. "I have known that you have feelings for Eve. I have known that you loved her – I actually thought that you were in love with her but didn't really know it."

Tristram nodded. "Yeah. Yeah, well, it did take a while, but I have come to realise that I do love her."

"I still love her too." Chris returned gently. "That isn't going to change any time soon."

"I'm sorry."

"These things happen. I know I told you a few weeks ago that I wanted my marriage to be over because I was so sick of Eve being...well, you know all about it, probably."

"I know that she has been very unhappy and difficult to talk to and hard to get a straight answer out of."

Chris grunted. "She talks to you."

"Actually, she only spoke to me at the start of the year. In the last few weeks she has been very hot and cold – and by cold, I mean extremely cold at times. It has been...well frustrating – but frustrating is really under-stating it." Tristram answered.

"That is the whole thing, isn't it?" Chris suddenly frowned. "She won't just decide what she wants."

"Agreed. I could live with one thing or the other. Either she is with you definitely – or she is with me definitely – either way, we could move on from this painful place towards something else."

"Yeah. That's it. I can handle one or the other but not this fucking limbo we're in."

"What are we going to do? How do we...deal with this?" Tristram asked carefully.

Chris considered him. "Give me a year. Stay away for a year, and then if she still wants you, go for it."

Tristram frowned. "A year? That seems rather...arbitrary."

Chris shrugged. "A year would give me time to prepare."

Tristram nodded. "I will stay away for a year..."

Tristram of the present shook his head.

I really wanted to mean that. To stay away for a year. But within two weeks Eve was texting me again and I answered.

The thought stung Tristram with guilt. He broke his word. His word was so important to his sense of self-worth – and he had broken it. Then he remembered the end of his conversation with Chris.

"If I can't be with her, I am glad that it is you." Chris suddenly announced. His sea-blue eyes were upon Tristram.

Tristram bowed his head. "That is nice of you to say."

"I mean it." Chris smiled sadly. "I would rather you than some other hobo off the street. At least I know you – you are honest, sincere, smart. You're a good man at least."

"I try to be..." Suddenly Tristram sighed. "I hate this situation, Chris. You don't deserve this at all."

Chris grunted. "Shit happens, eh?"

THE BAT AND THE RAVEN

A BAT BROUGHT Tristram back to the present. It was a large flying fox that flew above him and for the briefest instant, its shape was contained against the full moon.

"Whoa." Tristram smiled.

He suddenly remembered that he had seen something similar before...

It was a crisp, blue autumn morning. He was young – in year seven at high school. The full moon glowed against the early sky. Then he heard the beating of wings above him. He had looked up in time to see a large raven fly across the moon.

Religious, twelve-year-old Tristram had seen it is as a sign from God.

Wow. Jehovah, I thank you.

Tristram of the present frowned as he remembered something that he had forgotten for years.

116

The raven was a marker in the timeline of his life. That was what his twelve-year old self had decided.

Jehovah, I will stop grieving for Granddad Toby. His light was bright before it faded – and now it is my light that must brighten. Life is short, and we must do what we can before our light fades. I know who I am. I am your servant. I shall not ever lie or steal. I shall not ever murder or worship another god. I shall stop having unclean thoughts about women. I shall be strong. I shall be righteous. I shall be a man of honour. And though I know I will fall, I will always, always get up. Please, heavenly father, give me the strength to make the right choices.

Tristram of the present suddenly stood straight and with a defiant sigh, he strode across the bridge, north towards his parent's place.

The right choices? Tristram frowned angrily and began to march speedily up the hill. *My twelve-year-old self would be so disappointed in me. From the time the raven crossed the moon on that morning, how far have I fallen from grace?*

Suddenly a bark of laughter escaped him.

I will NOT be judged by my twelve-year-old self! I was self-righteous. I was bigoted. I was black and white in a world of vivid colours. I was judgemental. I was fearful. I was ignorant...So why am I so angry now? What's really going on here? Am I ashamed of myself?

Tristram's pace quickened even further at that last question. He began to jog lightly up into WyYung.

Am I? Am I ashamed of myself? Is that what is really going on here?

No! I am not twelve anymore. Nor am I a Jehovah's

*Witness. I do not believe that marriage is sacred to God –
because I do not believe in God. I do not believe a person has to
stay with someone they are deeply unhappy with – married or
not – just because they made a vow and signed a document.*

The above circled over and over in Tristram's mind and he
as passed through Wy Yung and up into the hills towards his
parent's home.

*Is this what you really believe? Or are you fooling yourself,
Jones?*

Tristram had jogged long enough. Breathing heavily, he
slowed to a walk. He was now less than a kilometre from home.

Another memory floated into focus. Another text message
from Eve...

"I don't know what I would do if you walked away, Tristram.
Things would get very...dark."

Tristram remembered his answer, then continued his march
home.

*"I will not walk away from you. I will be there for you no matter
how dark it gets. I will face all the hurt and all the fear and all
the judgement. I am yours, Eve. Everything I am, everything I
have – everything I will ever have – is yours. I love you."*

EVE'S DECISION

THE SIGN ABOVE HIS PARENTS' drive through at the top of the property hung unevenly on the chain.

"Tyntynder" said the wooden sign – aboriginal for "place of birds".

Tristram smiled at the din of the banjo frogs that echoed up from the dam in the valley below the property.

Pobble-bonk. Pobble-bonk.

It is good to be home.

Tristam smiled as he saw his jade Ford Falcon. He patted his pocket. He had kept one of his spare keys with him – force of habit.

Beside his car was an unfamiliar vehicle – a motorcycle. It was a hornet and looked well looked after.

Pyran's motorcycle.

Tristram could see the lights of the kitchen and the lounge down the hill, warm and welcoming. Pyran would be down there watching television with Russell and Holly. Teddy – the big golden retriever – would be asleep near the front door. The other little dogs – a tri-coloured corgi called Belle and cream maltese-shitzu called Pixie would be on the couch or on his mother's lap. They would start yapping as soon as he started down the path to the house.

Tristram pulled out his phone and read Pyran's message again.

"We need to talk. Dinewan is back and he has a message for you. See you tomorrow at Fred's funeral."

Tristram had replied asking what the message was, but Pyran would not say. He said that he would only tell him in person.

Pyran has our family's flair for drama.

Suddenly his phone chimed.

Tristram's pulse quickened. It was from Eve.

"So..." She had written. "I have just read something from a promising author."

"Yes?" Tristram texted back.

"Your Bunyip story. I wasn't in the mood to read it before this evening – too much shit going on with Chris and his mother. Sorry about that."

"That's OK. Thank you for reading it."

"Thank you for writing it and sending it to me. It cheered me up. And spooked me a little. I just wanted to connect with the author – hence this message."

Eve had added a side-ways smiley emoticon to her last message.

"You are very welcome." Tristram returned, with a smiley of his own. "I just got into Bairnsdale. My car looks ready. I could visit you."

That was stupid, Jones. That is forward and pushy, and she will politely decline.

His phone chimed with the response. "That would be nice."

Well, what do you know?!

"On my way." Tristram texted.

Tristram unlocked his car, climbed in and turned the engine on. He refrained from turning his headlights on, until he had slowly crept out of his parent's drive-through and was a hundred metres up the road.

He had a nearly forty-minute drive ahead of him – north, along winding gravel roads through bush-covered hills.

On the way, he listened to Billy Joel.

Finally, he found the bare dirt drive-way, marked by two tyre halves painted white. Slowly and carefully he navigated the bumpy and circuitous road, with ti-tree and young wattles brushing the sides of his car. The drive was corrugated and misshapen by tree roots and exposed rocks. It was almost another ten minutes before he reached the tiny bush cottage.

Tristram stopped the engine and turned off his headlights – and suddenly he was in another world.

The forest was tall and dark around him. The stars seemed more numerous here and brighter. Tristram caught at once the invigorating aroma of eucalyptus and a faint trace of wood-smoke in the warm spring air. Here too there were banjo frogs, but in far greater number than what he had heard at his parent's place.

The cottage was a hexagonal structure, made of pine logs stained to look like red cedar, and stone pillars faced with multicoloured slate. The windows were made with bamboo grids and the same white paper used to make the walls of traditional Japanese huts. The light glowing gently behind them was candle-light.

Tristram tapped lightly on the sliding door.

"Come in." Eve called. "Close it after you. There are mozzies."

"It is hot in here. You have the the pot-bellied stove going! Don't you know it is a warm night outside?" Tristram smiled as he entered. The smell of strong coffee and frangipani incense filled the room.

Eve was not immediately visible, as she was in the loft that was suspended over half of the cottage. The loft was Eve's bedroom, and it was accessed by a wooden ladder with wide steps. Under the loft was a small kitchen, and an alcove with a shower.

"I wanted some green tea. Then I wanted a chai latte. Then I changed my mind and had coffee." Eve grinned down from the top of the ladder. "I was thirsty, and now the coffee has made me thirstier."

"So, drink some water."

"No. I never drink water." Eve answered as she cimbed down the ladder. "It makes me feel sick."

Tristram noticed that Eve had dyed her long hair again – this time a dark cherry colour. It suited her.

"I like your hair."

"Thanks. I did it today."

Eve went to the old pot-bellied stove to retrieve her coffee. Then she turned to look at Tristram. Her dark almond eyes considered him over the rim of a tall, olive mug.

"Do you want a drink?" She asked.

"No, thank you."

Eve was hard to read. Tristram wondered where he was on the tight-rope of her mood.

Eve was dressed in tight jeans and a black tank-top. Her hair was free, and her feet were bare. She was sexy – but unreachable. Her shoulders were hunched and tense, her arms were crossed.

"So, what happened with Chris's mother?" Tristram opened kindly.

Eve frowned, and then took her cup and sat in the only piece of furniture in the room, an old, jade recliner.

"Just the usual shit that happens all the time these days..."

Tristram looked for somewhere to sit and chose a space about two metres away from Eve, on the slate floor. He sat, and he listened to Eve talk out her day.

Her complaints were the usual ones. She was tired. She was sick of being talked about. She was sick of the civility and passive aggression from Chris and his mother as they tried to run their business. Her moods ran from frustration, to guilt, to anger, to sadness, to longing.

Tristram was very familiar with Eve's grievances now, so without losing track of her actual words, he shifted his focus to the tones of her voice. He loved her voice. With patience, he knew the tones would change. Once the misery of her day had been expressed, her cadence would gradually shift. Instead of frowning at the floor with her shoulders clenched, she would look up every now and then. Tristram would be ready. Her dark eyes would catch his hazel ones, and she would know he was listening. A hint at a better mind space would flicker in their brief meeting of eyes. Soon her posture would relax, and grins of mischief would return.

After an hour or so, Eve's conversation seemed to reach an abrupt conclusion, followed by a decisive change of mood.

Tristram was unprepared for the spotlight of her attention. He was full of desire but had nothing to say.

Suddenly a pig grunted in his ear.

"Jesus!" Tristram exclaimed.

Eve laughed wickedly.

Tristram relaxed. "Shit, Truffles. I didn't know that pigs could sneak up on you."

Truffles was a small ginger pig with a cream patch on his right shoulder. His dark eyes beamed at Tristram as he continued to grunt a greeting. Tristram gave him a fond scratch about the ear.

"Truffles has been bothering me all evening for pats when I was trying to read your story." Eve smiled. Then she sighed.

"Why the sigh?" Tristram smiled.

Eve shrugged. "I should have taken him for a walk down to the river. I promised him earlier, but then I got side-tracked. Your fault – your damn book."

"Uh-huh." Tristram nodded with comic resignation at her cheeky smile.

He stood up.

"What are you doing?" She asked.

"Come on, honey. I won't be the reason for you breaking a promise to your pig. Let's go for a wander down to the river."

"OK, I'll get my boots on."

Tristram, Eve and Truffles wandered easily through the bright night without a torch. The track to the river was deeply rutted and steep. It was accessible only to good four-wheel drive vehicles. Moonlight gleamed in puddles on the track from earlier rain. Crickets and frogs chorused loudly from deep within the surrounding bush. A warm breeze made the shadows of the trees dance under the stars. As they got closer to the stony river the clay on the track became rich and pungent. Truffles relished digging his nose into the sides of the track as they carefully walked down the steep final curves.

The river was shallow and slow, with wide swathes of smooth river rocks interweaved with patches of soft, white river sand. The sky above the river sang with stars about the bright full moon.

. . .

"Perfect for some night-time skinny dipping." Tristram teased as they reached the edge of the water.

He turned to see Eve taking her boots and socks off. Then she took off her black tank top and shimmied out of her jeans. Without a word, she sauntered past him in a black bra and black undies. She did not look at him, but her smile was obvious as she entered the water.

Tristram tried to be nonchalant as he undressed down to his jocks. He faced away from Eve as he did so, planning to get into waist-deep water before facing her again.

"Where's Truffles?" Tristram called as he waded through the cool water towards Eve.

"I dunno, but he'll be alright." Eve answered. "Come this way, it is a good swimming spot just over here. Loved it since I was a kid."

In deeper water, they floated a few feet from each other, gradually moving closer to each other as they talked. The water now seemed to be a comfortable temperature, and it had a clean taste. Moonlight turned their every ripple silver.

"I have missed you." Eve whispered and took Tristram's hand.

"I wouldn't have known it from your recent texts and emails." Tristram murmured.

"I know." Eve sighed. "Last week I was ready to never speak to you again. I was very clear about that. But then you write to me, and write to me and write to me..."

"And you become so exhausted you just give up?" Tristram kissed her hand.

Eve shook her head. "Your writing usually upsets me.

You say things to tear me down, and then you say things to build me up. I know you think you are dropping truth bombs on me – and you usually are. It's not like I read your stuff and think you are factually incorrect – well most times. But it doesn't have the effect you want. It doesn't make me want you."

Tristram nodded. "I understand."

Eve grunted. "Do you? You get it so wrong sometimes...but then...when you decide to write a story for me, you make me remember that I love your mind. You make me doubt what I am doing. You cloud me, you silly bugger."

"I'm sorry for the lectures, eh?" Tristram sighed. "I reread what I have written to you over the last few months...and boy, do I write a lot of *intense* shit. I'm sorry. I feel very intensely... about us. About you."

Eve considered Tristram's face. She seemed serious at first, and then she grinned.

She let go of Tristram's hand and swam for the sand bank on the middle of the river. Without a word, she exited the water and walked to her clothes.

Tristram sighed with longing, rolled his eyes at his foolishness, and exited the water as well.

On the walk back to the cottage, Eve held Tristram's hand. They did not speak until they reached the front door.

"Well, this was fun, but my wet jocks are starting to chill..." Tristram grinned, as he paused at the door.

"So, take them off and hang them near the pot-bellied stove." Eve replied casually.

"Heh. Nah, she'll be right..." Tristram returned, taken aback.

Eve turned away from him and began to undress again. However, this time she took off her bra and underwear. Without looking at Tristram, Eve now naked, walked to an alcove where her shower was, and pulled the shower curtain across.

Tristram exhaled slowly, trying to quiet the raging arousal that was upon him.

"Don't go anywhere, I won't be long." Eve called as the shower ran. "Just washing the river off. Do you want a drink or something? The kettle on the stove should have some hot water."

"Ah...I'm good." Tristram answered and sat on the old jade recliner.

"You alright?" Eve asked.

"Yeah. Why wouldn't I be?" Tristram answered.

The running water stopped. Eve popped her head from behind the curtain. She had an elfish grin.

"Could you grab that towel over there?"

Tristram obliged and went for the dark green bath towel that was hanging from a thick string in front of the pot-bellied stove.

Eve took it from him and dried herself as if he were not in the room.

Tristram wasn't sure what to do with himself, so he decided to get back into his navy cargo pants and red t-shirt. Then he made tea.

He heard Eve go to another corner of the cottage. She sprayed herself with deodorant, before she slipped into some black cotton shorts and a purple T-shirt.

When Eve sauntered across the room to Tristram, her breasts had a gentle, intoxicating bounce.

Tristam realised that he was staring, so he quickly lowered his eyes to the mug of green tea that he was holding.

When he looked up again, Eve was standing solemnly in front of him. She gently took the mug from him and put it on the pot-bellied stove. Then she moved in and hugged him.

"I've made a decision." She murmured.

"What's that?" Tristram whispered in her ear.

"I'm going to stop jerking you and Chris around."

"Chris has been jerked around?" Tristram asked, with a trace of suspicion.

Eve sighed heavily. "Don't...over-think this, Tris. I was married to him, it is complicated. Only last week I was thinking of going back to him – that's why I wasn't talking to you anymore."

Tristram tensed. "Why...am I only hearing this now?"

Eve looked up into him, her eyes serious and imploring. "You and I have not had a happy ride. I was beginning to think that it would just get worse and worse between us until we hated each other. I say something to make you mad – or I don't reply to your texts and you assume the worst..."

"All of which could be avoided if we could just talk." Tristram answered, frustrated. "But you insist that it all has to be by text or email. You won't pick up the phone, when a simple phone conversation would make things right again."

Eve gave a censuring grin. "You see...that's another thing – I make a point about something I don't like and you always have something to say..."

"I'm sorry. Go on."

"I don't want to go on. That is my point. It is time for things to finally change."

Tristram waited for Eve to clarify, but she simply looked at him, waiting for his reaction.

"Eve...could you specify exactly how things are about to change?"

Eve sighed. "I don't want to be stuck in a cycle of going crazy, and of being hurt all the time. I want things to just be simple for a while."

"OK. I am right with you there...but what does that mean? Specifically, what does it mean for you and me?"

"Well, I don't know that there is a you and me."

Tristram blinked. "What?"

Eve continued to look at him sadly. "I know you think that eventually there is a happy ending for us, but I don't see it. I want to see it. But there is just so much shit in the way..."

"Are you going back to Chris?"

"Hell no." Eve frowned at him, as if he had suggested the most outrageous thing in the world.

Tristram frowned back.

"You just said that last week you were thinking of going back to him...whilst at the same time, you were technically still with me..."

"I still have feelings for him sometimes, but I will never go back to him. I was married to him for four years, been with him for seven. Surely you can understand that?" Eve rebuked.

"Yes, I can understand...but I thought we went over all that months ago? I told you that you and I couldn't go on whilst you still had hope for your marriage – and then *you* convinced *me* that it was over with. *You* persued *me*. Remember?"

"Come on, it was mutual."

"No, actually it wasn't to begin with. I know I have been very keen on you once we got going, but in the beginning, I was pushing you to fix your marriage. Remember?"

"Details..."

"Important details. And I am right about this detail, yes?"

"I don't know. Probably."

"Yes?"

"Alright, *yes*. But I have underestimated how powerful the past can be. I have made my decision though – the feelings are not enough to make me want to be with Chris again. Or anybody else."

"So...we are breaking up?"

"Were we together?" Eve asked with a shrug.

Tristram glared at her. "I thought so."

"Well, yes." Eve conceded, suddenly. "Actually, of course yes – we were together. I mean we hadn't technically broken up – but we weren't speaking for a couple of weeks."

"Because you asked me to give you space!" Tristram exclaimed.

"Please don't get mad." Eve murmered.

"Don't get mad? You swim with me almost naked, you walk around nude in front of me –"

"It's not like you haven't already seen everything." Eve shrugged.

"Eve, even to the most...forgiving person, you are sending out very mixed signals."

Eve smiled disarmingly. "Well, that is your fault."

"HOW!?" Tristram bellowed with comic exasperation.

Eve laughed.

Tristram wanted to laugh with her, but he was tired and angry.

"What about this is funny?"

"Nothing." Eve returned dejected. "Our situation is a cat's litter box."

"It's a *what*?"

Eve grinned ruefully and shrugged.

"A cat's litter box?" Tristram went on in disbelief. "That is the description that you present to me as the state of our relationship? A box of *sand*... filled with rancid nuggets of cat shit? It is has come to THIS, has it?"

Eve giggled, but Tristram was immune.

"And according to you, I always have something to say. Yeah? Well...You know why I always have something to say? Because there is *always something to say*."

Eve sighed gently. "I am not trying to start a fight here."

"Eve, why did you invite me here tonight?"

"I didn't. You offered to come out and I said that was OK."

The bluntness of her retort stung Tristram.

"Actually," he replied cooly, "you said that it would be *nice*."

"Well, until now it was nice." Eve mumbled.

Tristram stepped away from her. "I am sorry. It has been a very long day and I just don't have the morale for...this."

Eve seemed sad and frustrated. "Are you going to storm out?"

Tristram searched her face and felt his ire fade. "No."

Eve waited for him to say more.

Tristram looked about the room before shrugging helplessly.

"You see?" Eve began quietly. "It has become hard for us to just be close and talk. I know I have said some awful things to you and done awful things to you – and you have said some pretty harsh things to me – and I don't blame you for it. But we are in a pattern I don't want to live with. It always ends in hurt."

Tristram shook his head. "We always end up back together. We have had some pretty serious fights, but we always end up making up."

"But each time, we forgive each other a little less."

"What do you mean? Eve...I always forgive you. And I always forgive *completely*. I don't hold grudges; it is not what I do. There is no forgiving *less*."

Eve considered him seriously, and then her expression softened. The light of affection flickered in her dark eyes.

"I know."

Tristram again shrugged helplessly. "Well...my postion on this issue..."

"Yes?" Eve prompted, grinning at him.

"I am crazy about you." He announced, with comical defeat.

Eve blushed, looked to the floor and smiled.

Tristram sighed and smiled in return. "The only constant in this little drama, eh? I am mad about you. Whether I like it or not. And... on that note...is it time for me to get outta here or what?"

Eve suddenly looked miserable. Tristram felt instantly sorry for her.

"Eve..." He began as kindly as he could. "I know that you don't want to hurt me, and you don't want to be hurt anymore yourself. You want me to go, but you don't know how to get me to leave without a fight. Well, I am sorry for being angry just now, but it will be alright. I am just going to go, yeah?"

"I don't want you to go." Eve murmured.

"Well...if we are breaking up, I have to, don't I?" Tristram answered, trying to sound caring and not heart broken.

Eve did not answer, but stood tense and uncertain, with tears forming in her eyes.

Tristram moved in closer to signal that he was open for a hug but did not hold out his arms.

Eve stepped forward and embraced him.

In silence, they held each other. It lasted for several minutes.

"I have to go to bed now." Eve finally whispered.

"Fair enough." Tristram answered as he released her.

"Will you tuck me in before you go?" She grinned cheekily.

Tristram sighed forlornly "Do you have to be such a tease?"

"I was joking – but I do have something up there I want you to see." Eve rejoined.

Tristram raised his eyebrows, shrugged and said "OK...after you."

"No, you go first."

Shaking his head, Tristram climbed up the ladder to Eve's bedroom loft.

A king-sized canopy bed dominated the space. It was obviously an expensive heirloom or antique, made of rich red cedar. Intricate spiralling and rose-work decorated the pillars and the headboard. Fine white gauze curtains enclosed the bed, that had a scarlet satin cover draped carelessly over it.

The only other item in the tiny loft was a plain pine chest of drawers.

Just as Tristram was considering the contrast between the style of the bed and the cheap gaudiness of the chest of drawers, Eve leaped up onto his back.

She wrapped her legs around his waist and her arms around his neck.

"Give me a piggy-back to the bed. Ya, mule, ya!" Eve shouted playfully.

Chuckling, Tristram obeyed – the bed was only three steps away.

He turned his back to the bed, allowing Eve to flop down through the gauze curtain onto the mattress.

When he turned to face her, she was top-less.

RECURRING MOTIF

RAIN BEGAN to fall heavily on the tin roof and the sound filled the whole cottage.

"Crikey, that rain is loud. Wasn't it a clear night?" Tristram asked Eve, as she lay naked on top of him.

She looked up into his face, kissed him and then gave him a playful look.

"Didn't you notice the storm?"

"There was a storm?"

"Thunder and lightning. Were you distracted?"

They laughed together.

"You are the sexiest woman alive."

"You weren't too bad, I suppose." Came her cheeky reply.

Tristram grunted. "Better than our first time. Which was *my first time*. All those months ago."

"I thought that was awesome. I told you so, didn't I?" Eve said sweetly, stroking his chest.

"You did...but..."

"What? I wasn't lying."

"It couldn't have been very good." Tristram sighed. "How could it?"

"Tristram...it was a very beautiful night." Eve said sincerely. "I will always remember it."

"I remember the way I felt that night. I was the happiest I have ever been. And I am not talking about the sex, either. I am talking about the way you surprised me. I was in my house in Melbourne, it was around 11pm and I thought *you* were in Bairnsdale."

"Yup. But I was driving to Melbourne to meet you." Eve sang with a smile.

"You were sending me some very naughty texts."

"All part of the fun."

"You were talking about how it seemed like it was going to be ages before we could be together." Tristram grinned.

"All part of the surprise. The look on your face when I came up the stairs made the drive worth-while."

"I was amazed. Just *amazed*. It was the thing I wanted most in the universe and the very last thing on *Earth* that I was expecting. I was just so... delighted. I just picked you up and hugged you. We stood in the kitchen just hugging and smiling at each other. We must have looked so goofey to my housemate."

"Noel took the hint pretty quickly and went to his room."

"Then we were kissing on the couch. And then you...you held your arms above your head and signalled to me to take your top off."

Eve kissed his neck and whispered in his ear. "I remember. You said I had exquisite breasts and I said *they're yours*."

A wave of arousal went through Tristram, and he fondled Eve's plump breast. Her nipples had hardened again.

"How could I have resisted these wonderful boobs?"

"You couldn't." Eve shrugged, with comic vanity.

They kissed sensually for a few minutes. Another sexual storm brewed between them.

"Round three?" Tristram asked.

In answer, Eve rolled off him to the side of the bed, grabbed a condom, and then rolled back to him.

A few minutes later, they were resting again, and the rain had begun to ease. Tristram noticed a small bat fluttering across the ceiling.

"I have something I need to tell you." Eve began.

A wave of anxiety ran over Tristram.

"I'm listening." He answered.

Eve sat up and made eye contact in the dim light.

"Chris came over for a sleep-over last week."

"Right..." Tristram answered. "And...?"

"There's that look in your eyes. The look of tired anger that makes me sad."

"Did you sleep with him? Did you have sex with your ex-husband only a few days before having sex with me?" Tristram asked as calmly as he could.

Eve sighed and did not answer right away, which quickened Tristram's anger. Yet he held his temper.

"Well? I am entitled to an answer." Tristram persued.

"No." Eve groaned. "Don't jump to conclusions."

"You said earier that you were thinking of getting back with him last week. Then you say he slept over..."

"We had an agreement. We thought we would try a night of talking. But the agreement was that he would sleep on the floor, and I would be in the bed."

"You stuck to that?"

Another pause from Eve.

"Just...be straight with me." Tristram pleaded.

"We didn't have sex. OK? But we did hug on the bed for a few minutes. We just held eachother. That's all."

Eve watched Tristram's face for a reaction.

Tristram had no idea what to say.

"Are you mad? I guess I would be if I were you." Eve prompted.

"No. I am not mad. I am...I am sad. I feel sad for you and for Chris." Tristram answered.

Eve leaned down and kissed Tristram on the cheek. He calmed down immediately and began to gently stroke her arm.

"I loved him once. I still love him in some ways. But as we hugged, I knew I was feeling for the past, not the future. I knew he could never be my husband again. It felt terrible. I felt guilty. Then I felt angry. Then I felt sad. Then I felt love. I don't expect you to really get it." Eve whispered into Tristram's neck.

"I don't make that claim. But I don't blame you for it. These things are hard. These things are complicated." Tristram sighed.

"Tonight, I learned something." Eve continued. "I learned that it's not going to work..."

"This again?" Tristram murmured.

"Let me finish." Eve kissed his neck. "I learned that breaking up with you is not going to work."

"What does that mean? Does that mean we are together? That we are staying together?"

"I think so."

"You think so? See, now I am remembering more about that lovely night that you surprised me in Melbourne. There was a moody next day. And two days after that, our biggest fight."

"I know." Eve sighed.

"It was horrible. After that night, the best night – only two days later, the worst night, followed by a horrible fucking day. You basically sent me a text saying that you had decided to go back to your husband. A *text*..."

"That's not fair – we talked."

"We talked, because I drove the bloody three hours to Bairnsdale and came out here to talk to you. A lot of good it did, you were so damn cold." Tristram was getting angry as he remembered.

"You understand why. We talked about a few days later. Remember?"

"I remember the next day I went over to your old house and faced Chris. I had to tell him what happened."

"I had already told him. I didn't think it right that he heard it from you."

"That's right. When I arrived at his house, you were *there*. You told me that I could not keep coming to see you and I told you I was there to see him, not you."

"I remember." Eve murmured.

Tristram paused to remember Chris. His once good friend, with sea-blue eyes full of hurt and anger.

"It was the weirdest thing..." Tristram spoke sadly, as his memories became words. "Chris started out by saying that there are some things that could never be forgiven. And I told him that I understood, and that I was sorry – and also, that even though I very much regretted the hurt I had caused him, I felt that I had done nothing wrong. That surprised him."

"You had done nothing wrong?" Eve prompted.

Tristram shrugged. "Yeah, that is what I said. And even now, I think it is true. I did not enter into a relationship with you lightly, I thought about all the angles very, very carefully for weeks. I spoke with all the people that I respected. I did not decide to be with you until you convinced me that your marriage was over. I had told Chris of our feelings for each other before we had sex. I know that it sounds cold, but it comes down to this: marriage is not sacred in of itself. It is very, very important. It should not be entered into carelessly and it should not be given up on easily. But ultimately, the happiness of both people trumps the marriage contract. If you were unhappy with Chris, then you had a right to leave him. And just because I am his friend, does not mean that I am obligated to say no to the most important woman of my life. Do you get it, Eve? I was – and am – as serious about you as if I was considering you for my wife."

Eve bowed her head. "I know. It was part of what scared the shit out of me."

"The point is, when we had sex, I was convinced that it was the beginning of the most important relationship in my life, and the end of a very painful chapter. Then two days later – bam! A text proving that I was completely deluded."

"But you weren't. I had just freaked out. We made up a week later." Eve reminded him.

"Yeah...but at the time. I was in so much agony. And Chris, being the superior man that he is, could see it as he and I spoke. Even though he was so angry and betrayed, I could tell that he felt a bit sorry for me – as I did for him. He is a good man, Eve. Not the right man for you, but that doesn't mean he isn't a good man. In fact, he is a great man. Do you know how our conversation ended?"

"He didn't tell me."

"With a hand-shake. I told him that the last roadblock to getting his marriage back on track was gone – because at that point I thought we were well and truly *done*. Then he said to me, that I should not give in to hating – that hating would fuck me up. We shook hands and that was the last time we saw each other."

"When you left, he came into the kitchen shaking his head. He said, "How come I didn't deck him?""

"Sounds about right. He and I were good friends. It is the biggest sacrifice I have ever made. I don't know how to make it right. But I had to choose – be friends with him, be a man of honour – or choose true love. I chose true love, Eve."

Tristram lay back and closed his eyes. He suddenly felt very tired and vulnerable.

A moment passed in silence before Eve spoke.

"I haven't said that I love you. You have said it to me so many times. But I have not said it. But I do. I love you. I love you more right now than I have at any time before. It is time to give this a real go."

"Eve...can you...can we...?" Tristram searched frantically for the words.

"What?" Eve smiled.

"Can we just promise...to remember this moment? This one, *right now*. Can we hang onto these feelings...I mean, seconds from now we will still feel this...minutes, and hours too, probably...but as each second passes, it is a second towards the change in feelings. Will you stay on guard with me? As we watch the continuum of seconds between love and heart-ache – can we catch the first doubt, and run back to now?"

Eve thought about his outburst, smiled sadly and then shook her head.

"Times change, feelings change, there are no promises."

"It happens when you fall asleep, Eve." Tristram continued. "After we have sex, you go to sleep, and when you wake up your feelings have changed. Your mood becomes a sad anchor on the day that I can do nothing to lift. You withdraw into yourself and suck all the energy out of the room. It breaks my heart. It leaves me baffled and beaten and broken. And I can almost garauntee that I am predicting tomorrow morning. It is a recurring motif."

"No. It will be different this time. It is time for things to change."

Tristram felt pressure behind his eyes.

140

"I am going to stay awake." He decided. "You can sleep if you like, of course. But I am watching the seconds..."

They embraced and kissed, and then lay dreamily together as rain fell upon the tin roof again.

In the early morning, Tristram awoke and groaned. He had fallen asleep despite himself.

"Ah...fuck." He mumbled. "How long was I asleep for? Couldn't have been more than a few minutes."

Eve laughed gently beside him.

"Too bad, you fell asleep. And guess what happened once you did?"

Tristram smiled. "You changed your mind? We are breaking up again."

Eve gently straddled him, then slowly ground against him, intantly arousing him.

"No. Now give me a good fucking before you leave my bed. And then tell me when we are meeting up next."

THE WARNING

It was just before nine in the morning when Tristram quietly parked his car in in the drive through area at the top of his parent's place.

His lack of sleep was mitigated by the bone deep euphoria of love that Tristram felt as he reflected on his night with Eve.

Tristram doubted that his parents would be up yet, so he thought it just possible that he could sneak through the house and go down to his cottage for a couple of hours' sleep.

As he reached the top gate, Teddy the magnificent golden retriever was waiting for him. Tristram gave the big dog a whsipered and enthusiastic greeting. Thankfully, though Teddy was jumping up on him and wagging his tail, he was at least quiet.

"G'day boy, let's get down these stairs before the little dogs ruin my discreet arrival."

As if on cue, the corgi Belle started yapping, which set off Pixie the old shitzu-maltese cross.

"Oh shit. Shut up! Come here! Idiot dogs!"

Tristram laughed as he greeted the two little dogs, whose

enthusiasm always melted him. Belle leaped very high, and even though Pixie was now a very old dog, and rather crabby, she still wagged her tail and got up on her back legs.

Once down the steep brick stairs Tristram realised that he was never going to arrive unnoticed anyway. He could see right through the kitchen windows to the other side of the house that Pyran was sitting outside at the table and chairs of the al fresco area.

When Tristram entered the house, he was surprised by the menagerie that filled the lounge room.

Cages and plastic tubs that were covered in old bath towels and woollen blankets sat on the dining table. Four large "pouches" hung on hooks on the wall above the wood-heater. These were bags made by sewing up a sheep-skin rug so that the luxurious wool padded the inside of the "pouch". As he looked at them a small face poked out of one them. He recognised it as an Eastern Grey Kangaroo joey. It was well developed and had soft storm-cloud grey fur and glossy dark eyes.

Smiling, he quietly approached the pouches to see if the others had occupants.

The three dogs hampered his progress across the room, jumping up at him, panting and wagging their tails. Their brown eyes shone with joy. He patted and acknowledged them affectionately.

When Tristram finally reached the pouches, he allowed the curious joey to sniff and lick his hand before he looked in the other pouches. There was a second Eastern Grey joey in the next pouch across.

A twin to this one?

The third had a swamp wallaby joey.

The final pouch had a very sleepy occupant that made Tristram very happy. It was a baby wombat.

Tristram turned to see if Pyran had noticed his arrival yet.

Pyran had his back to him, seemingly oblivious, but turned sharply as Tristram opened the back door.

"There he is!" Pyran beamed. "Did you catch the early train, mate?"

The question took Tristram by surprise, but then it dawned on him.

They don't know that I came down last night.

Tristram smiled to himself.

"Good to see you, cousin." Tristram opened his arms.

They hugged, and Pyran wreaked of cigarette smoke and cheap beer. Tristram noticed that Pyran seemed gaunt and emaciated. His vivid green eyes moved erratically in dark hollows behind his greasy ginger fringe.

"You got my message, man?" He asked abruptly.

"Yep." Tristram replied, as they sat back down at the table.

"And?" Pyran prompted, staring into Tristram.

Tristram returned a kind but firm stare of his own.

"You tell me, Pyran. You are the one with all the information."

"Why is he back in our lives, man? Why is that creepy fuck back in our lives? And how the fuck did he track me down in Queensland? When all the shit that went down happened over in Western Victoria?"

Tristram shook his head. "How should I know? Didn't you talk to him?"

Pyran shuddered. He reached for a packet of packet of cigarettes. Tristram noticed that they were his mother's brand.

"I wasn't really able to ask questions. I was too busy shittin' myself. Man, that Dinewan is not to be messed with, eh? You met him. You know. He is a kadaichi, eh? A fairdinkum fucking witch doctor..."

"He is a mad old trickster, Pyran. Don't you remember? A

drugged fire and plastic human skulls. Theatre and no substance. He is to be pitied, not feared."

Pyran shook his head at Tristram's words. "I won't argue with you, man. You had your experience with him and I had mine. No disrespect, but there is more to this guy than you seem to have picked up. I think he's dangerous and you need to be really, really careful."

Tristram smiled, bemused. "Well, what's he going to do?"

Pyran frowned deeply. "I dunno. But he has given me something to give to you."

"OK. What is it? A black spot on a piece of parchment?" Tristram smirked.

Pyran nodded towards a yellow padded envelope on the table in front of them.

Tristram picked it up. "If there are five orange pips in here..."

"Man...can you just...just, be careful, alright? In fact, I'm not sure you should even open the fucking thing."

"I've got to open it."

"Yeah, I know! But fuckin'...tell ya what, use some tongs or something."

Tristram sighed. "Alright. No harm in being careful. I'll get some tongs and a long knife."

Tristram went into the house briefly to retrieve a chef's knife and some tongs. He held them up for Pyran's approval, and the latter nodded gravely.

Tristram frowned seriously, then held the envelope up to his ear.

"What are you doing?" Pyran asked.

"Listening for a ticking sound..."

"Very funny." Pyran drawled.

"Alright." Tristram conceded. "Let's get on with it."

He sat down, then held the envelope onto the table with the tongs and cut the top open with the knife.

"I can already see a feather in here." Tristram sighed derisively. "What's the bet it is an emu feather?"

"Is that all?"

"There is a folded page..."

Just as Tristram was about to reach for the page, a large black spider pounced from the inside of the envelope. It missed Tristram's hand by millimetres.

"Fuck!" They cried in unison.

The walnut-sized spider was extremely agitated. It perched on the edge of the envelope, raising its front legs in aggression.

"Jesus. That's a funnel-web spider." Tristram breathed.

"Sure is. *Fuck*. Look at the size of those fangs." Pyran agreed in horror.

"Deadly venomous."

"No shit. Glad you followed my advice with the tongs? Fuck..."

"OK...yes, I agree with you, I need to take this bastard a bit more seriously."

Suddenly the spider scuttled towards Tristram. It jumped off the table at him, but Tristram slid his chair back and was on his feet. He stomped on the spider and crushed it in fear and disgust.

He looked to Pyran and shivered.

"Fuck – another one!" Pyran shouted.

Another funnel web spider crawled out of the envelope. Then another, and another.

"Fuck this." Tristram snapped. He marched determinedly to a bench beside the back door and retrieved a can of fly spray. He sprayed the spiders vigorously. They curled up and died almost instantly. Then, holding the envelope with the tongs, he emptied the can of spray into it.

"That should do it." Tristram scowled.

"Depends what else is in there." Pyran sighed. "I'd still be careful, eh?"

"Fair enough." Tristram answered, as he used the knife to cut the sides of the envelope so that it could be completely opened out.

Inside, were another three dead spiders, a handful of dead and dried out meal-worms, an emu feather and the folded page.

The page was soaked in fly spray, but it was only folded once, so Tristram could carefully unfold it to make the message readable.

The witch doctor had written the following, in a beautiful, flowing script:

Dear Tristram,

I am delighted to advise that we will meet again soon.
There will be no theatrics this time. The upcoming experiences will be most assuredly authentic.

Fond regards,

Dinewan.

Pyran paled as Tristram read the letter.

"Alright, man, what's the plan?" He said.

Tristram stood rigid and angry, and then slowly, the faintest grin softened his face.

"What?" Pyran asked.

Tristram sat down and tossed the letter onto the table.

He flashed Pyran a cavalier smile.

"That letter is a challenge."

"Yeah? And?"

Tristram's eyes narrowed.

"And I accept. Bring it on."

FRED'S FUNERAL

It was the 21st of November.

The morning started with fog but became bright and hot by the time Fred Morris's memorial service began.

Tristram had expected a large crowd comprised of mostly Kurnai people, a few teachers from the Primary School and possibly even a reporter for the local newspaper. Fred was an elder after-all.

However, there were perhaps less than thirty in attendance. Furthermore, the only non-Kurnai present were Ivan, Pyran, Tristram and his parents.

Ivan arrived looking pale, serious and uncertain of himself.

Pyran was quick to recognise him and approach.

"Mr. MacAllister!" He beamed.

Ivan beamed back. "Pyran! How the hell are you?"

Another person approached Ivan. Tristram was astonished to recognise Terry Green – his one-time bully from his junior high school years.

Terry was shorter than Tristram remembered. He also seemed to have mellowed. His face was handsome and serious, but not brooding as it was back in high school. Terry's deep coffee eyes were still striking. In high school, it was because of the aggression and defiance that emanated from them. Now however, they appeared thoughtful and caring. His hair was neat and short, but not in the crew-cut he used to favour. Terry also appeared less muscular, though he did look lean.

"G'day, Mr. MacAllister." Terry smiled.

Ivan did not seem to recognise him.

"Good morning." Ivan answered with a warm smile.

"You don't remember me, do ya? It's Terry. Terry Green."

Ivan recognised him then. "Yes! Terry! Wow look at you." He shook Terry's hand.

Terry turned to Tristram. "G'day, Tristram."

Tristram stepped forward and heartily shook his hand.

They exchanged pleasantries and then it was time for everybody to take a seat.

The ceremony was simple and brief. There was no indigenous people's singing or music. No didgieridoo droned. No ceremonial smoke took place. It was like any other funeral Tristram had been to, only it seemed shorter.

Tristram reflected on Fred solemly. The ceremony just wasn't good enough. Fred deserved more than this simple white-fella-style funeral.

Tristram began to truly regret that he had not stayed in touch with Fred. Pressure built behind his eyes. He wiped a tear away.

Suddenly a memory of a conversation long ago floated into his mind.

. . .

"Remember what I said, matey. Ya behaved like a true warrior today...an' like all true warriors, ya mourn for the sacrifices dat ya made...but listen, little brother..."

Tristram smiled sadly at the memory.

"Ya see da sunlight through da trees? It's all yours, mate. Never stop lookin'. Can ya smell da gum leaves? Mmm. Never stop smellin'. And do ya hear dat all around ya? It's da voices of ya family, unna? Still got dem, brother. Never stop listenin'."

At that thought, Tristram turned to look at his mother and father. A deep love welled up within him, and he sighed at the thought of losing them.

When the ceremony was concluded, and they stood in the bright sunshine, an old aborigine woman called Kathy called out to Tristram.

Kathy was a friend of his mother's, who worked at her primary school, helping the teachers to engage with the koori children. She was an immensely cheerful and affectionate woman who delighted everybody she ever met. She was dressed in wild colours – not unlike his mother. In fact, the two of them had been cackling and cuddling fondly since they had come out of the building.

"Caw, look at ya!" Kathy burbled in a nasal drawl. "Ya got ya dad's big shoulders and ya mum's smile, eh? What did ya feed 'im, Holly? He's so tall!"

Tristram gave Kathy a big hug.

There was an old aborigine woman standing near Kathy, looking sour and stand-offish. Tristram decided to try and engage her.

"Kathy, I don't believe that I have met your friend." Tristram smiled at the old woman.

"This is Elsie. She's my cousin, unna? She spring from da mob dat used to be in Bung Yarnda." Kathy informed him.

Elsie was a total contrast with Kathy. Her hair was nearly pure white, her posture was slumped, and she wore a cheap looking black dress. She had scars on her legs and her forearms, and her eyes were a milky brown.

"Bung Yarnda?" Tristram asked.

"Lake Tyers." Kathy clarified.

"Oh..." Tristram replied awkwardly. Kathy was referring to the Aboriginal mission on Lake Tyers, and Tristram knew that the place had painful significance for a lot of Kurnai/Gunai.

"Did ya know him, boy?" Elsie asked Tristram bluntly.

"Yes." Tristram answered respectfully. "A long time ago. When I was a boy."

Elsie grunted, and then spat.

Kathy gave Tristram and Holly an apologetic smile, and then said something to Elsie in her own aboriginal language.

Whatever it was, it seemed to surprise Elsie.

"Dat true, love?" Elsie asked Kathy.

"Yeah, yeah. This is the boy. You know, Tris, Fred was an elder?" Kathy smiled.

Elsie sighed heavily.

Kathy covered her mouth. "Oops. Not allowed to say the name of the dead, unna?"

Tristram nodded. "Yes. Yes, I knew he was an elder."

"He was also a watchdog. In fact, he was da last watchdog. He used to let Elsie and da others know if there was any bad spirit or any bad magic men comin' into da area, unna?" Kathy continued.

Tristram raised his eyebrows. "Really? I didn't know that. So, who is going to watch out for the area now?"

Kathy laughed. "I don't reckon we got anythin' ta worry about, Tris."

Elsie did not seem to agree, but she said nothing.

The chatter turned to other trivial things and general catch-up. After a few minutes, Tristram and Pyran said their good-byes and left.

However, just before Tristram and Pyran reached his car, Elsie hobbled towards him.

"Oi, Tristram. Did he ever tell you about Ngooran?" Elsie began.

"Ngooran?" Tristram asked politely.

Elsie considered him for a moment. Then she shrugged. "Doesn't matter."

"Ngooran...that means emu." Tristram said kindly.

Elsie seemed to come to a decision. She reached into her handbag and pulled out a double feather – an emu feather.

"*Ngooran.*" She said with significance, handing him the feather. "His message come on da wind. You need to watch out for 'im. OK, boy?"

"Dinewan." Ivan suddenly interjected.

Tristram was surprised that Ivan was so close and eaves-dropping.

Elsie turned sharply and looked Ivan in the eye reproachfully.

"Ngooran. Dinewan. Emu. Same thing, unna?" Elsie finally answered. She turned to Tristram again, holding the feather up into his face.

"I understand." Tristram said, looking her respectfully in the eye.

"You watch out, boy." Elsie said again, an urgent care in her voice. "No more watchdog. OK? You watch out."

"I will." Tristram nodded solemnly.

Elsie then scowled at Ivan, and then hobbled away.

"I would take that warning seriously if I were you." Ivan began.

Tristram shrugged. "I already knew he was coming after me."

"Really? And are you prepared for that?"

Tristram grunted. "More prepared than last time we met."

"What are you going to do?"

"I am going to wait and see what happens." Tristram shrugged. "I am not sure what that old witch doctor expects from me. I don't have the opal anymore now than I did back then."

"Maybe he thinks you can get it back from the bunyip."

Tristram shot Ivan a withering look.

"The bunyip has nothing to do with it. Don't mix fantasy and reality, Ivan. The is no such thing as a bunyip. And the opal? The opal is lost – has been for a very long time – and that is the beginning, middle and end of it."

THREATENING GESTURES

It was now a night and two days that Tristram had not slept. Normally, Tristram would need to collapse at this point, but his mind stormed with recent events.

Lachlan had arrived at Tristram's parents' place only moments after they had all returned from Fred's funeral. After a couple hours of chatting, Lachlan, Tristram, Pyran and Ivan went fishing.

They chose to fish on the east side of the Mitchell river, where it ran south from Bairnsdale through lush green cattle paddocks, towards Lake King and the rest of the Gippland Lakes system. The scents of the gum trees, the grass and the cow dung were lifted out by the hot afternoon sun. They were carried leisuirely by the faintest breeze along the deep, languid river. Bees buzzed in the long green grass of the riverbank. Teddy, the big golden retriever, bounded with joy at the stimulating environment, his tail in a constant, vigorous wag.

The place they chose to fish was shaded by a magnificent old eucalyptus tree.

"Look, you hate it in Melbourne." Lachlan began.

"Here we go." Tristram sighed with a grin.

"You have always hated it. So, when are you going to finally get the guts to quit your shitty call centre job and move back down here?"

Lachlan had asked the question of Tristram many times over the years since he left Bairnsdale. In fact, it seemed to come up nearly every visit, when the two of them went fishing.

Today Tristram suddenly gave an answer that even he was not expecting.

"You know what? You're right, Lachie. You have always been right. And I have come to a decision: to hell with my fucking job at Emu Post. I am going to write my resignation letter tomorrow."

Pyran and Lachlan snorted.

"Just like that, huh?" Ivan answered, with a raised eyebrow.

Tristram nodded resolutely. "Yeah, just like that. I'll be outta there in a week. One of the advantages of being a casual employee."

"Have you saved money or anything?" Pyran asked.

Tristram grinned. "Nup."

"So...?"

"Yeah, I will need to find a job within a month or two."

"Where? Down here?" Ivan asked.

"Well, I am not going to commute from here to Melbourne everyday, am I?"

"Holy shit." Pyran shook his head, amazed.

"I'll believe it when I see it." Lachlan drawled as he cast another line out into the middle of the river.

"You'll see it." Tristram assured him. "And now I am a little worried about finding a job. I will actually have to solve that problem pretty quickly."

Pyran nodded thoughtfully. "Yeah, eh? You know, Terry has a pretty sweet gig. He's an artist."

"Who? Terry at the funeral this morning?" Tristram asked.

"Yeah." Pyran confirmed. "He and I had a good chat. I'm catchin' up with him in a couple of days. Gonna check out some of his paintings."

"Nice." Tristram grinned. "He's come a long way from the guy I fought back in High School."

"Oh fuck – was that him? Ha!" Pyran clapped.

"Yep."

"How time changes people, eh?" Ivan smiled faintly.

Suddenly, Lachlan raised his rod tip. The deep bend and heavy shakes in his rod, along with the crackle of line going out against the drag were sure signs that he had a decent sized fish on.

"Well, fuck me..." Lachlan beamed. "That was a soft bite, I thought it was a little tacker."

A beautiful, dinner-plate-sized bream was soon lifted over the reeds and onto the grassy bank. The sun gleamed in the silver scales of the belly that phased into a storm-grey about the spiky dorsal fins.

"Well done." Ivan smiled.

"Look at the big golden eyes and the blue nose." Pyran pointed.

Tristram whistled appreciatively. "That is a thumper, mate. She'd be over twenty years old at that size."

Lachaln removed the hook from the jaw, admired his catch and then tossed it back into the river.

"Too big to keep, I reckon. It has more value as a breeder. Ya reckon, Tris?"

"Too right." Tristram nodded with approval.

Lachlan reached for a pack of shag-tobacco and began to roll his own cigarette.

Pyran looked on longingly.

"Hey man, don't suppose I could bum a durrie off ya?" He asked.

Lachlan ginned. "A durrie?"

"He's a Queenslader." Tristram smiled.

"Heh. Yeah, that's no worries." Lachlan replied, as he extracted another cigarette paper and rolled a smoke for Pyran. "You smoke, Ivan? I know Tris doesn't. He's always naggin' me to quit."

"No thanks." Ivan answered politely.

"Cheers, eh?" Pyran said as he accepted the smoke, which Lachlan had also lit for him.

"So...you reckon you need a job?" Lachlan asked, rather pointedly, as he lit his own cigarette.

"Yep." Tristram answered.

"Can you use a shovel?" Lachlan asked.

Tristram shrugged. "Sure. Why?"

"Well, me old man reckons we can take on a couple of casuals for a couple of jobs up in the high country this summer. Probably two or three full time weeks in it." Lachlan continued.

"Oh yeah? What sort of work – just filling in pot-holes in roads or something?" Tristram asked.

"Yeah, a bit of that, probably. But you know we mostly look after the bridges. Replacin' timber, paintin' rails, diggin' out the big concrete drainage pipes. Odd jobs like that. Reckon you would be interested?"

Tristram thought about it. "Yes. Yes, I would, mate."

"Hey man, if you are taking on a couple of casuals, I wouldn't mind bein' the other one, eh? I know how to use a shovel." Pyran interjected.

Lachlan considered him and then Tristram in turn.

"Righto then. I will run it past Dad and let you know."

The cousins looked to each other and smiled.

"Thanks, mate." They said in unison, then laughed.

"You laugh now, but it can be pretty tiring work." Lachlan grinned. "But it will be a change from being in a bloody lab or an office."

"I will probably enjoy that contrast most of all." Tristram sighed happily.

Everything just seems to work out sometimes. He thought warmly.

Suddenly Pyran tensed.

"What the fuck?" He growled, looking across the river. He shaded his eyes with his hand.

"What?" Ivan asked. "I see. I see...Tristram, look."

Ivan stood up.

Tristram looked across the river and saw him immediately. An aboriginal man in an olive-green trench-coat, and a floppy hat the same colour.

It was Dinewan.

He was standing perfectly still and staring across the river at him.

Tristram's eyes narrowed, his jaw moved forward. Then he suddenly smiled coolly.

"Well, hello..." He crooned. "What are you up to, over there?"

There was no chance that Dinewan heard him. Even if they shouted across the river, it would only be faintly heard at the other side.

Pyran tried it anyway.

"OI, CUNT!"

"Pyran – don't –" Ivan warned. Yet Pyran angrily ignored him.

"CUNT! CAN YA HEAR ME?"

Dinewan made no sign that he had heard Pyran. He continued to stare across the river at them.

Pyran sighed, frustrated. "He shouldn't be fucking over there."

"Where should he be?" Tristram asked him, confused.

Pyran simply shrugged.

"He is trying to unnerve us. Is he succeeding, Pyran?" Ivan answered calmly.

Suddenly Teddy began to whine. He bounded over to Tristram and nosed him anxiously.

"Don't you start, Teddy." Tristram grinned and gave the dog a cuddle.

"Who is it?" Lachlan asked.

"Dinewan. He's a witch doctor. And a cunt." Pyran growled.

"I believe you have made that point." Ivan drawled.

"Oh yeah? Oh shit – is that the guy that fuckin' stabbed you in the shoulder when you went on band tour, Tris?" Lachlan demanded, suddenly enraged.

"Yep, that's the guy." Tristram answered, still patting Teddy.

The dog was increasingly anxious, groaning and nosing Tristram urgently.

"Teddy – calm he hell down, dog! He can't get us from over there." Tristram growled, losing patience.

Lachlan stood up with resolution.

"What are you doing?" Tristram asked.

"I've got a 22 on the back seat of me ute..." Lachlan glowered.

Tristram stood up. "Are you fucking kidding me?"

"What? He fuckin' stabbed you and now he thinks he can just fuckin' –"

"What are you going to do, shoot at him?" Tristram demanded.

"Fellas, let's settle down a bit..." Ivan interjected.

"Relax – I am not going to be able to kill the cunt from here – I was just going to fire a warning shot." Lachlan explained, deflated by the glares in his direction.

Teddy increased his whining and began to jump up on Tristram.

"Teddy – for Christ's sake!" Tristram groaned.

Suddenly a great big German shepherd appeared from the behind the gum tree. It was a powerful animal, with a dark face and large eyes.

As quick as the group noticed, more wild-looking dogs bounded through the long grass and descended the bank to surround them.

Tristram counted quickly – there were five of them – then two more joined from the left, another five from the right. They were mostly mongrels – a few looked like shaggy German shepherds, one looked like an American pitt bull, another looked like a Rottweiler – but these were clearly not pure-bred lines.

They had made their circle in silence, but now began to growl in unison. Dark eyes that showed the whites glared at them above bared teeth.

At the slightest movement of any person, they snapped their jaws in savage warning and inched closer in the pounce postion.

Instinctively, all men stood still.

Quickly, Tristram noted everyone's expression – surprise and caution were apparent in Pyran and Ivan – but Lachlan seemed terrified.

"Lachlan..." Tristram spoke to him quietly.

Lachlan made eye contact, and Tristram nodded to him reassuringly.

"Don't move and don't look them in the eyes. They will move on."

Teddy cowered behind Tristram.

Suddenly the growling escalated into savage, raucous barking. The leader of the pack began to inch forward, snapping viciously at Tristram. Just as it was about to pounce, Teddy found his courage and leaped in front of Tristram.

Never had Tristram heard Teddy bark so loud. It was a deep, powerful roar that surprised everybody. His back hair was bristling with outrage and his tail stood erect and defiant.

Now uncertain of itself, the leader of the pack backed away from Teddy.

Teddy pressed his advantage forcing the German shepherd back against the tree.

Tristram was so moved by Teddy's courage that he forgot his caution and found his anger.

"GET FUCKED!" He bellowed and charged at the lead dog.

Ivan and Pyran immediately responded by charging the dogs in front of them.

The animals dispersed and were soon about to regroup. However, suddenly at some unknown behest, they ceased their barking and bolted up the riverbank.

Teddy ran after them for a few metres, roaring triumphantly and now wagging his tail.

Everyone ascended the riverbank and looked up and down the gravel road, and into the paddocks that led to the flats of Jones Bay. The pack was out of sight within a couple of minutes.

"What in the fuckin' fuck just happened!?" Lachlan demanded, looking pale and shaken.

"You alright, man?" Pyran asked him.

"Yeah...I just fuckin' hate wild dogs!" Lachlan shouted.

"I'm not too fond of them, either." Pyran answered.

"Nah, you don't get it. I see them sometimes in the high country when pig-shootin', and they creep me out. They are

dangerous, man. I've never seen any this close to town before."
Lachlan continued.

"Dinewan is gone." Ivan interjected.

They all turned to look across the river, and sure enough,
the old aboringe was no longer there.

Tristram considered Ivan and a suspicion formed.

"Ivan, how the hell did he know we would be fishing here?"
He asked, pointedly.

Ivan stared Tristram in the eyes. "How should I know?"

Suddenly, a new conclusion slammed into Tristram's mind.
"You...it was *you*..."

"What?" Ivan snapped.

"On band tour...it was you that was throwing those plastic
skulls at me. You are Dinewan's fucking accomplice."

Ivan's jaw clenched, and his his eyes narrowed.

"You got me. It makes perfect sense." Ivan scoffed.

"It does, actually" Tristram growled back.

The two men squared off.

"What's goin' on?" Pyran asked, trying to deflate tensions.

"Ivan told Dinewan we would be here. Ivan is Dinewan's
little helper. He helped him try and trick me all those years ago,
on band tour, and he is helping him now. How else do you
think Dinewan found you on the Gold Coast, Pyran? A pretty
hefty coincidence, wouldn't you say?"

"You know my history with that man, Tristram. You know
what happened to my sister. You think after that I would be his
fucking accomplice? Think it through." Ivan sneered.

"All stories told by you..." Tristram returned, growing
angrier as conclusions exploded within him "All very theatrically told, too – like the stories the witch doctor tells himself.
What a manipulative spider you are."

Ivan slowly exhaled and then gave a horrible smile. "I
didn't know we were going fishing. I didn't know *where* we

were going fishing – we have come in *your car*. I didn't know – and still don't know where Pyran lives on the Gold Coast. I was in Japan for most of the last twelve years. I didn't know Fred had died until *you* emailed me. Shall I keep going?"

Suddenly Pyran interjected. "It was me, man."

Shocked, Tristram turned to his cousin. "*You?*"

Pyran looked defeated. "Yeah."

He then stood looking at the road, not saying anything further.

"Are you going to explain?" Tristram finally prompted, exasperated.

"I texted him." Pyran shrugged, miserably.

"*What!?*"

"Can we talk about this privately?" Pyran pleaded.

"No, we fucking can't! Everyone here has a right to know what the fuck is going on here!"

"Alright, look." Pyran sighed. "The cunt texted me at the funeral and asked where you were. I asked why, and he said he wanted to meet up and talk with you. I told him I would give you his number, and he said no, he wanted to speak in person. He asked where you lived, I told him that I wouldn't tell him..."

"He *texted* you? The witch doctor sends *texts?*" Tristram interrupted, incredulous.

"Well fuck, what do want from me? He has a fucking phone, he made me give him my fucking number." Pyran glowered, defensively.

"So how did he end up over there?" Ivan interjected, impatiently.

"Like I said, he wanted to meet Tristram." Pyran continued. "I told him we were going fishing, maybe I could ask Tristram if he wanted to meet somewhere public after that. He asked where we were fishing – I had no fucking idea, so I asked you on the way here, and then I texted him your answer. He didn't have another message after that, man."

"I can't believe you are only now telling me this!" Tristram shouted.

"I was going to tell you all this – very soon – when we were able to talk about it privately. Are ya hearin'me?" Pyran shot back.

"Fucking hell. Some warning would have been nice."

"Well, fuck. Sorry, man. I didn't think it would pan out like this. I mean how was I supposed to know he had a pack of wild dogs at his disposal?"

Tristram sighed and shook his head. He looked to Ivan and suddenly felt guilty and foolish.

"Ivan, I owe you an apology."

"Yeah, you do." Ivan returned, coldly.

"I'm sorry..."

"It's done. Forget about it. Let's move on." Ivan spoke rapidly. "Pyran, what is Dinewan's number? I have connections that can trace his phone. We'll find out where this fucker is and we can take the fight to him."

Suddenly, a mobile phone rang. It was Pyran's. He took it out of his pocket.

Tristram snatched it from him.

"Caller ID: Cunt – I am tipping it is him?" Tristram said, as he answered.

"Put it on speaker." Ivan demanded.

Tristram obeyed, and the sound of mocking laughter emanated from Pyran's phone.

"We are listening, Dinewan" Tristram calmly spoke. "What do you want?"

Beats of tense silence passed, before the voice of Dinewan drawled from the phone's tiny speakers.

"I'll be in touch, Tristram Jones. Not on this number. I am

throwing the phone away now. We shall meet in person, and you will be *all... alone.*"

He hung up.

The four men considered each other.

"Tristram, you will not face him alone." Ivan announced, a kindness in his face.

"Damn right, man. I'll be there with you." Pyran assured.

"Thank you." Tristram said to both.

"Well, you can fuckin' count me out!" Lachlan thundered.

They turned to look to him, and once he had their full attention, Lachlan gave a roguish smile.

"Nah, of course I'll be there. As long as one of you calls the dog-catcher first."

The tension broke with laughter.

"Alright. Let's go home." Tristram said. Then he turned to the loyal and brave dog beside him.

"You were such a good boy, today, Teddy. You really were."

Teddy smiled and jumped up to Tristram, wagging his tail. They hugged.

THE MISEMPLOYED ZOOLOGIST

IT HAPPENED FAST. Three days after the incident with Dinewan's dogs, Tristram was back in Melbourne and had resigned from Emu Post. As he was technically a casual employee, he did not need to give more than a week's notice. The days of his last week hurtled by with surreal speed.

On his last day, he was given a large card full of signatures from a few of the call centre staff, and comments wishing him well.

Tristram was touched to notice that only a few of the comments were generic versions of "all the best". Most were a little paragraph, reminding him of funny experiences that he had shared with them, or heart-felt thanks. Besides the card, he received nearly a dozen emails comprising a few paragraphs from some of the people in his team, fellow team leaders and staff from other departments.

He was surprised at how generous people were in their well wishes. With a tinge of guilt, Tristram realised that there was more to the relationships with his co-workers than he had really thought about.

Yet, when it came time to leave on his last day, he felt intensely liberated. Tristram took one last look at the vast floor of cubicles and fluorescent lights and computer screens. He considered with sympathy the people glued to the phones and computers, trying to service the multiple personalities of the general public.

No, I really will not miss this place. He thought happily. *I am finally free!*

Only two days later, Tristram was at work in a vastly different environment. Instead of fluorescent lights above him, it was a hot, blue sky. Instead of corporate attire, he was in an old navy t-shirt, black shorts and work boots covered in thick, pungent clay. Instead of looking at forlorn battle-ship grey cubicles and computer screens, he was taking in a vast swathe of the Victorian High Country. As far as the eye could see were steep, rolling hills that had been baked golden by a hot, dry spring.

His legs, back, arms and shoulders all ached from labor, yet Tristram was very happy.

On the third day of the job, they had spent the morning in a corrugated drainage tunnel that was about sixty feet long and four feet in diameter. It ran under a bend on a steep winding road, high up in the hills at the back of Omeo. Rains earlier in the winter had washed vast amounts of mud and debris into the tunnel to the point that it was almost blocked. The job was simple: Lachlan would drive the dingo digger into the tunnel as far as he could. There wasn't enough room for the machine to dig properly, so Pyran and Tristram took turns being in the tunned and filling the bucket of the digger manually with shovels. Lachlan would then back out, empty the bucket on a bank, and then start the process over.

Now, it was lunchtime. Lamb chops, sausages and onions

sizzled on a portable gas barbeque. Lachlan was the cook. As it was considered easier to operate the dingo digger than be in the tunnel working with shovels, he gladly accepted the job. They had a barbeque lunch every day that they were in the high country, and it was a perk that Tristram relished.

Heat emanated from the bitumen road nearby as cicadas sang. Small yellow and orange grasshoppers jumped away in waves whenever they walked through the dried-out grass.

"This beats the living shit out of being in a call centre." Tristram grinned as he got some slices of white bread and tomato sauce from the esky.

"I dunno, man. A cushy office job talking to people sounds alright to me." Pyran answered as he opened a can of Lemon Solo.

"Nah, mate. Trust me. It is tedious dealing with the general public. It is much better to be out here in the fresh air away from people."

"The air wasn't too fresh in the tunnel." Pyran smirked. "And I don't hate talking to people like you do."

"Are you not likin' the job, mate?" Lachlan asked Pyran.

"I didn't say that. I am enjoying it up here, eh? Good company makes a difference. Although my ears are still ringing from Tris makin' those monkey noises in the tunnel."

Lachlan chuckled. "That reminds, me, Tris. Vic-roads stopped by this morning. They were just checkin' up on us. You were in the tunnel and you started makin' your monkey shouts and it echoed really loudly."

"Shit, really?" Tristram smiled. "Ha! What did you say to the Vic-roads' blokes?"

"I said that everyone always says that a monkey can do my work, so I went and hired one."

Pyran clapped and laughed as Tristram shook his head.

"I reckon we'll have that tunnel cleared this arvo." Tristram opined.

"Yeah, I'd say so." Lachlan agreed. "We've made good time too. Dad quoted five days in the tender – we've done it in three."

"Does that mean less money?" Pyran winced.

"Nup. It means more fishin' time. That alright with you?"

"Fuck yeah." Pyran beamed.

"Perks of the job, eh, Tris?"

"Bloody marvellous." Tristram agreed as he placed a sizzling sausage into a piece of bread. Caramelized onions and tomato sauce completed the delight.

As the afternoon wore on, they did manage to clear the tunnel, but it took a couple of hours longer than they expected. It was a lot of time for Tristram to sit in the tunnel with his thoughts, as the further they cleared, the further the digger had to travel into the tunnel.

The constant drone of the digger engine and the loud whir of the exhaust fan from the other end of the tunnel blocked out all other sound. It was a background soundscape that made day-dreaming vivid and focused.

Tristram's mind always ran to Eve. He wanted to text her, but his phone had no reception up in the high country. When he had left, she had seemed distant again and yet would not admit to such a feeling. She told him that she was just tired from selling off all the pheasants with Chris and his mother. It had left her drained and depressed, and she didn't want to talk about it. Tristram was at least grateful that they had not broken up again. Not yet, anyway.

Tristram caught himself imagining unpleasant break-up scenarios with Eve and chided himself for getting worked up over things that hadn't happened. He decided to switch focus to his Masters.

Tristram now reminded himself that his career was supposed to be that of a zoologist and that his promotion to team leader at Emu Post was a distraction. In fact, even the job he was doing now was a distraction.

I am a misemployed zoologist.

The thought made Tristram smile. Then it made him sigh. Burt had really let him down these last few years – but he was *so close* to the finish line.

Before coming down to Bairnsdale, he had had a promising thesis meeting with Burt. Burt seemed to have recovered some of his energy, and he had some corrections for Tristram. Tristram laughed as he remembered their last conversation.

"I meant what I said about you being the second-best writer that I have ever had as a student – but it is working against you in places." Burt had said.

"What do you mean?"

"Well, look – for instance – this sentence, right here: 'toads were content to sit quietly as they awaited experimentation'. Beautiful English, but it is also anthropomorphic bullshit."

Tristram grunted. "Fair enough."

"And what the hell is this?" Burt continued with theatrical rage. "You have written here, in your Methods section: 'a teaspoon was used to pry open the toad's mouth'. A *teaspoon!?*"

"Yes, a teaspoon." Tristram fired back. "*You* said that I should bluntly report the facts – and the fact is I used a teaspoon."

"No, you most certainly did not."

"Yes, I most certainly did – it was what *you* told me to do!"

"Yes, I know, but you are not writing that you used a

teaspoon! Fuck that for a joke, you used a flat metal probe. Got it?"

Suddenly Tristram's reverie was broken by unexpected silence. The dingo digger had been turned off outside the tunnel and the exhaust fan had cut out.

"Oi Tris! Come outta there, mate." Lachlan called down the tunnel.

The aftertoon sun made Tristram squint as he emerged from the darkness of the tunnel.

"What's going on?" He asked. "I reckon we are close to done, but there is probably another bucket or two left."

"Get up here, quick as you can." Lachlan called urgently.

Tristram could see that he had driven the dingo digger up and out of the ditch that lead to the tunnel. Pyran was standing beside him with a shovel, looking concerned.

Tristram did as he was told.

"Got you outta there to be on the safe side." Lachlan explained, when Tristram had climbed up the sides of the ditch to meet him. "I reckon I heard some rumbling and Pyran heard it too."

"Rumbling?" Tristram asked.

"Like a landslide." Pyran nodded.

"I was thinkin' more likely a flash-flood." Lachlan said.

Tristram looked up at the clear blue sky. "Seriously? From where?"

"We couldn't see from this side of the hills, but there was a thunderstorm earlier to the north of us. A sudden down-pour of rain might not seem like much, but up here it gets concentrated and fast really quickly." Lachlan explained.

Tristram gave his friend an incredulous look. "Is that the excuse for finishing early, then?"

"I'm not shittin' ya, mate." Lachlan continued. "Dad has told me of a couple of really close calls up in these hills, and I have seen it myself. Little creeks and gullies up here can fill up in minutes and be higher than your head."

"Look there! Shit, Lachlan, you were right!" Pyran shouted as he pointed to the top of the hill that hung behind the ditch.

A waterfall had suddenly appeared in the grassy furrow of the hill. It started as a trickle but quickly grew into a rivulet that began to fill the ditch leading to the tunnel.

"Told ya." Lachlan said.

Fascinated, Tristram watched the water flow grow, fill the ditch, become frothy and then flow into the tunnel. The tunnel amplified the sound of rushing water so that it seemed that a creek had always been running underneath this bend in the road.

"We'll go over the road and just make sure that water is flowin' out the other side. Then we can pack up and head back to Benambra." Lachlan decided.

Their accommodation was at the small Benambra pub. It felt more like someone's shed decked-out as an entertaining area. There were stuffed trout on the walls, along with photos of fisherman taken in the various local creeks and rivers. There were old logging saws and antlers behind the bar, which was a big slab of polished red-gum.

When they entered the pub that afternoon, they greeted Robbo the bar-tender and owner, and the one other patron of the bar. Tristram began the same conversation with Robbo that he had had the previous two afternoons.

"You want VB or Carlton?" Robbo asked Tristram.

Robbo was in his early forties, blonde, sunburnt and surly.

"Robbo, it's just past four pm." Tristram sighed.

"What's that got to with the price of fish?"

"I don't want beer, I want coffee."

"Does this look like a café?" Robbo whined theatrically.

The other patron, a ginger-haired man with a handle-bar moustache, snorted derisively. He wore a navy singlet and had tattoos.

"Robbo, do you see a café in this bum-fuck town?" Tristram smiled charismatically. "Come on, man. Just give a mug of instant like you did yesterday and the day before."

"For fuck's sake, just have a beer. I'll give you the first one for free, just so I don't have to go and turn the bloody kettle on."

"I'll have a beer a bit later. After dinner, yeah? After you do me one of your big porter-house steaks."

"Can you believe this?" Robbo asked Lachlan and Pyran.

"I am ready for anothery, Robbo." Pyran beamed, waving an empty pot-glass."

"I don't drink beer." Lachlan reminded Robbo. "A bourbon and Coke will do me."

"You see?" Robbo's blue eyes blazed, as he poured another beer for Pyran. "Your mates get it. This is a pub. Not a café. We have alchohol. Or – if you are a soft-cock, we have soft-drink."

"I want a coffee. I'll give you five bucks – that's twice what you charged me yesterday."

Robbo shook his head. "You are a disgrace to working men everywhere. I am going to serve you last."

"Well everybody here has a drink, Robbo, so go put the kettle on." Tristram commanded.

"Pete? You ready for another beer. This one is free."

"Well, I'm not here to fuck spiders." The man with the handle-bar moustache drawled.

Tristram smiled good-naturedly as Robbo took as long as he could to pour Pete's beer.

After he had slowly brought the beer to Pete and come back, he gazed defiantly into Tristram.

"Have you decided what beer you want?"

"Coffee-flavoured."

"Go into the kitchen and make it yourself." Robbo sighed with disgust.

Everyone chuckled.

"Thanks, Robbo. Just to cheer you up, I am going to give you one of the new five dollars notes." Tristram announced, placing a note on the counter.

"What the fuck?" Robbo winced, snatching the note up. "Oh yeah, that is one of the new ones. Dunno what was wrong with the old ones. Pete, you seen these? What do you reckon?"

Pete raised his small brown eyes to consider the bill.

"Hmpf. They tell me they're fucked but I wouldn't mind a truck-load o' the cunts."

Pyran and Lachlan snorted their drinks.

Tristram came out with his mug of coffee, took a theatrical sip and then pantomimed extreme satisfaction to Robbo.

Robbo scoffed. "You are out of place here, mate."

"I know. I am supposed to be a zoologist." Tristram shrugged.

"You're a long way from the zoo, mate." Pete drawled.

"You actually a scientist?" Robbo asked incredulously.

"Not yet. Completing a Masters in animal physiology at Melbourne Uni. I am in the final stages, but the scholarship ran out, so I am doing a bit of work for Lachie and his Dad."

"Are you and your Dad only employing people with degrees, now?" Robbo teased Lachlan.

"Dean and Scotto were in here earlier sayin' you'd hired monkeys." Pete added.

"Dean and Scotto?" Tristram frowned.

"The Vic-roads boys." Lachlan explained with a grin. "It

was Tris here makin' the monkey noises they were talkin' about."

"Well that's a tertiary education put to good use." Robbo scoffed.

"So, what are ya gonna do when ya finish?" Pete asked, his curiosity seemingly genuine. "You gonna work in a zoo?"

"Nah, mate. There are only two types that work in zoos. Vets and people with shovels." Tristram grinned.

Pete smiled and nodded at the joke.

After they had enjoyed their enormous porter-house steaks, Pyran, Lachlan and Tristram had a few drinks. Pete had stayed around drinking, and as the night wore on, he joined them for a few rounds. They talked about fishing and hunting in the hills mostly, before Pete started asking Tristram more and more questions about zoology.

Tristram was flattered by Pete's interest, and so they talked long into the night about animals – Australian animals, and what made them so different from those found in the rest of the world. Even Robbo was taken in by Tristram's enthusiasm for the subject. Tristram found himself telling science anecdotes with the same style and humour as Professor Burt Whiteside.

"This is definitely your thing to do on this earth, eh?" Pyran drawled drunkenly, putting his arm around Tristram. "Talkin' shit about animals. You are a good at it, man. Tell your fuckin' supervisor to get his head out of his arse and get your Masters over the line."

Before they retired for the night, Pete drew a map to a remote fishing spot that he knew of for Lachlan, Pyran and Tristram to try out the next day after work.

It would be a fateful location.

THE SIGHTING

"You RECKON your Dad might do us a favour for a bit of cash?" Lachalan asked Tristram the next morning.

They were eating a hearty meal of bacon, eggs and sausages that Robbo's wife had cooked.

"What do you need?"

"I told Dad on the mobile last night that we were a couple of days ahead of schedule. He reckons that rather than goin' back to Bairnsdale today and comin' back next week to paint those bridge rails, we should stay up here and get it done. It will save comin' back up here next week just to do a day job."

"Yeah, OK. What do you need from my Dad?"

"Well, we don't have the paint up here. I thought that job was next week, so I left the paint at my place in Bruthen. I was just thinkin' maybe Russ wouldn't mind pickin' it up and drivin' it up this morning, so we can finish the job this afternoon." Lachlan explained.

"I see. Normally, I reckon Dad would do it, but I've got a feeling he has a doctor's appointment today." Tristram mused.

"Ah well. Just a thought." Lachlan shrugged.

Tristram thought about the problem. "Maybe Ivan will do it. I will give him a ring."

Ivan kindly agreed, and so that morning as they waited for Ivan to bring the paint from Bruthen, Lachlan, Pyran and Tristram drove to a remote wooden bridge deep into Alpine National Park. They spent an hour and a half sanding down the white, flaky rails of the bridge as a pristine stream gurgled underneath them. Morning sun drenched the soaring eucalypt forest and glowed in the vivid green fronds of towering tree ferns. Multi-coloured, smooth river rocks were cleansed by fast, clear water. Birds whistled and flitted about the bush. Electic blue dragon-flies zig-zagged around them.

When Ivan finally arrived on the scene in his red Land-cruiser, Lachlan, Pyran and Tristram were fishing from the bridge.

"Oh...I can see it's a hard life for you boys." Ivan called with warm smile.

"G'day Ivan. How was the drive up?" Lachlan answered, striding over to meet Ivan.

"Beautiful." Ivan said, as they shook hands. "You can keep the cash, mate, it was a genuine pleasure driving up here. The scenery is breath-taking. I took a few corners a bit wide, looking around too much."

"Thanks, Ivan." Tristram beamed and shook his hand.

"You're a life-saver, mate." Pyran added, also shaking Ivan's hand.

"No worries. Let's get the paint out of my vehicle, eh?"

. . .

Ivan decided to hang around and talk to them as they worked. Lachlan suggested that Ivan oversee the fishing rods and Ivan was delighted to accept the duty.

The wooden rails received two coats of thick white paint in very quick time, less than two hours. In that time, Ivan landed a three-pound brown trout. He cleaned and filleted the fish, then used their portable gas barbeque to cook it with butter. Since he was cooking already, he added burgers and sausages for his companion's lunch.

After lunch, Lachlan decided to wash the paint brushes in the stream.

"Don't worry, the paint is not lead-based or anything – it won't hurt the environment." Lachlan assured Tristram.

As soon as they put the brushes in the water the river downstream went pure white.

"It will clear up in a minute." Lachlan said with more hope than conviction.

Thirty minutes and much chiding later, the stream appeared to be in its original pristine condition.

The water looked so tempting that before they left, they all stripped down to their jocks and sat in the stream. They laughed and chatted the remainder of the afternoon away, feeling like kings.

"Before going back to the pub, do you wanna check out that fishin' spot Pete showed us last night?" Lachlan asked.

The agreement to do so was unanimous.

Pete's fishing spot was on the way back to Benambra. It was accessed by a bumpy dirt and gravel road that ran through hilly, golden paddocks that were surrounded by large stretches of bushland. They had to open and close four farm-gates. They felt that they were in the middle of nowhere. Eventually the road cut roughly into the side of hill that was very steep. In the gully far below, a small stream barely two metres wide lazily flowed.

As the light faded to rose gold, it glowed hot in the dry grass on the ridges of the hills. A chill grew in the shadows.

No fish were caught, but no one minded.

With thoughts of juicy porter-house steak and mushrooms, and a session on cold, bitter beer, they left the stream – and Tristram's fishing tackle-box – behind.

"So, do you want VB or Carlton?" Robbo asked Tristram, when the latter had approached the bar.

"Carlton Draught, thanks, Robbo." Tristram grinned.

"*What!?*" Robbo shouted. "Don't fuck with me – you know where the kettle is."

Laughter filled the pub, and many drinks were poured.

Later that night, warm with beer and a full belly, Tristram remembered that he had left his fishing tackle-box behind.

"Fuck it." He waved dismissively. "I can't even remember at which spot along that stream I left it."

"Let's go get it." Ivan offered. "I haven't been drinking, because I am going to drive back to Bairnsdale tonight."

"You sure?" Tristram asked.

"Yeah, let's go. I have got a spotlight, we can scan along that little river. We might see some wildlife whilst we're at it. Lachie, Pyran – you wanna come or stay here?"

They had been driving for five minutes in Ivan's Landcruiser when Pyran suddenly wailed drunkenly from the back seat.

"Shit! I should have grabbed a traveller!"

"Traveller?" Ivan asked Lachlan, who was sitting in the front passenger seat, due to being too tall to be comfortable in the back.

"A drink for the drive." Lachlan smirked.

"I think there is half a bottle of Coke back there." Ivan offered. "It may be a little warm. I don't usually drink it, but I brought it up for you fellas this morning."

"Thanks anyway, but unless you have something to mix in it you defeat my purpose." Pyran answered, before chuckling stupidly to himself.

"There is a cask of red wine on the second row of back seats." Ivan grinned. "I doubt it is very nice wine, though. It was given to me ages ago and I have just left it there."

"Now you're talking!" Pyran whooped, then un-clicked his seat-belt to look over the back of his seat.

"Seriously, cousin?" Tristram drawled. "You can't wait until we get back to the pub?"

"Ho, ho!" Pyran shouted triumphantly, holding up the cask of wine. "Claret, eh? Let's give it a whirl!"

He lifted the nozzle to his mouth and took an indulgent sip.

"YUCK!" Pyran concluded, and they all laughed.

"Mix it with the Coke." Lachlan joked.

"Good idea." Pyran grinned, acting immediately.

"He's not doing it, is he?" Ivan asked, as they ascended a steep dirt road up to the first farm-gate.

The sound of wine being squirted into the Coke bottle was Ivan's answer.

Lachlan's laughter boomed from the front seat.

"I call this concoction...kwine!" Pyran announced, proudly.

"Kwine!" Tristram clapped appreciatively. "Brilliant!"

"You want the first sip?" Pyran offered.

"Hell no!" Tristram laughed.

"Your loss." Pyran replied, then took a swing from the bottle.

"Well, what's the verdict?" Tristram winced.

"It is delicious!"

"Bullshit."

"Try it!"

"No thanks."

"I'll try it." Lachlan called.

Pyra handed him the bottle.

Lachlan took a swig then raised his eyebrows.

"Actually, that is not as bad as I thought it would be."

Suddenly, the Landcruiser stopped.

"Boys, we are at the first gate, who is going to open and close it for us?" Ivan asked.

"I will do the first two gates." Tristram announced. "Pyran can do the second two."

"Fair deal." Pyran declared, then gulped down more of his kwine.

After Pyran had opened the third gate and closed it, he leaped onto the tail bar of the Landcruiser and grabbed the roof-cage.

"What are you doing?" Ivan called.

"I'm ridin' on the back. She'll be right." Pyran called.

"Drive slow, he'll be right." Lachlan assured.

"I am not sure this is a good idea." Ivan said.

"Nah, he'll be right. There is plenty of step back there and he can hang onto the roof cage."

"He still has his kwine bottle with him." Tristram smirked.

Pyran thumped the back window.

"What's the hold up? Get going!" He called happily.

Ivan shrugged, and then drove slowly down the steep hill to the final gate.

After the final gate was opened and closed, Pyran did not get back in the vehicle, but again jumped on the back.

"I'm havin' fun on the back, keep goin' – I'll ride here until we get to the river!" Pyran shouted joyously.

The other three occupants of the Landcruiser shook their heads and laughed.

On the last hill before the river, as they crawled along a bumpy dirt road that cut into the side of a steep hill face, Ivan rode the break and let gravity take them down to the stream in the gully below. At one point, they were going a little too fast for Ivan's liking, and he over-compensated by tapping the break too hard.

A sicking thump was heard behind them.

Tristram turned immediately to check on Pyran.

"STOP!" He shouted. "Pyran's fallen off the back!"

Ivan stopped the vehicle, turned and pulled the handbrake.

They leaped from the Lancruiser and ran to the back of the vehicle.

"Fuck! He's gone down the hill face!" Tristram roared. "I'm going after him. Ivan, get your first aid kit! Pyran! PYRAN! CAN YOU HEAR ME?"

Lachlan had an LED headlamp on, but its reach failed before the bottom of the gully. All they could see were goat-tracks that ribbed the hill, black-berry bushes and other small shrubs. They could hear the trickling of the stream below, but they could not quite see it.

"Can you see him, man?" Tristram asked Lachlan.

"Not yet, but I can see where he went down – look at those broken bushes there." Lachlan answered.

Suddenly they heard Pyran's laughter from the darkness.

"I'm alright!" He shouted.

Lachlan and Tristram exchanged a relieved smile.

"I'll come down to you." Tristram called.

The hill was too steep to walk down, so Tristram attempted to descend by climbing. Within he seconds he slipped and then slid on his backside, feet-first into the darkness.

"Fuuuuuuuck!"

Ivan came to Lachlan's side with the spotlight and the first aid kit. The spotlight was much more powerful than Lachlan's headlamp. They could see Pyran and Tristram lying on a muddy bank beside the stream, laughing uproariously.

"Fuckin' idiots." Lachlan chuckled.

"Lachie, we could use some light down here!" Tristram called.

"Yeah, yeah, I'm comin'." Lachlan called back.

"Careful, it's splippery *as*!"

"No shit!" Lachlan laughed. "But I'm not as pissed as you cunts."

A second later, he too slipped, his large frame crushing what remained of the small shrub that Pyran and Tristram had slid through.

Lachlan's momentum carried him further than the other two, so that when he hit the muddy bank, he stumbled past them before crashing face-first into the river.

Pyran and Tristram, helped him out of the shallow water. The three of them then collapsed into hysterical laughter on the muddy bank.

Suddenly a deep, guttural growl reverberated around them.

For an instant, they thought it was a thunder crack.

They froze and looked all around for the source.

White eye-shine gleamed at them from behind a scrubby little tree that was about thirty feet away. Those eyes were large and appeared to be about four feet above the ground.

No sound carried through the gully, save the slow trickle of the stream and the heavy breathing of the three men.

The animal blinked.

"Is that a bull?" Tristram whispered to Lachlan.

"It would have to be. Look at the size of it." Lachlan whispered back.

"I can't make out it very clearly – are you judging by the size of the eyes?"

"Yep."

"Is cattle eye-shine usually white?"

Lachlan shrugged. "Blue, usually. I s'pose it can be white."

"It sounded like a bloody lion." Tristram breathed.

"Yeah, eh?" Pyran agreed. "Could it be a wild dog?"

"Nah – too big. And wild dog eye-shine is green or yellow." Lachlan answered.

The eyes blinked again.

"Fuck, that's a big head. Those eyes are like head-lights." Pyran whispered.

The animal was just within the reach of Lachlan's headlamp, but a satisfactory look at it was not possible with the scrubby tree between them.

"We need to get a little closer." Tristram whispered.

"Mate, if that is a bull and it charges, we're fucked." Lachlan hissed.

"Good point." Tristram answered.

Beats of silence passed. Lachlan kept his headlamp fixed on the eyes.

Then the eyes lifted – from about four feet above the ground, to six feet. They paused, blinked, and then rose to more than twice as far as the men were expecting.

White eyes now gleamed at them from above the scrubby tree.

Suddenly a more powerful beam of light from behind them flooded the scene, and the extraordinary monster was revealed.

A giant, kangaroo-like creature glared at them. It was

standing on its hind legs. Its fur was a dark, mottled grey, with a a thick and dark mane about the neck. A predatory animal for certain, it snarled, revealing enormous rows of canines.

The second, powerful beam of light came from Ivan, who was standing half-way down the hill, having crept carefully down to meet the others.

The eyes of the giant creature were now dark and dreadful. The eyes had whites, giving them an unsettling human quality.

The bunyip considered each of them in turn, staring right into their faces. It sniffed the air, then focused directly on Tristram.

Tristram got goosebumps. He noticed that Pyran and Lachlan had instinctively moved in right beside him.

The bunyip's eyes narrowed and then it turned to be squarer on with them. It leaned forward, and its back legs tensed. Its ears were pinned back, and its eyes had a terrible focus. It was going to charge.

Suddenly an audible click broke the tension.

The bunyip's large rabbit-like ears pricked up. It looked at Ivan.

Tristram turned and could make out Ivan's shape behind the powerful spotlight.H He was pointing a handgun.

Tristram turned back to the bunyip, which was staring at Ivan.

The bunyip rose up on its rear legs again. Then, with a snort of contempt, the monster leaped up onto the opposite face of the hill, and out of the light. They felt the ground shake with its landing.

By the time Ivan and Lachlan had tracked their lights to the new location, the creature leaped again, and again, and within seconds it was out of sight. They heard the ground shake twice more with the landing from each powerful leap, then heard no more.

Ivan scrambled down to them, and when he reached them, they all burst into excited whoops and cheers.

"WHAT THE FUCK DID WE JUST SEE!?" Lachlan roared.

"WE JUST SAW A BUNYIP!" Pyran shouted.

Ivan's sapphire eyes locked onto Tristram. "After all these years...after all these years..."

Tristram nodded understanding. "It's real. The bunyip is REAL!"

CRYPTOZOOLOGY

"Why are we discussing this bullshit?" Burt demanded playfully.

Tristram and Burt sat opposite eachother around a small weather-beaten coffee table. The cafe had a funky feel. Jazz music oozed through the tiny space that was cluttered with second-hand couches and mis-matched tables and chairs. Surrealist paintings screamed on green and purple feature walls. Burt's eye-watering red Hawaiin shirt completed the clash of styles and colours.

Two cafe lattes and a dog-eared copy of Tristram's Masters Thesis sat between them.

"Cryptozoology is interesting. I just wanted your thoughts." Tristram grinned.

"Cryptozoology includes Big Foot, the Loch Ness monster and unicorns." Burt grunted.

"It also includes plausible things like panthers or other big cats in the high country."

"I have seen no convincing evidence of those in recent

years, either. Did you see a big cat whilst you were down in Bairnsdale?"

"No – it was a native animal. And it was up in the high country, near Benambra."

"Thylacine?"

"No. Although Tasmanian tigers were reliably reported as recently as the mid-seventies."

"Bullshit."

"And there is a guy in South Gippsland who thinks he will soon have footage of a living thylacine. A high school teacher, I think. He has some footage already of one on a beach near Lochsport – but I dunno, it could be a mangy fox – the film is hardly conclusive."

"Uh-huh. What do you think you have seen?"

"I think I have seen a specimen of megafauna."

Burt's eyes twinkled. "Megafauna, eh?"

"Oh yes. I am certain of it."

"And? What sort of megafauna?"

"Some sort of giant macropod. A very large, very tall kanga-roo-like animal with a flat face."

"Sounds like *Procoptodon goliah* – the giant short-faced kangaroo."

"That was my first thought as well. They are a well-repre-sented taxon in the fossil record so far. And wide-spread – these animals have shown up in digs in South-east Queensland and New South Wales."

Burt leaned back and considered Tristram bemused.

"How tall was it?"

"About 14 foot tall when it raised itself up."

"Jesus! And how did you arrive at that estimate? How far away were you?"

"We were about thirty feet from it, give or take." Tristram held

Burt's eyes as he spoke. "As for the estimate, it was standing beside a gum tree and its head was level with the first fork. The next morning, we went back, and I measured the distance between the base of that tree and the first fork. It was fourteen feet."

"Footprints?"

"That is what I insisted we come back to measure."

"And?"

"Over-night heavy rain in the hills had caused minor flooding that caked the whole area in mud and debris."

Burt laughed merrily. "How fucking convenient."

"Still..." Tristram returned. "We saw what we saw."

Burt stroked his beard, smiling. "Well, fuck my old boot, Tristram."

"Interesting, right?"

"Sure. But a few questions need answering first."

"That is why I am discussing this with you. I need a sceptical, scientific view of our sighting. And maybe some ideas on what to do next."

"Alright. So... tell me more about this sighting. I assume this was at night?"

"Yes."

"What were you doing? Were you fishing? Spotlighting?"

"We had gone for a drive to look for my fishing tackle box that I had stupidly left behind that afternoon. We didn't find it. But it was on the way back that we saw the animal. I'd say it would have been about one am."

"We? How many is 'we'?"

"Four. Myself, my cousin Pyran, my mate Lachie who Pyran and I were working for, and Ivan – my high school English teacher."

"Hmph. Pick the odd one out."

"Yeah, it was an odd situation before the animal showed up. I have told you about Ivan. Ivan MacAllister."

Burt nodded. "He's the madman who believes that the bunyip in your novella is real?"

Tristram laughed. "He's not a madman. I don't think so, anyway. He thinks that the bunyip that I wrote about in my novella is probably a repressed memory of what Pyran and I saw up there when we were kids. After our sighting, I think he may be right."

"Whoa! Hang on. Pyran is the red-haired kid in your novella, isn't he? So, this is the same Pyran?"

"Yes."

"So, you and Pyran both believed you had seen this animal in roughly the same geographic area when you were young?"

"Well – not exactly. Pyran certainly does. Ivan thinks it is possible. I have always maintained that we never saw the bunyip – that it was our imaginations."

"OK. I can see a worrying theme here already. But go on. Where did you see the animal this time? Was it crossing the road? Feeding on the side of the road?"

Tristram smirked. "It was at the bottom of a gully, actually. We would never have been down there to see it, but my cousin Pyran fell off the back of the Landcruiser and rolled down the hill."

Burt shook his head and snorted. "Do tell."

"Look – Pyran was riding on the tail-bar of Ivan's Land-cruiser, as we had a couple of farm-gates to go through and he was the guy that we had opening them for us, and then closing them behind us. Ivan was driving along the side of a steep hill. The road was a bit bumpy and Pyran lost his balance. It was Pyran's fault. He should have hung on with both hands. But he was holding his kwine bottle and taking a swig instead of watching the road."

"Kwine? What the hell's kwine?"

"Coke mixed with red wine. Cask wine." Tristram grinned.

"Oh Jesus."

"Look – I know. I know, alright? Pyran thought the cask wine was disgusting so he mixed it with the half bottle of Coke that Ivan happened to have in his vehicle. He said it tasted good – but I seriously doubt that."

Burt winced and laughed. "Sounds delightful."

"Anyway, we backed up and then parked. There was no way to drive down the hill – it was too steep, so we made our way down the hill on foot. Well, I say on foot – we really fell and slid down on our arses..."

Tristram then recounted to Burt the sighting of the giant animal. He tried to use non-emotive language, but the climax of the story got the best of him.

Burt seemed to enjoy the tale, but he shook his head skeptically none-the-less.

"I'd love to tell you that I believe you, Tristram, but it has the whiff of a shaggy-dog story with no punch-line."

Tristram nodded. "Fair enough."

"You do actually believe it, though?" Burt asked with more kindness.

"Yes." Tristram nodded emphatically. "Absolutely yes. This happened and there is an animal out there that is new to science. My question – and I would like your help with this – is how do I prove the animal exists?"

Burt shrugged. "The usual. Find fur samples, take plaster casts of footprints, find remains of prey and look for teeth marks on the bones. You could set up camera traps. You know – all the usual tricks people are still using to to try and find a thylacine."

Tristram sighed. "All sensible suggestions – but we have tried this before. There is a hell of a lot of country for that beast to hide in."

"Still, there would have to be evidence of this animal some-where up there. It is telling that people have lived in that area for decades now and yet we have not had any reports or evidence of this creature until now. Remember, if you have seen one then there must have been a population of them at some point. Yet no reports – ever."

"It is a good point – aside from the fact that the Kurnai people have known about it all along. But yes, no non-indigenous people have reported this animal as far as I know. If it is an apex predator, as I suggest, then it would be a solitary animal most of the time and would have a low population density. There may be no sightings because it is a secretive animal. The Kurnai elder who told me about the bunyip said that it was a *thoughtful* creature – that it watched what humans did and decided not to make itself known to them." Tristram suggested.

Burt's eyes lowered in thought, and he let out long exhalations through his nose. Tristram waited for mockery, but Burt surprised him.

"Tree kangaroos...have the largest brain relative to body size of all the marsupials. I know of some behaviouralists who believe that tree kangaroos are actually as intelligent as some higher primates. They have told me that they think that tree kangaroo numbers are under-reported these days because the animals are clever enough to actively avoid detection by humans."

Tristram thought about it. "So, we have a precedent – potentially – for an animal intelligently avoiding detection by humans."

Crows feet tightened about Burts eyes. "Possibly. Tree kangaroos are obvious candidates for Australia's ecological homologue for primates. They live in trees, have a diet so varied that their young spend five years at their mother's side learning what they can and can't eat. They can use their front paws for more than just walking. Their eyes face more forward like a primate's eyes – and as I have just said, they have a large brain."

"Ecological homologue..." Tristram mused. "That's a very interesting notion. Like the wildlife of New Zealand. The only mammals there are bats – all the other niches that are usually filled by mammals are instead filled by birds. For example, the ten-foot-high emu-like birds – the moas – would occupy the niche of ungulates everywhere else."

Burt nodded. "Yes – zebras, wildebeest, buffalos and so on in Africa, bison, horses and deer in America; moas in New Zealand – and here in Autralia, we have kangaroos."

"Lions and leopards in Africa, tigers and leopards in Asia, pumas in North America, jaguars in South America – *giant eagles* in New Zealand – eagles big enough to attack *moas*..." Tristram beamed.

"In Australia, the leopard or lion equivalent is the extinct thylacoleo – the marsupial lion." Burt added.

"And our equivalent of wolves and hyenas would be the thylacines – Tasmanian tigers." Tristram continued.

"Until they were displaced by dingos on the mainland, brought across from South-East Asia about seven thousand years ago. The list goes on – we have quolls instead of weasels or small cats, possums instead of squirrels or wood-peckers."

"Woodpeckers?"

"Yeah. We have the striped possum instead of woodpeck-ers. And that animal is remarkably similar to Madagascar's aye-aye – a small lemur. Both animals listen for prey crawling under bark, and both extract grubs with a long, thin and specialised finger."

"So, the big question: what is the homologue of the bunyip? I think it is obvious." Tristram grinned, holding Burt's gaze.

"It is our equivalent of a bear." Burt grinned back. "It is a large, often solitary, opportunistic predator."

"Exactly, yeah, at least in size, I think it matches the bear. It probably is kangaroo-like as most of the marsupials in this country are kangaroo-like." Tristram opined.

"Maybe." Burt frowned. "Although the lineage of bears is closely linked with wolves and to a lesser degree, the big cats. Why would this bunyip not be more like a marsupial lion? It sounds like it is an ambush predator like thylacoleo."

"It stood up on its back legs like a kangaroo." Tristram assured excitedly.

Burt snorted. "Of course, you have seen one."

"Yes, I am telling you I have."

"How do you know that what you saw is actually a predatory animal? You are leaping to the conclusion that you saw a bunyip – and the stories from aborigines all say that it is a predator. But what if you saw a giant short-faced kangaroo - *Procoptodon goliah* – as you first thought? What if your first impression was the correct one?"

Tristram shook his head. "Definitely not a giant short-faced kangaroo – this animal is unmistakably a predator. It had a long, wide snout like a lion, and a huge saggital crest for the attachment of powerful jaw muscles."

"Gorillas have a huge sagittal crest – and they are herbivores." Burt countered.

"It had large, forward facing eyes, like the big cats and bears and other predatory animals."

"Again, primates have forward-facing eyes – and many are not hugely carnivorous."

"It had a mouth full of canines – it bared its teeth briefly before it took off." Tristram persisted.

"Canines are no garauntee of carnivory either, but alright. You are convinced it is a predator." Burt conceded and then chuckled.

"I think bunyips surprise their prey from the water's edge." Tristram explained. "I think they spot their prey on the far bank of a deep pool or billabong. I think they *slide into the water as quietly as a crocodile.* They swim along the bottom and watch from under the water. Then they launch themselves out of the water using their enormous kangaroo-like back legs and grab their prey with their front legs and their powerful jaws."

"You think they attack like crocodiles? From the water – as opposed to from cover near the water?" Burt asked, bemused.

"Yes." Trstram nodded.

Burt frowned. "Nah. Ockham's razor – take the simplest explanation. It ambushes from cover near the water's edge. Otherwise you have an animal that requires other aquatic adaptations."

"Like a thick *tapetum lucidum?*" Tristram grinned.

Burt grunted with appreciation. "Oh yes? Did you get a good look at the anatomy of its eyes?"

"The eye-shine was incredible. It was like a pair of LED torches shining back at us. Bright white – the brightest eye-shine I have ever seen. It must have had a thick *tapetum lucidum* to reflect that brightly."

"Or the large size of the animal means it has larger eyes to reflect light back to you. But you could be right, it may be indicative of a thick *tapetum lucidum* – and that in turn could be an indicator of aquatic adaptation." Burt conceded.

"Yeah. I think it leaps from under the water, making use of its powerful kangaroo-like legs. Remember that the kangaroo mode of locomotion is a lot more energy efficient than eutherian mammals. Enormous energy can be stored in the elastic tendons of their legs."

Burt shrugged. "Sure. You make a plausible case."

"I also think my crocodile-style of hunting theory is good because there are no stories of bunyips up north. I think that the range of the bunyip would not overlap with crocodiles, because crocodiles have had millions of more years to get good at hunting like...well, crocodiles. Therefore, they out-compete bunyips up north, but in cooler southern Australia, where crocodiles cannot live, the bunyip has the advantage of being a warm-blooded mammal that can exploit what would normally be the crocodile's niche."

"So, the ecological homologue of the bunyip is not a bear but a crocodile." Burt grinned.

"Maybe I should talk to some crocodile hunters for advice on finding this animal?" Tristram grinned back.

"If your theory of being an aquatic or semi-aquatic hunter is correct, then you should get some maps from the Victorian water-board and look for likely habitat. Something with deep pools that have adjoining pasture for prey animals." Burt suggested.

Tristram nodded thoughtfully. "That may narrow things down a bit at least. Although there would still be hectares and hectares of ground to cover."

"Not necessarily." Burt countered. "The home range of this animal is probably no more than a few kilometres. You have one comfirmed sighting. Maybe use a radius of say 20 kilometres around that point. Look for all potential habitat in that area and set poisoned baits."

"Poisoned baits!?" Tristram scoffed.

"If you want to slow the animal down and make it easier to find, that is one way to do it." Burt shrugged.

"Or kill it."

"That would really slow it down." Burt joked.

"I can't believe you suggested that." Tristram frowned.

"What? It is perfectly reasonable. There is a population of these animals, so killing one would not be the end of the world."

"What if it goes into a cave somewhere and dies? Or sinks to the bottom of a billabong?" Tristram asked.

"Attach a tracker to the poisoned baits." Burt shrugged.

"What if the bunyip does not eat carrion?"

"Then attach the tracker to collars on prey animals."

Tristram considered Burt, who was watching him with a michevious twinkle in his eyes.

"I will give your suggestions some thought." Tristram finally announced.

Burt chuckled heartily.

"In the meantime, how are you going with reading my thesis?" Tristram asked.

"Oh Jesus." Burt sighed ruefully. "You have more chance finding this bunyip than getting anything productive out of me."

THE NEW WATCHDOG

"But you are turning thirty!" Saffi shouted down the phone, exasperated.

"So, what? I don't want a party. I don't want a fuss being made." Tristram growled back.

"A few friends over is hardly a fuss being made. Why can't you celebrate these things like a normal person?"

"Look, why is this so hard to understand? You are a social person – you like people, you like parties. I am an anti-social person. I don't like people, I don't like parties. It's my birthday, I should be allowed to be left alone if that is what I want."

"You want to be miserable and alone for your thirtieth birthday?"

"Who said anything about being miserable?" Tristram fired back.

"Well, we should at least go out to dinner. Maybe the Wy Yung Pub or something?"

"Look, I appreciate that you want to do something nice for me, but I don't want anything. I just want to enjoy the day without any pressure or obligations."

"We'll pay for dinner!"

"That's not why I don't want to go out. I don't want to go out because, well, I don't want to go out."

"Why do you have to be so difficult?" Saffi groaned.

"What is difficult about doing absolutely nothing?" Tristram pleaded.

Eventually, Tristram negotiated a barbeque at his parent's place with a few friends over.

The thirteenth of December 2008 was, in East Gippsland, one of the last days with any rain before a heatwave dominated the summer. It was relatively cool in the morning, before becoming a clear, hot day that relaxed into a warm evening. The moon was full and golden as it rose over the rolling hills, and Tristram decided to see it as a good omen.

Fortunately, it was also a Saturday. This meant that Saffi and Sam didn't need to take time off their work in Melbourne but could drive down on the Friday night. Noel, Tristram's housemate in Melbourne, had also come down for the weekend.

Jase also surprised Tristram, catching a bus from Ballarat, which was even further away.

They sat outside in the al fresco area on a variety of old camp chairs. Small fairy lights gleamed amongst the grape vine and jasmine that crept up the wooden pillars and ran along the roof. Languid flames flickered on citronella candles on the glass out-door table. The sprinklers in the garden hissed softly and frogs sang from the nearby fishpond.

Jase played his acoustic guitar, and Pyran tried to jam with him on Holly's old guitar.

Holly was in constant motion – briefly joining the conversation at times before disappearing back into the house to feed her various wildlife charges. They had been moved temporarily to Holly and Russell's bedroom. Before his parents could lay down to sleep that night, they would need to move two cages: one with a tempermental galah and the other with a clumsy magpie. They would also need to move three plastic tubs each with a different possum species inside: the baby brush-tail, the tiny feather-glider and sugar-glider. Hanging from draw handles on their chest of draws, they had four make-shift pouches made with sheep-skin rugs. The occupants were two eastern grey kangaroo joeys, a swamp wallaby joey and Wilbur the baby wombat.

Inside on the kitchen table, empty beer bottles sat beside small glass feeding bottles in sterilizing solution.

Swirling chatter was punctuated by raucous laughter.

Lachlan had started the evening telling jokes designed to shock and disgust a polite audience. However, his was not a polite audience. Noel, Saffi, Tristram and Sam each escalated the smut of every topic of conversation to hilarious heights.

They were drinking crisp, bitter beer, except for Lachlan who drank bourbon and coke.

It had been a nice day, with lots of birthday texts and emails. However, one important text did not come until after dinner.

"Happy Birthday." Eve texted, with a smiley face.

Relieved, Tristram texted back straight away.

"Thanks. I have missed you. You are not droping by?"

"I don't feel up to it. But I wanted to wish you a good birthday. You deserve it."

"I appreciate that. Thank you. Perhaps I will see you soon?"

"Maybe. It's your birthday so I am being nice. But tomorrow I am not holding back."

Tristram sighed. *What does that mean?*

Suddenly Russell interrupted Tristram's train of thought.

"Is that a text from Eve?"

"Yeah." Tristram replied.

"Is she coming over?"

"No. She has other commitments." Tristram shrugged.

The others around the table exchanged meaningful looks.

"She knows it's your thirtieth birthday, right?" Russell asked.

Tristram glared impatiently at his father. "Yes."

Russell frowned, puzzled. "Then why isn't she..."

"She can't make it. It happens. I am going to catch up with her later." Tristram barked.

Russell blinked. "Tris... Does Eve love you?"

The question caught Tristram completely offguard.

"I don't know, Dad."

"You don't seem happy."

"I'm fine. It is just a challenging stage."

"How many more challenging stages will there be before things finally stabilize?" Saffi asked pointedly.

"I don't know." Tristram sighed. "There can't be too many hurdles left, surely?"

"Well, relationships are not so much a set of hurdles." Noel interjected. "They are more like a wheel – a wheel that you have to run on for the rest of your life."

Tristram chuckled. "I know we keep breaking up and getting back together – so far we have not broken up again. I dunno, eh? It is all part of the...what? The love equivalent of the hero's journey?"

Noel scoffed. "Love is not a hero's journey. It's a fool's errand."

Laughter ran around the table.

"You are taking it up the arse a bit." Saffi sighed. "It makes me angry. You are being a chump. I need a stamp that says 'CHUMP' – in capital letters, so I can jam it on your forehead."

Tristram frowned good-humouredly at his sister. "Thank you..."

"She's right." Sam suddenly said, with a quiet seriousness that took the group by surprise.

Tristram considered Sam, who was tipsy but lucid.

"Any more to that thought?" Tristram prompted.

Sam frowned in thought, then answered. "You are a chump. I'm not saying that to be mean. But you are. Relationships *are* a wheel. The patterns keep going – so whatever is set up in the beginning is just going to go on and on. You guys have a fight – Eve stops talking to you or whatever – you end up really hurting and feeling distraught and depressed – and then it is you – always you – that does all the work to try and get things back on track. It is not good enough. It is really not good enough."

Tristram nodded appreciation for Sam's words.

"Man, you should take note of your friends, eh?" Pyran added sincerely. "I don't really know anything about this Eve chick or your relationship – but the people around this table know you well and care about you, so I'd take what they say seriously, eh?"

"I do." Tristram assured them, with a quiet smile. "But I love that woman. I have to keep going."

"Love is supposed to be exciting." Russell interjected. "You are supposed to feel great, you are supposed to feel enthusiastic. Tris...what you are going through, just doesn't look like love. I'm sorry, son."

Tristram sighed. "Can we give this topic a rest now?"

The group agreed, and Lachlan steered the next conversation back into the gutter with some deeply sexist jokes.

· · ·

At about 8.30pm, they were joined by Ivan, who had brought Terry with him.

"Hello everybody." Ivan flashed a charismatic smile.

"G'day." Terry grinned shyly. He was dressed in a smart casual teal shirt and blue jeans. He was the best dressed of everyone there, who lounged around in shorts and t-shirts.

"Terry! Mate!" Pyran smiled broadly.

Everybody stood up to greet the newest vistors.

"The other birthday boy!" Tristram beamed, as he gave Ivan a hug.

"Happy Birthday, fellow Sagittarian." Ivan chuckled.

"G'day, Terry. Thanks for coming." Tristram grinned, shaking his hand.

"Thanks for the invite, eh?" Terry grinned back.

"No worries, mate. I'm glad Pyran suggested it. Thanks for picking him up, Ivan."

"My pleasure." Ivan smiled.

After Ivan and Terry had shaken hands with everyone about the table, they each took a seat.

"Beer, fellas?" Sam offered.

"Yes, please." Ivan answered.

"No thanks, I don't drink, eh?" Terry replied.

Lachlan raised his eyebrows.

"No worries – there's plenty of soft-drink goin' around. You want a coke?" Sam replied.

"Yeah, thanks, that would be great."

Lachlan reached into an ice-filled esky and gave Terry a can of coke.

"I've got plenty of bourbon here if you come to your senses." Lachlan drawled with a cheeky twinkle in his eyes.

Terry laughed gently. "Cheers, mate. This will do me, eh?"

"So..." Ivan began, his eyes sparkling with enthusiasm. "Did you talk to your supervisor about our sighting?"

Saffi rolled her eyes. "About the wild dog you saw?"

Lachlan grinned and shook his head. "We have a sceptic."

"She didn't believe my Tasmanian tiger sighting either." Sam added with a sympathetic grin.

"No shit?" Tristram asked Sam. "You saw a thylacine?"

"Yep. I am confident I saw one out at Sarsfield one night in the summer after we all finished year twelve." Samuel answered.

"Where'd you see it?" Pyran chimed in.

"It ran across the highway, just before the turn-off to Mum and Dad's."

"What time?" Tristram asked.

"Oh, it was early in the morning, eh? Probably three am or thereabouts."

"A likely story." Saffi teased. "This is Sam, remember. He is not exactly good at spotting wildlife."

"Oh what? What are you talking about?" Sam responded indignantly.

"You *do* remember our trip along the Great Ocean Road a few months ago?"

"Yeah? Why...what happened...?"

"I saw a whale." Saffi explained to the others. "I told everyone in the car, "look – a whale" and there's Sam, looking in the paddocks *"where, where is it?""*

Sam scoffed into laughter, that was immediately echoed by everyone at the table.

"You are so mean to me!" Sam chided.

"Just keeping it real, sweetie." Saffi smiled cheekily and kissed him.

"You ever see a Tassie tiger, Terry?" Tristram asked.

"Nah, eh? But I have seen the bunyip." Terry smiled.

Suddenly, Terry had their undivided attention. But he said

nothing further, instead looking with mild confusion at the faces fixed on him.

"You're just going to drop that bomb-shell and leave it at that?" Ivan asked incredulously.

Terry shrugged, then grinned. "I reckon it is the same bunyip Tristram would have seen up in the high country, all those years ago. Do you remember? When you went for a walk just before dawn with an elder who just recently passed away?"

Terry then made friendly eye contact with Tristram, who eyes had narrowed in thought.

"How did you know about that?" Tristram asked.

"The old fella told me a few things, eh? That's why Elsie and the other women have made me the new watchdog."

Pyran was the first to react. With a beaming smile, he put his arm around Terry.

"Congratulations, mate. I am sure you deserve the honour, eh?"

The sentiment was echoed around the table. Terry grinned shyly and shrugged.

"So, what does that mean?" Saffi asked.

"Oh, I dunno, eh? I don't really think it's an official Kurnai thing – just a sort of complimentary title that the old fella was given by a couple of the older ladies back in the day. Fred was always looking out for the area, you know? He would always tell Elsie and her cousins if something new or strange was happening. He reported any interesting visitors. They called him the Watchdog." Terry explained.

"You used his name." Tristram observed.

Terry nodded. "Yeah, I used his name. It is mostly only the older people that shy away from naming the dead. And some of the younger ones, depending who they are, I s'pose. But I am not superstitious or religious, eh?"

"You're an atheist?" Tristram smiled appreciatively.

"Yep. I like the stories and the Dreamtime and my culture, sure, but I also like to keep a grip on reality, eh? No offense to anyone here who might believe in Jesus or something."

A gentle scoff ran around the table.

"You are pretty safe to say that here." Lachlan grinned.

"So, Tristram..." Ivan began expectantly.

"Yes?"

"You saw a bunyip on our camping trip with Fred all those years ago? And you chose to hold out on that information?"

An accusation distorted his smile.

"I didn't see a bunyip." Tristram sighed sadly as he remembered. "Terry, you seem to know what I saw..."

Terry nodded. "It was an old burnt out tree."

"And Fred pointed to that old tree, and he whispered urgently – *do you see him? Do you see him, Tristram? Look, but not too long. Stop looking if he looks back.*"

"And you couldn't see anything but the tree." Terry smiled nostalgically. "But he kept goin' at ya, until you agreed that you could see the bunyip. Did he dig his bloody bony fingers into your shoulder?"

"Yes!" Tristram exclaimed. "You too!?"

"Yep. Cained for a couple of days." Terry grinned.

"Yeah, I had bruises – I remember that." Tristram said, absently rubbing his left shoulder.

"I don't understand." Ivan frowned.

"Neither did I, at the time." Tristram shrugged. "Actually, even now I have no idea what he was up to."

"He was protecting the real bunyip." Terry replied, matter-of-factly.

"Did he yell you that?" Ivan asked.

"Yes." Terry nodded. "Old Fred really believed he had seen a bunyip. But he didn't want anyone else to go looking for it. So, whenever some young fella got a bit too interested in the stories of the bunyip – such as yourself, Tristram – and me – and more than one of my cousins – then we would get the early morning trudge up the hill to go and look at that burnt out old tree."

The implications of what Terry was saying seeped into Tristram like blood soaking into paper towel.

He remembered how he had pitied Fred. He remembered the energy and bewildered sadness of the drunken old man.

"Mate, you have no idea how what you are saying...*hits* me." Tristram began, as his thoughts led to words. "You've turned a very important memory upside down."

"Sorry." Terry shrugged, with empathy.

"No, I am sorry, actually." Tristram continued. "At the time, I assumed that Fred was just a mad old drunk. It made me question what I thought I had seen as a kid. It confirmed in me as a teenager, that what I saw when I was ten years old was just my imagination."

"Maybe that was what he intended." Ivan interjected. "Fred wanted you to doubt that you ever really saw a bunyip...I wonder...I wonder if that is my fault."

"What? How?" Pyran frowned.

"Maybe I showed a little too much interest in finding the bunyip back then. I did go with you boys up into the high country with a lot of hunting and tracking equipment after-all. Fred knew you, but he didn't know me."

The group thought about Ivan's hypothesis.

"It seems to make sense." Tristram concluded.

"So, the bunyip is an old burnt out tree?" Saffi shrugged. "Bit of an anticlimax. You will need to write about something else in your novel, Tris."

"Are you writing a novel about the bunyip?" Terry asked.

"Yeah." Tristram grinned. "I have a way to go though, before it is finished."

"Do you mind if Tristram writes about the bunyip?" Pyran winced at Terry.

Tristram, Saffi and Lachlan scoffed.

"What? I am serious, you guys." Pyran added sternly. "It's not our culture, eh?"

"Actually, the bunyip legend is probably a mix of Aboriginal myth and fairy tales of European origin." Tristram replied.

"Come on, man." Pyran chided. "The bunyip is clearly an indigenous legend. And anyway, haven't you written about the rainbow serpent as well?"

Tristram shifted uncomfortably in his chair. "What if I have? It is my culture too."

"No, it is not."

"Pyran, I consider all the world's stories my culture. You wouldn't be getting on your high horse if I was writing about Thor or Hercules." Tristram growled.

"Would you write about Mickey Mouse?" Pyran demanded.

"No, but that is different."

"It is not different, man. The Rainbow serpent and Tiddalick the giant frog and every other legend of the indigenous people is their intellectual property, eh? Just because they didn't write it down doesn't mean it isn't theirs."

"So, what are you saying? That the rainbow serpent is the copyright of indigenous people?" Tristram asked.

"Yes, exactly. Don't you think that they should have some rights over how their stories are used?"

Tristram thought seriously about the question.

"I don't know. Do the people of Athens own the stories of Zeus, Ares, Apollo and so on?" He shrugged. "I don't think the Rainbow serpent is the same as Mickey Mouse. Walt Disney created Mickey Mouse – I reckon if you can't pin down the specific author for a story or a character, then it is public domain."

"There is a term for this." Saffi rejoined. "Cultural appropriation."

"Yeah, but which culture is being appropriated? For example, which tribe came up with the Rainbow serpent?" Tristram asked.

"It doesn't matter." Pyran shrugged. "It belongs to all indigenous people."

"Pyran, it is not as simple as that." Ivan interjected. "You do realise that before the British invasion, there were maybe five hundred or more different tribes or nations of aborigines? There were hundreds of mutually incomprehensible languages. Saying that the stories and legendary characters of one tribe belong to all tribes is a bit of a stretch."

"Agreed." Noel joined in. "It would be like treating Europe as one culture, without acknowledging the vast differences between the Germans, the English, the French, the Norwegians, the Swiss and the Spanish and so on."

"I still think we should not just write about their Dreamtime culture without considering the wishes of the indigenous people." Pyran objected forcefully. "I mean, we have taken everything from them, surely the least we can do is not take their art and stories – I mean it is all they have left."

"What do you reckon about all this, Terry?" Lachlan asked.

Everyone paid Terry their full attention.

Terry shrugged and then gave a bemused smile. "Am I the spokesperson for all indigenous Australians, am I?"

"Fair point." Ivan nodded with a hint of chagrin.

"I am interested in your opinion, mate, if you would care to give it." Tristram persued.

Terry thought about it, before he answered. "I think that if people draw inspiration from indigenous culture, it will generate interest in that culture. That interest will help keep it alive. As long as it is done respectfully, I think it is a good thing."

The group nodded appreciatively.

"Well said." Pyran grinned. "I suppose that is a good way to look at it."

Terry nodded at the compliment.

"So, Tristram..." Ivan began, his sapphire eyes dark and keen. "What did your supervisor, the great Professor Burt Whiteside, have to say about our sighting?"

"He thought it was bullshit, of course, but we hashed out a few ideas on what sort of animal the bunyip might be." Tristram answered.

"Any thoughts on how to track it down?" Ivan asked.

"Yeah, actually. He thinks we should put poisoned, live baits near creeks that have access to both pasture and nearby shelter big enough for a bunyip – caves, giant old dead trees and so on. He thinks we should get some maps from the water-board and identify locations that fit the bill within a twenty-kilometre radius of our sighting."

Ivan nodded thoughtfully.

"Hang on a minute." Terry frowned. "Are you talking about tracking the bunyip?"

"Yeah." Tristram shrugged.

"You reckon you have seen the actual bunyip? Is that what you were saying before, when you were talking about a sighting?"

"Yeah – but you know there is a real bunyip." Tristram rejoined. "You just said before that Fred used the burnt-out old tree to cast doubt in the minds of people who wanted to look for the real thing."

Terry stared at Tristram. "The *real thing*? There is no real bunyip. Fred thought there was – but it was all just story-telling – like Santa Claus and all that."

Saffi smirked, as Pyran, Ivan, Tristram and Lachlan searched each other's face to see which one, if any of them, would claify the matter.

"We saw a bunyip." Pyran informed Terry decisively.

"*What*!? Where?" Terry laughed, incredulous.

"Up in the hills near the Alpine National park – past the back of Benambra, in the High Country." Lachlan answered.

"Bullshit." Terry scoffed.

It was Tristram who then took up the task of describing their sighting of a few days before.

Terry listened with wrapt attention, his eyes growing wide with wonder at the description of the bunyip. Lachlan, Ivan and Pyran also added to the tale with their own observations and feelings.

Sam, Saffi and Jase listened with sceptical interest.

"That is fuckin' amazing, eh?" Terry smiled, shaking his head.

Suddenly Holly was behind Terry, cradling the baby wombat.

"Watch your language and hold this." She said, taking Terry by complete surprise.

"Mrs. Jones! Oh what..." Terry laughed as he was handed the wombat. "Oh...g'day little mate."

"That's not to be eaten." Russell joked.

Saffi sighed loudly. "Inappropriate, Dad."

Terry was delighted. "What's his name? Or her name?"

"That's Wilbur the wombat. He was playing in the lounge with Belle before, so I thought he could say hello to everybody before I feed him and put him back to bed." Holly smiled.

"Oh wow..." Terry beamed. "He's like a human baby, eh?"

Wilbur was indeed the size of human baby, covered in chocolate fur with grey highlights.

"The poor boy was found beside his mother. She was hit by a car and was lying dead on a road near Bruthen. We think she must have had mange, as this little boy is showing signs of the infection. See the scabby patches near his back legs? We are treating it with a bit of Cydectin."

"Yeah, seen a lot of mangy wombats about this last year, eh?" Terry winced. "Leaves them in a horrible state, eh? Covered in bloody wounds, fly-blown. I hope you get over it soon, little mate."

"Here – you might as well feed him." Holly said, handing Terry a small bottle of warm milk made from special formula.

Charmed, Terry fed Wilbur, who's small front paws gripped the bottle like a human infant. The wombat rapidly drained the bottle with gleeful slurping noises. His tiny beady eyes gazed sleepily up at Terry.

"I wonder if the bunyip is an animal just like this one? Just like all the animals we have in this country?" Terry wondered aloud.

"Like a marsupial?" Tristram asked.

"Yeah, I suppose." Terry shrugged. "But I really mean...you know, like this – flesh and blood. Needing to be raised up from a baby by a mother bunyip."

"Old Fred used to say that the bunyip was like a man. Part animal, part spirit." Ivan offered.

Terry nodded. "I reckon all animals are part animal, part spirit."

Wilbur finished the bottle and pushed it away. He half-closed his eyes and made satisfied gurgling noises which made everyone laugh.

"I'll take him now, or he will fall asleep on you and you

won't be able to move." Holly grinned, scooping Wilbur up in her arms.

The evening wore on with more jokes, drinks and stories. At around midnight, Terry advised that he had better be going.

"I will walk you to the car." Tristram smiled.

"Actually, Ivan, man – I don't suppose you wanna do me a favour?" Pyran chimed in.

"Yeah?"

"Can I come into town with you? I wanna do a Macca's run, eh?" Pyran grinned.

"How are you going to get back here afterwards?" Tristram asked.

"Ah fuck...yeah, don't worry about it." Pyran said, deflated.

Ivan laughed. "I don't mind dropping you back."

"You sure?"

"I'm sure. Come on."

"Fuck yeah!" Pyran whooped. "You are such a legend, man!"

Pyran, Ivan, Tristram and Terry ascended the stairs to the top of the block. The full moon hung bright above them, so much so that they could make out each other's facial expressions very clearly.

Once they were at Ivan's Landcruiser, Terry turned to Tristram.

"So...being the new watchdog, I do have to sorta warn you about something..."

"Yeah?"

"There's an old fella who has come to town. He calls himself Dinewan. You know him, don't you?"

"Yes, we do." Ivan answered, his face now dark and serious.

"I don't know him." Terry continued. "He's not from around here. I heard he came down from Queensland?"

"That's where I saw him a few days ago." Pyran confirmed. "Up on the Goldcoast."

"Years ago, I first encountered him further north than that – up near Noosa Heads." Ivan added. "Then Tristram and I ran into him again in Western Victoria. Dinewan gets around, I guess."

"Cool. So, no problem then?" Terry asked, searching their faces.

"He is not excactly a friend." Tristram confided. "I don't wish him any harm, but I can't say he feels the same way about me."

Terry nodded. "Fair enough. Yeah, well, he's been gettin' in the ears of a few of our young lads. He has been asking about you and where you live. I don't think he knows you live here. If you like, I can make sure it stays that way – or at least, you know, make sure my guys keep their mouths shut."

"I would prefer that he didn't know I live here." Tristram admitted. "But on the other hand, this address is hardly a secret. Tyntynder Wildlife shelter is publically listed – the address is very easy to get."

"Should I get some of the boys to suss him out?" Terry asked.

"You mean beat him up?"

Terry seemed disappointed. "No. I don't organise gang-bashin', Tristram. I mean do you want me to find out more about him?"

"Not on my account, mate." Tristram answered. "Just warn your guys that the old man has mental health issues, and that he can be dangerous."

"How so?"

"He once attacked me with a knife. Recently he menaced us with a pack of dogs." Tristram answered.

"Don't forget the package he sent full of fuckin' funnel-web spiders." Pyran interjected.

"And he sometimes has venous snakes on him." Ivan added.

Terry raised his eyebrows. "Fuckin' hell, boys. I gotta hear more about all this."

"Well, those are the high-lights." Tristram shrugged. "Ivan and Pyran can tell you more as they drop you back home. Just tell anyone you know that is dealing with him to be very careful."

"Will do." Terry answered, then smiled broadly. "Gotta say it's been an interesting night, fellas."

THE ABDUCTION

Almost as soon as Ivan, Pyran and Terry left, Tristram went down to the cottage. He was deeply tired and still slightly drunk. Looking forward to a deep and delicious sleep, he slipped out of his clothes into a pair of black boxers. He couldn't be bothered finding a t-shirt to wear, so he decided to go to bed top-less.

He took a moment to consider his reflection in the small mirror next to his bed.

Could stand some improvement.

Tristram grimaced, noting that where a six-pack should be, a four-pack sat above a bulge of belly fat. Flexing his pecs and biceps, he promised himself to work-out soon.

Tristram stood beside his bed taking several deep, slow breathes. In only a moment, he was calm and sleepy.

However, when he finally pulled the doona back, he was confronted by a coiled black snake.

"*Fuck me!*" He breathed.

The animal raised its head. Its tongue flickered rapidly, and its beady black eyes were fixed on Tristram.

"A red-bellied black snake." Tristram thought aloud. "Fuckin' hell. You scared the shit out of me. I always thought a snake might come in here one day, but far out...why are you in my *bed*?"

The snake let out a hiss and raised its head higher, flattening its body, ready to strike. It had a bright scarlet belly.

"OK...no need for threats, girl – you are probably a girl at that size...how big are you? Hmm...at least six or maybe seven feet...Jesus...I wonder if you are the one taking gold-fish from Mum's pond?"

Tristram moved very slowly back-wards towards the door.

Suddenly another snake slid into view, coming from underneath Tristram's bed. It was a large tiger snake.

Then an ornament from the shelf above the mirror was knocked to the floor. Another tiger snake leaned out from the shelf, it's glossy black eyes on Tristram, its tongue rapidly flickering in and out.

Tristram began to breath rapidly, wondering if the snake on the floor or the snake on the shelf would strike at him first. Then the red-bellied black snake hissed again and opened its mouth wide.

Finally, another snake made its presence known, sliding out of shoebox on Tristram's desk beside the door – an enormous eastern brown snake.

Carefully Tristram reached behind him to the doorknob, and slowly turned it. The snakes hissed in unison as he opened the door, the hinges creaking loudly.

The black snake suddenly leaped off the bed, and before it hit the floor, Tristram stepped through the door and slammed it shut.

He half-expected to see snake heads pushing from underneath the door to get out, but there was no movement that he could see.

Then he noticed the dark, still presence of dogs. Four large german shepherds; two to his left and two to his right. Their ears were erect, watching him intently.

Tristram carefully considered each animal. Unlike the dogs at the riverbank a few days ago, these dogs showed no aggression.

"Good evening, Tristram."

There was no mistaking the low drawl of Dinewan. Yet, Tristram could not see the witch doctor yet.

"You know, in Victoria you need a license to keep snakes." Tristram returned. Then he winced, silently wishing he had some better remark.

Dinewan laughed gently but said nothing in response.

An awkward pause passed, then Tristram spoke again.

"So, what is happening here?"

"Follow the dogs."

"Can I get dressed first?"

A faint whistle was the only answer Tristram received.

The german shepherds' ears twitched and they seemed to become animated. The two animals to his right began to walk together up the path towards the top of the block. The two animals to his left growled at him. It was obvious where Tristram needed to go.

Gingerly, Tristram made his bare-footed way across the gravel of the path. Then the dogs herded him onto the grass and up into the orchard. As they walked up through the orchard, he could see through the trees to his right the lights from the lounge room's southern windows. The blinds were down, so he could not see in – and therefore he realised grimly, that no one could see out. He knew that his parents were still up with Lachlan, watching television, oblivious to his plight.

Tristram wanted to shout out, but he was undecided. In seconds, the dogs had guided him firmly past the opportunity, and up to the gate at the very top of his parents' property. It was already open, and a moment later, Tristram was walking barefoot along the gravel road, the canine sentinels surrounding him.

Only a few metres down the road he saw a beaten-up old panel van. In the dark, its colours were uncertain, but Tristram guessed that it was once white – but was now painted over with surfing imagery and slogans.

As they approached, the panel van's engine spluttered to life. Tristram was guided to the barn-doors at the rear of the vehicle.

The dogs then sat silently around Tristram.

Unsure of what to do, Tristram looked around him for Dinewan. The witch doctor was nowhere to be seen.

The panel van continued to idle. Tristram took note of the license plate.

He waited for the doors to open, or for some instruction from Dinewan. Neither happened.

Tristram thought about kicking the alpha dog and making a bolt for his parent's place. Tristram considered each dog in turn.

Which one of you arseholes is the alpha?

Finally, Tristram considered opening the van's doors. Surely, that was what he was expected to do. But what horrible surprise was waiting inside the van?

With a resolute sigh, Tristram reached for the handle, turned it and opened the doors.

A cloud of fruity smelling smoke billowed out onto the road. Tristram waved the smoke away and peered into the belly of the van.

Aside from what looked like old woollen blankets, the vehicle seemed to be empty. Tristram could not see the driver – there was a metal cargo barrier.

Suddenly an impatient voice barked from the front seat.

"When you're ready, princess."

That was not Dinewan. Who was it?

Tristram climbed into the back of the van, and before he had time to turn around the doors were slammed behind him.

The van lurched forward, and they were away.

Tristram coughed at the smoke that filled the dark interior. The woollen blankets seemed to be saturated with the fruity smoke.

This smoke smells familiar.

"Oh *fuck*." Tristram shuddered as he realised what it was. "Not this shit again. Fuck!"

I am probably going to start hallucinating. How the hell do I control my mind through the experience?

As Tristram was bounced around in the back of the van, he felt for a breeze that would give away a crack in a window or a panel that would let in fresh air. Eventually, he decided that the rear doors were his best chance. He pressed his mouth against the crack where the doors closed and tried to breath fresh air from outside.

Unfortunately, whenever the vehicle braked his face was slammed against the metal door, and when they went around a corner Tristram was thrown about.

To mitigate the impacts, Tristram wrapped himself in the woollen blankets. However, every movement caused smoke to puff out of the blanket. It seemed there was no escape from the smoke.

Tristram had no clue which direction they had travelled. Eventually, the vehicle's speed slowed, and there were multiple bumps and jolts. He suspected that he was being taken out into the bush somewhere.

Am I going to be killed and buried in the middle of nowhere?

No, Dinewan wants something from me. I will probably live through this.

Probably...

THE QUINKIN MISTAKE

WHEN THE VAN FINALLY STOPPED, it continued to idle. Tristram by that point had lost his sense of time.

How long have we travelled? An hour? Two? Where are we now?

Tristram heard the driver get out and walk around to the back doors. The doors were violently opened, and the outside world was revealed.

There was no trace of the person who had opened the door. The rear lights of the van cast red light upon white sand that seemed to trail off to a dark lake.

"Get out." A gruff voice commanded.

Tristram cast the blankets off him and did as he was told.

As soon as he set foot on the ground, the panel van sped away from him across a sandy plain.

The sky was pink, and a myriad of stars seemed to cause pin-pricks to his eyes. The full moon hung high in the sky, gleaming bright blue.

Just breathe. I'll get you through this.

Tristram frowned at the familiar voice. Then he smiled.

Magician?

Yup. It's been a while, eh?

Tristram suddenly burst into a stupid giggle.

Something funny?

"Oh, my god!" Tristram shouted. Then continued to laugh so hard that he fell to his knees.

Tristram enjoyed the feeling immensely, and it seemed that the more he laughed, the funnier everything was. Minutes went by, as he lay on his side in the sand, laughing for reasons he could not begin to understand.

Finally, Tristram sat up and considered his surroundings. He was on a sandy stretch of ground that was running beside a lake. The lake seemed to be surrounded by dense bushland. At first, the lake seemed to be reflecting a bright pink sky. Yet, when Tristram looked at the sky itself, he noticed that it was not pink anymore. The full moon was gleaming white again in a satin sky awash with stars.

"Ah...it's wearing off, is it?" He asked himself.

Then he noticed a rainbow coloured bonfire about fifty metres away.

Rainbow coloured flames...guess I am still under the influence.

Tristram stood up.

Can I hear the ocean?

The magician answered in his mind.

Probably, but you cannot trust your senses. Things will go smoother if we don't worry too much about what is actually happening.

Tristram looked again at the bonfire and saw that there was a large sign behind it.

"Guess I am supposed to go read that." Tristram announced and then chuckled some more.

I think you are supposed to be afraid. The Magician observed, a smile in his voice.

"Well, I am not."

As Tristram got nearer the sign, he saw that it was hand-painted on a big slab of cardboard. The message was in red capital letters.

MIND YOUR MANNERS. SPIRITS HERE.

Tristram shook his head and smiled. Then an involuntary shudder went through him.

Spirits? There are no such fucking things...right?

Right. The Magician confirmed.

Soon Tristram noticed a large arrow drawn in the sand. It pointed away from the lake now behind him towards a stand of stunted looking eucalyptus trees about a hundred metres away. With a resigned sigh, he marched towards the stand.

The sand was cool and loose on his bare feet at first, but the further he walked, the firmer the sand became until he was feeling dry roots, leaves and sticks.

As he approached the trees, he was slowly able to see them in more detail. They turned out to be dead and twisted pillars, reaching up to the stars in tortured dismay. Their aspect was unsettling, and a cold air seemed to be slowly rolling towards him from their centre.

Tristram paused a few feet from them.

He turned to look at the bonfire, which now seemed very

far away. Then he considered the stand of dead trees in front of him.

It's a bad idea to go into the trees. You can too easily be ambushed.

Suddenly a loud and terrible laugh shattered the silence. It sounded bestial and demonic.

Tristram stood his ground and searched the shadows in front of him for the source.

Again, there was a horrible, guttural laugh...

"ROWAL...huh-huh-huh-huh-huh-huh."

The Magician laughed. *That is an animal call.*

Tristram breathed a sigh of relief as he recognised it.

"I know that sound." He said aloud to whomever may have been listening. "I hear it nearly every night. It is a male brush-tail possum."

No answer was returned.

"DINEWAN!" Tristram shouted, angry now.

Suddenly a chorus of voices harshly answered him.

"*Shhhhhhhhhhhhhhhh!*"

Tristram was now afraid. He began to slowly back away from the foreboding shadows of the dead trees.

Breathing rapidly, Tristram frantically searched the scene in front of him.

Spirits or not, I am outnumbered.

Suddenly clicking sounds emanated from the shadows.

Then Tristram felt a poke in the ribs.

He screamed and turned to face his attacker, but there was noone and nothing behind him.

Instinctively, Tristram put his arms in the air above him and displayed his empty hands.

A guttural voice rumbled from the shadows. "Dinewan?"

"Yes?" Tristram answered. "Dinewan. Do you know Dinewan?"

More clicking sounds were heard.

The spirits are talking to eachother. The Magician observed.

"Dinewan?" Rasped another voice with the same questioning tone.

They don't know that word. Dinewan is a word from a tribe a long way from here. The Magician explained.

"Dinewan. *Ngooran.*" Tristram clarified. "Dinewan. Emu. *Ngooran.*"

"Ngooran..." Multiple voices repeated, as though an understanding had been reached.

Beats of silence passed.

"Why don't you show yourselves?" Tristram called, trying to sound calm and brave. "Come on out."

His answer was a loud whisper.

"*Ngooran...wait. Wait...*"

Tristram waited.

He could hear rustling and incoherent whispers.

Then suddenly a large creature was hurled from the centre of the stand of trees. It crashed to the ground, but then immediately it was on its feet and running at Tristram.

Tristram stood his ground and a second later realised what the animal was.

The emu hissed savagely at him as it charged. Its powerful footfalls seemed to shake the ground.

Just at it was about to reach him it reared its head up high and fanned the feathers of its neck and chest.

Tristram raised his open palm and extended it at the animal.

The emu was successfully bluffed, and so did not kick him. It instead it stopped in its tracks, then turned clumsily on the spot before dashing away along the sandy shore of the lake.

Uproarious laugher and clicking emanated from the centre of the tree stand.

"NGOORAN!" Voices shouted gleefully.

"Very funny!" Tristram barked at the shadows. "Now, why don't you come out and face me."

The laughter stopped abruptly.

Tense seconds passed.

Then suddenly, multiple animal eyes appeared. The moonlight gleamed in the *tapetum lucidum* of each eye.

They blinked intermittently like fairy lights winking on and off.

Tristram froze and waited.

A long, thin, black appendage waved out above the eyes – then another and another.

Tristram shuddered.

It's a giant spider.

Don't be so sure. The Magician murmured.

What other creature has multiple eyes? Tristram thought in reply.

Look at the eyes again, Tristram. The Magician instructed.

Tristram obeyed and saw that they moved and blinked in pairs.

I see.

Not a giant spider.

No.

But what sort of creatures are they?

Thoughtful clicks and hoots began to break the silence.

Finally, the head of one leaned out from the shadows.

The creature was pitch black. Perched on a neck as long and thin as a broom-stick was a round, bald head about the size of a rock-melon. Large, gleaming white eyes stared at down at

Tristram. In the moonlight, Tristram could make out a very flat nose and a wide, lipless mouth. Where ears would have been on a human head, a rounded, fleshy protrusion the thickness of a banana angled down to just past the jawline, giving the suggestion of an arrowhead.

The other spirits lifted their heads out of the shadows, and they also had long, thin necks, and the same fleshy protrusions where ears would be on humans.

The first creature looked to the other four, then hissed. It raised a long thin arm, the same thickness as its neck, above its head. At the arm's end was a hand that resembled a long-legged spider. It curled the fingers into a fist, and the other four creatures nodded in unison. In solidarity, they also raised clenched fists.

The spirits seemed familiar to Tristram. He was sure that he had seen their ghostly likeness in photos of indigenous cave paintings.

Suddenly, the first creature stepped out with awful purpose from the shadows of the twisted trees. Its body seemed impossibly thin, and its legs were no thicker than its arms. It towered above Tristram, seeming to be more than twice his height.

Though its eyes were white and pupil-less, they were not expressionless. The creature glared down at Tristram in a most predatory way.

Don't break eye contact. The Magician commanded.

What do I do!? Tristram thought in reply.

Stand your ground.

Against spirits?

What else can you do?

Now the first spirit strode to Tristram. With surreal disgust, he realised that it was not genderless. It was male.

As it strode, an enormous, flacid penis swung between its legs.

It stopped about eight feet away from him.

Now that it was closer, Tristram could see that its intensely thin torso had ribs and a diaphragm. The small belly moved in and out as it breathed.

Breath. It is not a spirit – but an animal after-all? A primate?

Then the creature spoke, in a loud, rasping whisper.

"I...have...come...out."

Its aspect was defiant.

"Pleased to meet you." Tristram returned, trying to sound polite and brave. "I am Tristram. What is your name?"

The creature's eyes narrowed.

"Why...are...you...here?"

"I was brought here. By Dinewan. Ngooran." Tristram answered.

"Ngooran?" The creature scoffed. "He...wants...you...dead."

"And you?"

"We...want...you...gone."

"I am more than happy to leave." Tristram assured. "I am sorry to have trespassed. I meant no disrespect."

"We...want...you...ALL...gone." The creature growled.

"All?"

"ALL!"

The other four beings had stepped out from the trees, and they were wielding thick gum tree branches like clubs.

"I am the only one here. The only one besides Ngooran." Tristram answered.

"You...take...message." The creature pointed, its long finger only a foot away from Tristram's face. With wonder, he noted that it had a fingernail.

"Message? I would be honoured. What is the message and who is it for?"

"Message...for...your...people...   Get...out...or...all...
will...burn."

Tristram shuddered at the malice that emanated from the
being.

His companions were equally fierce.

"BURN!" They hissed in unison, brandishing their
weapons.

"Who shall I say the message is from?" Tristram asked.

The creature stood tall and proud, and put its hands on its
hips.

"The...Timara... Quinkins."

The Timara Quinkins? Tristram thought, confused at the famil-
iarity of those words.

Aha! The Magician laughed. *That is a mistake!*

Tristram frowned. *Mistake? Why?*

The Quinkins, Tristram! The Magician cheered happily.

Then Tristram remembered a story book from his early
childhood and relief flooded through him.

"The Timara Quinkins?" Tristram smirked. "You are a long,
long way from home."

The quinkin seemed confused.

"I remember the Quinkins. There are two types, are there
not? The tall, thin Timara that like to play tricks on children.
And the short, fat, ugly Imjim that bounce on knobby tails and
try to lure children into caves and turn them into Imjim."

"How dare you!" The creature glowered.

However, the spell was broken. Tristram could now see the
wires – literally.

A few feet behind the Timara in front of him, Tristram could make out the puppeteer – dressed in head to toe in black.

"The Quinkins are not a Kurnai legend." Tristram boomed. "They come from the stories told by the Kuku Yalanji people in Far North Queensland. The game is up, Dinewan!"

"We shall teach you some manners!" The quinkin threatened.

Tristram suddenly grew irritated.

"No, I am going to teach YOU some manners!" He shouted, then suddenly charged past the quinkin towards the shocked puppeteer behind it.

"Wait-wait-wait-!" The man pleaded to no avail.

Tristram kicked him hard in the balls.

With a yelp of pain, the man fell to the ground, and the quinkin also lost balance and crashed to the sand.

"You fuckin' cunt!" A man yelled from the shadows.

Tristram saw other figures coming out from the stand of trees. They ran towards him.

He turned back towards the bonfire in the distance and ran.

OUTNUMBERED

Tristram ran along the shore of the lake, energised by the shouts and footfalls behind him.

Where can I go?!

Once he reached the bonfire, he turned to assess his persuers.

Seven. Four dressed in black – the other puppeteers. The other three look like bikie gang members – heavy boots, jeans, beards. Who the fuck are these people? Where is Dinewan?

Tristram scanned the edge of the lake and then the land around him. There seemed to be sandy road between a clump of banksia trees about fifty metres away.

Where does that road go? Where am I?

Suddenly he saw headlights coming from the road towards him.

It was the beaten-up old panel-van that had brought him here.

Its headlights were focused on him, he realised. The engine roared. It was coming towards him as though to mow him down.

The men were now getting close and began to fan out in a semi-circle.

Decisively Tristram strode into the surprisingly warm waters of the lake. He registered that the the lake was salty. Once he was in knee-deep water, he stopped again to consider his situation.

The men stood at the edge of the water. The panel van had stopped just behind them, the engine still idling, its headlights in Tristram's face.

"Turn your high-beams off, you pack of cunts!" Tristram shouted with a hint of humour.

They ignored him.

"Come out of the water! Now!" A burly, bearded man commanded.

"Fuck you!" Tristram shouted back.

"Where do you think you're gonna fuckin' go?" The burly man barked.

Good point.

Tristram looked across the lake behind him. He could see only dense bush on the other side.

I could swim across. I am going to have to. But then where will I go?

"Well?" The man persisted, his hands on his hips.

Fuck it. I am gonna have to figure this out as I go.

Tristram dived into the water and began to side-stroke across the lake.

"Are you fuckin' serious!?" The man called after him.

As Tristram swam, he heard a heated argument go on behind him.

Suddenly, there were surprised shouts.

Tristram turned to see what was going on.

A Landcruiser had appeared on the beach. Its headlights were off.

Its engine suddenly roared, and the Landcruiser, armed with its heavy steel bull-bar, rammed the panel-van from behind.

The men on the beach began to curse and shout as the Landcruiser revved its engine again. It pushed the panel van into the lake. The water reached the van's engine and it cut out. The driver of the panel-van began to climb out of the window.

Tristram felt a surge of joy as he recognised the landcrusier as it backed up the beach by the bonfire.

Ivan!

"WOO-HOO!" Tristram cheered, punching the air.

He then swam back to shore with free-style as fast he could.

When he reached the shore, he was confronted by the driver of the panel-van. He was shorter than Tristram and seemed only a few years older than him. He was a skinny, blonde Caucasian with a crew-cut.

"I wouldn't start something you can't finish, cunt." Tristram glowered, as the enraged man strode up to him.

Before Tristram was ready, the man punched Tristram in the face. Tristram rolled with the punch, which did not have much force, and swung back.

He was too slow, and his opponent ducked the blow and returned another to Tristram's stomach.

Tristram had braced for the punch, but it still hurt.

Angry now, Tristram finally found his advantage as the man threw another punch.

This one Tristram simply caught. He then used his height and strength to violently shove the man backwards off his feet.

As the man went to get up, Tristram kicked him as hard he could in the ribs. His oppent was lifted off the ground by the force. He did not get up – he was winded.

Then Tristram looked up the beach towards the Landcruiser.

Ivan and Pyran had exited the vehicle and were now surrounded by seven attackers.

Ivan stood relaxed with his hands by his sides, but Pyran was in a boxer's stance.

A dark-haired Caucasian man ran to Pyran, and to Tristram's delight Pyran smacked him hard and fast with a right cross. Then another straight after. The man fell.

Tristram ran to join the fight.

As he drew close, Pyran had engaged another attacker. This one was a short, wiry, dark-skinned man with black curly hair. He had the look of a cold, practiced streetfighter.

They circled each-other, both bouncing and switching stances.

Tristram realised that everyone had stopped to watch them fight.

Pyran's green eyes were narrowed and angry. His opponent's brown eyes were cool – too cool.

Cousin, this guy is dangerous.

No sooner had the thought crossed Tristram's mind, Pyran moved in for a punch. His opponent responded with a quick and devastating Muay-thai low side kick.

The onlookers winced at the sickening sound of Pyran's shin splintering from the force.

Pyran screamed and fell to the ground.

The other men whooped, cheered and jeered.

Horrified and outraged, Tristram strode towards Pyran's opponent.

The man smirked at Tristram and raised his fists into a fighting stance.

Tristram responded by facing him with an open-handed Aikido stance.

Suddenly Ivan's deep voice cut across the scene in a low, powerful roll.

"I'll take this one."

His authority was not questioned.

He stepped quickly and yet casually towards the water, beckoning to the man that had downed Pyran.

The fighter followed, and the other men fanned out to watch.

Tristram went to Pyran's side.

"You alright, man?"

"I think that prick fractured my shin." Pyran groaned. "But I'll be right. Ivan's outnumbered, man."

"Pyran, I think we are about to see one hell of a fight." Tristram said with quiet excitement. "Ivan is a black belt in more than one style."

Pyran, wincing, looked to Tristram.

"Yeah?" He said, with a hint of humour. "Well then, get out of the fuckin' way so I can see."

Ivan's opponent bounced and danced around him. Cocky and mocking, he snarled at Ivan. He widened his eyes.

"You saw what I did to that other bitch." He sneered. "You really want next?"

Ivan said nothing.

"Oh look, boys, he's too cool for school." The man continued.

"He's in over his head." Another man jeered.

"No time for smack talk, player?" Ivan's opponent smiled cruelly. "Don't know what to say?"

Ivan yawned pointedly, and the men around him laughed, including his opponent.

"OK. Let's do it, bitch." The fighter smirked.

He circled Ivan, then veered left and right, changing his stance.

Ivan barely moved. He was alert but not tense. His face was unreadable, his eyes never leaving his opponent's. His stance was perfectly balanced, he did not lean on his front nor his rear leg.

Suddenly, the attacker threw a feint punch. Ivan did not move an inch, as if he knew the blow would never connect.

The attacker then bounced more energetically, before he threw a quick but again feint punch. He then shot off a quick but powerless kick that Ivan parried easily.

Ivan smiled ever so faintly.

For every attack that came, Ivan moved only precisely as much as he needed to. He dodged the kicks and the punches by the narrowest of margins by either leaning slightly out of the way or taking a small step. At all times he seemed relaxed, balanced and in control.

Finally, Ivan's opponent made a decisive and poweful kick to Ivan's abdomen. However, Ivan had slid imperceptively to the side of the kick's trajectory and turned his hips. With a quick low front-kick, Ivan took out his enemy's knee, then stepped through and struck the man forcefully in the face with his opposing fist.

The man fell and did not move.

Suddenly three other men ran at Ivan. One of them was the burly, bearded man that had ordered Tristram out of the water.

Ivan moved to the engage the burly man to his right. The man threw a right hook, but Ivan simply blended smoothly with the arc of the strike, taking control of the attacker's arm so that by the end of the punch, the man was off balance and turned more than he had intended. Ivan completed the technique with an efficient push at such an angle that the man could not resist being thrown into the other two men.

The three fumbled and scrambled as they attempted to separate from each other, but Ivan took advantage of their confusion with calculated hip and shoulder shoves to any man about to to stand up. Finally, the big, bearded man went to grapple with Ivan, by reaching to grab his shoulder with one hand, with the intent of striking him with the other.

Tristram recognised Ivan's technique in response: *nikyo* – a pronating wristlock on a bent arm that results in sudden, intense nerve pain. The shock of the *nikyo* brought Ivan's opponent immediately to his knees. Ivan instantly kneed the man hard in the face, shattering his nose.

Ivan was ready for further assaults by the remaining two men, but they now stood still in awe of him.

"Are we done?" Ivan drawled.

The men nodded.

Suddenly, four more men approached the group, from the road amongst the banksias.

It was Terry, two other young koori men, and Dinewan.

THE AGREEMENT

"OK. Which one of you arse-holes are going to explain what the fuck is going on here?" Ivan demanded of the men around him.

Now that that the heat of battle had passed, Tristram could consider the men that had abducted and assaulted him.

In the fire-light, which was now no longer rainbow-coloured, Tristram realised that the men dressed completely in black – the puppeteers – seemed now to resemble artists more than combatants in stealth gear.

One of them, a young indigenous man with large, kindly eyes, answered Ivan.

"The guy comin' towards us can tell you what's goin' on." He said, with a nod towards Dinewan.

Despite the warm night, the witch doctor was in his trench-coat and wore long beige trousers. He had one bare foot, the other in a long leather boot.

The witch doctor's unusual gait contrasted with the cool march of the young men around him.

"*Dinewan...*" Ivan rumbled. His sapphire eyes were narrowed and dangerous.

"Ivan MacAllister." Dinewan drawled, lifting his chin so that his orange eyes gleamed out from under the brim of his floppy hat.

"Alright..." Tristram called over everybody. "Let's pick everyone up and go sit around the fire. We'll talk this out. Yes?"

The idea seemed reasonable to everyone, and so as Tristram helped Pyran to the fire, he saw the other men raise the two fighters that Ivan had knocked out.

Terry walked to Tristram, to take Pyran's other side.

Terry nodded to Tristram, a twinkle of humour in his eyes.

"They took ya in nothin' but your boxers, mate? Worst birthday ever, huh?"

Tristram and Pyran chuckled.

"My name is Tristram." Tristram began, once all were seated. "I'm guessing you knew that already. I know Dinewam – as I suppose you all do..."

Dinewan sat cross-legged and apart from everyone else. He was silent and unreadable. He did not react to the attention paid to him.

"The guy with the shattered shin next to me is my cousin, Pyran." Tristram continued. "That's Terry – and these lads with you, Terry...?"

"Simmo and Matt." Terry answered.

"Good to meet you, Simmo and Matt." Tristram smiled.

The lads, who looked to be in their late teens, smiled and nodded. Simmo was lanky and cheerful. He had dyed his short hair fire-truck red. Matt was short and stocky and serious. His hair was also short and dyed platinum blonde.

Tristram then gestured to Ivan, who stood with crossed arms, glowering at Dinewan.

"And the bad-ass guy who beat the shit out of you all single-handedly is my English teacher from high-school, Ivan."

There were grunts of acknowledgement from all in the circle.

"So – I see five puppeteers, and four non-puppeteers." Tristram continued. "Anyone want to make introductions?"

In moments, the people around the fire became relatable human beings, rather than varations on a thug stereotype. The non-puppeteers were cousins and friends of Simmo and Matt. The puppeteers were travelling artists, all the way from Far North Queensland. They were travelling the country, meeting with various indigenous comminuties, and performing small shows with their amazing puppets. They were going to finish the trip with a big show for the Adelaide Arts Festival.

"You ever read children's books about the Quinkins? The imjim and the timara?" A shy puppeteer asked. His name was Wilson.

"Yes." Tristram nodded. "I still have some of the books by Percy Trezise and Dick Roughsey."

"Yeah – one of our shows is based directly on one of their books, eh?"

"Oh...righto. That's wonderful." Tristram beamed.

"We just spent a week in Bung Yarnda."

"Where's Bung Yarnda?" Tristram asked.

"You're sitting beside it." Terry answered with a grin.

"What?" Then Tristram remembered. "Bung Yarnda – Lake Tyres! Oh! Fuckin' hell – so that's where we are!"

There were chuckles from some in the group.

"The story-tellers here are staying at the mission." Terry

continued "That's where they met our local boys here – and this travelling witch doctor."

"OK. This is starting to make some sense." Tristram nodded. "They are pretty amazing puppets, by the way. I will admit that you had me for a few moments there – I was believing in the super-natural."

Wilson grinned with pride.

"They are expensive puppets." A sterner puppeteer called Kevin interjected. Tristram noted that he was the big, bearded man that had barked at him to come out of the water. He was the biggest by far of the group, and the last man that Ivan had taken down. Kevin's nose had stopped bleeding, but it was clearly broken and swollen. Blood was drying in his beard.

"Yeah? They look it." Tristram nodded.

"Each one cost about ten thousand dollars." Kevin continued. "That's why we came after you when knocked one to the ground."

"Well you can't blame me for that." Tristram rejoined, bemused.

"And you kicked Wilson in the balls." Kevin added coolly.

"You can't blame me for that either." Tristram answered. Then he turned to Wilson. "Although I am sorry about that, man. If we had met under more reasonable circumstances, I am sure we'd get along alright."

Wilson shrugged. "Water under the bridge."

"Water under the bridge!?" Ivan boomed over the scene. "You kidnapped Tristram from his own home and attempted to terrify him with your *very expensive* puppets. And just what the hell were you doing when we arrived on the scene? You had him trapped in the water – I saw you hooning towards him in your panel-van – were you trying to run him down?"

"I would've braked before I hit him." The blonde driver mumbled defensively. His name was Chris.

"Oh well, that's mighty decent of you." Ivan growled.

"Don't forget that I was also drugged." Tristram added coolly.

The puppeteers frowned.

"What do you mean?" Kevin asked.

"Dinewan drugged me. Check the blankets in your van. Note the fruity smelling smoke that puffs out when you move them. It is some sort of hallucinogenic compound." Tristram rejoined.

"We don't know anything about that. This was supposed to be a prank played on a local racist arse-hole." Kevin explained.

"Thanks. How do you know I am a racist arse-hole? The colour of my skin?" Tristram glared.

Kevin shrugged, sheepishly.

"He told us about you." Wilson answered quietly, pointing to Dinewan. "He is an elder. We took his word, eh?"

"You took his word that he was an elder?" Pyran sneered.

"Come on, man." Terry chimed in. "He looks the part, eh?"

"I suppose, yeah, he does." Pyran shrugged, then winced at the pain in his shin.

"Look, it was a prank, alright?" Kevin sighed. "It fucking backfired and got out of hand. But we've had our fight, and there are no serious injuries."

"Speak for yourself." Pyran grumbled. "I think my shin is fractured."

"Yeah? And what about Alpaca?" Kevin fired back.

"Alpaca?" Tristram frowned.

Kevin nodded towards the curly haired fighter that had taken Pyran down, and then been knocked out by Ivan.

Alpaca was rubbing his jaw. "I'll be right."

"You were knocked out." Kevin glared. "You might have a concussion."

"I've had worse." Alpaca shrugged.

"Why do they call you Alpaca?" Tristram asked, with a twinkle of humour in his eye.

Alpaca shrugged. "They are cunts."

Wilson giggled. "Look at him. His neck is a bit long and his head looks like an Alpaca – look at that curly Alpaca hair."

Some of the other's laughed.

"He spits like an Alpaca, too." Kevin added, with an affectionate grin.

"Fuck off." Alpaca grinned, softening his street-fighter look. He then made eye contact with Pyran. "And sorry, eh?"

A silence ensued, as the group watched Pyran. At first, he seemed unforgiving, but then he gave a charismatic smile.

"Apology accepted, Alpaca." He nodded to his opponent. "All's fair in love and war, eh? I wasn't gonna go easy on you, so I shouldn't hold a grudge against you for lettin' me have it."

"You boys got off easy." Ivan suddenly growled, his voice cutting down the jocular and forgiving mood of the group.

Uncertain smiles, nods and shrugs were Ivan's answer.

"Actually, Ivan..." Tristram interjected. "How did you guys know I was here?"

"You can thank Simmo and Matt." Terry answered. "We met them at Maccas and got talkin'. They said there was a prank going on at Bung Yarnda. They were gutted they couldn't be here. We had a suspicion that Dinewan might be up to something. So, we decided to give 'em a lift."

"Rightio then. So now we come to the architect of this night's drama..." Tristram crooned, holding Dinewan's gaze.

The witch doctor stared quietly, with an ironic grin.

"Well?" Ivan prompted. "Explain yourself, Dinewan."

Dinewan yawned, then smirked at Tristram.

Tristram imitated Dinewan's yawn and smirk. The others laughed.

"Are you just going to sit there and say nothing?" Tristram

scoffed. "Of course, you are. All your tricks have been laid bare. Your monsters turn out to be puppets. It's like the finale of a Scooby-doo cartoon."

"Yeah." Pyran sneered, then put on a cartoon villain voice. "And I would have gotten away with it too, if it weren't for you meddling cunts."

The reference got a laugh from everyone except Ivan.

"What did you say in your letter to me, Dinewan?" Tristram continued. "Your letter packed with funnel-web spiders? You said that the up-coming experiences would be *most authentic*. Certainly, the quinkin puppets are better than your plastic skulls, but really, what did you think you were going to achieve tonight?"

Dinewan suddenly spoke. "It is not yet time."

The group waited for him to continue, but he said nothing.

"Not yet time." Tristram shrugged theatrically. "You retreat into ambiguity."

"I don't expect you to be convinced." Dinewan sighed.

"Convinced of *what*?"

"It is not yet *time*. I took advantage of an opportunity to teach you some respect, before the important *time* really comes."

"Are you talking about the rapture?" Tristram mocked.

"I'm talking about magic." Dinewan answered seriously.

"Ah...right." Tristram nodded sarcastically.

Dinewan sighed, then smiled to hide his frustration. "I cannot convince you. You will not be convinced until it is too late."

"You're full of fucking shit!" Pyran shouted.

"We know. And *he* knows." Tristram soothed. "This is sad. This is a sad state of affairs."

Suddenly Ivan strode towards Dinewan. He towered over

the witch doctor and fixed him with a very cool stare. Both of his fists were clenched.

"Dinewan, I want some fucking straight answers. And I am going to get them, or I am going to beat you bloody."

A tense silence followed.

Dinewan did not seem afraid, but neither was he defiant. He held Ivan's gaze with a thoughtful pity, before he blinked.

"Alright." Dinewan finally answered. "Ask your questions."

If Ivan was surprised, as the others were, at Dinewan's sudden compliance, he didn't show it.

"Did you cause the car accident with me and my sister?" Ivan began.

Dinewan winced. "No. It was just an accident. Your sister hit a kangaroo. I do not control kangaroos."

Dinewan watched Ivan blink with confusion.

Ivan seemed unsure of himself in the face of Dinewan's seeming earnestness.

"If you don't believe me, ask Charlotte." Dinewan persisted.

"*What?*" Ivan hissed, suddenly enraged.

Dinewan raised a placating hand.

"Ivan, I was a friend of your grandmother. And I now am a friend of your sister, Charlotte. She tracked me down about two years after the accident. You would know that, if you were not so fearful of contacting her."

Ivan blinked, his face pale.

"You are friends with my sister after what you did?" He sputtered.

Dinewan held his gaze. "I didn't do anything, Ivan. Unless you believe that I have magic powers. Which at that time, I did not have – as I don't have at this time."

"Shut up. Just shut up!" Ivan snarled. "Magic? Fuck off!"

Dinewan sighed. "You don't believe in magic?"

"Of course I fucking don't, you old charlatan!"

"Then you make my case for me, is my point." Dinewan countered. "Like I just admitted, I don't have power over kangaroos. I was on foot and miles away from you when you had your horrible accident."

Ivan seemed at a loss for words. He put his hands on his hips. He then ran a hand through his hair.

"Any more questions?" Dinewan prompted, indignantly.

Tristram was about to ask the witch doctor how he found Pyran in Queensland, but Ivan suddenly fired another question.

"Did you put a taipan in Adrian's shirt?" Ivan asked, his eyebrows raised in accusation.

The group watched in wrapt attention.

Dinewan blinked, considering his answer. He then opened his trench-coat and pulled out a beige, cloth-bag. He placed it on the ground.

"I gave that boy a bag like this one." Dinewan answered, a sadness in his voice. "There is a snake inside this bag. An Eastern brown. Fat and warm and fast. Also, very deadly."

"*What the fuck?*" Alpaca gasped.

The group looked with alarm at the beige cloth bag and the old man who put it there.

"Your point?" Ivan snapped.

"Adrian...*knew* there was a taipan in the bag that I gave him."

"Why did you give him a taipan?" Tristram asked.

"It was payment in advance for an *opal*." Dinewan answered, meaningfully.

"An opal you never got." Tristram added quietly.

"Yes." Dinewan grimaced. "An opal I never got. An opal that you, as a foolish little boy, *lost*."

"You gave a teenage boy a deadly snake – one of the deadliest snakes in all the world." Ivan scorned. "You knew what could happen. His death is on your head."

"No, his death is on *his* head!" Dinewan snapped with a sudden ferocity. "He was running from the police, with a taipan in a cloth bag. A cloth bag tied with a *very secure knot*. He must have undone that knot as he was running – his intention, probably, to throw that deadly serpent at the policemen running after him. It would have been very provoked by the frantic movements of the boy as he ran and fumbled with the bag. Is it any wonder that he got bitten?"

Ivan gave a derisive smile and shook his head. However, he had no rebuttal.

Dinewan seized on it. "No apology, Ivan MacAllister?"

"Apology? For *you*!?"

"You accused me of having a hand in two tragedies. In both cases, utterly ridiculous." Dinewan glared.

"Don't you try and turn this around." Ivan pointed. "Don't you fucking dare – you are hardly an innocent party!"

"You fucking stabbed Tristram!" Pyran shouted. "What do you say to *that*!?"

At that outburst, another tense silence followed.

Dinewan's eyes sparkled dangerously, but it was clear that the point had hit home.

"You sent me a letter with venomous spiders." Tristram added, quietly and firmly.

"I knew you would be careful opening it." Dinewan shrugged. "I told Pyran to be careful with that package."

"You put a red-bellied black snake in my *bed*." Tristram answered.

"Fuckin' hell." Terry breathed.

"And then there were the other snakes you put in my room. Two tigers, a brown snake – any others that I missed?" Tristram continued.

Murmurs of disbelief ran around the group.

"I knew you would be careful. And even if you weren't – I had milked those snakes." Dinewan retorted.

"Oh *bullshit*." Tristram fired back.

"No. I am telling the truth. I wanted to scare you, not harm you." Dinewan insisted.

"You fucking drugged me with a hallucinogenic compound." Tristram persisted.

Dinewan scoffed. "Harmless."

"That is debatable." Tristram sighed impatiently. "Being stabbed in the shoulder is not. I still have the scar."

Dinewan sneered. "A scar? What about the scars you have left?"

"You mean me, personally?" Tristram raised an incredulous eyebrow.

"Yes." Dinewam answered, with a defiant pursing of his lips.

"I am not a great man, Dinewan, but you cannot hold me accountable for whatever the hell has happened to you in your life."

"But I CAN. And I DO." Dinewan snapped bitterly.

"Explain." Tristram replied, holding the witch doctor's gaze with sincere attention.

Dinewan shifted uncomfortably. An awkward silence had time to ripen before Dinewan finally spoke again.

"Where do I start, Tristram? How do I convince you of a truth so simple that I can hardly find the words to describe it?"

"What a cop out." Ivan sneered.

Tristram held up a silencing hand.

"Dinewan, I will wait for you to find the words. I am very interested to hear them." He implored.

Dinewan scoffed in frustration. Then a thought occurred.

"We all have a part to play. The way a society turns out is

dependent on how each member plays their part. Do you understand?"

Tristram nodded. "So far, yes."

Dinewan leaned forward. "Do you agree?"

Tristram thought about it. "Yes. Yes, I do."

"What part are you playing?" Dinewan asked, opening his palms.

Tristram shook his head. "Um...ordinary citizen, I suppose. What part are you playing?"

Crows feet tightened about Dinewan's eyes. "A spokesperson for the aggrieved."

"Well, why are you taking it up with *me*? You need to take it up with some politicians. I am not in power." Tristram shrugged and sighed.

"Oh, but you *are* in power. Don't you see? Which of us indigenous brothers here can take up our cause and be listened to? Who needs to hear the message? The politicians, you say, but they listen to the majority. And the majority, Tristram, is not *us*. Do you understand?"

Tristram nodded. "I am just one person. I cannot make the difference you are talking about. I am not in anyway...special."

"Agreed." Dinewan drawled.

"Well then, what the hell?"

"Tristram, it is painfully obvious that you are not special. But by chance, yes, you actually can make a difference. Because by chance a special magic found its way to you."

"The bloody opal again?"

"The opal is just one manifestation." Dinewan waved dismissively. "There is another."

Tristram stared at Dinewan. "The bunyip?"

"Yes." Dinewan grinned. "You saw a bunyip all those years ago as a little boy. Maybe because you had the opal. I don't know. But if you saw it once, you can see it again. That is what I came here to convince you of."

Tristram nodded understanding. "By frightening me with very realistic quinkin puppets. If I could be made to believe in the quinkins, I could be made to reconsider my memories of the bunyip as real and not just imagined. And then what? We hunt for the bunyip together?"

"Surely, once you believed it was real, you would go and find it. Ivan, and you, would find it. And what great attention you would have, Tristram, should you be the one to show the bunyip to the world." Dinewan's eye's sparkled with enthusiasm.

Tristram smiked and shook his head. "But the quinkins aren't real. All you have done is shatter the illusion."

Others in the groups exchanged looks of pity and amusement. Terry made meaningful eye contact with Ivan and Pyran – it did not escape Dinewan's notice.

Tristram suddenly stood up. "I am sorry, but you seem to be suffering the same delusions and fantasies as last time we met. Sadly, I think we're done here."

Dinewan winced, then looked to the ground.

"Alright." Ivan boomed. "Show's over. Let's all get out of here."

"Before we do, I don't suppose you could give us a hand pulling our van out of the water?" Kevin asked, respectfully.

Ivan sighed, then nodded with a grin. "Yeah, I can do that. Let me get my snatch strap outta the Landcruiser."

"Pyran and I will stay with Dinewan for a bit." Tristram announced.

Ivan looked quizzically at Tristram, then to Dinewan, then shrugged.

"Alright then. The rest of you with me." Ivan rejoined.

· · ·

Once they were alone, Tristram raised an incredulous eye-brow at Dinewan.

"Identity politics? Seriously, you pulled that move?"

Dinewan fixed Tristram with a bemused look. "Pardon?"

"You said you were a spokesperson for the aggrieved."

"I am."

"That's not why you are pulling all this shit." Tristram countered. "You don't care about the plight of your fellow indigenous people. You are after the same thing you wanted from me all those years ago. The tear of a monster. If not an opalized fragment of a bunyip fossil, then you want fresh marrow from the bones of a freshly dead bunyip."

Dinewan smiled wickedly. "What an extraordinary accusation."

Tristram smiled back. "Let's make a deal."

Dinewan tilted his head. "A deal?"

"Your puppet show was totally redundant. I believe in the bunyip, because only a few days ago, Pyran, Ivan and I came face to face with one up in the high country."

Tristram watched Dinewan's face closely to gauge the witch doctor's response.

Dinewan considered Tristram, showing neither surprise nor enthusiasm.

"Go on." Dinewan finally responded.

"Do you believe me?"

"I suppose so." Dinewan shrugged. Then he fixed his gaze on Pyran.

"It is true." Pyran confirmed. "Although I don't know why the fuck Tristram is telling you about it."

Dinewan turned back to Tristram. "Well then, what is the deal?"

Tristram nodded. "You back off, stop sending me horrible packages, and putting snakes in my bed and all your other witch doctory busllshit. And I will keep you apprised of our bunyip hunt. If we find the bunyip..."

Dinewan leaned forward, a predatory gleam in his eyes. "You will bring me its head."

"No." Tristram shook his head. "Such a rare animal shall not be killed."

"But if you find it *already* dead...." Dinewan rejoined. "Then you will give me its head?"

"No, I will not give you its head or any other part of it." Tristram barked.

The witch doctor shook his head.

"This will not do, Tristram."

Tristram sighed and reconsidered. "Alright...OK...if it is dead – and only if it is dead – I will bring you its head so that you may examine it."

"*Examine* it?" Dinewan mused.

"Yes. You can examine it. Then you will finally have the treasure you have chased for most of your life."

The witch doctor grunted.

"*Then*," Tristram added derisively, "you will experience the great anticlimax that is reserved for all monomaniacs."

"And if it is not dead?" Dinewan grimaced.

"I am not going to let you – or anyone else – kill it." Tristram warned. "I will protect this animal, Dinewan."

"So, if you find it, and it lives, I get nothing whatever?" Dinewan scowled.

"You will get proof – footage – fur samples – its dung, if you like. You will be in on the zoological find of the millennium. You can share the fame of its discovery with us. It may well be a source of great wealth for you. That is not nothing." Tristram offered.

Dinewan narrowed his eyes at Tristram.

"Remember the moral of the story, Tristram? The story I

told you all of those years ago – about the Great Emu spirit who lost his wings? You remember what he needs to be whole again?"

"He needs a monster to cry for him." Tristram answered.

"Tears of a monster to heal the broken man." Dinewan recited with significance.

Dinewan then exhaled through his nose and lowered his eyelids in thought.

Tristram patiently waited.

Finally, the witch doctor nodded. He then fixed his bright orange eyes on Tristram. Though they were shadowed under the brim of his hat, the fire was suddenly reflected in them, giving them a supernatural glow.

Pyran shuddered.

Dinewan grinned. "Tristram Tobias Jones, I accept your proposal. I give you my word that I will not harass you or anyone else whilst the *hunt*... is on. In return, you will bring me the dead bunyip's head – and *it will be dead*...so that I may take a knife to its eye and extract my tears."

Tristram nodded solemnly.

"Do you know what happens if you fail to keep a promise to a witch doctor?" Dinewan drawled.

"I am a man of my word." Tristram rejoined, holding Dinewan's gaze.

"Well then...we have an accord." Dinewan smiled wolfishly.

He offered a hand, and Tristram shook it.

GREENER PASTURES

"Here, talk to Tris." Holly said, then handed Tristram the landline phone.

Tristram was just walking past and had no idea who had called.

"Hello?" He asked politely.

"Tris! I'm so worried, Tris. God! Holly just said Pyran was in the hospital!"

Tristram moved the phone a little away from his ear.

"Hello Aunty Hester. He's alright. He has a fractured shin, but he's alright."

"How did it happen? Was it that bloody motorbike? I knew he'd have an accident one day, I just knew it! But you can't stop your kids when they are adults. You can tell them how bloody stupid they are being, but you can't stop them. Oh god! He is OK?"

"Yes, yes, he is OK. You can talk to him, he's right here."

"What!? Holly said he was in hospital!"

"Well, he was, yesterday, but we just picked him up this morning."

"Holly didn't say that! She just said he was in hospital and then started talking about her bloody animals!"

"Well, you know my mother..." Tristram sighed.

"And then she hands the phone to you and wanders off! Seriously! She says my son is in hospital, she has a wombat with mange, the magpie needs feeding and an echidna with a sore beak has escaped – and then she says 'here, talk to Tris'!"

"The bottom line, Aunty, is that Pyran is OK and he can assure you of that because he is right here..."

Pyran hobbled across the room on his crutches.

"I'm going to put him on. Hang on..."

Tristram handed the phone to Pyran, who rolled his eyes and smiled.

"Well, this will be a barrel of laughs..." Pyran murmured before he spoke to his mother. "Hi Mum."

Tristram decided to see if there was anything worth having for breakfast in the kitchen cupboards, as Pyran continued to try and reassure Hester with plausible lies about a minor motorbike accident.

On the top shelf of the cupboard, about a foot higher than his head, Tristram saw a handsome ringtailed possum sitting on a box of Nutrigrain. It had a couple of Nutrigrain chain links in its front paw. Its wide burnt-orange eyes considered Tristram as it munched casually.

"Mum..." Tristram called. "Do we have another ring-tailed possum?"

"Yeah, haven't you met Ottie?" Holly called from the lounge room, as she gave a wallaby a bottle of milk.

"Ottie?"

"He was found near the Ottway ranges. He arrived a couple of days ago."

Ottie was now leaning forward, and his back legs were tensing. His eyes were keen, sizing Tristram up.

"Do ringtails jump?" Tristram asked, deciding not to break eye contact with the possum.

On cue, Ottie jumped and landed on Tristram's shoulder.

"OK." Tristram drawled. "That answers that. Are you going to bite me now?"

Ottie gently sniffed Tristram's cheek – then gave him two small licks.

"Huh." Tristram smiled with delight. "What a nice little fellow you are."

"Look, Mum – I dunno, alright?" Pyran whined. "I mean, don't get me wrong, I'd love to be home for Christmas, but plane tickets are expensive and with the Christmas rush comin'...oh yeah? You already got me a ticket? Shit. I mean thanks. Nah – I meant thanks – come on, Mum."

Pyran turned and gave an exaggerated look of surprise.

Tristram absently patted the possum as he listened to Pyran's conversation.

"When is it for...? OK...yeah, I guess I will get a train ticket to Melbourne..." Pyran sighed, running his hand through his hair.

"I'll drive you." Tristram offered.

"Hang on, Mum." Pyran covered the receiver. "Nah, man, I will catch the train, eh?"

"I have to go to Melbourne in the next day or so anyway. I have to get my thesis and data from Burt. I may as well drop you off at the airport." Tristram explained.

"You sure?"

"Yeah – I could use the company on the way up." Tristram grinned.

"Cool. Thanks, man." Pyran grinned back, then resumed talking to Hester. "Hey Mum, Tris is going to Melbourne anyway for his university stuff in the next day or so, so I guess this is gonna work out alright...yeah, I will be there. And yes – for the millionth time – I am ALRIGHT. You're gonna see that in a couple of days anyway, aren't you? OK? Alright...yep..." At the end of the conversation, Pyran blushed. "OK. I love you too, Mum. Bye."

The next day, two hours into the drive back to Melbourne, Pyran suddenly interrupted the casual conversation with a forceful announcement.

"Man, this just doesn't feel good. It doesn't feel right. I'm tellin' ya, as soon as I can afford it, I'm flyin' back down, eh?"

Tristram nodded understanding, as he drove.

"Can't just up and leave right before we find the bunyip." He said.

"Right! That's fuckin' right!"

"Is it?" Tristran raised an eyebrow.

Pyran sighed back, with comical disdain. "Isn't it? Arsehole?"

"What makes you think that we are going to find the bunyip anytime soon? If indeed at all?" Tristram asked, seriously.

Pyran scoffed. "Because we *saw it*. We know it is *real* – we know that our efforts are not a waste of time. We know where to start looking. We know there is only so much ground to cover before we find its trail, its lair – the thing itself. Ivan is an obsessed, smart, resourceful man who will find that thing in fuckin'...days – weeks at most."

"He already looked for it for months and months and never found hide nor hair of it." Tristram answered.

Pyran was agape. "What!? *When?*"

"Years ago. After our camping trip when we were in high school, when you were last down here. Remember that little trip, when we met up with Fred?"

Pyran exhaled at the revelation. "Did Ivan go back up and keep looking by himself?"

"Yes, he did." Tristram answered, with a spark of anger in his voice.

"And he never told you about it until when?"

"The other night. After our stoush with the Quinkin puppeteers."

"That mother-fucker." Pyran groaned.

"It makes sense, I suppose." Tristram sighed. "I don't really blame the guy. He was certain that the creature existed, and it would have been a lot harder to track it down with you, me and Jase along. So yeah, he went and had another look. And another and another – every spare weekend, every school holiday."

"Cunt." Pyran pouted.

Tristram smiled at his cousin. "Yeah, alright. Still, he says that he would have let me know if he had found it. I believe him."

"Well...fuck. Still – this time its different." Pyran answered. "This time we have a fresh sighting, newer technology and time to go looking. Ivan or you or both of you or bloody Lachie – he's a hunter – point is, it is going to happen this time. For sure."

Tristram sighed. "Maybe. I don't know."

"Surely you reckon it is worth throwing everything we can at finding the bunyip?"

Tristram nodded reluctantly.

"Come on! Tomorrow, you will be talking with that lazy arse-hole of a professor and it won't be about your thesis – it will be about the bunyip." Pyran insisted.

"Actually, it better be about my thesis. I need to get it done finally, so that I can get a real job in zoology and not be employed anymore in these bullshit call centre roles." Tristram sighed.

Pyran suddenly seemed quiet.

Tristram noticed.

"What did I say?"

Pyran considered Tristram. "You don't get how lucky you are, do you?"

"Meaning?"

"You just...you think that a call centre job is just shit. You probably thought painting bridge rails with Lachie was shit. That the work is...beneath you."

Tristram frowned. "You think I am judging Lachie or call centre staff or something? Because I don't. They are great people – most of them – I actually respect them, I don't judge them."

"Nah, man. You kinda do, eh? I heard you say to Ivan that you consider yourself a failure – yet as a so-called failure, you are doing pretty well. I mean, I would love a call centre job. Talking to people, helping them out and getting thirty-eight or forty grand a year. That would make so many things possible for me. The job you quit that you thought was the lowest point in your career, is way better than the best job that I could ever get."

"Well...why couldn't you get a call centre job? You are very personable; I am sure you could get one." Tristram reassured.

Pyran sighed. "I made some bad choices, man. It is not easy to recover from them, you know? The Goldcoast is not that big a place – if you have a reputation for hanging around with aborigines, you are pretty much written off."

"How can that be true?"

"Are you kidding me?"

"No, how can that be true? Get a hair-cut, get some nice interview clothes and apply for whatever job you can get. No one is going to ask you if you hang out with indigenous people or any other people – I mean what the hell? Their Human Resources department would never allow it."

"It's not that easy."

"Who said it was easy? Like it or not, man, there is a market. And yes, it does discriminate, but it's not personal. The more skills you have, the better your value to the market. That's it."

"And if you don't have any skills?" Pyran winced.

"What are you talking about? You have skills."

"Not marketable ones, man." Pyran insisted.

"You start at the bottom then. You accept the low-skilled job, you do that job well. By doing that job well you will get recognised as someone who is reliable enough to train further – so you will get more skills, and then you will have more value to the market and then you will get more money. Success is a ladder – it doesn't much matter which rung you start on, as long as you get on the bloody ladder and climb as best you can."

"Sure thing, man." Pyran scoffed. "It is easier for you – you have a university degree. I didn't even finish year twelve."

Tristram rolled his eyes. "Am I blinded by my priveledge?"

"Kind of, yes."

"For fuck's sake..."

"You don't see your advantages. You can start way higher on the ladder than me or my friends."

"Do you think I got the job at Emu Post because I had a zoology degree?" Tristram countered.

"Doesn't matter what your degree is, what matters is that you have one. They see that bit of paper as a symbol of someone worth employing. I have no chance whatsoever of getting a symbol like that for myself."

"Pyran, my degree was no help to me in learning to service Emu Post customers. It did nothing for my customer service skills. It did not inform my initiative in helping others or looking at the systems in the workplace to see if I could improve them. I was asked to step up as team leader only because I knuckled down on the entry-level role."

"Asked to step up to team leader? *Asked*? And yet you go on as if you are a failure. If that is what failure looks like, I'll take it." Pyran sneered.

"You know what? I do see myself as failing in my career, because the career I am trying for is that of a zoologist. However, there is no need for that failure to hold me back in a job that I have to do in the meantime. I have done the best I can in the job I don't like. Fuck it, I have done the best I can in this Masters that I don't like. Have you done the best you can with your lot, Pyran?" Tristram challenged.

"Fuck off."

"Is that the best you can do?"

"You don't understand."

"What don't I understand? That's an easy dismissal for you to make, man." Tristram returned.

"OK. Alright, let's see if I can get you to understand something. Let's say you go into a supermarket. Let's say you want to buy milk, and you have enough money for milk. What happens?" Pyran asked.

Tristram frowned, confused. "What is supposed to happen?"

"Just tell me what happens. You go in..." Pyran prompted.

"OK. I go in, I walk to the dairy section, I grab the milk, I go to the registers, I pay, I get out of there." Tristram answered.

"Good. Nothing to it, yeah?"

"What's your point?"

"Now imagine that a black fella wants to buy milk. Will his experience be the same?"

"What do you mean? That he can't buy the milk or something?"

"No, he can buy the fucking milk. But his experience *is not the same*. Imagine what happens as soon as he walks in the door. How do the other white customers react to him?"

"I have never heard any racist taunting if that is what you mean, but I suppose it does happen." Tristram offered.

"It happens plenty, man, but in most cases, what happens is that the other customers notice the black fella and *change their behaviour*. They may not say anything, they may not be rude, they may even grin politely as they move away. But they react in a different way to the black fella than they do to any other stranger. He can see it in their faces, in their looks. He is judged. And then what happens as he grabs the milk? Do the staff pay a little extra attention? You know, to see if he is going to try and hide something in his pockets? And the person at the register?"

"I can see what you are saying." Tristram nodded seriously as he imagined the scenario.

"That's just buying milk." Pyran continued. "Imagine a whole day, a whole week, a whole *life* of this type reaction from most of the people around you. How will you feel, going to a job interview? Confident?"

Tristram nodded again. "OK. That is a genuine disadvantage to indigenous people. So...what's *your* excuse?"

Pyran sighed heavily, then gave a conceding shrug. "I don't have an excuse. You're right, man. You're right."

The cousins were silent for a few moments.

"I'm not right." Tristram finally said quietly. "You're right, Pyran. It is not a level playing field at all. If there is a prejudice against you that impacts your self-worth, you will not have the morale to do the best you can. And if you are not doing your best, you will not get good results. These not so good results compound over time, so that as your life goes along and your youth fades, and your potential is wasted, you will spiral into a pit that you can never get of."

"Yep. That's about it, eh? And the opposite is true – if you start in a good position, you get good results which encourage you to try harder and get better results and up the ladder you go, wondering why everyone around you just doesn't climb like you do." Pyran answered.

"What is the solution?" Tristram asked.

Pyran scoffed. "If there was one, we wouldn't have anything to talk about."

"There are plenty of cases of people with tough backgrounds reaching astounding success."

"Luck." Pyran waved dismissively.

"Hard work." Tristram countered.

Pyran looked at Tristram. "Luck AND hard work."

Tristram smiled. "OK."

"We can't do anything about our luck – but yes...alright, yes...we can do something about how hard we work. You give me the shits, cousin. You give me the fucking shits." Pyran grinned ruefully.

Tristram laughed.

"We are both lucky, man." Pyran continued. "We saw a bunyip. And that beast is going to change everything for us, man. You don't have to worry about your masters – you will have first dibs on the zoological study of the fucking millennium. I know you work hard, man, but talk about some unbelievable luck."

"Unbelievable being part of the problem." Tristram frowned, thoughtfully.

"Well, more hard work it is then. Find this bunyip. Secure our future. I'm counting on you, man." Pyran joked.

Tristram shook his head, smiling. "I'll give it a red-hot go."

THE MASTERS

"Hɪ Dᴀᴅ..."

"Tris? What's wrong?"

"Um...Dad...I don't know what to do..."

"What's going on? What's happened?"

Tristram didn't want to be too early at Burt's house, so he went for a very short walk to a small reserve at the end of a quiet street. There he found a swing and indulged in twenty minutes of reflection. He swung high and drank in the blue sky, relishing each rush up to it, and each fall away.

When he finally did approach Burt's house, he was surprised to see Burt and Nathan preparing to leave.

"Tristram!" Burt waved from their red sedan. Then he wandered over.

"Did you forget about our appointment?" Tristram asked.

"Yes, I fucking did." Burt answered sheepishly.

"But I reminded you *yesterday*."

"I know. I am without excuse. I totally forgot. Nathan and I were just about to pop down the street for some shopping."

Tristram nodded to Nathan, who sighed petulantly from the front seat of their car. He was a slender Greek man with large, sleepy brown eyes.

"Hello, Tristram." Nathan called, his voice a mix of pity and annoyance.

"Hi. I'm sorry to inconvenience you." Tristram said, attempting a polite smile.

"It's fine." Nathan yawned. "I will wait in the car, Burt."

"We won't be long." Tristram assured him. "I am just here to pick up whatever Burt has done on my thesis and my data."

"OK." Nathan grinned, yet it seemed a wince.

Burt ushered Tristram into his Edwardian home. Tristram noted the high dark ceilings, and the numerous bookshelves.

"That book you lended to me is not read yet." Burt began. "I felt guilty, I thought I really shouldn't read it whilst I have not made any progress on your thesis."

"It's all good. As I said, I am going to get help from Reginald and maybe Harold." Tristram answered.

He didn't want to be angry with Burt, but he didn't want to be friendly either.

"Well, I don't think they will be able to help you." Burt answered bluntly.

Tristram turned to look his supervisor in the eye.

"Well, that may be so. But I have to try and see, don't I?"

"I deserve that rebuke." Burt smiled. "Let me get my so-called notes on your thesis."

After much swearing, muttering and moving of card-book boxes and piles of books, Burt found what he was looking for and handed it to Tristram.

"Jesus Christ, that was harder than it should have been." Burt chuckled ruefully. "No wonder I have been dragging my arse, eh?"

Tristram did not respond to the professor's attempt at self-deprecating humour.

Burt noticed, and a nasty twinkle appeared in his eyes.

"Is that everything, Sir?" Burt asked, holding Tristram's gaze.

Tristram looked back with defiance. "I also need the raw data."

"Well, I have some bad news for you there. It's gone." Burt returned coldly.

Tristram's eyes narrowed. "What do you mean it's gone?"

Burt shrugged and sighed. "I honestly thought I had the disks somewhere, but I don't."

"It's all on your computer. Where's your computer?"

"*My* computer – my personal one – is behind you. My *work* computer, on the other hand, was disposed of without my permission by those useless cunts from the university IT department. I asked to keep it, but they must have assumed it was old and for security reasons destroyed it."

Tristram's stomach sank as the implications of what he was hearing hit him.

"That means...that means I can't submit. I won't be able to finish."

Sympathy and guilt emanated from Burt. "You haven't saved it anywhere else?"

"No. You *know* that I haven't. You have a Mac; the software was on your lab computer – I have a Windows PC. We transferred the analysed data and graphs to PC format, but all the raw data – the data I need to finish my thesis...was all on Mac disks."

Tristram felt intense pressure building behind his eyes, but he was damned if he was going to break down and cry in front of Burt.

"Well, this is deeply – and I mean *deeply* – shit-house." Burt anwered quietly. "But it is probably for the best."

Tristram held the corrected copy of his thesis to his chest and said nothing.

Burt continued. "Look, let's get real here. I just can't keep pretending that this Masters of yours has a chance. The material is just not there."

"But you said...you said I had about two weeks to go..." Tristram murmured in surreal disbelief.

"I know I said I could pull it together, but I have been deluding myself. And I have been leading you on. I guess when all is said and done, I am extremely guilty of wasting your time."

"So...what? This is it. This is all you have to say?" Tristram asked, looking at the floor. He could not bring himself to look at Burt.

"Look, I know this seems big. But really, what is actually going to change for you? You have been in the same postion for how long now?"

"Six years. Six years, Burt, since you told me I had two weeks to go."

"Shit. That's longer than I thought, but my point remains. Look at you, you have a job. One that suits your skills."

"I told you that I quit the call centre job."

"Well, in all honesty, you should try and get it back."

"I don't want to be a fucking call centre worker. I want to be a zoologist." Tristram growled.

"Well, be as pissed off as you like, but face the reality. You are not going to make it in science."

Tristram shook his head in disbelief. He wiped his eyes.

"I did the work. I did the experiments. You said…"

"Tristram, you were never really focused on this project. You day-dreamed a lot – I saw you reading a lot of classic novels when you should have been reading papers. A lot of the time I watched you doing a whole lot of nothing. I should really have kicked your arse a bit more, but I was distracted by my own bullshit problems – as you know. I have told you all about them."

An awkward silence followed. It was broken by an impatient toot of a car horn.

"Ignore him." Burt smiled kindly. "This is important."

"This is over." Tristram suddenly decided.

Tristram turned and marched down the wooden hallway to the front door. Burt hurried to keep pace with him.

"I will check all the boxes for those disks." He offered.

"What's the point?" Tristram sighed.

"Well, if I find them, Ryan might be able to read them and convert what's on them into a format you can use. I won't hold you back if I find the data. You can still try to work on this Masters with Reginald and Harold."

"If you find the disks." Tristram shook his head. "Which we both know you never will."

"Tristram, wait." Burt implored as Tristram left the house.

Tristram turned to face Burt.

Burt looked sad and guilty. "I am not trying to be an arsehole to you. I am trying to be straight with you. You are a talented, intelligent person and you should not have had to deal with this shit. I am happy to explain your situation to…well, whoever it needs explaining to."

Tristram held Burt's gaze as coldly as he could.

"Later, Burt." He said and walked away.

. . .

"It's over, Dad." Tristram cried on the phone when he got back to his place in Melbourne. "My career as a zoologist is over."

Nothing Russell said could help Tristram feel better.

NEW YEAR'S EVE

IT WAS a warm New Year's Eve.

"Why is Wilbur so covered in sarcoptic mange?" Tristram frowned, as he fed the baby wombat in the al fresco area.

Ugly patches of dry, wrinkled skin were red and flaky about the wombat's back legs, front legs and the bottom of his face.

"We are not sure." Russell answered.

"Aren't you treating it?" Tristram asked angrily.

"Yes, we are treating it. Unforunately, the medication is not easily absorbed into wombat skin. The mites are tough." Russell explained, patiently.

"Are we forgetting to treat some days? Wilbur is looking horrible."

"Your mother and I have been treating him exactly as the vets have instructed."

"The pouch. Mum had another wombat a few weeks ago that had mange. Tilly – she has put Wilbur in Tilly's old pouch."

"Your mother washed the pouch."

"Clearly, she didn't use disinfectant."

Russell sighed. "Tris...listen...you know how careful your mother is – she knows what she is doing. She always washes the pouches in antiseptic. You know that we sterilize all our tubs and cages – we use Vetinary grade antiseptic – F1o."

"She must have forgotten. I am not meaning to criticise her, Dad – but she has had a lot of animals recently, and she is well – you know – Mum."

"Your mother may indeed still be recovering from her nervous breakdown, but you know better than that, son. She takes better care of all these animals than anything else in her life."

"The fact remains that this wombat, under our care, is covered in mange. He is covered in bare patches and cuts and scabs..."

"We are well aware of it. Your mother has tried moisturiser to make him feel a bit better, but the mites get under his skin and cause itching. And you know wombats, they just keep scratching, even after they are bleeding."

"I don't get it. I just don't get how this happened. He had hardly any mange at all when we got him, now he is covered in it! The poor bugger. The poor little bugger."

"Tris, *we are treating him.* The treatment works, but it takes a few weeks. As you can see, he is still relatively healthy. He is still feeding. He will be alright."

Tristram sighed in frustration.

Wilbur finished his bottle of milk, and then gazed sleepily up at Tristram. The satisfied gurgling noises made Russell chuckle fondly.

"Can you nurse him a while before he goes back in the pouch?" Tristram asked. "I have to get changed."

"It is still a couple of hours to midnight, Tris. You have plenty of time. Why don't you relax?"

Tristram sighed. "I guess you are right. I am going to have a shower now, anyway, and try and cool off."

That morning, Tristram had met Eve near Picnic Point by the Mitchell River.

Eve had parked her car in the shade of an old peppercorn tree and was sitting beside it.

It was bright and hot, and bees buzzed in the long grass by Eve's hatch-back. Eve was in a black tank top and wore large, dark sunglasses.

Heavy, fast rock from the band Nine Inch Nails blared from her car speakers.

"So..." Tristram began amiably. "Will I see you at Lakes Entrance tonight?"

"Probably." Eve shrugged.

"It was your idea." Tristram reminded her.

"No, it was your idea." Eve returned. "I just went along with it."

"You're right. I suggested it. But it was you who said we should dress up. I am supposed to bring a single red rose."

"And to be dressed all in black." Eve added.

"Yes. I will be. But if this is a bad idea...?" Tristram let the question hang, as he tried to gauge Eve's mood.

Eve sighed. "It's a good idea. I will probably be there."

"Probably?" Tristram prompted.

"Yeah, probably. I probably will be there." Eve answered.

"Could you please take your glasses off so that I can see your eyes? It may help me to know what's really going on here." Tristram asked, with a tentative smile.

Eve took her glasses off, grinned at him, and then looked at the ground.

"Thank you. That clears it up." Tristram sighed with comic dismay.

"I am glad." Eve rejoined, deadpan.

"Look..." Tristram began, as kindly as he could. "If you are not sure about this, then we shouldn't do it. It's OK if you don't want to."

"I think we should go." Eve answered.

"So, you *will* be there?"

Eve nodded. "Yes."

"OK then. It is settled. I will meet you there."

"Mm-hm."

"Eve...are you alright?" Tristram asked.

"I'm tired, that's all. And I have to go soon. Mum needs some help with some stuff." Eve answered.

"Fair enough. Well, alright, I will get out of your hair and see you later." Tristram smiled.

"See ya." Eve grinned back.

Tristram had then left.

At twenty minutes to midnight, Tristram stood near the foot-bridge at Lakes Entrance that led to the Ninety Mile Beach. As agreed with Eve, he was dressed all in black – a black satin, long-sleeved dress-shirt, black dress slacks and black dress shoes. He also carried the promised single, long-stem red rose.

The small sea-side town was packed with revellers – most of them in their late teens and early twenties. There were glow-sticks, sparklers and cleavage everywhere Tristram looked.

The police were in attendance in large numbers. They patrolled on foot, slowly in cars and there were two on horse-back. Their sober and yet good-natured watch contrasted with the drunken cheer of the youths that swaggered around them.

Music from the eighties blared from a carnival stand, and

temporary merry-go-rounds and jumping castles were fully and joyfully occupied.

Above the din of the crowd, Tristram occasionally noted the cry of swans and seagulls, and he wondered what the local birdlife made of the human celebration of New Year's Eve. He looked away from the human-made lights of the town and towards the bright stars south, above the beach that he could hear but not see.

He sighed fondly and longingly up at the Southern Cross.

Ngooran...free to roam the sky without fear, for Narran the moon is not hunting you tonight.

On a hot night like this, Tristram would normally be out somewhere wading in the Gippsland Lakes, hunting for prawns, flounder and flathead with Lachlan.

Tristram had at first attempted to dispel some of his anxiety and kill time with a walk up and down the long Main Street of Lakes Entrance. Before long however, he realised that it was a bad idea. He had showered only forty minutes ago, but he was starting to sweat already.

Dressed all in black in mid-summer? We did not think this through. Where is she?

Everywhere Tristram looked in the crowds he would see a woman who might be Eve only to be disappointed. Voices argued in his mind.

She'll be here. She said she would be here.

Actually...

She said she would probably be here. Probably. Why did she say "probably?"

Because she seems to like hurting you.

That's ridiculous.

Is it?

What did she start doing when you told her sincerely, that it hurts you when she ignores your text messages? She ignored them even more.

It was not deliberate. You are melodramatic.

Am I? Actually – yes – I can be.

She is not going to have you stand around all dressed up, with a single rose, and not show up. She would message you.

Tristram checked his phone again. No messages.

Perhaps she messaged, and it has been delayed? It is New Year's Eve.

Test that theory.

Tristram sighed, then sent a message to Lachlan.

"Happy New Year, big fella!"

Not a minute later he got Lachlan's reply: "You too, mate!"

Tristram checked the time. It was now two minutes to midnight.

Tristram stood at the agreed meeting place by the foot-bridge, and frantically scanned the crowd.

Maybe she was here just a few minutes ago and didn't see me and so assumed that I had stood her up?

No. Eve would have to know that you could never do that to her.

Maybe she had an accident? Maybe she is stuck in traffic?

Suddenly, with raucous enthusiasm, the crowd began to count down the last ten seconds of the year.

Eve was nowhere to be seen.

The fireworks began to thunderous cheers and applause.

Each explosion lighted the crowd in multicoloured flashes.

Eve was painfully absent.

How long should I wait? What should I do?

Pressure built behind Tristram's eyes. The most awful feeling sank into his chest.

People around him were hugging and cheering.

So much partying.

Tristram felt wretchedly out of place.

This is a nightmare. This is the worst thing that could have happened. She has stood me up.

No. There has to be another explanation. Eve would not be this cruel. She would not humiliate me like this.

Tristram tried a text to Eve. It would not send.

It is New Year's Eve – everybody in the country is texting right now.

Tristram tried to ring but could get no signal.

What can I do? What can I do?

Tristram jogged through the throngs of people, looking everywhere for Eve.

Finally, he decided to just leave.

As he reached the top of the hill near the Kalimna Hotel, he decided to stop at the lookout. It had views of the Gippsland lakes and the ocean beyond.

He still wasn't sure that Eve was not in Lakes Entrance. He would need to wait, just in case she called, wondering where he was.

It could all still be a misunderdstanding.

Forty anxiety-ridden minutes later Tristram finally got a signal, rang Eve and she answered.

"Hello?" Eve said. There was a party going on in the background.

She must be here. Tristram sighed with relief.

"Eve. I'm at the look-out – I am so sorry, I couldn't find you. Where are you?"

"I'm at Chris's place." Eve answered, deadpan.

She is at Chris's place...?

"...Did you say you are at Chris's place?"

Tristram was flabberghasted. His heart beat wildly and he became short of breath.

"Yes."

"You are at Chris's place. You are back with your ex-husband?"

"No. I am not back with him." Eve answered firmly.

"You are not here. You are not here...why are you not here?"

"I didn't want it to turn out this way. I was going to come. But I couldn't find the right moment to leave this party."

Tristram had no words. All he could do was stand agape.

"Are you there?" Eve finally asked, quietly.

"You couldn't find the right moment to leave Chris's party...?" Tristram repeated back to Eve, his anger growing.

"Can I talk to you?" Eve answered, as if to try and check his anger.

"About what? What possible justification can you offer for this blatant kick in the guts?" Tristram demanded.

"There's something you don't know." Eve began.

"Yeah? And you couldn't send me a message? Ring me to let know that you weren't coming? Instead you let me come here, dressed in black with a single red rose to just stand around as the countdown begins and wonder...but you say...there's something I don't know. No! NO! This is not good enough! THIS IS JUST NOT GOOD ENOUGH!" Tristram roared.

He then calmed himself, aware of people coming up the road.

"I'm sorry." Eve answered, in shamed tones. "The time just kind of went by...and then the moment passed, when I knew I would not get there in time. I don't know why I let the moment pass, but I did."

Tristram shook his head.

"I know all I need to know." He said levelly.

"Will you let me explain?" Eve was trying to sound rational and cool.

"No. What is there to explain?"

"I'm sorry." Eve murmured.

Tristram hung up.

He stood at the look-out and helplessly stared across the lakes to the ocean.

"Happy New year, mate!" A young man shouted.

Tristram smiled politely.

The cheer was repeated by a group of young men and women staggering by.

"Happy New Year!"

Tristram waved to them and smiled. "You too!"

I have to get the fuck out of here.

Tristram drove in a state of miserable disbelief.

He decided to drive through the bush, Colquhoun State Forest, just outside Lakes Entrance, rather than the Princes Highway back to Bairnsdale.

The pressure pounded behind his eyes, his chest was being squeezed. His hands began to shake.

The road was an unsealed, ungraded bush track. It was very bumpy, he was driving too fast, taking corners wide and slipping on the sandy patches.

I'm fucking losing it. Pull over.

Tristram stopped. He turned the engine off.

The sudden quiet slammed into him. He felt utterly alone.

A sob escaped – and then he cried.

After a few moments he realised with surreal wonder that his crying had caused the windshield to fog up.

He calmed himself.

What do I do? What can I do?

He decided to drive home.

When he reached the turn-off to his parent's place, he suddenly decided to keep going.

Tristram drove north, until he was bumping along the heavily corrugated bush track to Eve's hexagonal cottage.

He did not stay long. With quick, careful steps, he entered the cottage, climbed the stairs to loft, and lay the rose on Eve's pillow.

Then Tristram left.

SANDCASTLES

"Am I allowed to talk to you yet?"

Eve had texted Tristram two days after New Year's Eve.

Tristram shook his head at the text bitterly. He was sitting in the al fresco area of his parent's place, reading in order to distract himself from thoughts about any aspect of his current life. It wasn't working.

He attempted a reply, but in the end could not think of what to say, so placed his phone on the table and went to make himself a coffee. When he came back, there were further messages.

"I am so sorry. I haven't been able to think straight for months. I have been trying to work out why I did not meet you at Lakes. A part of me wishes to god that I had gone, another part is glad I didn't. Not glad. Glad is the wrong word. I hate hurting you. I am sorry I have been such a cunt to you. Maybe it's my brain's way of saying that I don't want to be with you. But then I have missed you so much in the last two days. I can't stop thinking about you or the rose you left on my pillow. I am going to keep it. I am going to dry it and keep it. Are you there?"

Tristram sighed and fought back tears.

I just don't want to do this anymore. But I love you. I don't know what else to say.

"I'm here." Tristram texted back.

"How are you?" Came Eve's text.

"Can we talk?" Tristram texted back.

The beep on his phone was the answer – another text from Eve.

"I don't think I can handle a conversation on the phone or in person. Do you mind so much if we just text?"

Tristram sighed.

"As you wish." Tristram typed back. "How am I? I am tired. I am bitter. I am sad. And I wish that I didn't still love you. But I do."

"I am sorry."

"Instead of being sorry can't you just make a decision about us? A decision that lasts?"

"I wish I could."

Tristram typed "fuck off" – then deleted it. He had no idea what to say, but his anger had begun to simmer.

"I am going to visit my brother in America in two days." Eve texted.

Tristram raised his eyebrows.

"For how long will you be gone?"

"Just ten days. I wanted to try and improve things between us before I went."

"Are we broken up or what?" Tristram texted.

"I don't think we should be together for now. I need time to think. I need to be away from you, from Chris, from everybody else and just be me."

Tristram nodded to himself and typed back. "I understand."

"You could probably do with a break as well?" Eve texted. "It can't be good for you in the sand-box."

Tristram grinned sadly at the reference to their earlier conversation.

"Our relationship in the cat's litter box? It has taken everything out of me recently." He texted back.

"There isn't much you can do with a situation like ours, eh?" Eve returned.

"If our relationship really is stuck in the sand-box for now, then I will still sit in it." Tristram returned.

"And do what?"

Tristram wiped his eyes.

Good question. What the hell can you do?

A thought occurred that made him chuckle inwardly. He shared it with Eve.

"I will make sandcastles."

"You always have an answer." Eve replied. She included a smile emoji.

"Have a great time in America. I will not write to you or text you until you contact me. Fair?"

"Thank you. I think it is for the best." Eve answered.

"It is a promise. I will miss you."

"I know I will miss you. Goodbye for now. Thanks for texting with me. I feel a little bit less shit now."

I wish I could say the same. Tristram thought.

"Goodbye for now, Eve."

BUSHFIRES

The cattle-truck-driver never noticed the witch doctor.

His blue-heeler however, had been aware as soon as the old aborigine had sauntered up to the driver's side window. She bared her teeth and gave a low growl.

Orange eyes held deep brown ones.

The dog licked her lips submissively.

Both remained silent thereafter.

Dinewan then climbed up the back tyre and through the wooden slats of the truck with surprising agility. He then lay flat on the floor of the single trailer.

A small truck. He mused. *I have seen them with three or more trailers – all with double decks and they carried different cattle than this one.*

He sniffed the air and considered the swirling scents of fresh sawdust, old wood, diesel fumes, and pungent cow dung. Closing his eyes, the witch doctor focused on the scents and tuned out all but the smell of the Hereford cattle that were contained in the trailer earlier that morning. The smell of their skin and their breath lingered faintly around the trailer. Dinewan smiled.

Such big powerful animals, yet so fearful that their advantages don't matter.

Dinewan looked through the slats at the Bairnsdale sale yards.

Kangaroos will never be sold in sale yards.

Suddenly Dinewan was aware of heavy footsteps.

The driver. Hurried steps – decisive. His business is concluded here, and now we go north up into the hills.

The diesel engine coughed into life and the vehicle vibrated in response. The driver allowed the engine to warm up for a couple of minutes and then they were away.

Dinewan shivered with excitement. He had been looking forward to this.

The bright hot morning could not reach him in the back of the truck, but he glimpsed it through the gaps in the wood panelling. He longed to be out in it, but they would not be out of town for a few minutes yet.

Omeo.

Dinewan mused on the name of the town that they were heading towards.

An aboriginal word. It means high hills and mountains. A kurnai word? Or the long forgotten Jaimathang tribe? Never really knew any of them...

Dinewan sat up once they were into the winding road through bush covered hills, that eventually followed the stoney Tambo river in the steep valley. He relished the speed and the fresh, hot air.

Dinewan climbed through the panels and up onto the wood-slat roof of the truck.

The wind nearly stole his hat, so he crumpled it up and

shoved it into his trouser pocket. His coat flapped wildly about him and the truck rocked below him. When the truck took a sharp bend in the road, Dinewan gasped as he felt certain that he would be hurled into the steep ravine. He imagined his body smashing against a thick gum tree, before tumbling through tree ferns and sharp scrub into the stoney river below.

Yet he could hold on...

With a thrill that he had not experienced since he was a little boy, Dinewan raised himself onto his hands and knees... and then he stood up.

A wild euphoria took the witch doctor. He raised his arms up and smiled so wide that his lips cracked and bled.

It is time! It is time!

Dinewan could feel every baked inch of the country he was flying through. Every dried blade of grass, every parched leaf, every sheath of bark on miles and miles of eucalyptus forest. The searing blanket of summer sun, the constant oven-hot winds from the north. The dams and swamps and creeks that have dried out. Cracked mud and dust where once frogs sang and birds swam, and animals drank. The soaring blue days were now coming to a head...

The fuel is ready!

Dinewan bent his will upon the sky. Channeling the fevor that years of waiting had seared into him, he chanted his magic words.

He continued his chanting gleefully and with fierce expectation.

Thick white clouds with glowing edges rolled into each other above Omeo as the truck finally reached the out-skirts of the town. An intensely charged darkness loomed over the valleys and steep hills. The bright blue day was now all consumed by a rumbling shadow.

Jolts of joy ran through the witch doctor with each white flash of lightning.

Very little rain fell.

The fires started in several places.

THE PARTS WE PLAY

THE MONTH of January crawled by, dry and burning as it did so.

Hot nights were good for prawning, but Tristram's longing and restlessness robbed the activity of its joy. He went only once, spent barely an hour out in the water and then firmly decided that he was done for the summer.

Everything was measured now to the nearest dollar. Instead of following every whim to drive into the bush, or go fishing by the river, Tristram mentally calculated the cost of the petrol. It was always too much.

He had no job yet, and money was running out. His time however, seemed interminable.

Ivan was on constant adventure – reporting back every three days or so on his progress with the bunyip hunt. Ivan had flown drones with cameras up and down gullies and gorges. He had set up camera traps. He went on very long treks, following streams and creeks, systematically exploring according to the maps from the Forestry Department. He found no footprints, no scats and no hair samples.

Tristram began to tire of Ivan's text messages, often sent around two or three in the morning.

"Nothing yet." Was all he ever said.

Tristram wanted to go with Ivan but did not ask. He could not pay his way.

Ivan seemed to want to be by himself anyway. Tristram sympathised with Ivan's antisocial instinct.

Lachlan was Tristram's only Bairnsdale friend left, and he had suddenly become very busy fighting fires that had started in the high country. Those fires were growing in intensity and had begun to spread relentlessly towards the coast.

Every day, every hour, Tristram longed to contact Eve. However, he had made good progress in keeping his promise to not do so. He did write texts and emails but then deleted them without sending them. He had a habit of writing that was hard to break.

Bright blue days began to give way to smoke-stained skies.

Finally, on Australia Day, January 26th, Russell was fed up with his eldest son's morose inactivity and decided to intervene.

"What are you waiting for?" He asked Tristram, as he sat sadly at the table of the al fresco area.

"Huh?" Tristram frowned.

"You are just waiting. You are sitting around as if you are waiting for something to happen. What are you *waiting* for?" Russell asked with a kindly impatience.

"Um...I dunno." Tristram shrugged.

"Is it a text from Eve?"

"No. I won't be getting one of those anytime soon."

"A message from Burt Whiteside?"

"That's a dead end. So, no."

"A call from work?"

"No – I have no job – you know I have no job – what are you getting at, Dad?"

Russell sighed. "I know that you are going through a lot. But you seem to be just waiting, as if you expect something to change shortly if only you wait."

Tristram glared at his father.

"What are *you* waiting for, Dad? You are about as busy as I am."

"I am waiting for the shit to hit the fan, actually. There are fires in the high country that are out of control and a lot of people are very worried." Russell answered pointedly.

"What are you going to do about it?"

"Have you noticed all of the mowing that I have been doing recently? The gutters that have been cleaned out? The fence-posts cleared of long grass and that there are no piles of flammable leaves, sticks, clippings and prunnings and what-not laying about and endangering our property?" Russell countered.

Tristram blushed. "If you wanted my help you could have just asked."

"Tris, I'm not criticising you." Russell assured.

"Then what are you doing?"

"I'm just making an observation. You are waiting. I want to know what you are waiting for."

Tristram sighed and looked at the ground. "I'm waiting for some sort of clue, Dad. Just some...clue...as to what to do next in my life. That's all. And I haven't got it yet. I don't know what happens now – with Eve, with my zoology career, with my empty bank account and the bills I have piling up. I don't know what to do."

Tristram wiped away a tear.

"Things will get better, mate. They will."

Tristram grabbed his coffee cup and stood up. "I'm having another coffee, you want one?"

"No thanks, mate." Russell smiled. "We love you, you know?"

Tristram blinked.

"I'm sorry, Dad." He murmured.

"Sorry? For what?"

Tristram shook his head. "I know I am bringing everybody down...and I just can't seem to help it."

Russell moved to Tristram and hugged him.

When the hug finished, they turned to see Terry standing at the back door.

"G'day." He said with an uncertain smile. "Am I here at a bad time?"

"No, Terry, it's good to see you." Tristram smiled, wiping his eyes. "To what do we owe the pleasure?"

"I was just wonderin' if you wanna go fishin'?" Terry asked.

Russell clapped Tristram on the shoulder and answered for him.

"Yes, yes he does."

They decided to fish near a place called "the cut" on the eastern side of the Mitchell River. It was a short drive down-stream from where Lachlan, Pyran, Ivan and Tristram had fished after Fred's funeral and been confronted by Dinewan's dogs. Here the river ran deep roughly west to east in the valley, with the crumbling, red limestone bluff marking the southern bank. The Eagle Point look-out was at the top, about eighteen metres above the water. It had views to the east of the Gippsland Lakes and the long Silt Jetties, and the valley and the mountains to the north – Mount Taylor the largest of these. The Silt Jetties, a natural structure formed over thousands of years, formed a narrow bridge of land covered in scrub on each side of the river for eight kilometres into Lake King. "The cut" was a break in the northern silt jetty that allowed the river to flow into Jones Bay – a shallow lake that was part of the whole lake system.

Terry and Tristram sat under gum trees a few metres away from "the cut" and fished facing the sandy orange bluff on the other side of the river.

"Happy Australia Day, mate." Tristram said, as they cast their lines out.

Terry grunted and Tristram realised he had probably made a faux pas.

"Not exactly a day of celebration for indigenous people, eh?" Tristram added in a conciliatory tone.

"Invasion Day?" Terry agreed but smiled at Tristram. "Yeah, plenty of blacks don't take too kindly to Australia Day being on 26th of January – the anniversary of the first fleet. Mind you, some take it in their stride and just accept that we are celebrating what is good about Australia. Myself? I don't give a fuck – but I'll take the day off."

Tristram nodded thoughtfully. "I think we could change the date, eh? To show that we have grown up as a country and accepted that we have a black history."

"What difference would it make?" Terry shrugged.

"It would make a symbolic difference – and we as human beings are moved in important and significant ways by symbols." Tristram offered.

"I suppose." Terry answered. "I use plenty of symbols in me own art. But I dunno if people think about these things as much as you and me, eh? I reckon if you try and change the date you'll piss off a whole bunch of other people who think you are messing with their traditions. It's kind of ironic."

"Well, maybe keep the date but make an important change to it." Tristram replied, thinking aloud. "Like...well, I am thinking about ANZAC Day."

"I don't see the connection. And good luck connecting the sacred digger mythology to anything other than ANZAC Day or Remembrance Day." Terry warned.

"I mean no disrespect. In fact, I am trying to find a way to show exactly the opposite. There is an important solemnity to ANZAC Day that most Australians understand and respect. It is a public holiday which most of us do enjoy, but we understand that there is something very serious we need to reflect on. That is the horror of war, and the fact that brave soldiers – and their families and their communities – paid a horrible price for the society we have today – and that we should honour that sacrifice. I was thinking that maybe on Australia Day, we could have a similar solemn remembrance for the First Nations. It would be wrong to call the theft of Australia from aborigines a sacrifice – because a sacrifice is voluntary. But you can see what I am getting at?"

"Sure. I think you mean well, but who wants to turn a celebration into a sombre memorial?" Terry answered.

"Well, can't it be both? Perhaps in the morning, just before sunrise say, we could reflect on the horrors of the past and vow not to continue them. Then later in the day, we can have the usual celebrations – including a celebration of the wonderful indigenous culture that survives and grows."

"That may not be a bad idea." Terry mused. "And you are right about symbols. When Kevin Rudd apologised officially as prime minister, it was appreciated by a lot of indigenous people."

Suddenly Tristram smiled. "Do you remember in Ivan's English class we did that exercise of writing a symbol for a horrible experience?"

Terry nodded seriously. "Yep. I've never forgotten it. Those days in Ivan's class were a turning point in my life."

"Really?"

"Yeah." Terry grunted with faint amusement. "It started with you, funnily enough. When we fought, and then we had to go and see Mr. Gurnard. I realised something. You had a kind of power that I just didn't have at that time."

"What do you mean?"

"It took me a while to figure it out. Actually, I didn't really figure it out on me own. It was Ivan that explained it. It was about words. You had the power over your situation because you had the power over words."

"You could beat me up, so a fat lot of good my words were." Tristram grinned.

"Heh. You put up a reasonable fight. But that's not what I'm talkin' about. I had sat in Mr. Gurnard's office so many times and every time I felt like I had no control over what was going to happen next. But you sat there in as much trouble as I was, but you were as bold as brass and just *spoke*. And Mr. Gurnard listened. So did other teachers. They listened to you in a way that they wouldn't listen to me. They respected you – and because of that, you had a power over your situation that I just didn't have. A power over *adults*. And I reckon it was because of your way with words."

Tristram nodded thoughtfully. "Language is power...isn't it? You are on to something there."

"I reckon that's why God is such a hard thing for people to shake." Terry added, turning to make eye contact with Tristram. "In the beginning was the *word*, and the *word* was *God*."

"Hmpf. I thought you said you were an atheist?"

"I am. But there is something to this business of linking power over words to power over the world – and linking God to that power is not a hard step to make, eh?"

"As easy as slipping on a banana peel." Tristram grinned. "But probably more dangerous."

"Heh. But you agree, eh? There is no denying that those

that have power of words, have power over the world." Terry persisted.

"Yes, I agree. Are you going somewhere with this?"

"The other night, Dinewan pointed out to you that if you spoke up for the Kurnai, things would change. You wouldn't have a bar of it."

Tristram thought about it. Terry was now frowning out over the river.

"As I said to Dinewan, there is is nothing special about me – nothing that makes me a likely spokesperson in that regard." Tristram shrugged.

"Unless you find the bunyip, yeah?" Terry prompted.

"Yeah, sure, OK. When I am one of two or three people that prove the existence of an amazing, large predatory marsupial in the high country of Victoria, I may in that fifteen minutes of fame have the attention of a lot of people. But what is the message? Hey, I found a bunyip – now give Australia back to the aborgines?" Tristram challenged.

Terry grunted, bemused. "Yeah, eh? I guess one point doesn't really follow the other."

"Let me ask you a question. What person in all the word could make a case to the Australian people that they are the descendants of invaders and that they are living on land that was never ceded, and that they should give that land back?"

"I dunno. I guess nobody."

"Do you own a home by any chance?" Tristram asked.

"Nup. The bank owns about two thirds of it."

"So, you *do* own a house? Even if you have a mortgage, you actually own a house?"

"It's not much, but yeah, I do."

"Well you own more land than I do, mate. In fact, there is not one square inch of Australia that I can call mine – I am renting my house in Melbourne. Given property prices, and the lack of wage growth in this country, I can't see me ever owning my own home anyway."

"It's not really the point though, is it?" Terry answered good-naturedly.

"Well, what is the point?"

"Seriously? Our rightful heritage is denied to us and is instead being enjoyed by the descendants of the cunts who killed our people and stole our land. I reckon that is about the size of it." Terry returned, with a sardonic twinkle in his eyes.

"What is different between you and I right now, as we sit on this riverbank? We are both fishing for bream with local prawn. We are enjoying the same nice view of the Eagle Point Bluff – and neither of us own it, but we can both come here and appreciate it." Tristram offered.

"We are not quite having the same experience, mate. Though I see what you are getting' at." Terry nodded, thoughtfully.

"How is it different?" Tristram asked, making eye contact with Terry to show that he was sincerely interested in the answer.

"The local black fellas know the history of that bluff. A whole clan of us, men, women and children, were rounded up at the top there, like cattle. We were then forced over the edge, and shooters took out anyone who survived the fall – shooters probably sitting exactly where we are now. The bodies were then washed out to sea." Terry answered solemnly, his eyes on the orange cliff.

"Is that true?" Tristram asked softly.

Terry shrugged. "I doubt you will find a written record of it anywhere. But us black fellas have passed the stories down from that time. Stories of how they cut the balls off the men to see how far they would run. How they buried babies up to their neck and kicked their heads off, just for fun."

"That is horrible. And though I don't doubt that the first settlers murdered many of the Kurnai, that last detail sounds made-up to me."

"Why would any body make that up?" Terry frowned incredulously.

"It sounds like the barbarity of the Spanish in the South Americas. The British were very keen to distinguish themselves from the Spanish in that regard – it was illegal to kill aborigines, you know." Tristram answered.

"Was it? Oh well, guess it never happened then." Terry scoffed. "Of course, it is well documented these days that the population of the Kurnai went from about two thousand in 1840 down to just one hundred and thirty-one only thirteen years later. Where did they all go, Tristram? Did they all just die of the flu?"

"You're right, mate. I'm sorry – it seems petty to squabble over the particular details when it seems pretty clear that violence and cruelty and murder were committed against your ancestors by the first settlers." Tristram rejoined.

"By your ancestors, do you reckon?" Terry asked.

"I don't think so. But then who would admit to it?" Tristram answered. "Anyway, I am sure that there are murderers in both of our family trees somewhere."

"Well, I am not full-blooded aborigine, eh?" Terry joked.

"Heh. Well, since we seem to be provoking each other at the moment, I have a personal question to ask you." Tristram grinned.

"Oh yeah? What?" Terry grinned back.

"It is about the part of your genetic heritage that is not indigenous..."

"Oh shit – you're not going to get the nose calipers out are, ya?"

"No – no. What I want to know is this: do you identify as Koori? As Kurnai or Gunnai?"

"Yes, I do. I am proud of my genetic heritage, as you put it."

"What about the non-aborginal part of that genetic heritage? What is it – British? Scottish?"

"Yeah, probably."

"Well, those nations have made some very worthy contributions to humanity and democracy and so on. Are you proud to be related to them?" Tristram challenged. "Or is the Kurnai race somehow superior?"

"Oh, you cheeky cunt!" Terry laughed.

"You see the problem with identity politics? No matter what race – or what mix of races a person is – in the end you have to judge them as an individual. You cannot give them any credit or blame for their genetic heritage."

"True, true." Terry nodded. "But Ivan has beaten you to that argument, mate – by about what? Fifteen years?"

"Yeah?"

"Back in school he told me straight that if I was going to avoid the most common fate for koori kids, which is to drop out of school and basically be doomed to poverty, I would have to come to grips with a pretty cold reality. And that reality is that playing on white-guilt or indulging white-resentment would have very little currency for my future."

"Jesus. He said that to you? In those words?"

"Well, do those words sound like me? Yeah, he used those words, as far as I can remember. And he looked right into me, eh? A strange look, that I will never forget. It took me yonks to figure out what that look was, eh? It wasn't disrespectful. It wasn't cold. It wasn't harsh. It wasn't pity, or anger or shame."

"What was it?"

"Truth." Terry answered, raising his eyebrows. "He was telling me straight."

"Was he right?" Tristram asked, thoughtfully.

"I dunno. But he wasn't bull-shittin' me, eh? He wasn't talkin' down to me or telling me "stiff shit". Well, actually he was, but I could tell that he was trying to help me find a more useful attitude to life."

"Did he give you any pointers?"

Terry grunted, then smiled faintly. "He said to work with the world, and not against it. And then one day, if you are influential enough, you may change it for the better. But if you get bitter, you will get beaten – and half of the beating you will give to yourself."

Tristram nodded. "It's pragmatic, I suppose."

"So...I do have a reason for inviting you out today..." Terry said, with a cheeky sparkle in his eyes.

"Oh yeah?" Tristram sighed with smile.

"Dinewan wants to know how the buyip hunt is going. He promised he would't hassle you, so..."

"He asked you to take me fishing?"

"Yeah." Terry grinned and shrugged.

"And why did you agree to help him?"

"We've been talking a lot, eh? A few deep and meaningfuls. Dinewan is much more than some crazy old misfit, mate. I am not sure what he is trying to accomplish, but the more he talks, the more he kinda persuades, you know?"

"That's the skill-set of the huckster." Tristram grunted.

Terry shrugged good-naturedly. "Maybe, yeah. Anyway, he is just up the road."

"Really?" Tristram frowned.

Terry raised a placating hand. "But he will not come here, if you would rather he didn't."

Tristram considered Terry. Then he shrugged.

"Alright. That's fine. I'll talk to him."

Terry gave a "coo-ee."

A few minutes later, the witch doctor shuffled into view. Despite the hot day, he was in his trench-coat and long trousers. One foot was in a long leather boot, the other bare, as Tristram was accustomed to seeing.

"Any bites?" Dinewan asked congenially.

"Nothing yet." Tristram answered.

"You should try snake's heart." Dinewan returned with a lupine smile. "It never fails."

"You got some handy?" Terry grunted.

"As it happens..." Dinewan began.

"No thanks!" Tristram expostulated.

Dinewan chuckled. "As you wish."

Tristram gestured for Dinewan to sit down, and so he did.

"Thank you." Tristram began. "For seeking permission to talk to me. You didn't need to do that, but I appreciate the gesture."

Dinewan nodded. "I didn't want to risk being seen not upholding my end of a bargain."

"Fair enough. You should know that Ivan and I are for our part, doing our best to track down the bunyip. At least – Ivan is doing everything. I would join him, but I can't really pay my way, so I am waiting around just like you are."

"What have you tried so far?" Dinewan asked.

"Everything we can think of, eh? Ivan has set up camera traps along likely water-ways near where we saw the bunyuip last. He is flying drones with cameras up little valleys, gorges and streams. He is even staking live goats beside possible hunting grounds near the water-courses. I don't know what else we can do." Tristram explained.

"Perhaps a good fire to flush it out." Dinewan drawled, with a knowing look out at the river.

"Bushfires are growing in intensity in the high country at the moment." Tristram answered.

"Yes...I heard." Dinewan nodded. "What can you tell me about your sighting?"

Tristram then recounted the sighting to the witch doctor, whose orange eyes gleamed with interest.

"Hmm. I think I have identified the common thread." Dinewan mused, when Tristram had finished.

"Yes?"

"You."

"Uh-huh?"

"Yes, Tristram. You are the common link. Don't you see? The bunyip remembers you, remembers your scent. It was down in the gulley where you had been fishing that afternoon – it was following your scent, where you left your tackle-box." Dinewan explained.

Terry shook his head. "That's a bit of a stretch."

"Agreed." Tristram answered. "You are assuming a lot there. You are assuming that the bunyip we saw was the same bunyip that I saw as a kid, and that it can remember a scent from all those years ago. A scent that I am sure would have changed anyway, over the years."

Dinewan shrugged. "It is a testable hyposthesis. Try scenting the goats with your scent."

Terry and Tristram chuckled derisively.

"I'm serious." Dinewan smiled, holding Tristram's gaze. "What is the harm in trying? Scent the animals with some clothing that you have worn."

"Sure, sure. That doesn't sound creepy at all." Tristram smirked.

"When was the last time you washed your bed-sheets?" Dinewan asked.

Terry burst out laughing.

Tristram shook his head, bemused.

"It is an easy enough thing to try." Dinewan smiled, disarmingly.

"I think it's a bit bat-shit, to be frank. But... *it is* easy enough to try." Tristram conceded. "I'll text Ivan the idea right now. I doubt he will get the message though, if he is up in the high country."

As Tristram texted Ivan, still shaking his head, Terry saw his fishing rod tip move, indicating a bite.

"No need for snake's heart after-all." Terry grinned, as he reeled the fish in.

It was a very small bream.

"Ah well. Better than nonthin'" Tristram grinned. "So, Dinewan, aren't you sweating like mad in that heavy trench-coat? It's thirty-eight degrees, man."

Dinewan's eyes sparkled with mischief.

"What sort of magician would I be without my magic cloak?" He replied.

Tristram returned a friendly smile. "You do play the part well."

"I play it with *conviction*...yes." Dinewan answered.

"Terry and I were talking about our chat out at Lake Tyers. Or as we should call it, Bung Yarnda." Tristram began.

"Yes?"

"You seem to have decided that you are the spokesperson for the aggrevied indigenous people. And that I should decide to be the spokesperson for the white invaders."

Dinewan considered his answer before he spoke.

"We understand our world better through drama. We act things out in order to understand them. So then, we need actors. I am playing my part, you should play yours."

Tristram shook his head. "I decline the part you would have me play. I do not relate to the white invaders. I do not buy into this sins-of-the-father bullshit. We take on responsibility for our *own* actions, not those of people who came before us. I had no more choice in being related to the white invaders than you did being related to the displaced indigenous people."

"You could take responsibility anyway – voluntarily. The innocent man Jesus Christ took on all of the sins of all people who would accept him and paid the price with his life." Dinewan countered.

"You mean he gave up his long weekend." Tristram fired back. "He was alive again three days later, remember?"

Terry smirked and then straightened his face.

Dinewan grimaced and then shook his head. "You dismiss the big ideas so easily."

"Dinewan, I am not a Christian. I haven't been a Christian for years." Tristram sighed impatiently. "Don't tell me you are a Christian?"

"I am not a Christian, no. But I respect the power of Christianity's most important idea: that the wickedness of humankind cannot be helped by humans, so God sent his son to voluntarily take on all sin." Dinewan explained.

Tristram shook his head in confusion. "Do you want me to take on the crimes of British colonists upon my self and then what? Allow you to spear me in the leg or something? Just what the fuck are you driving at?"

"You know, Tristram, I am not at all sure what I expect from you – or the person who *would* take on the part in this drama. I just know, instinctively, that a drama *is* being acted out. Think about it. From our earliest days, we shaped and shared our understanding of life with drama and music. The drama and music that was powerful to all who watched it, survived. *Then* we had words – you see? Words that captured what we understood from the acting out – words that become our myths and legends. The stories of the Dreamtime. And our stories are still being told, don't you see? But we are not moving forward with our one, Tristram. We will not understand what to do next until we *act it out*. We *act out* that which we are trying to understand."

Dinewan seemed sincere and frustrated.

Terry and Tristram looked to each other.

"I think I almost understand." Terry mused. "There is the idea that in the beginning there was the word. But there was life before words, eh? Maybe the whole point of life is to act things out and try things – you know – the whole point of... well...art? Art comes first. It is our first attempt to understand."

Dinewan nodded encouragement.

Tristram frowned reluctantly. "If you have things that you need to work out...to me, that seems a private matter. An expression, artistic or otherwise, of the *individual*. You don't just drag other people into your...what? Artistic experiment?"

A new thought seemed to dawn on Dinewan. "Participation in the drama is voluntary for some, and not others. The parts that we are all assigned are by chance, it is true. But the actor, flawed in life, can perfect a moment on the stage. It can be a moment that changes the story, moves it on, completes it, perhaps. That is what our lives are. A chance for meaningful actions."

"This is all very deep and poetic, but the fact remains that your meaningful action in all of this, Dinewan, is to kill an amazing animal in the hopes that its magical tears will make your life right again." Tristram challenged.

"The tears of a monster to heal the broken man. The blood of Christ for the sins of all people. It is about powerful ideas – don't you see that?" Dinewan implored.

"It's fucking shit." Tristram growled. "It is is right up there with the Chinese using tiger penis to cure erectile dysfunction, or locking up bears in cruel little cages, alive only to have their bile extracted. Just because a stupid idea is a revered cultural tradition does not mean that I have to accept it. *All* ideas need to be critically examined for their merit based on the best information we have – and no idea – not even ideas from the culture of a dispossesed people – are to be exempt from that examination. Let's not use white guilt as a trump card every time reason and science go against traditional customs."

Terry winced. "I thought we were making some diplomatic progress here, man."

"Look – indigenous people have a serious, historical grevience with non-indigenous people that still ripples through our lives today. No escaping that. They also have opportunities unavailable to their ancestors – access to technology, knowledge, modern medicine and the art of the rest of the world. It does not wash away the blood on the hands of the invaders. But it is a silver lining available to those who take advantage of it. All I am saying is...don't go chasing bunyips for their souls, witch doctor – join the world of today and get some professional help."

Dinewan chuckled merrily at Tristram's rant.

"I decline to accept your lecture on how I should live my life." Dinewan finally responded. Then he became abruptly cold. "Don't mistake our uneasy truce for rapport."

"Yeah? Well, don't you give me any bullshit." Tristram responded, returning the cold glare.

Dinewan grunted. "Well then, that's that I suppose."

With a grimace of pain, he got to his feet, and without any further word he shuffled away from them down the road.

"I'm sorry." Tristram murmured to Terry. "I hope you don't read any disrespect to you or indigenous people in general from what I just said. I don't do identity politics, man. It was personal – and it was personal to just *him*."

Terry shrugged. "You're not wrong, mate. But you're not

right either, eh? We were getting somewhere and you let being right get in the way of doing right."

Tristram sighed and nodded. "I find it hard to accept that, mate. Which makes me very worried that it might be true. I don't know what to do. I don't understand the part he would have me play in his little show, nor what good it would do, nor what wider relevance it would have for anybody else."

Terry nodded thoughtfully. "Well...it's not like you have to work it out right now. I'd help you, but I've got no bloody ideas either. So, as they say in the classics...fuck you."

They made eye contact and then laughed.

They fished happily until evening, catching only small bream. When Tristram was finally home, he discovered that his bed-sheets were missing.

"Huh." Tristram grunted to himself. "I guess Ivan got my text."

OVER

ALL HOPE WAS LOST. There was nothing left to try. There was nothing left to say.

Yet, there was plenty to feel. Too much to feel.

Tristram always knew that life would throw challenges his way. Some would be a test of strength, some a test of intellect, some a test of patience and perseverance. Some would be moral tests. All of them, in some way or another, would be tests of character. Tristram knew this.

He also knew that some tests he would fail – and so, he would have to pass the test of dealing with failure.

Tristram knew that his heart may be broken and that too, would be a test. He knew that people he trusted may betray him. He knew that people he loved would get sick and die. He knew that the girl he loved with everything in him may not requite his love. He knew that he may hear the news of her in another's arms. He knew all of this.

Yet this night, Tristram found himself totally unprepared to deal with the test he now had to face. Everything he feared the most had happened, and he was unable to do anything about it.

Eve had started a sexual relationship with someone else.

It was someone he knew from high school – someone who went on his last Senior Band tour.

As he lay on the couch in his parent's lounge room, trying not to vomit, trying not to cry, he knew that it was Saturday night, and Eve would probably be having sex with Bruce McIntyre again. She would be gasping, moaning, and writhing on top of him as Tristram lay only a few miles away, devastated and alone. As Tristram's tears would finally come, Eve would be groaning with pleasure as Bruce mouthed her breasts. As Tristram's body would rack with violent sobs, Eve would shudder with orgasms. When the sex between Bruce and Eve would finish, they would whisper 'I love you'. They would make lover's jokes, and then do it again. A different position this time. Maybe doggy style. Would it be slow and sensual this time? Or hard and fast?

Tristram got up, went to the toilet and threw up. So much for the roast chicken dinner that his father had prepared. It would not nourish him.

"I'm sorry, Tristram. Bruce is everything I ever wanted or needed in a partner and I adore him."

"You know this after what? Three weeks?" Tristram had murmured with surreal detachment.

"Yes." There was a cold stubbornness to her answer.

"You just blocked me out. We wouldn't even be having this conversation if I hadn't called you from an unknown number. You just fucking well blocked me out." Tristram was getting angry and nauseated.

Eve sighed. "It was the only way. I just couldn't handle talking to you. Every time I thought about what we did I felt sick inside. It took a long while for me to realise this, but I blame you for your part in the break-down of my marriage."

"*What*?! How can you say that after *you* pursued *me*? After

I tried to help you sort your marriage out, after you convinced me that you were going to end it with him regardless of whether you and I got together?"

"I don't want to go over it again." Eve murmured. Again, there was a cold, stubborn quality to her tone. "I have moved on."

"Without talking to me?!"

"I had to block you out for my own sanity."

"What?"

"You cloud me. I can't think straight with you around me."

"You don't think I deserved a fucking explanation?! You don't think you should have told me that you had started to see Bruce?!"

"It was none of your business."

"*None of my business?!*"

"I had to tell Chris. I owed him an explanation because I was married to him – but I didn't have to tell you anything."

"Fuck...You." Tristram hissed. "Fuck you, Eve – how dare you!?"

"Look, if you're going to shout, I'm going to hang up. I can't handle this."

"OK. OK, I'm sorry I shouted just now..." Tristram could hardly believe that he was apologising.

"I am not saying that I have handled this well." Eve continued. "In fact, I have handled it very badly. But it doesn't change anything. Tristram, it is over. I told you that it was over and that I would not be responding to you – you persisted. Even though you promised you wouldn't."

"Of course, I persisted! I love you!"

"Stop. Just stop. This isn't helping, OK? I know you are hurt. I know there is nothing that I can say to make you feel better about this. But I can't talk to you anymore. I'm sorry but blocking you out is the only way for me to be happy again."

"You fucking shallow bitch." Tristram hung up savagely.

And then what happened? Tristram asked himself. *I called her back and apologised. And we spoke for an hour. And in that hour, I tried to make HER feel better.*

What did I say at the end of the call?

"I know it is over between us, Eve. I know. But I want you to know that I love you. I always will. If you ever want to claim me as your friend, and nothing else, I will be there for you. OK? I wish you and Bruce the very best, alright?"

There was silence on the other end.

"Alright?" Tristram whispered tearfully.

"Alright." Eve finally answered.

There was a dreadful silence then. There were just no words on either side.

Finally, Tristram found a voice, and with as much good will as he could muster, he said: "OK. Well, I guess everything has been said, hasn't it? So, I suppose I will say...goodbye."

There was another silence.

"Eve?" Tristram prompted.

"I don't really know how to say good-bye. I can't think of a right way to say it." She mumbled.

Was that shame in her voice? Or was she just uncomfortable?

Tristram swallowed hard. "You just say good-bye."

Eve sighed. "OK. OK...Goodbye, Tristram."

"Goodbye, Eve."

End call.

That was a week ago.

As Tristram ran the call over and over again in his mind he suddenly roared aloud.

"Now just what the FUCK was that?!"

Be her friend – be there for her, love her, after this cold, shallow abandonment? How weak and pathetic I must have sounded!

What can I do now? Send her a text message describing this wretched heartache in the bitter hope that I might interrupt their sex and make her feel bad? Take all the nice words back? Go over to her house and slap her one? Just what the hell can I actually DO?

Tristram leaped off the couch and marched out the back door. He jogged up the steps and then ran as hard as he could up the gravel road.

His body screamed to do violence. He would hurt – he would viciously hurt. He would break noses and bruise flesh. He would fracture ribs. He would make them all pay. None could withstand him.

Terrible, horrific fantasies accosted him.

I never wanted this. But did you really think that you could do this to me and then just walk away, scott-free?

I will hurt you. I will apply all my intellect, all my imagination and all my strength into punishing you.

A new voice broke into his thoughts.

And then what, Tristram?

Then I will run. Then my life will be changed forever. Then I will find a way to die.

Too soon his legs hurt from the sprinting. Too soon he was short of breath. His energy could not match his rage.

Tristram pushed himself harder. He ran up into the hilly farm country until it he couldn't run anymore.

His head throbbed. Huge pressure had built behind his eyes. His neck felt contricted and his chest heavy. His legs burned.

He heard a car approaching.

Tristram did not want to be seen, so he ran towards a dead

gum tree beside the wire fence of a huge cattle paddock and hid behind it.

He sat down heavily behind the tree and gazed miserably out.

I won't hurt her. I won't hurt any of them. It is not who I am.

So, what can I do with all this anger? NOTHING! I can do NOTHING! Nothing except direct it inside and choke myself with it!

Finally, Tristram cracked. The first sob escaped and then he was bawling. Hot tears coursed down his face and his body shook so hard it hurt. Tristram could not even sit up properly.

All he could do was cry.

PUT AWAY CHILDISH THINGS

Lachlan, tired and horrified, arrived at Tristram's parent's place about four in the afternoon. He had been at one of the bushfire fronts near the tiny town of Suggan Buggan.

The sky was dark with smoke-choked clouds that had glowing, orange edges. The wind was hot and relentless.

The garden was wilted, the grass dead and dry.

As Lachlan wearily descended the steps, he could hear a heated argument coming from the other side of the house.

"It is breath-taking arrogance!" A familiar voice barked. Lachlan recognised it as Peter, a Jehovah's Witness who lived in Bruthen. He was surprised to hear him speak in anger.

"Science is arrogant?" Tristram scoffed. "How so?"

"It is arrogant because it assumes it can explain everything eventually, without any credit given to the Almighty Creator." Peter replied.

"Right. It is much humbler to claim that you *know* that there is an Almighty God, and that I must subject myself to his will – which you also claim to know – based on a collection of discredited and immoral fables from Bronze-age Palestine."

"Immoral fables!?" Peter laughed incredulously. "I cannot believe that I am hearing this. What a marvellous result your studies have produced in you. I suppose you think of our Lord Jesus as immoral now!?"

"He is the most immoral idea in the whole bible."

"Oh Tristram! Tristram, Tristram, Tristram. Come *on*." Peter scoffed.

Tristram's eyes narrowed. "I am being deadly serious."

"Really? Fine. Fine! I can't wait to hear your argument!" Peter provoked.

"Peter, are we really to accept as moral, the idea that we can be redeemed for our bad behaviour by the torturing to death of an innocent human scapegoat? That is what Jesus is – he is a scapegoat."

"He is *not*... a scapegoat."

"Peter, he is referred to in the bible as *the sacrificial lamb*. That's the only progress we make in the bible – we go from scapegoats in the old testament to one sacrificial lamb in the the new testament." Tristram smirked.

"OK. So, you have just undone your scapegoat argument, haven't you?"

"*Huh?*"

"You know that there is a difference between scapegoats and the sacrifice of our Lord. Your wit betrays you." Peter smirked back.

"And it escapes you. Let us consider the scapegoat in a little more detail, shall we? A benighted tribe of illiterate peasants come together to cast the wickedness of the group – the *responsibility* for that wickedness – upon a poor hapless goat. That goat is then killed – often tortured cruelly before it is killed. And then the conscience of the tribe is wiped clean by that atrocity – just as our sins are washed away by the blood of the lamb, Jesus. It is medieval, dark age, repugnant bullshit that has no place in our modern societies."

"Our Lord and Saviour shall not be trivialised by comparison with scapegoats." Peter retorted coldly. "He was an innocent man, a *perfect* man – who generously took on every sin of every person who would believe in Him upon his flesh. If you were *there*, Tristram, I wonder if you would not feel shame as you looked upon Him, suffering and dying."

"If I was *there* – at Golgotha – the skull place – I would indeed feel shame. Shame that I thought such *barbarism was necessary*. Shame that rather than accept full responsibility for my mistakes, I would put them onto an innocent man and watch him be brutally punished for them." Tristram rejoined.

"I can see your point, and it is noble in its way, but I am saddened by your misunderstanding." Peter answered. "If you really could take a moment to imagine yourself at the scene. To see his pain and anguish. To look into his face and see why he was doing it. You would be moved. I know you would be moved, Tristram, as you always were a compassionate young man."

"Peter, if *you* were there – I hope you would notice *two others* on torture stakes. I hope you would also look into *their* faces. In fact, I hope you would notice all the crosses and stakes and reflect on just how many other human beings were tortured to death in the way of Jesus." Tristram countered.

"They did not choose to go through it for all of mankind." Peter sighed.

"Right. They did it for shits and giggles. It is barbaric nonsense, Peter. Why couldn't your god simply forgive all men without the need for the shedding of innocent blood?"

"It is not for us to dictate morality to Jehovah, Tristram. We are to accept it or reject it as it is."

"Howdy, all." Lachlan interrupted.

"Lachlan!" Peter smiled. "You look beat, old son. You just come in from the fires?"

Lachlan shook Peter's hand.

"Yeah. Been up past Suggan Buggan for the last sixteen hours." Lachlan croaked. "Sorry, I can't talk – my throat's buggered, eh?"

Lachlan was red-eyed, covered in soot and reeking of fire-smoke. His face was the most care-worn that Tristram had ever seen.

"Sit down, Lachie – I'll get you a big glass of water, mate." Russell said, gesturing to a chair.

"Thanks, Russ. Crikey, Peter, how can you wear a shirt and tie in this weather?"

"I am visiting a few folks – just popped in to check on these heathens." Peter smiled.

"Yeah, well good luck with that. I heard Tris givin' ya the third degree. He hates Christians now." Lachlan grinned, cheekily.

Tristram smiled and sighed. "I don't hate Christians."

"He wouldn't piss on one that was on fire." Lachlan persisted.

"I am sure that if Tristram saw a Christian on fire, he would find a way to put the fire out." Peter said, putting his hand on Tristram's shoulder.

"Like a wet cricket bat." Lachlan suggested.

"No..." Tristram answered with a dry grin. "Thoughts and prayers."

Peter groaned. Lachlan laughed appreciatively, then coughed.

"Touché, touché. Tristram was always a challenging student." Peter sighed fondly. "But one day he will see the truth again and realise that his science doesn't hold all the answers."

"I already see that, Peter. Science has *some* answers though – unlike religion, which has *none*." Tristram answered bluntly.

"Here we go." Lachlan sighed. "Bloody red flag to a bull."

Russell appeared with an enormous glass of water, and a jug.

"Thanks, Russ." Lachlan said, before he drained the glass in four gulps.

"I thought it might go down fast." Russell chuckled. "That is why I brought a jug out. I'll leave it here on the table, and you can help yourself."

Russell then took a seat next to Lachlan.

"Cold water. You have no idea how good this is." Lachlan sighed.

"I guess you couldn't take a sip out of the fire-truck hose – too much pressure?" Tristram grinned.

"Yeah, but even if the pressure wasn't too high, you couldn't drink it. We had boiling water coming out of the bloody fog nozzles this mornin'."

"What?" Peter frowned.

"Yep." Lachlan confirmed, making meaningful eye-contact with them. "The fire was that hot in one spot, we were slippin' through melted bitumen, and we were worried the tires were gonna catch fire. A couple of fire-fronts came at us so fast we just had to pull into a paddock and prepare for a burn-over. Luckily, it went over relatively quick and we were in an open area. Still – there was boiling water comin' out of the fog-nozzles."

"The fire was that hot that the radiant heat boiled the water as it was coming through the hose?" Tristram asked in awe.

"No – it was that hot that it boiled all the water we were carryin' in the tanker. All two thousand three hundred and ninety-five litres of it."

They shook their heads in fearful wonder.

"That's hard to believe." Tristram mused, diplomatically.

"I'm not shittin' ya." Lachlan sighed.

"I believe you." Tristram assured.

"Tris, do you know how hot bushfires can get?" Russell asked.

"Tell me."

"The energy of a big fire can be as much as *one hundred thousand* kilowatts per square metre. The radiant heat can melt metal and vapourise a human being."

"Shit. How do you judge a safe distance from the fire?" Tristram asked.

"Four times the height of the fire is a rough guide for a safe distance. You don't always get the luxury of keeping that distance though." Lachlan answered.

"I'm glad you made it out of there, man." Tristram murmured sincerely.

"Me too. Been more than a few times these last few days when I thought I was gonna go the way of the dodo." Lachlan drawled before he drank down another glass of water.

"Speaking of dodos, have you seen a picture of a dodo, Tristram?" Peter suddenly asked.

"There's a non-sequitir." Tristram grunted.

"I reckon my granddad ate one of those..." Lachlan added, a tired twinkle in his eye.

Tristram smirked. "It tasted mid-way between platypus and koala?"

Peter smiled patiently. "I do have a point. Humour me. Have you ever seen a picture of a dodo?"

Tristram shrugged. "Sure."

"It is probably wrong. Does it look like this?" Peter pulled out a magazine article from his pocket and showed Tristram.

"That is probably the most famous image of the Dodo – Edwards Dodo, by Roelant Savery." Tristram replied.

"Well done. It was painted in 1626. It has been copied numerous times. So, you agree, that this is what dodos looked like?" Peter persisted.

"That is what I think a dodo looked like." Tristram confirmed. "So?"

"Is that your *scientific* opinion?" Peter asked, a smug sparkle in his deep brown eyes.

Tristram sighed. "As that animal has been extinct for over four hundred years, and all we have are drawings and stuffed specimens, yes, that is the current scientific view on what dodos look like."

"Well, sorry to burst your bubble, Tristram, but science has been wrong about the dodo for hundreds of years. The painting is wrong in several important details, according to the latest studies done on remains and subfossils. Your confidence in science must be shattered." Peter announced triumphantly.

Tristram chuckled gently and shook his head. "Hardly."

"Hardly? Fair enough, you need more proof that scientific truth is not eternal? Well, there is plenty of it out there if you care to look. But I have made my point."

"Which is...?"

"Which is that you stand with unjustified confidence in your opinions, based on *science*. The image of the dodo was scientific opinion for hundreds of years, and yet suddenly, new evidence comes to light that science was *wrong all that time*. The solid ground beneath your feet suddenly looks very tenuous."

"Actually, it is even more solid." Tristram shrugged.

"*What?* Come on, Tristram, have the honour to concede the point."

"Peter, your example only increases my confidence in science, because it shows that science has improved and corrected an error in its understanding. You will notice that it was *more science* that disproved the painting – not scriptures from the bible. You are resting just as confidently on science as I am."

"You are being evasive. All I am saying is that you have faith in science, just as I have faith in the truth." Peter rejoined.

"That is a false equivalency." Tristram waved dismissively. "If science was like religion, you would have a bunch of people denying the new evidence about the dodo. They would insist that we respect the ancient wisdom of the painting from hundreds of years ago. No argument would convince them to disregard the painting. In fact, most of them would sit smugly waiting for yet more evidence to come to light that the painting was right all along."

Russell laughed. "Touché."

"Well, nevermind the dodo, then." Peter shrugged good-naturedly. "There are still so many things that you scientists cannot explain."

"You should be grateful that we can explain anything at all, given that we only just evolved from monkeys." Tristram retorted.

"You believe in evolution, of course." Peter rolled his eyes.

"I am *convinced* of evolution – that is not quite the same thing."

"You should apply that critical mind of yours to evolution – you will see that it does not exactly stack up. The fossils that supposedly prove human evolution can all fit on the surface of a billiard table." Peter glowered.

Tristram frowned. "That is not true – and even if it were – where's *your* billiard table full of evidence? I'm sorry, Peter, but I don't think we should have this conversation. Evolution is informed by a wide range of disciplines – genetics, geology, paleontology, botany, zoology, chemistry and so on. Your view is informed by Bronze Age texts from Palestine."

"They are the *holy* scriptures. Not just any ordinary text. And *they* are informed by the word of Jehovah, the Almighty Creator of the universe. What information could be more important than Jehovah's word?" Peter rejoined piously.

"The truth!" Tristram barked.

"Jehovah's word is the truth. It is our spiritual food, as you used to know with all your heart."

"That is what I believed as a *child*." Tristram growled angrily. "Forget it, Peter. I am not one of your lost sheep. I am a goat – and not a scapegoat, either. I don't need your spiritual food. Secular humanism is all the nourishment I need now, as an adult. It is time to put away childish things."

Peter considered Tristram sadly. Then he bowed his head and quoted the book of John 6:48-51.

"I am the living bread that came down from heaven. If anyone eats of this bread he will live forever; and for a fact, the bread that I will give is my flesh on behalf of the life of the world."

Peter watched Tristram for his reaction.

Tristram narrowed his eyes moodily, and then gave a mean grin as he answered.

"I feel for the disciples at the last supper, I really do. Jesus basically goes completely nuts on them. Drink this wine – it represents my *blood*. Eat this bread, it represents my *flesh*. At this point they must have been shifting in their chairs, quietly grateful that there was no *mayonnaise* on the table."

At that, Russell and Lachlan snorted into laughter.

Peter's face flushed with anger.

"I am done here. I wish you all to be safe from the fires coming towards us." He announced with controlled anger.

Then Peter left, firmly shutting the back door behind him.

Russell clapped. "Good to see some life come back into you, son."

Tristram sighed with deep self-reproach.

"Don't clap. Don't applaud what I just did. I was an arse-hole." Tristram answered.

"You were funny." Lachlan countered. "Fuck 'em if they can't take a joke, I say."

"You know Peter, Lachlan. Bruthen is a small town. How is he thought of?" Tristram persisted.

"Bloody do-gooder and door-knocker."

"And?"

Lachlan shrugged. "Nice bloke. Good bloke. Always helps out with the school and the CFA and all that. He'd give you the shirt off his back."

"Exactly." Tristram sighed, miserably. "And he has been an ear to you Dad, when you were going out of your mind during Mum's break-down. He always went out of his way to pick me up and take me to Kingdom Hall when you and Mum didn't want to go anymore. He sincerely believes that he is a slave for Jehovah God, that Armageddon is around the corner and that it is his duty to try and save our eternal lives. And I just treated that man with contempt. And you both laughed with me in his face."

Russell sighed. "Don't over-react, Tris. Peter may be a good man – even a great man, but he was pretty arrogant in the way he was presenting his ideas. If he can't stand his idea's being mocked and challenged, then the fault is with him, not you. Besides, you can catch up with him later and smooth things over. You know he will forgive you. His religion gives him no choice."

Tristram grunted appreciatively.

"Well, he may be right about Armageddon being around the corner." Lachlan sighed heavily.

"I know." Russell nodded seriously. "I will be up at 4am tomorrow – got to be up at Swifts' Creek early to assist with the first aid stations supporting the fire-fighters. They are expecting the fire-front to expand even further and speed up. Efforts are being redoubled everywhere."

"Tell me about it." Lachlan added. "I've been fightin' fires non-stop. Just did sixteen hours. Day before was fourteen, day before was fifteen. Managed to save a couple of properties up past Suggan Buggan, but this fire is unstoppable. It is the worst I've seen; the worst Dad has seen. Even Pop reckons he's never seen one like this."

Lachlan then shared some of the horrors that he had witnessed.

THE WOMBAT

IT IS ALMOST HERE...

The moon has risen early this evening and it glows blood red. The air is thick with the acrid sting of bushfire smoke. If the northerly winds are as strong as predicted, the fire will be on the north side of Bairnsdale by tomorrow evening.

And then it will be here.

Tristram sat outside on the dry grass near the orchard beside his parent's house. In the unpleasantly hot semi-darkness, he watched the sprinkler make slow turns on the apex of the tin roof. The gutters had been scoured and blocked so that they could be filled with water. His father had organised the family to place stainless steel buckets of water at strategic places around the block – two every three meters on the verandahs – four on the verandah of Tristram's cottage. They were stainless steel buckets because in the heat of an on-coming bushfire, plastic ones would melt.

Hot wind brought tidings of the approaching monster. The

sky was smeared with ash, and oily black cinders fell like snowflakes. An orange haze blanketed the district. It stung the eyes and burned the throat. The dry heat was oppressive and unbearable.

Tomorrow would be another over forty-degree day, with fierce northerly winds.

Yesterday morning, the fire travelled at a speed of forty kilometres an hour.

That was big news.

However, by the late afternoon, raging northerly winds were fanning the furnace at one hundred and twenty kilometres an hour.

That was unheard of.

The fire front itself was over seventeen hundred kilometres long. Over one hundred and sixty thousand hectares of bushland in the high country of East Gippsland were burnt. Over six thousand sheep and four thousand cattle were dead.

What horrible numbers - a cold summation of sickening horror. Do these numbers recall the piercing bleat of sheep as their wool burns and their fat blisters? The panicked stamping of hundreds of hooves in a cyclone of fire? The tumultuous rattle and twang of barbed wire fences, as doomed animals hurl themselves in a blind, desperate attempt at escape?

Tristram brooded, as he remembered Lachlan's updates.

And what of the guttural wailing of cattle lying in hot black paddocks, their legs literally obliterated from underneath them? Their bloody blackened stumps twitching as their red eyes roll, and their jaws mindlessly run through the motions of chewing their cud? Can statistics assault the eyes and nose, with the searing mist of vaporised eucalyptus oil and roast beef?

Gum trees thick with decades just smash apart as the intense heat rolls into them. The heat is so fierce that it can melt metal — rail-way lines disappear, melting into the scree. Fire hurtles through the forest canopy with a terrifying ROAR. It takes the breath away – literally. Possums and koalas do not have the air to squeal as they are burned to their bones. Wombats suffocate in their burrows, even though they are up to two metres underground. Only the fastest kangaroos and wallabies can stay ahead of the flames – but where can they go when a blaze of this magnitude consumes their world?

Tristram suddenly noticed Teddy, padding towards him. He waited for the dog to reach him, then gave him a big cuddle. Teddy licked his face, then sat down beside him.

For a few moments, Tristram sadly patted Teddy's head and shoulders. Whenever he got lost in thought and stopped patting, Teddy would groan then shove his big snout under Tristram's hands, urging him to continue patting.

"Oh, am I not serving you well enough?" Tristram smiled weakly. He kissed Teddy on the head. "Bugger off, mate. Leave me alone, eh? I am not good company."

He gave Teddy three firm pats on the rump, and the dog understood that that was the signal to move on.

As Teddy sauntered away, another creature ambled towards him from the darkness.

"Oh no..." Tristram groaned.

Wilbur the wombat heard his voice and then rushed toward him.

Tristram did not feel like giving the poor mange-afflicted wombat his attention. Unlike Teddy, who would move on after a pat, this needy creature would nip him as soon as he stopped scratching its back.

As Wilbur got close Tristram heard its unusual whisper-like call.

Kyuh-kyuh-kyuh-kyuh-kyuh.

When it reached him, the wombat sat expectantly between his legs.

Tristram sighed, then massaged and gently scratched the creature's back. Wilbur was covered in ugly scabs that were dyed blue by the treatmet for sarcoptic mange. The infected skin was dry and cracked and bleeding in places. The poor creature itched terribly, and would scratch and scratch, causing himself yet more damage.

As predicted, when Tristram absently stopped massaging the wombat, it nipped him on the thigh.

"Ouch!" Tristram growled, then slapped the wombat gently on the nose.

It didn't seem to register the rebuke.

Tristram hadn't wanted to get up from where he was sitting, but now he angrily decided to take the wombat back to the house and then go to his cottage and try to sleep.

When he got to the front verandah, he handed the wombat to Holly, who was smoking with Russell.

"Here, could you please take Satan's Guinea Pig, give him a feed and then stash him in his pouch?" Tristram asked gruffly.

Russell snorted. "Satan's Guinea Pig?"

Tristram was already marching away.

"Good night." He called without turning around.

Tristram was half-way down the path to his cottage when he heard a familiar call.

Kyuh-kyuh-kyuh-kyuh-kyuh.

"Oh, for Christ's sake."

Wilbur was running down the hill behind him.

Tristram picked the creature up us soon as it reached him, then stormed back to the house.

This time he didn't hand the animal to his mother.

"He likes you." Holly smiled.

"He is a pain in the arse." Tristram muttered.

He took the wombat inside, dumped it on the couch, then went back outside, shutting the door behind him.

When Tristram got down to the cottage, he lay in bed with the covers off. It was unbearably hot, and he sweated heavily.

Tristram was steeped in misery and self-pity. Anger, hatred, grief, longing, and fear of the future kept him wide-awake.

Just as he was indulging in imagined, savage arguments with Burt and Eve and every member of his family, he heard a call getting closer to his door.

Kyuh-kyuh-kyuh-kyuh-kyuh.

No! Fuck!

Tristram covered his ears.

Maybe if I pretend I am not here, he will go away.

Tristram lay still, holding his breath as he listened to the wombat pace near his door.

It stopped moving. Then the scratching on the door started.

If I ignore him, he will give up and go away.

The wombat did not give up. It knew that Tristram was inside, and it kept scratching.

Scratch...scratch...scratch...scratch...

Tristram's anger simmered as Wilbur continued to scratch the door.

The animal's stupidity lends it enormous patience. Listen to that methodical, consistent, relentless scratch...scratch...scratch.

"PISS OFF!" Tristram suddenly roared.

The scratching stopped for a moment. Then began again.

Scratch...scratch...scratch...scratch...

Tristram groaned, then tried to ignore the scratching.

Minutes went by, and the scratching never skipped a beat.

Scratch...scratch...scratch...scratch...

What is wrong with that fucking creature? Why can't it just leave me the fuck alone? Surely it can tell that it is not fucking wanted right now?

Scratch...scratch...scratch...scratch...

I am trapped. Trapped in my own shitty, sweaty, uncomfortable, spider-infested bed-room by a relentless, scabby, dumb, fucking...

"For crying out loud!" Tristram shouted, leaping to his feet. He opened the door and picked the wombat up.

"Fuck you!" Tristram snarled into its face with gritted teeth. "Do you understand!? I don't want to deal with you! Leave me alone!"

With that savage rebuke, Tristram jogged a few steps up the path towards the house, lowered the wombat to the ground and gave it a rough shove up the hill. He then marched back to the cottage, went inside and slammed the door. Even as he did, he could hear Wilbur running after him.

Kyuh-kyuh-kyuh-kyuh-kyuh.

Seconds later came the methodical, relentless scratching.

Scratch...scratch...scratch...scratch...

Tristram again tried to wait out the endless scratching, but again his anger exploded.

He opened the door again.

"Fuck off!" He wailed. "Won't you please, just fuck off?!"

Wilber sat on his feet, so he lifted his right foot and propelled the wombat a few feet away.

Wilbur landed clumsily, then immediately turned and ran to Tristram.

Kyuh-kyuh-kyuh-kyuh-kyuh.

Tristram, fully frustrated and enraged, grabbed the wombat and threw it up the hill. He calculated the throw to be something that would not hurt the animal too badly.

Wilber landed with a thud. However, he seemed to take the

event in his stride, because he immediately ran back to Tristram.

With disbelief and yet further anger, Tristram tried the experiment again, this time hurling the wombat further and more roughly.

Wilber hit the gravel of the path and slid a little. Then he got up but hesitated before he ran back to Tristram.

Kyuh-kyuh-kyuh-kyuh-kyuh.

Tristram threw him savagely again. Again, Wilbur hesitated before running back.

"You see? Is the message starting to sink into to your thick skull yet?" Tristram growled.

This time Wilber stopped just a few feet away from Tristram. Then he started hiccupping – the sign of distress in a young wombat.

"I don't feel sorry for you." Tristram hissed. "I fucking don't. This is what you get for being relentlessly stupid and selfish. You can't force your needs from a person, Wilbur!"

At the sound of Tristram's voice, Wilber approached again.

"No, no, no, NO!" Tristram barked.

Again, he picked up the wombat and marched up the hill. Halfway to the house, he stopped and threw Wilbur again.

Wilbur landed heavily this time.

He hesitated, and then started to move towards Tristram. However, Tristram was waiting for the first sign of such a move and so he rushed to the wombat, picked it up and roughly threw it again.

"This is going to keep happening, Wilbur, until you fucking get the message."

After another two throws, Wilbur did not move to Tristram. He stood uncertainly in place, hiccupping pitifully. Finally, the animal did something that Tristram did not expect. It sat down and did not move.

"Good." Tristram murmured. "About time."

Slowly, Tristram walked back to the cottage, listening for the call and the rapid foot-steps of the wombat. However, Wilbur did not move.

Feeling resentful, guilty and miserable, Tristram shut himself in the cottage and lay on the bed.

Minutes went by. There was no scratching at the door.

Tristram was unable to enjoy his hard-won peace. An absurd, and yet obvious truth sat on his chest. He had hurt the feelings of a creature that wanted his love.

Tristram got up, opened the door and looked up the hill. He could make out Wilbur's forlorn figure in the darkness, still slumped in the same spot.

What if I have accidentally caused him a serious injury? I had better go and check.

With a sigh, he walked towards Wilbur.

Wilbur did not move.

As Tristram leaned down to examine the creature, he saw something that broke his heart.

It was a single tear in each of Wilbur's eyes. The wombat was crying.

Tristram sat down beside Wilbur, completely drained of anger and full of remorse.

"I am so sorry, little wombat." He whispered.

He moved to pat Wilbur, and the wombat flinched and hiccuped.

"Don't be afraid, Wilbur. I am so sorry I hurt you."

Tristram tenderly scooped the wombat into his arms and cradled it until its hiccups stopped.

"You just didn't know what else to do, did you?" Tristam sighed, gently stroking Wilbur, who had now calmed down.

"You just needed to feel looked after. You are itchy all over and you can't help but scratch and make it worse. All you wanted was what you should be able to get from your mother. But your mother was killed, and so you look to us. How could I not understand that? You have the needs we all have. We all need..."

Tristram felt tears run down his cheeks.

"We all need love, Wilbur. Don't we, eh? And even in the face of rejection, we keep going because...what else can we do? What else can we do?"

NIGHT VISION FOOTAGE

TRISTRAM FED WILBUR UP at the house, sitting in the lounge room, which was barely cooler than the hot night outside, due to the bleak efforts of an evapouritive cooler.

When the wombat was sleeping finally in his pouch on a hook on the wall behind the fireplace, Tristram made himself a coffee.

Holly quietly approached him as the kettle gurgled to life.

She hugged him, and he hugged her back.

"I have something for you." Holly said.

She placed a small dark purple cloth pouch in his palm. It had a drawstring pulled tight.

He opened it and found a pewter coin inside. On one side was an image of two Christian Knights with a cross on their shields, riding the one horse. The words "SIGILLUM MILITUM XPISTI" encircled the image. On the reverse was an even cross, surrounded by the words "*Non nobis domine non nobis sed nomini tuo da glorium.*"

"Thank you." Tristram said, turning the coin over and considering the words. "Do you know what it says?"

"I know what it means." Holly answered. "It means from humble beginnings."

Tristram raised an incredulous eyebrow. "I don't mean to be impolite...or ungrateful, but I don't think it says that."

"That is what it *means*." Holly insisted, with a shy grin.

"Sigillum...sigil? Militum – military? The last word is probably "Christ" – sigil military Christ – hang on. I know what this says. Seal of the army of Christ – this is a Knights Templar coin?"

"Yes!" Holly beamed. "Well done."

"I will have to Google what the back of the coin says." Tristram grinned.

"*Not to us, Lord, not to us, but to your name give glory.*" Holly translated.

Tristram sighed. "Why are you giving me this?"

"To remind you of where you are going." Holly answered. "I haven't counted you out yet, Tris."

"Counted me out yet for what? Becoming a soldier for Christ? Didn't you hear about my fight with Peter earlier?" Tristram rejoined.

"I heard your argument with Peter. You were both very loud. It reminded me that I wanted to give you this coin." Holly smiled. "And it has nothing to do with Jesus. Look at the image of the knights."

Tristram gave a bemused sigh, then reconsidered the coin.

"They look like they are on a quest." Tristram offered. "A quest for glory, but not their glory, that of Christ. Am I a missing something? I think *you're* missing something, Mum."

"They are sharing a horse." Holly pointed to the coin. "Do you see?"

"Yes?"

"Why are they sharing a horse? The Knights Templar did not share their horses. This is a picture of the beginning –

before they were great. They were poor, so they had to share a horse – but it did not stop them from persuing their vision." Holly explained.

"I think I see what you are getting at." Tristram nodded.

"They will acheve great things – but their beginning was humble. From humble beginnings." Holly smiled.

"I like the image, Mum." Tristram murmured.

"Will you look after it? Or will you dismiss it as more of my spiritual rubbish?" Holly asked with a defensive laugh.

Tristram looked her in the eye.

"I will look after this, Mum. I promise. And thank you."

They looked at the coin again, focusing on the knights.

"I think the two riders are you and Ivan." Holly mused.

Suddenly, they heard a car pull up at the top of the block.

Belle and Pixie began yapping immediately, bolting out the back door and running up the steps.

"I wonder who that is at this hour?" Holly asked.

They heard the chain on the gate being opened, and then saw that it was Ivan descending ths stairs.

"Speak of the devil." Tristram frowned.

A shudder went through him.

Ivan marched straight through the front door. He had a lap-top with him.

"I have something to show you." He said to Tristram, a wild sparkle in his eyes.

He had completely ignored Holly.

"Hello, Ivan." Holly said pointedly, with a censuring grin.

"Hello, Holly. Sorry for my bad manners – it has been a long few days." Ivan grinned, and looked quickly around the room. "Is Russell still up?"

"No, he has to be up early tomorrow. He going to meet

some CFA and Red Cross people at Swifts Creek and he is going to help at one of the relief points for the firefighters. He used to teach first aid, as you know." Holly answered.

"Ah yes. Good work. They will be glad to have Russell up there – his humour will be good for morale." Ivan nodded.

Holly could see that Ivan was keen to talk to Tristram.

"Yes, I am sure he will be useful. I am going to put the hose in the pond to top it up. We do it at night so that the water doesn't evapourate straight away."

Holly then went outside.

"Sit down and look at this." Ivan directed, opening his lap-top and placing it on the dining table.

Tristram obeyed and waited patiently for Ivan to load the video. Ivan looked furtively about the room to make sure that they were alone, then clicked on the media window to make the video play in full screen.

The footage was grainy, blurred and dark green. A white goat wearing a black cape was tethered by chain to a stake. It was on stony ground by a mountain stream. The brightest points were the goat's eyes and the stars were visible above the black shape of forested mountains.

The goat seemed nervous, as it tried to chew the cloth cape fixed to it with a belt.

Then, a few feet behind the goat at the water's edge, a pair of enormous white eyes appeared, glowing under the surface.

Tristram held his breath. His heart-beat rose.

The size of the animal watching the hapless goat was terrifying. Tristram could not make out its body yet, but the eyes seemed about the size of headlights.

It happened suddenly and was over in less than three seconds.

"*Jesus!*" Tristram breathed.

"Yeah, eh?" Ivan agreed. "I have watched it a dozen times and it still scares the shit out of me."

"That's brutal. That's so fucking quick and brutal." Tristram answered.

"Let's watch it again in slow motion." Ivan suggested.

"OK. Slow it right down, I want to pause when we can see the whole bunyip."

Ivan obeyed, and they watched the footage again.

"Stop!" Tristram barked and stopped the film just as the bunyip leaped. "Look at the time-stamp – let's go back to the one second mark. Jesus, look what has happened in the first bloody second."

Before the first second had passed the bunyip had exploded from the water's edge and covered the distance between the stream and the goat without touching the ground. It filled almost the entire screen behind the goat. Its giant eyes flashed, its ears were pinned back, and its fore-legs were held tight against its sides. Its jaws had opened to show alarming rows of long, sharp canine teeth. The goat had only turned its head half-way towards the bunyip.

"How far away from the water's edge did you tether the goat?" Tristram asked.

"About eight metres." Ivan answered.

"It covered eight metres in less than second? And look at the size of it. How much power would you need in those back legs to propel that bulk through water and then air across eight metres?"

"A fucking shit-ton. Remember that in Melvin Dubrelle's account, a bunyip kicked a full-grown horse up into the fork of a tree."

"OK, let's keep watching." Tristram clicked on the screen.

During the next second of film, the bunyip's jaws snapped brutally across the goat's neck and shoulder girdle. The bunyip's forelegs came forward at the same time as its humongous back legs. The back legs then landed, and as they did, the bunyip slid so that it was now side-on to the camera.

At the start of the third second on the counter on the screen, the bunyip's legs had taken all of the weight of the landing and were springing back up. The goat's corpse swung as it was lifted up and out of the shot, the chain and the stake it was attached to lifted out of the stones as easily as a tooth-pick is removed from an *hors d'oeuvre*. Then the great bunyip leaped out of the shot, leaving a mountain stream scene that showed no signs of the drama that had taken place.

"Well, well, Ivan. This is amazing footage." Tristram shook his head in awe.

Ivan snorted. "The understatement of the fucking century."

"Now what? What's the plan?" Tristram asked eagerly.

"Now we go up into the high country and collect the specimen." Ivan's eyes sparkled.

"Collect the specimen?" Tristram blinked. A horrible premonition sank into him.

"That goat was poisoned. The bunyip should be dead very soon if it is not already." Ivan replied without a trace of remorse.

Tristram blinked. "You poisoned the goat? *Why?*"

Ivan frowned at Tristram. "How else are we going to get our specimen?"

"You have this amazing footage – *isn't that enough?*" Tristram hissed.

"No. It is not enough." Ivan snapped. "That footage is only

three seconds long and not the greatest quality. We could be accused of faking it."

"*What*!?" Tristram scoffed. "Fuck off!"

"Look at it again. Imagine that you have never seen a bunyip – what does this look like?" Ivan persisted.

"Like no other animal on the planet!"

"Wrong. Watch again. Pause on the best glimpse of the bunyip."

Shaking his head, Tristram did as requested.

As he looked, he realised that Ivan had a point.

"Tell me that is not a grizly bear." Ivan challenged.

Tristram sighed. "A weird looking grizly bear...but you're right. We can't get a good look at its long ears as they are pinned back. The tail is never in the shot either – I thought I saw that – but it is clearly not there in the film."

"You see what you expect to see." Ivan added.

"What about the leap from the water?" Tristram countered.

"Is that water?" Ivan asked. "Or is it leaping out of the shadows of a ditch?"

Tristram sighed. "Yeah. OK. I concede your points. But surely we could have set up a better camera and done this again?"

"The fires are bearing down, Tristram. I felt it was our only chance – to be sure – to be absolutely sure of our prize – that is why I poisoned the goat. With a carcass, we can be assured of our place in history." Ivan explained. "The good news is that I attached a tracker to the goat's ear. We can go up there and start tracking it immediately."

Tristram felt ill at the thought of the bunyip struggling with poison in its system.

"How far could it have gone from where it took the goat, I wonder?" He asked, trying to master his feelings.

"Not far. The poison acts fast. It will be close to the stream somewhere in the valley, most likely – and not too far from the bridge." Ivan answered.

"When did you get this footage? Last night?"

"Yep. I was up there this morning, and I saw that the goat was gone – but so was the stake and chain. Seeing as there was no sign of what we just saw in the footage, I assumed that I had not hammered the stake in well enough and the goat just pulled it and wandered up into the hills. It wasn't until I reviewed the footage half an hour ago that I knew otherwise. I came straight here, Tristram."

Ivan made meaningful eye contact with Tristram.

"Thank you." Tristram murmured.

Ivan smiled and then suddenly hugged Tristram.

It seemed that neither man expected that to happen, so it was brief.

"We have to get going." Ivan began. "The clock is ticking. The chance that someone else will come across our bunyip is increasing every minute."

"Well, no one is looking for it – no one *knows* to look for it, so that is in our favour. Also, with the fires up in the high country it is highly doubtful that there will be much traffic up there, and what traffic there is will be focused on moving through as quickly as possible."

"True. But that's the other risk – the fire." Ivan returned, holding Tristram's eyes.

Tristram nodded. "You're right. You're right, if we wait the bushfire may destroy the bunyip."

"Exactly."

"So, we better get going." Tristram said as he stood up. However, a new thought occurred. "Although – maybe we should get up there at first light?"

"Why the delay?" Ivan asked.

"We can find it faster in daylight, for one – less chance of missing it, in case the tracker has fallen off or become damaged. It will also be safer – safer on the drive up, and safer should the bunyip be still alive and dangerous."

Ivan considered Tristram and then nodded.

"Alright. Alright, that makes sense. I realise that I need to get some equipment ready anyway, and if someone hasn't spotted the bunyip yet they are very unlikely to see it between now and early tomorrow morning."

"OK then."

"OK then. Right. Well, I will get going and pick you up just before sunrise. When is that, around six-forty am?"

"Sounds about right. Yes, it's a plan. I'll be ready. I doubt I am going to sleep. It was a shitty night for sleep before you arrived with this bomb-shell." Tristram grinned.

Ivan clapped Tristram on the shoulder.

"See you soon." He beamed, then scooped up his lap-top and left.

Tristram paced the lounge room as a thousand wild thoughts and fantasies accosted him. He was sweating, and he had a headache.

He could not shake a feeling of dread.

Suddenly he was aware of holding the little purple pouch with the pewter coin his mother had given him.

I need to put this somewhere safe.

He remembered that he had a little wooden box hidden under the bed in his cottage. In it were pennies that he and Pyran had purchased cheaply at the Flea Market on the Gold Coast, when they were about twelve years old. They had thought that they may stumble across a penny with a rare imperfection that would make them super rich. Tristram smiled at the memory. The pennies filled the box and underneath them was a round silver fifty cent piece – the most valuable coin that his younger self had.

Probably worth about five bucks max. I wonder if it is still there?

Tristram went down to the cottage and checked carefully under the bed. A memory of venomous snakes made him shudder.

He found the little wooden box, heavy with pennies.

Would the silver coin be there?

Tristram moved the copper pennies aside.

What Tristram discovered made him cry harder than he had in a long time.

When he finally stopped, he put the purple pouch safely amongst the pennies and the round silver fifty cent piece.

Sleep was going to be impossible.

Time seemed at once interminable and yet fleeting.

What can I do with the time I have left?

Finally, he decided to get his own lap-top out and set it up on the dining table. With a deep breath, he opened the Word file of his novel and began typing.

Tristram found that he was in the zone – the words flowed easily, and three hours disappeared.

He paused at one point and let his eyes gaze into the middle distance. He must have drifted into a short sleep because he had a dream of the bunyip.

It lay dead on its side upon cracked earth. A single tear glistened on its closed, sad eyes.

INTO THE FIRE

It was early morning when I pulled up into the drive through at the top of Tristram's parent's place. Though in a hurry, I took just one moment to notice the view.

The sun had risen bloody, and dimly glowed in the orange haze that oppressed the landscape. I could barely see the hills. The astringent smoke saturated everything. Holly's normally lush garden was dry, wilting and distressed. The heat lay heavy through the night, and the wind had just picked up from north. It would drive the miles and miles of intense fire-front from the high country right towards Bairnsdale.

It was going to be a nightmare of a day.

I found Tristram sitting calmly at the dining table, typing at his laptop.

He must have heard me as I came down the steps, as the dogs barked. I stood at the door and waited for him to turn around, but he continued typing.

"Are you ready?" I called pointedly.

Tristram typed a couple more sentences before he answered.

"Very, very shortly…"

"What are you doing?" I asked impatiently.

"Sending you an email." He answered, turning to look right at me.

"Ok…?" I responded, confused.

Tristram smiled at something only he seemed to know. He hit send, then stood up.

"Let's go." He sighed.

The roads were eerily quiet at first. Then, as we got past Bruthen and up into the winding roads through the bush, we began to pass a stream of vehicles heading back towards the coast. Utes, sedans, station wagons, four-wheel drives – packed with belongings and worried faces. Old couples, young families. Eyes wide with surreal dread.

"Shall we turn the CB radio on?" Tristram asked.

No. I don't want you to hear anything that might scare you into insisting we turn around.

"It doesn't work." I answered.

"Hmpf. Foreboding place names that we are passing, wouldn't you say?" Tristram grunted.

"I don't know; I am driving a bit faster than I should, so I am focused on the road."

"*Prices Downfall. Battle Point. Haunted Stream. Devils backbone.* You know there is usually a sad or tragic story behind these place names."

"I don't doubt it. Maybe you can look some of them up when we get back. Unless of course, you will be far too busy *writing about us*, and how we drove through serious bushfire danger to retrieve the zoological find of the fucking millennium!" I exclaimed.

"You are right. This should be fun. This *is* fun, Ivan." Tristram nodded, detached.

"Fun? *Fun?*"

"Yes. Isn't it?" Tristram seemed bemused.

I shook my head and laughed.

"What?" He asked.

"I don't understand you, Tristram. You should be on the edge of your seat. You should be excited. Or at least, you should be scared. You should be anything but fucking...*blasé!*" I shouted at him.

In my excitement, I was speeding, and we took a bend too quickly. We were on two wheels briefly, and then we experienced a heavy thump as the vehicle recoconnected fully with the road.

"Slow down, please." Tristram asked levelly.

"What's wrong? Where is your perspective? Has that bobble-headed girl and that blustering old failure of a professor completely destroyed you?" I demanded.

Tristram looked sad and did not answer.

"Come on, man! *Come on!* Sure, you will need time to deal with this stuff. But what a distraction this very morning should be. Think about it! We might actually die today, if we are not seriously careful."

Tristram shrugged. "That is not likely. We may have our way cut off by the bushfires, but we will head to a gully or back to the river."

I glared at him. "Worst case scenario, you and I will be trapped between fire fronts with no access to safety. Things may turn *that fast.* Are you not taking me seriously?"

"I am taking you seriously. I am sorry, Ivan. I just feel... empty, you know?"

"We are going to come back with a FUCKING BUNYIP!"

"Will we?" Tristram shook his head. "Don't count your chickens, man. We will see."

"Tristram..." I decided to try a different tack. "Don't you deserve some kind of reward for all the *shit* you have been through?"

Tristram frowned, confused. "What shit?"

I scoffed incredulously. "What shit? Seriously?"

Tristram nodded, then shrugged. "You mean my recent heart-aches, faliures and disappointments?"

"That is a pretty casual way to put it." I persisted. "You are down, my friend, and not for trivial reasons. You have been betrayed by a mentor you love, you have hit a seemingly impassable road-block to your zoology career, you have no job – in fact, you cannot even get back the job you hate because there is no vacancy at Emu Post. You are running out of money, and you have rent and bills to pay in Melbourne – which you can't afford to drive back to. You have endured two years of a very toxic relationship that took everything out of you to try and save – and in the end, Eve just blocked you out and moved on and expected you to to just be a man about it... and to just...let her go – without a fuss."

Tristram bowed his head and sighed. "What reward do I deserve for all that? It was my fault."

"What? How so?"

"I betrayed a good friend and gave up my sense of honour for a shot at true love. But what grounds did I have for thinking that it really was true love? Didn't I just rationalize away my friend's marriage? As for my stalled zoology career...I failed my Masters, because I did not have the character to properly challenge my supervisor and the University – and I did not have the drive to complete it despite the obstacles. I have no job, because I quit the job I had – at a time of year when very few companies are hiring. I have been very selfish, and very fearful...and foolish. The shit I have gone through? It is a natural result of my bad decisions, that is all."

A moment passed as I considered Tristram's response.

"No." I decided. "That just isn't fair."

"Life is not fair. In fact, let's be glad for a moment that it isn't. I don't think I deserve a reward – or for that matter, further punishment. My life so far has been very lucky. I got to do zoology, and I had a great honours project. I have had a comfortable life with all the food, clothes and so on that I need. I have great family and great friends." He turned and smiled sadly at me. "I have also had some wonderful teachers."

"Thank you. And as one of your teachers, let me give you another lesson. There is life after heart-break."

"Was there?" Tristram asked suddenly, searching my face for the answer.

"Huh?" I asked, taken aback.

"Ivan...you were in Japan for what – nearly twelve years? A huge chunk of your life – and yet in these last few weeks I have not heard you say a thing about it."

"I am not hiding anything." I rejoined. "It has never been relevant in any of our conversations."

"Did you have any important relationships in Japan?"

I blinked. Then shrugged. "Yes."

Tristram was watching me very carefully. He was waiting for me to say more. I didn't want to say anymore, and yet I if I did not say anymore it would seem that I was indeed hiding something.

"Tristram...I had a wife, in Japan."

"And a child." He said, as if he already knew about my little girl.

"Yes." I answered, before I had even registered the question.

"What happened to them?" Tristram asked gently.

I gripped the steering wheel hard and felt an intense pressure behind my eyes.

I had retorts flying through my mind.

Why do you assume something happened to them? You don't know anything about my life.

"Hiroko was killed by the Boxing Day Tsunami." I answered finally. "That was in 2004. She was with her best friend on a scuba-diving holiday in Ao Nang, Thailand. Our little girl...Keiko...died four years later. She was bitten by a habu viper near our home in Okinawa."

I waited for Tristram to say those most useless of words "I'm sorry". I feared he would try to touch me, to comfort me with some empty gesture.

Yet he said nothing. He stared at the winding road in front of us, deep in melancholy empathy.

I turned to prompt him. "So now you know."

He nodded. "Do you stay in touch with Hiroko's family?"

I frowned, confused. "Erm...no."

He nodded again, unreadable. "Your own family? Charlotte?"

I sighed and shook my head at his question.

"Ivan...who do you talk to?" Tristram asked, kind concern in his face.

I took a few seconds to think, before I answered him.

"Well, I just spoke to you."

Tears came to Tristram's eyes. He wiped them away. "Well...no matter how shit my life gets, your's seem to be even shittier."

An awkward second passed. Then an ironic smile found its way to both our faces.

The tension broke and we both laughed.

"Sorry. I don't know what I should have said, but I shouldn't have said that." Tristram grinned ruefully.

"It was the truth, mate. I expect nothing less from you." I answered fondly.

"Well, I don't know about that either, but I do try to see the truth and then tell it as honestly as I can. Hopefully, I can learn a bit of tact as well."

"Well, I have a question. A question that I have had for years..." I began.

"Yeah?"

"What was your sin against the spirit?"

"You've lost me." Tristram frowned, confused.

"The sin against the spirit – the thing symbolised by the opal in the paws of the bunyip. Do you remember that, back in high school all those years ago?"

A sudden revelation seemed to come to Tristram.

"Huh. *That*...ha!" He clapped.

"Well?"

"Oh man! It seemed so important at that time. In fact, it seemed like a death sentence. It *was* a death sentence. A final judgement. I was convinced that I was doomed and that the rest of my life was just a waste of time before the final judgement." Tristram answered, shaking his head with disbelief.

"A final judgement for what?" I persisted.

"Masturbation." Tristram beamed, and then laughed heartily.

"Masturbation? That was the big issue dominating your guilty conscience?"

"Yep. Masturbation. The most normal and trivial of teenage behaviour."

"I don't understand..."

"You shouldn't. It is very, very stupid."

"So, jerking off is your great sin against the spirit?"

"Not exactly. Sinning against the spirit is when you deliberately sin in Jehovah's presence. I was so hormonal one night, that even after praying, I masturbated, pushing Jehovah's presence to the back of mind so that I could focus on the intense experience that I was having. Then suddenly, for the first time, I ejaculated. And then the great shame washed over me."

"Surely God would forgive you for that?" I scoffed.

"Well, that is what I tried to clarify in one of my bible studies. I wanted to know if what I had done counted as sinning against the spirit."

"And?"

"As far as I could work out, I had technically committed that sin. I was very careful in how I posed the question to Peter, my Jehovah's Witness elder. Heh. I didn't just spell it out. In fact, looking back, I was impossibly vague. I just couldn't be clear about what I was asking. Poor Peter had no idea that he was confirming that I was doomed."

"That is terrible. That is just terrible that you felt that way." I answered kindly.

"And I couldn't talk about it. That made it so much worse – I just couldn't confess it to anybody. I had to keep it a secret. A disgusting, shameful secret. The righteous boy on the outside, the condemned sinner inside. A white-washed grave – clean on the surface, but rotten within. My life as the well-behaved student, the boy who would be a man of honour...a lie – but a lie known only to me."

"So how did you come to use the opal in the paws of a beast as the symbol for your predicament?" I asked.

"The opal was the most precious thing I was ever given. I lost it, stupidly, just as I lost my chance to be with God by stupidly giving in to my animal urges." Tristram shrugged.

"Wow." I sighed.

"Yeah. My younger self thought that was deep, but really I was just an ignorant wanker." Tristram replied, then laughed heartily at himself.

. . .

The drive was little over an hour. We passed Swifts Creek, and then Omeo and Benambra.

Just outside Benambra was a roadblock, with a relief station.

I slowed down, and made out to pull in and park, as if we were going to assist.

Suddenly we noticed Russell, standing in jeans and a white shirt with the Red Cross logo. He was talking to a policeman and a couple of fire-fighters.

He noticed us, then looked confused and slightly alarmed. He walked towards us.

"Wave to your father." I said.

"Huh?"

"Just wave to your dad, Tristram, as if we are supposed to be here, but we are just passing through."

We both waved before Russell go too close.

We pretended not to hear him call out after us we drove around the roadblock and away.

Tristram seemed deeply uneasy.

"What's up?" I asked him.

"That wasn't the last time I am going to see my Dad, was it, Ivan?"

"Of course, not." I scoffed. "We will be careful."

As we drove deeper along the winding mountain roads, I needed to turn my headlights on. The sky was roiling black above the forest. Bright firebrands crossed over-head like shooting stars.

We had no idea where the fire was. We could have driven straight into hell around every corner, and we would have had nowhere to go.

Finally, we descended into a winding, deeply forested valley. At the bottom was the wooden bridge that had its rails painted only a few weeks ago, by Lachlan, Pyran and Tristram.

Before we got to the bridge, we saw the great body of the bunyip on the other side of the river, in a small clearing. It was in plain sight.

"There it is!" Tristram gasped. "Oh my god!"

I stopped the car near the bridge without crossing it and did a quick three-point turn, so as to point the Landcruiser back where we came.

"You are not crossing the bridge?" Tristram asked.

"No. If the fire comes upon us quickly, the bridge may catch fire, leaving us nowhere to go. Come on, Tristram. We have no time at all to waste!"

THE MONSTER

THE BUNYIP LAY STILL in a small clearing. The song of the stony mountain stream was the only sound.

The enormous animal lay on its side, the great hump of its back to the clearing's entrance. From that angle, it really did look a gigantic kangaroo. The scale of the creature was utterly compelling, as though we had come across a beached whale. Its fur was thick and deep brown, with silver tips on some of the fur. Its head was very lion-like from behind, with a shaggy charcoal grey mayne.

We stood a moment in awe. Was it dead?

The stiffness of its enormous back legs, jutting out in an unnatural looking stretch seemed to suggest that it was indeed lifeless.

A sticky pile of loose feaces that could have filled a wheelbarrow stank nearby, like dogshit. A cloud of flies was upon it, and they were buzzing lazily about the giant corpse.

I was truly amazed. I was delighted. I greedily took in the scene and longed to run around to the other side of the animal to take in all of its magnificent bulk and gaze into its fearsome face.

Yet Tristram would not move.

His expression was one of wonder, horror, and sadness.

Blinding lightning suddenly flashed all around us.

A terrifying thunderclap boomed almost immediately after, making us jump.

Then the hot wind came, first through the canopy high above us, and then through the entire forest. It seemed that the trees had suddenly come alive to warn us of the approaching hell.

"We don't have much time, Tristram." I said, as tactfully as I could.

Tristram seemed to be in shock. "What are we doing?"

"A very quick film documentation of what we are seeing. Then we need to get the fuck out of dodge." I answered.

Tristram absently took out his phone.

"Fuck the phone camera, Tristram." I laughed. I showed him my digital video camera. "We're using this. I came prepared. Now, you're the zoologist. Quick! Take us through what we are seeing."

Tristram seemed to snap out of his reverie.

"Right." He breathed. "Let's do this."

He walked carefully to the middle of the giant creature, his eyes never leaving the back of the bunyip's head.

"This is the highest point." Tristram called, projecting his voice. "Here, at the hips. As you can see I can barely get my hand to touch the top. I am six feet tall."

"Good." I encouraged, gazing through my camera as it recorded. "Keep going. Let's get a look at that head."

"Actually, let's save that until last." Tristram countered.

He pointed to the tail.

"Alright mate. I'll follow your lead." I answered.

"The tail is thick with muscle, which suggests that it is used actively in swimming. It's more like a crocodile's tail, rather than a kangaroo's. The fur is extremely short on the tail, unlike the fur on the rest of the body, which is shaggy, like a grizly bear. OK – let's pace the length of the tail out."

Tristram paced carefully the length of the tail. When he passed the out-stretched legs, the one above the ground finished with the foot at Tristram's head height.

"You saw it – five paces, so that is roughly five metres or fifteen feet." Tristram said.

Then Tristram pointed up to the foot that hovered just above him. It had grey leathery pads and was the size of Tristram's torso. The middle toe was the largest by far, with the most intimidating claw. There was a pair of smaller toes with claws on either side

"Note the webbing between the toes. And the claws on those toes."

The claws were thick, black, and sharp. The longest one was as long as my forearm.

"There is no mistaking the kinship of this animal with kangaroos. The body shape is so much like them. The claws are well developed – thick at the base, then tapering sharply. They are not blunted. I would say they are used for defense and for fighting with rivals, rather than digging."

Tristram pointed to the animal's enormous scrotum. It could have contained two basketballs.

"This is a male." He paused to reflect on the discovery.

Suddenly the wind picked up speed and more violently shook the trees in the forest around us.

A sound like distant jet engines suddenly dominated the scene.

The sky darkened even further. The ominous boom of

explosions carried down the mountain and reverberated through the giant trees.

"Let's wrap this up." I shouted, but the thunder drowned me out.

"What?"

"I said, let's wrap this up!" I called again over the growing din.

Tristram nodded, then moved towards the forelegs.

"How remarkably human-like – the great big paws on the end of the forelimbs!" He shouted. "Don't they look like a man's hands – with long fingers – with sharp black claws!"

"The head! Move to the head, Tristram!" I urged, as a terrible climaxing of thunder pounded around us.

Burning twigs, leaves and other firebrands began to rain down upon us.

I focused the camera on the great head of the fearsome bunyip.

Tristram was silent, he seemed in awe.

I did not prompt him to speak, I simply moved in beside him, and filled the frame of my camera with the predator's face.

The head was the size of a wheelbarrow. It's long, kangaroo-like ears were tucked along behind the saggital crest that was pronounced as it is in big dogs, for the attachment of powerful jaw muscles. The neck was thickly clad with a dark, leonine mane. Black, parched leathery lips were partially curled back in a dying grimace. Frightening canines gleamed in grey gums. The great eyes were closed in miserable pain, and I reflected on the long, luxurious eyelashes.

The nose was wide, and the nostrils were facing upwards, they way they are positioned in crocodiles.

Suddenly the nostrils twitched.

Then the eye opened.

Bleary and semi-conscious, the deep chocolate eye considered us.

The whites of the eye gave it an eerily human quality.

"Ivan! It's alive! It's alive!" Tristram shouted, as we unconsciously stood back from the giant creature.

Lightning flashed, and thunder smashed the air around us.

"That is a shame. Truly, that is tragic." I said, lowering my camera to make meaningful eye-contact with Tristram. I knew what needed to be done and I knew that I was about to encounter resistance.

"What?"

"Tristram, you know what needs to happen, don't you?"

"What are you talking about?"

"Hold this." I said, handing him the camera. "I'll be back in a few seconds."

"What?" Tristram frowned confused, then understanding dawned. "Oh Ivan...what have you decided to do?"

"We are out of time, Tristram. So, I don't have time to convince you that what I am about to do is for the best. If you cannot stand to watch, that is fine."

"You are going to kill it?"

"Yes, I am. Only minutes before that bushfire does the same thing anyway. Look at it, Tristram – it's done. It cannot escape the excrutiating death by horrendous fire that will also kill us if we don't hurry the fuck up. So, I am going to give it a quick death, and I am going to take its head, its feet and its tail."

"What the *fuck*!?"

"Calm down. You're a scientist. Think about it rationally." I insisted.

Tristram considered the stricken creature before him.

"No." He decided.

"Tristram – I'm sorry, but we are not debating this."

"Oh yes we are! There is life in this animal yet. It has a

chance to crawl from here into the river, where it may yet survive. Ivan!"

I had walked away from him. It did not matter to me what he was saying.

I jogged across the clearing, then across the bridge to the Landcruiser. I opened the back and retrieved a chainsaw and my handgun, a Glock G-19.

When I turned around, I saw that Tristram was waiting for me on the other side of the bridge. He glared into me and put his hands on his hips.

I met his eyes and started the chainsaw.

"We can help it." Tristram called. "Listen! The river – look!"

The sound of rushing water from the river seemed to have grown and joined in with the terrifying roar of the approaching bush-fire.

"IVAN!" Tristram shouted. "The river is in flood! There must be a storm on the other side of the ranges. It is causing a flash flood, so there must be a lot of rain coming! It may slow the fire and allow the bunyip to recover!"

"Even if that is true – and I don't think it is – we would be surrendering the greatest fortune of our lives."

"Bullshit." Tristram holds up the camera. "We have this. It is more than enough."

He held me with an authoritive stare. I had no answer.

Tristram nodded decisively. "That's it, then. Let's put this camera in the car and then try and drag the bunyip closer to the river."

The white-hot anger over-came me.

With a sudden round-house kick I slapped the camera from his hands. It bounced off the white bridge rail and then clattered back on to the bridge timbers. I then strode over to it and jumped on it, until it was utterly destroyed.

I turned to stare him down – but he had rushed me.

I lifted the chainsaw instinctively, but he had flanked me, and placed one hand on the handle of the chainsaw, as he stood shoulder to shoulder with me. I turned to face him and walked straight into one of Aikido's training forms – Tristram had moved into a position where he could fold my wrist back on itself.

I rolled out the lock, but in so doing had to let go of the chainsaw. When I was on my feet again, I saw him toss it over the bridge rail into the rapidly rising stream.

His defiance sealed his fate. I intended to finish him.

We faced each other and began to circle on the bridge.

"Ivan, I know you can beat the shit out of me. Please don't." Tristram began.

"Not confident in your Aikido? I wouldn't be either. You got stupidly lucky with that bullshit form of *kotegaeshi*." I growled.

"I know. I am as surprised as you are. Can we call it quits, or what?"

"Sure. You just let me past so I can get the axe out of the Landcruiser." I countered.

"No deal." He replied, with a twinkle of humour.

"Have it your way."

I closed the distance between us fast and decisively. I had smashed Tristram twice in the face with my fist before he managed his first feeble block, which I knocked out of the way to strike him again.

Tristram took the hits and tried to grapple with me, but I was prepared for his feeble attempts at Aikido locks and holds this time. I didn't let him touch me.

Tristram, like most people who study martial arts, was not ready for a real fight. Real fights are dirty. Real fights are unfair. Real fights are ugly and brutal.

Blood poured from his smashed nose as I corked his arms and legs with with leisurely blows.

Finally, I swept his right leg out from under him and let him crash to timbers of the bridge.

He did not get up.

"Did we learn anything?" I asked him coldly.

I then kicked him in the floating ribs and marched to the landcruiser.

I retrieved my axe and walked back.

Tristram was on his feet again, breathing heavily and looking bloody and beaten.

"Hi." He groaned, with an ironic smile. Then he implored me with his eyes to back down.

"Tristram, if you haven't understood how determined I am to have my way by now, then you deserve to have your teeth knocked in, and your knees taken out."

Tristram looked very frightened.

I moved to pass him, and he stood in my way, holding my eyes.

"Are you fucking stupid, Jones!?" I wailed in disbelief.

"Please, Ivan. Don't hurt me anymore." Tristram pleaded.

"You are pathetic!"

"I know. But have some mercy, please. Think of Charlotte..."

"*What*!?" My eyes must have narrowed.

"Think of Hiroko...and little Keiko. They are watching you, Ivan, right now. They are behind you. Keiko has forgiven you for neglecting her and letting her get killed. She says you're not a bad father." His eyes gleamed with mock pity.

I saw nothing but whiteness for a split second. I raised the axe back, to give it the mightiest swing I could, and with the intention of splitting his skull, I struck.

However, Tristram was ready. He was committed to his

response, and he moved with arc of the swing and guided it past him, then he span under it to put me in an over-shoulder arm-lock. He had then disarmed me of the axe. Rather than attempt a hold-down, he shoved me away so that I fell backward.

He threw the axe into the raging stream. Then he looked down at me, determined, strong and powerful.

However, I wasn't anywhere near beaten yet.

His face showed fear and disappointment when I stood up again.

"I know what you did." I snarled through clenched teeth. "Well done, you clever bastard."

"What did I do?"

"You deliberately made me angry. You knew that I would be slower if I was angry. Well, I am still angry. And I have not finished fighting yet."

I moved in and he charged in to meet me.

He tried to box and failed hopelessly. My reflexes and training were far superior, and he landed not one punch. However, that was not his intention. He took three of my hits deliberately so that he could land just one Muay Thai style front kick.

His strategy worked, and he lifted me off the bridge with the force.

Unfortunately, for him, I came back and just pummelled him. He tried to kick again, but that put him off balance and I swept his leg and slammed him mercilessly down to the bridge.

He rolled away as I tried to stomp on him.

Before he could get back on his feet, I got down on the ground beside him and punched him hard in the face. He tried to cover his face with his hands, but I kept slapping them down and hitting him.

Finally, his head lolled, and I thought I had knocked him out.

Breathing heavily, I stood up and back from him.

Rain began to fall.

It was thick and heavy all of a sudden.

With surreal detachment, I noticed that the raging torrent of muddy frothy water was now almost level with the bottom of the bridge.

"Can we go home now?" Tristram croaked.

I snorted in disbelief. "You are conscious after-all?"

"Barely." Tristram grimaced, he sat up and frowned at the change in the river.

"Well, you can take a few hits, Jones, I will give you that much." I sighed. "But you can't fight for shit."

Tristram nodded. "I have learned that much."

Then, groaning with pain and trembling, he got to his feet.

"If you don't sit back down, I swear to god I am going to break your legs." I warned him.

I was not over the fight. Not by a long shot.

"Ivan, it's over. I know I can't beat you in a fight, but that's not what is going on here."

"What the fuck are you talking about?" I hissed.

Then I saw it. Or rather, I did not see it. The bunyip was no longer in the clearing – which was now flooded.

"It began to try and find its feet when you went to get the axe." Tristram explained. "I wasn't trying to beat you. I was trying to stall you."

In utter rage I strode to the rails beside Tristram and looked frantically for signs of where the bunyip went. However, there was no trace of it anywhere.

I pulled out my Glock and searched the banks of the stream for a target. I could see nothing.

"The rain is a God-send, but that fire is apocalyptic, Ivan."

Tristram implored as he moved behind me to lean on the opposite rails. "It may be slowed down, but it is probably still coming toward us."

As if to underline his point, lightning blinded us, and thunder boomed, shaking the bridge.

We turned to look up the opposite hill and saw the first red fire-balls igniting the canopy at the top of the ridge.

With surreal slowness, I turned to face Tristram, and I pointed the Glock straight at him.

The rain fell heavier, and the sky grew pitch black. I could barely make out his silhouette against the frothing river behind him.

Ours eyes were locked.

Tristram's eyes were pleading again.

I narrowed my eyes and stared right into him, just as cold as I have ever been.

He sank back against the rail, as if to cower before the bullet struck.

Then suddenly he leaped over the side into the flash flood.

I rushed across to the rail that he had just cleared.

Tristram was taken away in seconds. He could barely keep his head above water, then he went under, then he was up again. Then he was swept around a bend and out of my sight.

I stood for seconds...minutes...blinking in disbelief as the lightning flashed, the rain fell, and the water boomed below, shaking the bridge.

Suddenly I felt out of breath. My head pounded. My neck felt constricted.

I put the barrel of the Glock in my mouth. I so very nearly pulled the trigger.

Then I braced and pointed the gun at the spot where Tristram had disappeared and fired.

I let off all fifteen rounds.

Then I screamed and screamed.

I kicked the rails, then smashed down on them with my fists, trying to splinter the wood.

All I accomplished was pain and bloody hands.

Then I was silent, letting the rain drench me and the rumbling bushfire that was now probably no more than five hundred metres away rumble and crash and sizzle as it met the downpour.

It was as dark as night. Only the white froth of the flood hurtling under the bridge provided any relief from the blackness.

Suddenly, an eerie chill lay upon me. I got goosebumps.

I was being watched.

Worse.

I was being stalked.

Very, very slowly, I turned towards the great shadowy presence that was blocking the bridge back to my Landcruiser.

I stood horrified.

The enormous bunyip had managed to creep half-way along the bridge without my sensing a *thing*.

It took up more space than my Landcruiser would have, its hips were almost touching the white bridge rail on each side.

With the fire rapidly rolling down the hill towards us, and the roiling stream underneath us, there was no escape.

The bunyip was in the pounce position, with its large rabbit-like ears up and tracking me.

It was a deep black shadow in a world of shadows, but I could make out the whites of its eyes. Those huge, predatory eyes with an intense focus right on me.

Slowly, I braced myself and aimed my gun between its eyes.

The bunyip did not move. We stared each other down.

Suddenly, it walked forward, like a giant kangaroo.

I pulled the trigger.

An empty click was the response.

Click. Click. Click.

Of course. I had fired them all after Tristram.

A new, cold dread washed through me.

Then the fire was suddenly close enough to throw a hellish red light upon the scene.

The viscous tapetum lucidum of the bunyip's eyes glowed, reflecting the approaching flames.

It moved two more steps carefully towards me, so that it was only six feet away.

Then it stood up. It towered above me, a snarl upon its giant maw.

Its great eyes blazed with hell-fire.

Then the wind came with renewed force.

It blasted down from the road behind the bunyip.

It was a wind thick with cold rain. The chill that hammered into my front contrasted with the baking heat I could feel intensifying behind me.

Then suddenly, the monster wretched.

It bent forward with a wince of pain.

It vomited the remains of my poisoned bait. A stinking pile of goat fur, flesh and bones now lay at my feet.

Then, the bunyip gave me one last look.

Sad disgust.

Its enormous back legs tensed and suddenly it turned and sprang away in an astonishing leap that ended on the other side of the bridge.

A second leap took it a further twenty metres away, crashing through the scrub beside the thundering muddy river.

Its third leap took it totally out of my sight, but I felt the ground shake from its landing.

I ran to my Lancruiser, jumped in and sped away from the

approaching bushfire that was towering in the forest behind me.

My windscreen wipers were at full-speed, my headlights were on, and yet I could barely see through the drenching rain.

In what seemed no time at all, I was sitting with surreal horror in the bungalow of my Aunty's house in Bairnsdale. I didn't know what to do with myself, so I absently checked my email.

There was the message from Tristram, sent only that morning.

It was his unfinished novel.

I cried and cried.

Then I started writing.

FINDING TRISTRAM

RUSSELL HAD SEEN Ivan's landcrusier rush past the firetrucks. Russell had seen only Ivan, looking shocked and grief-stricken.

Tristram was not in that vehicle. Why did Ivan look so upset? Where was Tristram?

A cold, horrible premonition formed in the pit of his stomach.

"Russ, good news, mate. Just heard from Darryl, all this heavy rain has put a massive suppression on the fires. Obviously, it is too early to tell if we are safe, but it is pretty bloody encouraging, eh?"

Russell nodded absently to the fireman.

He then grabbed his mobile phone from his pocket and searched frantically for Ivan's number. It was not in his address book.

Russell then tried to phone Holly, but there was no reception.

Russell's heart had begun to beat very fast, and his breathing was shallow. He started to feel dizzy and panicked.

A fury suddenly found him, and he jogged over to his jeep.

"Russ, where are ya goin'?" Called the fireman.

Russell was determined to catch up to Ivan and beat an explanation out of him.

Yet, only a few metres along the road, Russell had a change of mind.

Tristram is not with Ivan. Tristram is still out there.

Fear, anger and panic duelled within him. Then Russell caught sight of his reflection in the rear-view mirror. It took a second to recognise that those terrified blue eyes were his own.

You need to think rationally. Rationally.

Russell took a deep, long breath.

I know where they probably went. I know where to start looking.

Russell drove just as fast as he could. He took many corners far too wide, but he reasoned that on-coming traffic was very unlikely. He hurtled along deeply forested roads, and then finally along an old gravel road that he had not driven on for years.

He reached the campsite, where they had all camped all those years ago. Where Stewy took the kids fishing, and they had barbequed and laughed and talked around the fire. The hill Russell had climbed in the night and howled with grief at the passing of his father.

Russell barely recognised the place now – rotting timber picnic tables, rusted bins, weeds and blackberry bushes sprawled about the clearing.

The river was still there.

It was a clear, shallow, stony mountain stream back then.

But now a muddy, frothing, torrent raged in its place. The thunderous noise rose up, as black flakes of ash rained down. The clouds above ached with a bruised light.

Russell strode to the stream's edge, scanning for the track that used to run along it.

Is it still here? Is it under water?

Then Russell heard a familiar voice in his head. It was right inside his ear. It startled him.

This way, Russell.

With a chill, Russell recognised his dead mother's voice. His heart pounded frantically as the hair raised on his arms, and the back of his neck.

Then he saw the narrow dirt track beside the rushing stream. It was in plain sight now, but only a moment ago he could not see it.

Russell followed the goat track towards the shallow cave that he knew must appear soon. As he trudged, the river seemed to slow down. The flashflood was subsiding.

As he walked, his dread grew in him.

Had he really heard his mother's voice? Or was he hallucinating?

Her voice was cold. It was matter-of-fact. It was very sad.

Russell shook his head and began to jog.

Finally, the path rose a little between two big old eucalyptus trees. He knew that once he passed those trees, he would see the cave. He would find Tristram.

Suddenly his father's voice was in his ear.

Slow down, Russell.

Russell stopped in his tracks.

"Dad?" He whispered.

Pressure had built behind Russell's eyes. His throat felt

constricted, his chest hurt. Russell had been moving quickly without breathing properly, and he was now suffering.

He was suddenly weak and shaking. He fell to his knees.

*Breathe...*he told himself.

Russell concentrated on breathing.

Moments passed, and the stream rushed on, seeming to lose volume.

A sudden memory of Tristram as a little boy floated into Russell's mind.

One night, when they were camping at Coffs Harbour in Northern New South Wales, Russell had found a very large green tree frog hopping in the damp grass at the edge of the caravan park. He had caught it gently and cupped it carefully in his hands. He then decided to go back to their family tent to wake the kids up to show them. Tristram, barely five years old, and very sleepy, blinked in the torch light. The frog suddenly leaped from Russell's hand and landed on Tristram's face.

He had expected Tristram to scream with fright, but that is not what happened.

Tristram had smiled with deep delight.

The light changed in the forest around Russell.

The clouds parted, and a shaft of light fell beyond the gum trees just ahead of him.

Russell found his resolution. He stood up slowly, exhaled, clenched his fists and then moved on.

When he passed the two gum trees, he saw the cave. A waterfall ran over its entrance. The darkness of its entrance contrasted with the light that gleamed in the waterfall.

Then he saw the body. Lying in the fetal postion beside the stream. It was covered in mud, sticks and leaves.

He had found Tristram.

DEATH AND JUDGEMENT

DEAFENING THUNDEROUS WATERS.
    Terrifying speed.
    Swept along in foam.
    Sharp, explosive bursts of pain.
    River rocks and stones pummel the body.
    Above the water, the roar of wind, fire and flood.
    Below the surface, clinking of thousands of river rocks.
    You must lie straight, feet forward.
    The sides of the gorge soar up high.
    Lightning flashes.
    The trees cling to the sides of the mountain.
    The roiling stream powers along through the gorge.
    There is nothing to swim to.
    Only rapids to survive...somehow.
    Keep your head up.

Tristram is propelled across rapids.
    He is swept around bends into falls and then more rapids.

Into the white foam, his feet slam into boulders, then his backside is bruised as he is carried along.

Protect your head.

Tristram has his hands behind his head, his elboes pointed up.

He is through a set, now rushing down a straight, deeper section of river.

Relief, relief from the pounding stones. They clink and rumble *en masse* in the depths below him.

Tristram looks up as he is swept along.

The sky is deep black and scarred with swirling, bright firebrands like shooting stars.

Tristram is hurled against a massive boulder.

He is now under raging water, with rocks smashing into him.

Each impact sends sharp, bright pain through him.

He cannot breathe.

He cannot see.

Get up. Stand up. Or you will die.

Tristram pulls himself up the boulder's face.

He reaches the top, then the waters sweep him over it and away.

Fire and water rage.

Piercing explosions on both sides of the gorge above him.

With deep horror Tristram watches an enormous old gum tree burst into flame and then through some astonishing force become uprooted.

It crashes down the mountain, rolling heavy, fast unstoppable.

The river pushes Tristram to meet the giant, flaming tree.

It pounds into the river only metres in front of him

It explodes upon the water.

Violent steam.

Searing radiant heat.

Tristram ducks under the water as he is swept through its canopy.

He closes his eyes and covers his face.

A thousand scratches and cuts.

Then down.

Down.

Desperate, Tristram reaches for a branch, or a rock or anything.

He catches a branch – or does it catch him?

The roiling river squeezes his torso against the straining branch.

He cannot breathe.

Rocks are pounding his rump and legs.

Under or over the branch – you can't stay here.

Tristram looks ahead.

A fall into blackness only feet away.

Tristram manages to get over the branch and hang onto it.

The river strives to peel his grip away.

I can't hang on!

I can't let go!

A sudden moment of clarity comes to Tristram.

Surreal wonder, as the water thunders around him and the bright red hell booms and crashes above.

This is it.

Take a moment. Your last moment.

An actor, flawed in life, can perfect a moment on the stage.

What will I do?

Jehovah God, help me, please.

God will not help you. He does not exist.

You had your life. Now complete your last moment.

I don't want to die. I don't want to die.

Tristram sobs as his arms tire and burn intensely.

It doesn't matter what you want.

What is left to do but have courage? Man up!

Seriously?

Fine!

Courage? To do what? Let go?

The courage to be ordinary.

You were ordinary.

I was ordinary.

An actor, flawed in life, can perfect a moment on the stage.

All I have are fleeting seconds to try to understand before the blackness of forever.

No audience here but me.

Sea-blue sad eyes of Chris Saintly. A friend betrayed.

I hurt a dear friend so very badly.

Tristram loosens his grip.

I failed the test.

I deserve this. I deserve this.

Tristram lets go.

Tristram falls.

A violent crack of the head against rock.

Blackness.

Pain. Darkness. Crushing weight of wet earth and debris.

The demon with horns leers.

I am in hell.

How can I be in hell?

Worms creeping through my hair.

Not my eyes, please!

I am rotting. I am conscious as I rot.
The demon is a cow...
Sharp pain.
Water is rushing by.
Can I move?

Tristram gasps as electic ribbons of pain lash his body.
Heavy weight of mud and sticks and stones.
The demon...is a dead cow. A cow caught in the flood that
took them here.
Where is here?
A cave.
The pounding sound of water somewhere above.
Tristram climbs the pile of debris towards a dim light.
Every move, sharp pain.
Gasping. Groaning.
Tristram is at the top of the mound.
The light of day behind the curtain of water.
Unsteady slide to a debris covered cave floor.
Covered in pungent mud.
Scratched and cut and slashed and bruised.
I must get up.
Tristram stands.
He walks.
Each step seems to tear muscle.
Get on the other side of the waterfall.
Tristram carefully wades through water that is calf deep.
He reaches a hand to touch the waterfall.
It is steady but not too powerful to walk through.
He steps into the waterfall.
Cold!
Clean...

Tristram steps through and then blinks at the brightness.

Afternoon sunlight bathes the temperate gorge. It gleams in the wet limestone, and glows in the vibrant green tree ferns, vines, and trees.

In front the water deepens, but he can see that there is a bank of debris-covered river-rocks only a short swim away.

He sits down and gently floats.

The current takes him slowly across the pool.

Tristram reaches the shallow end. He groans as he crawls out of the stream to sit on a sun-warmed patch of river sand.

Headache.

Everything hurts.

What will I do? Where can I go?

Tristram sobs.

Then he sees it.

He is being watched.

The bunyip is perched on a limestone ledge, about twenty feet above the far bank of the stream.

The intense focus of the predator.

It is enormous. Powerful. Angry.

A fearful rumbling growl echoes among the rocks and trees.

Tristram gets to his knees.

He looks up just in time to see the monster jump...

It crosses half the distance between them and lands with a smooth dive into the centre of the pool.

Tristram senses it travelling the distance to him underwater.

He gets to his feet and runs.

Only a few metres away, he stumbles and falls.

He hears the monster surface behind him and leap from the water.

He turns to see it kangaroo-walking rapidly towards him.

It opens its fearful jaws and roars.

Bone crushing teeth snap.

It charges.

I am going to to die.

A memory flashes.

A little boy cries out in the seconds before the strike.

The name of God.

"JEHOVAH!"

The monster is still charging.

Peter's voice.

"You cannot call upon Him this time."

What can I do?

Good-bye, sorrowful one.

Ivan's voice.

"Your name is like a battle-cry."

A savage indignation explodes within Tristram.

I will not be CONSUMED!

Tristram stands, throws his shoulders back, his chest and jaw forward in defiance. He glares into the face of the charging bunyip.

Your name is like a battle-cry.

The Bunyip has closed the gap and stands up.

Its ears are pinned back, its mouth gaping wide for the attack.

Tristram roars, with all the life and outrage in him.

"TRISTRAM!"

The bunyip pauses.

Its mouth closes.

Its great dark eyes narrow in thought.

"TRISTRAM!"

Tristram thumps his chest once in defiance.

He glares into the eyes of the monster.

The bunyip lowers its forearms to its sides.

It sniffs the air between them.

Breathing rapidly, Tristram stands his ground.

With wonder, he realises that the bunyip is considering his scent.

Then the bunyip slowly extends its right forearm.

It extends the claw on the equivalent of its index finger.

It motions taking a tear from its eye and then holds it high above Tristram.

Tristram gasps.

He tells the bunyip with his eyes.

I remember!

Then the bunyip extends its left front paw. It is closed. It is holding something.

Impossible... Tristram shakes his head in disbelief.

Emotion overwhelms him.

The beast opens its paw.

In its palm glitters a brightly coloured opal.

Tristram falls to his knees.

His eyes fill with tears.

The buyip holds the opal out for Tristram to take.

Tristram cannot move.

I can't take it back.

The bunyip holds its palm above Tristram's head. It slowly turns it.

The opal drops from the bunyip's paw.

Sunlight flashes in it as it falls.

It touches Tristram's palm and he closes his hand around it.

Tristram bellows.

All of his life's loves, sorrows, fears and wonders surge through him. An explosion of intense sensual memories – years of life experience felt in an instant.

He slumps into the fetal postion, helpless.

I must be dying.

"When the brain perceives that death is imminent, there is a surge of neural activity. This is perceived as one's life flashing before one's eyes."

Four years old, drowning in the river.

Dad pulled me out of the water.

"It is the brain's way of frantically searching through memories for a similar experience, and therefore a solution, to the current threat of death."

Dad is not here now.

Tristram looks up and sees the bunyip is gone.

The storm of memories and feelings eases.

His energy is failing. He is cold. Sound is fading. His vision is growing dim.

Tristram sees something that proves to him that he will soon be dead.

Across the stream, watching him, stand Toby and Joan Jones.

He sees pity in their faces.

Tristram hears his father's voice.

"TRISTRAM! TRISTRAM!"

Good-bye, Dad. I'm sorry...

Russell gently and urgently slapped Tristram's face.

"Tristram! It's me. It's Dad. You're not dead! Do you hear me? You are NOT DEAD!"

"I'm sorry, Dad." Tristram murmured.

"Oh thank God! Thank God! Thank God!"

Tristram was suddenly aware that Russell was crying.

Tristram felt a sharp pain jolt through his body.

"Fuck!" He winced.

Russell had sat him up.

"I'm sorry, I'm sorry!" Russell soothed. "Where does it hurt?"

The pain was dying down.

Tristram looked again across the river.

Toby and Joan were smiling. Toby had his arm around his wife, and they were looking at Russell and Tristram with pride.

"Dad...?" Tristram croaked. "Do you see them?"

"See who?" Russell answered.

Toby continued to smile, his blue eyes sparkling. Then he spoke. The familiar voice from Tristram's early childhood carried over the rushing stream.

"I love you, boys."

TEARS

THERE WAS a community memorial at Howitt Park two days after the flooding in the high country. The skies were grey with water now, instead of smoke and ash. A refreshing wind curled around the small, steep hill of the park. The Mitchell river ran brown and full through the valley that had started to green.

The park from some angles seemed an island, as the main bridge from Bairnsdale crossed the river to the south of it, and to the west a foot-bridge crossed the back-water just before it joined the main river. Its famous long slide took advantage of the steep hill and the low continuation of the valley at its foot was flat and grassy – perfect for Sunday markets.

Today no children played on the slide. No market activity took place.

A couple of hundred people had gathered about a small group of white canvas marquees. They were dressed mostly in black.

Uniformed firefighters, police, forestry and State Emergency Service workers wandered purposefully about the scene.

Dinewan watched from the shadows of the nearby main bridge.

So far that morning, he had not seen anybody that he recognised.

Suddenly, he let out a long and impatient sigh.

I will learn nothing from here.

Dinewan quietly strutted and hobbled his way through the crowd, his trench coat pulled close about him, and his green floppy hat hiding his orange eyes.

His nostrils twitched at the savoury smell of sausages and onions frying.

He listened...

"The house was gone. Nothing left – we lost everything."

"The kids found the dogs. They will never get over it. They will never get over it."

"Borrowed a mate's tractor yesterday, and the neighbour's Bobcat survived the fires. He was lucky, the fires swerved just before they got to his place. Anyway, I sent the wife and kids back up to my folk's place in Traralgon. They don't need to see me burying their horse, and the pigs and what's left of the chooks."

"We lost everything. We lived there thirty-eight years, raised our family there. There was no time to take anything, and now its all gone. There is literally nothing left."

"We have no savings. This has broken us. We are homeless."

"The cows were screaming all morning. We had about forty head or so just lying in the soot, no legs. Eyes rollin', mouths frothing. We shot them one after the other, and it was just hell. It was just hell."

The witch doctor watched the expressions of all of the ordinary people, expressing grief, loss, and horror. He was determined not to be moved by them. However, their unaffected humanity – their empathy, their humour and their courage, cracked the shallow *schaden fraude* he was expecting to relish.

Suddenly, his reflection was interrupted as a policeman offered him a warm cup of coffee or tea.

"Thank you, no." Dinewan mumbled.

"Did you or your family lose anything in the fires, or...?" The young officer asked, kind sympathy in his blue eyes.

"Nah, we were lucky. I am just here to...observe."

"Observe?"

"Pay my respects. You know what I mean?" Dinewan bowed his head.

"Fair enough. Good on you, mate. I reckon if we kept the regime of bushfires that the Gunai/Kurnai people used, there would have been a lot less fuel out there and the fires would not have been as intense, eh?"

"That's possible. I guess we all act...according to our lights." Dinewan suddenly frowned, as if he was having an epiphany.

"That's the truth, eh? Well, good luck to you." The officer grinned politely.

"You too." Dinewan answered, absently.

Then he heard a child trying to comfort his mother.

"Mummy don't cry. It's going to be alright." The boy was fair-haired, blue-eyed and probably only four or five years old.

The young woman smiled at her son and wiped her eyes.

"You're right, you're right. It's going to be alright."

Dinewan watched her face as she hugged her little boy. He saw the truth. She was grieving and afraid of the future.

"I'm so sorry." The witch doctor murmured sincerely.

"Not as sorry as you're going to be." A dark, cold voice answered right beside his ear.

Startled, Dinewan turned to see the pale, frightening face of Ivan MacAllister.

"You." Dinewan breathed incredulously.

"Let's take a walk, arse-hole." Ivan commanded.

Dinewan felt a blade point on his solar plexus.

"Where are we going, Ivan MacAllister?" Dinewan sighed, sadly.

Ivan pointed to his Landcruiser, parked nearby.

They drove in a weary, cold silence.

The rain fell lightly on the windscreen.

Ivan's windscreen wipers were not going. Whether they were broken, or Ivan was not aware that they were needed was unclear to the witch doctor.

Ivan was unshaven and smelly. His eyes were red, and they stared out from deep, dark circles. His clothes reeked of old sweat and astringent fire-smoke.

They finally pulled up in a residential street close to the centre of town.

"Out you get." Ivan growled.

Dinewan was then guided with the threat of a knife up a cracked concrete driveway, past an old pale blue weather-board house.

The beige, fibre-glass panelled bungalow at the end of the driveway was an ominous shambles.

Inside was an old bar stool standing in the middle of clear plastic sheeting. All the furniture that would normally have occupied the space – a single bed, a desk and two chairs – was piled up in one corner and covered in plastic sheeting.

"Take a seat." Ivan drawled.

Dinewan crossed the plastic sheeting and sat on the stool. He faced Ivan, his hands clasped casually on his lap.

"It's not a question of if I am going to kill you." Ivan began. "It's a question of how."

Dinewan raised his eyebrows sardonically, then shook his head.

"You don't believe it?" Ivan asked. His voice was level, clear and cold.

Dinewan sighed. "No, I believe it."

"Is there anything you want to say?"

"Nope."

"Do you want a choice in how I kill you? Knife? Gun? Shall I just choke you to death?"

Dinewan snorted, then stared right at Ivan. "Do you have a spear?"

"A spear?" Ivan smiled awfully. "I am so sorry, I don't think I have one handy."

"Over there." Dinewan answered, nodding towards a wooden broom across the room. "Use your knife to cut a spear point out of that broom handle."

Ivan considered the witch doctor and then grunted. "Resourceful, aren't you? Very well, as you wish. It won't take long to make."

Ivan went for the broom, then came back to stand a few feet from Dinewan. He placed his foot on the broom head and then unscrewed the wooden handle from it. Then he kicked the broom head aside.

"Remember to cut away from yourself." Dinewan drawled.

"Right." Ivan nodded with a grin. "Wouldn't want to hurt myself."

"Safety is important." Dinewan grinned back.

They both shook their heads as Ivan began to carve a point into the boom handle.

"Tristram is dead?" The witch doctor asked casually. He was surprised at how his heart beat at the thought.

"Yes, yes of course he is dead." Ivan answered, without looking up from his carving. "You must have heard the news on the radio or seen it on television."

"No, I had not." Dinewan answered. "How did he die?"

Ivan looked up and saw Dinewan's bright orange gaze piercing him.

"He drowned."

"*Drowned?*"

"That's right. He drowned. Right in the middle of an apocalyptic fire."

"You were there?"

"Yes. Well, no. I did not see him die. I saw him jump into a river that was in flash-flood. I saw the river sweep him away, around a corner." Ivan continued to carve.

"So, he is dead. Drowned. They found his body?"

"Yes. Covered in mud and sticks and stones. He was very badly bruised, I am sure. Imagine being in a giant washing machine with thousands of river rocks, spinning at horrible, horrible speed. It's a wonder the corpse was identifiable."

"I didn't think he would die. Not really." Dinewan mused, sadly.

Ivan looked at him sharply. "Well, you can't predict everything, can you?"

"Was it worth it?" Dinewan asked, simply.

"Was what worth it?" Ivan snapped.

"The whole adventure. All of this longing, all of this planning, all of these wild dreams..."

"You tell me, arse-hole. What did you expect from all of this?"

"Something meaningful." Dinewan shrugged.

"Well, you're going to die shortly. Does that provide some meaning?" Ivan returned, and continued to carve. The spear point was quite developed, yet Ivan continued to work on it.

"I don't know. I suppose I am about to find out."

"Yup."

"Did you see the bunyip? Was it dead?"

Ivan stopped carving and threw the knife to the floor.

They held each other's gaze.

"Time's up." Ivan said.

Dinewan answered, his voice barely above a whisper. "*I'm ready.*"

Ivan began to breathe heavily and rapidly. He braced the spear in front of him. Then he spoke.

"The bunyip was dying when we saw it, but it was not dead. I was going to kill it. Tristram stopped me. He fought me. I beat him, and I beat him hard. But he won. The bunyip escaped as we fought." Ivan announced.

A beat of silence passed.

"Did you throw Tristram into the river?" Dinewan asked.

"No. He jumped, because he thought I was going to shoot him."

"*Were* you going to shoot him?"

Ivan blinked. "Yes."

"I see."

"No."

"No?"

"I don't know. I have thought about that for the last...days...nights...all, all the time. All of time since..."

"I see. You may or may not have shot Tristram, but because of you, he is dead in either case." Dinewan concluded with pity.

"Yes." Ivan breathed. "Yes."

"And you have worked out how to answer the question. The question of whether or not you were going to shoot Tristram." Dinewan leaned forward, his eyes spearing into Ivan.

"Have I?"

"If you can plunge that spear into my heart, then you could have shot Tristram."

Ivan blinked. Then he glared coldly into the face of the witch doctor.

"You're right. I think that would answer the question."

"Do what you're going to do then, Ivan MacAllister." Dinewan sneered.

Ivan's eyes narrowed, his body tensed.

Dinewan sat up straight on the stool and took a deep breath...

Then suddenly a new voice cut across the scene.

"Well, this is a bit melodramatic."

They turned and there was Tristram, standing in the doorway.

Ivan dropped the spear.

Dinewan exhaled sharply.

"You're not seeing a ghost." Tristram continued. "And you are right on with the giant washing machine analogy. That flooded river pounded me with rocks, and I am in fact bruised all over."

Tear sprang from Ivan's eyes, yet he was not sobbing. He stood and stared.

"Tristram Jones..." Dinewan breathed with wonder.

"They found your body..." Ivan murmured in disbelief. "I heard it on the radio, they found your body. There is a memorial service for you down at Howitt Park – we just came from there..."

Tristram shook his head. "It wasn't me. Obviously. That was a young forestry officer. They attempted a river crossing to escape the fires, and the flash flood caught them unawares. It is very sad. They were well known in the community."

"But...how did you get out of there?" Ivan asked.

"My Dad saw you drive past looking shocked and distraught. Then he drove to the campsite with the cave, and the pool and the waterfall. And by sheer good luck, that is where the flash flood washed me down to."

Ivan gasped. "Unbelievable. I am so happy that you made it. I am so sorry...for everything – I don't know where to start..."

"I am not here to confront you, Ivan." Tristram sighed.

"Tristram..." Ivan croaked. "I was going to finish it for you."

"Finish what?" Tristram asked, holding Ivan with stern eyes.

"Your book." Ivan grinned sadly, then wiped away his tears. "You sent me your book before we went up into the high country, remember?"

Tristram exhaled then smiled. "Holy shit. Yes, I did."

"As soon as I got here, I thought of your email. I don't know why. You said it would make sense later, and it just came to me. It was your unfinished novel. And so, not wanting to think about anything else, I threw myself into the task of trying to finish it."

"Right. Well, I will finish it, Ivan." Tristram returned. "And what happens here will be the end of it, I think."

"Are the police with you?" Ivan asked, looking at the floor.

"No." Tristram answered. "No one is going to come around

asking questions, although my Dad has very mixed feelings about you."

"I don't blame him."

"I told him that you were helpless to save me after I 'fell' into the river, and that you were driving for help and probably went into shock." Tristram explained.

"Why didn't you tell him the truth?" Ivan asked, humbly.

"I wanted to talk to you first. Anyway, Dad took me to the hospital, and through some miraculous luck, I have no broken bones – just a metric shit-ton of bruises. I was given some painkillers and then I went into a deep sleep. When I woke up, an hour ago, I came looking for you. I expected to find you here, and I was going to get your help to find Dinewan."

Ivan looked up, blinked, and then pointed at Dinewan.

"He's right there."

The three of them laughed and the tension eased.

"Thank you for that." Tristram grinned. "Now, Dinewan, I have something for you."

Tristram approached Dinewan slowly, a closed hand outstretched.

Dinewan noticed the yellow and purple bruises on Tristram's swollen hands. Sympathy flashed ever so briefly across the witch doctor's face.

"Dinewan." Tristram began. "I could not kill the bunyip. And so, you will not be able to extract your monster's tears. But I think you know that tears extracted in that way would not work for you anyway. Tears of a monster to heal the broken man. Surely, these must shed voluntarily?"

Dinewan exhaled slowly and then nodded.

"White people murdered your people and stole everything that they had. I continue to benefit from that atrocity just by being white. Meanwhile, you and others still suffer just for being black. That is not fair. And I can't fix it." Tristram spoke kindly and firmly.

Dinewan nodded and sighed. "No. You can't fix it."

The two men considered each other with mild surprise.

"Something you said has been echoing in my mind." Tristram continued. "You said: an actor, flawed in life, can perfect a moment on the stage. You are playing one part, and you have been asking me to play another. And I have been refusing to play it, because I don't think identity politics serves the greater good. And yet...as an individual – I can – for the purpose of our personal version of the drama writ large – voluntarily take on the role of the guilty white man."

Dinewan tilted his head. "Why would you do that?"

"I am not sure, to be very honest with you. But as you and Terry were saying, sometimes we act things out in order to try and understand."

"What have you to say for yourself then? Spokesperson for the invaders." Dinewan drawled, his orange eyes gleaming.

"I say that I am sorry. I say that I care. A great wrong has been done that cannot be undone. Justice, true justice, is impossible now."

"If you cannot fulfil the requirements of justice, then what else is there?" Dinewan returned coldly.

Ivan answered quietly. "Revenge. Small, petty, but that is all your people can hope for."

"Yes, revenge is one understandable response." Tristram replied. "There is another."

"Yes?" Dinewan stared.

"Your people can forgive my people." Tristram said simply.

"How can we forgive so much?" Dinewan's eyes narrowed.

"I don't know. I cannot tell you how to forgive. My part in this, is to say that I am truly sorrow and that I want to share the future with you."

"Words? All you have are words?" Dinewan blinked sadly.

"No. We also have symbols. I offer you this…"

Tristram held out his hand.

In his palm, the opal glittered brightly.

Dinewan's eyes widened in astonishment.

"Is that…?" He began.

"You tell me. Is it a magic opal, witch doctor?" Tristram asked, as he handed the opal to Dinewan.

Dinewan's eyes teared up as looked at the jewel.

"It is so very beautiful."

"It is a symbol." Tristram explained. "It does have some financial value, probably two or three thousand dollars. I am not sure. But the value for me is far greater. It was given to me a long time ago by Granddad Toby. He gave it to me and told me a fantastic story about it, to try and comfort me because I was so sad and terrified of him dying. I lost this opal only a few days later, and I have felt hollow ever since. Only recently did I find it again – and already I am giving it away to you, because I truly want a meaningful gesture of reconciliation between us."

Dinewan's lips trembled. His bright orange eyes considered Tristram intently.

"A symbol? A good one, Tristram. A tear of a monster after-all."

"The tear of a monster to heal the broken man?" Tristram grinned, trying to master his feelings. A tear formed on his left eye.

Moved, Dinewan stepped to Tristram and held out a hand for Tristram to shake.

As Tristram reached for it, Dinewan placed the opal back into Tristram's hand. Very briefly, he held Tristram's hand in both of his.

He then lifted a hand, extended his index finger, and tenderly lifted the tear from Tristram's face.

"I prefer this tear." Dinewan murmured.

They made meaningful eye contact, and then Dinewan turned away and shuffled towards the door.

As Ivan and Tristram watched, Dinewan's walk changed. He no longer strutted on every second step but stood tall and walked. In only a few steps he reached the door, so that neither Ivan nor Tristram could be sure that they had just seen a change in his walk.

Dinewan turned one last time to face them. His eyes were no longer orange, but deep brown.

"I was not the first Dinewan." He announced.

"How many have there been?" Tristram asked with a warm smile.

Dinewan's eyes sparkled, and he smiled back. "Good-bye, Ivan MacAllister."

"Good-bye, Dinewan." Ivan nodded respectfully.

"And good-bye, Tristram Tobias Jones."

"Good-bye, Dinewan." Tristram smiled again.

"My name is Matthew Hood." Dinewan said thoughtfully.

He paused to let the statement sink in, then he bowed his head in good-bye, walked through the door and was never seen by Ivan or Tristram again.

Ivan and Tristram stood in wonder for a few seconds, then Tristram moved to stand in front of Ivan.

He held out his hand and Ivan shook it, gratefully.

Then Tristram pulled him into a hug.

When the hug finished, Tristram said "Let's get out of this kill-room, eh?"

Outside, the rain had stopped but grey skies remained.

Tristram and Ivan walked to the end of the driveway and stood in the street.

"What do we do now?" Ivan asked. He seemed so very tired.

Tristram shrugged. "Life goes on."

"Sure, but...what is left? What is left?" Ivan persisted, looking miserably at the road.

Tristram answered. "Go and have a bloody shower. Then book a flight to Queensland, and then go to bed and sleep deeply."

"Queensland?" Ivan frowned cofused.

"That's where Charlotte lives, isn't it?" Tristram smiled kindly.

"I don't think..."

"Don't resist this idea, Ivan." Tristram interrupted. "Just put aside your years of bullshit and go and see your sister. Don't try and second guess what will happen when you do, just do it."

Ivan nodded slowly. "OK..."

Tristram nodded at Ivan, then turned and limped away. He stopped after a few steps and turned.

"Ivan, for what it's worth, I have decided to believe that you would not have pulled the trigger on me. I suggest that you decide to believe the same thing."

Ivan had no answer. He raised his hand in good-bye, and the two parted ways.

As Tristram walked down the soaked street towards his car, the clouds suddenly parted behind him. Every drop of water turned bright gold, and all the colours of the gardens grew vivid and magnificent.

RIGHTFUL HEIR

LIFE IS *a cascade of picturesque moments slipping though our fingers.*

Tristram was reminded of the thought as he was underwater and running out of air.

When Ivan and Tristram parted ways, after the last time that they saw the witch doctor Dinewan, they did not see each other at all for a handful of years.

Tristram recovered from his deep bruises in about three weeks. In that time, he borrowed some money from his grandfather Stewart MacDougall, so that he could pay the rent in Melbourne whilst he searched for a job.

Within three weeks, he got a job as a phone agent, taking calls for the tax office. He hated taking calls, but he hated being unemployed even more. Hence, he put his shoulder to the wheel and worked. It was enough to eat well, pay the bills and pay his grandfather back within a few weeks.

Months went by in a kind of low-grade depression, but eventually Tristram was given a chance to help with the real time management of call volumes and schedule adjustments. The role came with two great improvements: he did not have to take calls and he got a pay rise. Again, Tristram put his shoulder to the wheel and worked.

His life was a grey treadmill of work and not very much else.

However, within a couple of years, Tristram had been promoted twice more and now had a very comfortable wage. It came with more disposable income than Tristram had ever had, and so he began to enjoy a few material luxuries.

He bought hundreds of books, a laptop, a digital piano, a didgeridoo and a pair of West African djembes. He went on safari in Kenya with his younger brother Jase, Jase's girlfriend and another couple they knew. He would never forget standing on the great plains of the Masai Mara, and seeing wild chee-tahs, lions, zebras, wildebeest, hippopotamus, elephants, giraffes and rhinocerous. However, it was a visit to the slums in Nairobi, and the orphanages of Dr. Charles Mulli on the farms in the out-skirts that warmed his heart the most. He made a couple of life-long friends, including a Shotokan Karate cham-pion whom he took all over East Gippsland when he came to Australia two years later.

Tristram ate out with friends, bought a new saxophone and then he got into keeping reptiles. He accumulated a host of Australian pythons and some turtles. In his lounge room, he even had a pair of rare pig-nosed turtles from the Northern Territory, swimming in a large, beautiful aquarium.

As much as Tristram enjoyed the material improvements to his life, a dissastisfaction and impatience continued to grow in him. One day, he was looking at a photo of himself posted on social media and got a rude shock. He was fat. Not just a little over-wieght, but clearly a fat person, with a double chin, man-boobs and a big gut. He had never thought of himself as a fat person – for some reason, the mirror did not show him this. The photo on the other hand was undeniable.

Tristram used his healthy disposable income to buy good quality gym equipment. In a few months, he had a complete semi-professional gym in his backyard shed. He researched fat-loss diets and started weight training.

After many false starts, he made progress. He found a work-out buddy, who committed to getting buff along with him. They kept each other honest, stuck to a plan and after a few months got some good results.

Tristram went back to Aikido, and then he added Pencak Silat to his weekends.

Almost three years had passed, during which Tristram physically improved to the point that, to his surprise, he attracted a little interest from the opposite sex.

Then came an unpleasant experience. An attractive woman wanted to go out with him, but he politely declined. He did not expect to be asked out, and he did not expect to decline an attractive woman asking him out.

His reaction confused him. At first there was the thrill of flirting and the idea of a sex life. Yet, there was also a deep, fearful resistance. Suddenly, Tristram felt as if he was being trapped. The closest analogy he could give for the feeling, was like being bullied as a little boy.

The solution was not as simple as dismissing the emotions. Tristram understood that it was a classic case of "once bitten, twice shy", but that understanding was not as powerful as the response of his limbic system.

He decided to abandon the idea of a love-life, and instead turn his energy towards more rewarding endeavours.

Tristram went and got his scuba-diving license in Portsea, near Melbourne with Saffi. His intention was to fulfill a childhood dream of scuba-diving on the Great Barrier Reef.

Very soon after this decision, Ivan contacted him on Facebook.

"Hi Tristram. Small world – your sister was looking up diving and snorkelling adventures on the Great Barrier Reef and she came across the company that Charlotte, Bill and I run out of Cairns, doing day trips to some of the outer reefs. Fancy a dive? We have a very nice boat. Mates' rates of course."

How could he say no?

A month later, under a warm and clear blue sea, Tristram was running out of air.

He was off the coast of Cairns in Tropical Far North Queensland, finally scuba diving on the outer regions of the Great Barrier Reef.

His scuba tank was half empty in only a few minutes.

They had swum through grey and white coral reefs and seen a few fish.

Ivan swam close to him, making meaningful eye-contact with Tristram as they pointed out the beautiful gropers and the wrasse – large, impressive fish with vivid blue, purple and turquoise colours.

Tristram had enjoyed what he had seen so far, but it was not "under-water Las Vegas" as his mother had described her experience off Dunk Island years before. As much as he appreciated some of the pretty fish, and the intermittent stag-horn corals, he also noted plenty of dead reef, with ugly brown algae. The terrible price of climate change.

The most surreal part of the experience was the sound-scape. Hundreds of parrot-fish constantly chipping away at the coral. Their waste was the fine white sand that makes tropical beaches so distinctive.

Tristram checked his oxygen levels. Time was almost up.

The lead diver tapped his tank to get the groups' attention. He had found something worthy of note.

In a cave within the reef, the largest puffer fish that Tristram had ever seen, sat alertly watching the group. It was the size of a coffee table, and beautifully patterned in chocolate and white dots.

The diver gave the group a thumbs up, which in dive code means "surface".

Tristram took a last longing look at the puffer fish. The dive was already over.

Life is a cascade of picturesque moments slipping through our fingers.

Tristram surfaced into bright sunshine. At first, it was a surprising silence. He could not hear the parrot fish anymore, just the excited chatter of the thirty or so snorkellers on the shallow part of the reef they had been brought to.

He swam to the enormous white dive-boat, a two-story catamaran, and sat on the wide metal lattice platform that was submerged at the back of the boat.

A tanned, middle-aged woman with familiar sapphire eyes smiled at him, and took his flippers off.

"How was your first dive on the reef?" She asked.

"It was wonderful, thanks, Charlotte." Tristram smiled. "Your brother was showing off though, chasing the groupers."

Ivan approached behind Tristram. "You missed a sea turtle, mate. You were too busy looking at some sea anemones. But don't worry, this won't be your last dive."

"It is for today." Charlotte chimed in with an apologetic smile. "But you can still snorkel for a while. We will be here another hour."

"Yeah?" Tristram asked.

"Yeah, of course. Bill will take the tank off you and the BCD and regulators and what-not. You can probably ditch the shorty wet-suit as well."

Five minutes later, Tristram was free of his heavy diving gear and neoprene wet-suit. He sat on a bench contemplating the snorkellers swimming to the boat and back. It was a relief to be in a simple water-resistant pair of board-shorts, and a t-shirt, breathing normally. He found that diving was a slightly suffocating experience. Each breath from the tank seemed to be only *just* enough.

There were several attractive women on the boat, and in the water nearby. Most of them were tourists from Japan, Germany and Great Britain. Tristram noted with a sigh of sadness that he could observe attractive women without the slightest hint of lust within him.

Sexy is an observation without desire for me now. I must be getting old.

Then a Caucasian woman a few feet from him dropped her white towel.

She had her back to him. Her long auburn hair, wet from her recent snorkelling, played over her bare tanned shoulders. A bathing suit patterned with red and white hibiscus hugged her lean, yet curvaceous figure. As she bent down to pick up the towel to dry her hair, Tristram was aroused.

Whoa. Perhaps I thought too soon?

Tristram grinned faintly to himself and shook his head at his lechery.

I don't suppose you would turn around, you potentially gorgeous thing?

As if to grant his wish, the woman turned to face his direction, her face under the towel.

Her white ample cleavage jiggled as she leant forward, drying her hair. Tristram was electrified with lust.

Then she lowered her towel and caught him staring.

Oh shit!

Tristram turned away immediately.

What is wrong with you, Jones? You are not some horny teenager for Christ's sake. Show a bit of restraint.

"Tristram?" Called a mellow female voice.

She was smiling at him, with bright hazel-green eyes.

With a flush of joy he recognised her.

Regina Wilde!

"Hey...wow. Hello." Tristram fumbled, sheepish.

"Ivan said you were aboard. I thought I might not get to catch up with you, because you were in the dive group, whereas I am just doing the snorkelling. How did you find it?" Regina began amiably.

Tristram just kept smiling at her fondly, completely unaware that he had failed to say anything in response.

"Well?" She prompted, with a hint of humour.

"Well, what?" Tristram grinned.

"Did you enjoy the dive?"

"Oh shit – yes, yes I did. Sorry. I can't believe after all of these years I am talking to Regina Wilde." Tristram finally answered.

She frowned at him quizzically. "You assume that I am still a Wilde?"

Tristram shook his head confused. "Why wouldn't you still be a...oh..."

Of course...you would be married by now...

Tristram groaned with ill-concealed dismay.

"Yes?" Regina scoffed.

Who is the lucky BASTARD? Oh fuck...don't tell me...

"Oh Jesus Christ!" Tristram blurted out, as his thoughts led to words. "Did you end up marrying Ivan?"

"*What!?*" She gasped and then laughed heartily. It was music.

"Sorry, that was tactless." Tristram smiled disarmingly.

"That's right – you were jealous of him, even when we were finally together all those years ago." Regina answered, still giggling.

"I was." Tristram shrugged. "So, who did you marry then?"

Regina's eyes twinkled with mischief.

"I am not married. I have been engaged – twice – to the same unworthy guy, but he cheated on me more than once, borrowed a lot of money from me and still hasn't paid it back. He broke my heart so many times, and I just couldn't seem to extract myself from that toxic relationship, until about three years ago."

"I'm so sorry to hear it." Tristram beamed.

"You look sorry." She drawled with good-humoured sarcasm.

Tristram laughed. "I *am* sorry! It sounds awful, but I am just...so very pleased to see you."

"I'm pleased to see to you too." Regina grinned at him.

An old chemistry reignited in that instant. It sparkled in their eyes.

"I was going to go snorkelling – do you recommend it?" Tristram asked.

"Of course. It's amazing." Regina returned.

"I've never been."

"But you just went scuba diving...?"

"Yes. But, ironically, whilst I have been diving, I have never tried snorkelling." Tristram shook his head. "I do everything backwards."

"Grab your face-mask and snorkel. I'll show you some beautiful things." Regina promised.

Tristram obeyed, and then together they approached the platform to enter the water.

"I don't know why so many scuba-dive on the reef." Regina mused. "All the life is in the top couple of metres – that is where the light and the warmth is."

"Yeah, eh? Zoology taught me that, but I for some reason failed to make the connection until just now." Tristram shrugged.

"It's not the only connection you have failed to make." She grinned knowingly.

"Oh?"

Regina shook her head and chuckled. "I can't believe you thought I married Ivan."

"Why was that so unbelievable?"

Regina shook her head again with an enigmatic smile.

They sat on the edge of the platform, with their feet in the water.

Charlotte helped them with their flippers.

"Have fun, cousin." She smiled at Regina.

Wait – what!?

"*Cousin?*" Tristram asked, as he felt an impending epiphany.

"Yeah. Charlotte is my cousin." Regina smirked, holding his gaze. "So is Ivan. Is an age-old penny dropping yet?"

"What the...?"

"My mother's maiden name was MacAllister."

Tristram's jaw dropped. He put his face in his hands and lay back against the platform groaning in disbelief. Then he laughed harder than he had in years.

Regina laughed with him.

"What's the joke?" Charlotte asked, smiling.

As Regina explained to Charlotte their situation, Tristram looked back up to the back of the boat and saw Ivan watching them.

His sapphire eyes beamed with happiness. He nodded knowingly to Tristram.

Ivan set this up.

"Come on, chump." Regina commanded. "You are going to be blown away by what's just over there. It is like underwater Las Vegas, man."

Regina and Tristram swam together across a myriad of vibrantly coloured organisms. In the warm, clear water amongst the corals and teeming fish in endless variation, a deep euphoric wonder grew in both of them. In hazel eyes, and hazel-green eyes, the future glowed with promise.

Life has wonderful surprises.

Dear reader,

We hope you enjoyed reading *The Hunt For The Bunyip*. Please take a moment to leave a review, even if it's a short one. Your opinion is important to us.

Discover more books by Tristan A. Smith at https://www.nextchapter.pub/authors/tristan-smith

Want to know when one of our books is free or discounted? Join the newsletter at

http://eepurl.com/bqqB3H

Best regards,

Tristan A. Smith and the Next Chapter Team

AUTHOR BIOGRAPHY

Tristan A. Smith is a mis-employed zoologist who has finally committed to be being an artist. He completed a Bachelor of Science with Honours in zoology at the University of Melbourne, but now works as a Workforce Manager in a call centre. As it turns out, there is not much call in the market for someone who can do heart surgery on cane toads. Tristan's original plan in life was to be a scientist. The problem was that whilst he enjoyed learning about science, he hated doing it. He marvels at those that persist in science and is awed by their collective accomplishments, but that path is not for him. Tristan has long left the lab and prefers to go into the wild, the Australian bush, where his imagination is fired by stories old and new. *Bunyip* is his debut novel. It will not be his last.

The Hunt For The Bunyip
ISBN: 978-4-86750-516-8

Published by
Next Chapter
1-60-20 Minami-Otsuka
170-0005 Toshima-Ku, Tokyo
+818035793528

6th June 2021

Lightning Source UK Ltd.
Milton Keynes UK
UKHW041840140621
385519UK00001B/235

9 784867 505168